HEART
of
Gold

OTHER BOOKS AND AUDIO BOOKS
BY JEANETTE MILLER

Montana Summer

HEART of Gold

a novel

JEANETTE MILLER

Covenant Communications, Inc.

Cover photography by McKenzie Deakins
For photographer information please visit www.photographybymckenzie.com

Cover design copyright © 2015 by Covenant Communications, Inc.

Published by Covenant Communications, Inc.
American Fork, Utah

Printed in the United States of America
First Printing: March 2015

20 19 18 17 16 15   10 9 8 7 6 5 4 3 2 1

ISBN 978-1-62108-792-2

In memory of my grandmother, Claris Cronkhite, who made Meadow Vista as dear to me as it was to her.

Special thanks to:

MY WONDERFUL FAMILY AND FRIENDS, who support and encourage me.

My mom, Janine Hutchinson, for sharing another adventure with me as I researched Gold Country.

My dear friends in Meadow Vista: my sweet friend Larisa AhMu and the AhMu family; Anne Wegner, my grandmother's dearest friend and next-door neighbor; Marvin and Beverly Green, family friends and gracious hosts; and everyone who welcomed my family each summer while we stayed with my grandparents.

Marilyn Huff, my first cousin once removed, for sharing her Fair Oaks home, a kayaking adventure, and delicious food with Mom and me.

Marty Kent, for arranging kayaks and equipment, and providing instructions on how to get into a kayak in the first place.

Kourtney Ashton, for words of praise brought to me by her mom, Katrina, every six months, as I struggled to finish this story.

Stacey Owen, my fantastic editor, and everyone at Covenant who played a part in publishing this book.

Reluctance

Out through the fields and the woods
And over the walls I have wended;
I have climbed the hills of view
And looked at the world, and descended;
I have come by the highway home,
And lo, it is ended.
The leaves are all dead on the ground,
Save those that the oak is keeping
To ravel them one by one
And let them go scraping and creeping
Out over the crusted snow,
When others are sleeping.
And the dead leaves lie huddled and still,
No longer blown hither and thither;
The last lone aster is gone;
The flowers of the witch hazel wither;
The heart is still aching to seek,
But the feet question "Whither?"
Ah, when to the heart of man
Was it ever less than a treason
To go with the drift of things,
To yield with a grace to reason,
And bow and accept the end
Of a love or a season?

-Robert Frost

Chapter 1

A GUST OF ICY WIND slashed across my face. Blinking away the chill, I touched the crusty remains of the brittle rose bushes in front of my new house, wondering what color the blooms had been. But it was late January, and the lifeless bushes in front of the cracked cement porch would keep their silent secret for the rest of the season.

A movement on the frozen, straw-colored grass caught my eye. I stooped to pick up a crumpled wrapper creeping its way over a dirty patch of snow and tossed it into the garbage bin with a leaden sigh.

Moving back to my home ward in Meadow Vista should be exciting, full of anticipation and energy. Even if I'd bought an old rambler. But I felt . . . well, I didn't really know what I felt. But somehow I identified with the roses.

"Hi, Mommy!"

I looked up and tugged my mouth into a smile for my daughter, Katie. Wearing a bright pink coat and sparkly, multicolored snow boots that lit up with every stomp, Katie was the epitome of vivaciousness and joy, all rolled into a three-year-old bundle. It was my little girl who kept me going each day. Without Katie, I could have easily remained in a state of apathy after my husband, John, died so unexpectedly.

"Hey, sweetheart. Do you like your new room?" I asked. She'd been exploring the inside of our new, empty house, happily discovering magical places only a child could imagine.

"Uh-huh." She nodded vigorously, her pigtails bouncing like miniature Slinkies. Then her little nose scrunched up. "But where's my toys and my bed?"

I scooped her up and sat with her on the porch step for a moment. "In the moving truck with all of our things," I said, stroking Katie's soft cheek. "Tomorrow we'll move everything off the truck and into our new house."

Katie's eyes ignited. "Then I can have my toys?"

"Yep. All of them."

I was rewarded by the tightest hug a three-year-old could give and felt warmed inside in spite of the chilly morning. How I loved my little girl!

Back in Ohio, when I first told John I was pregnant, I'd been so excited. We'd planned on waiting a few years first—well, actually *he* was the one who wanted to wait, and I had reluctantly agreed. After we both graduated from UC Davis, we moved to Cleveland, where John settled into his new engineering job and I became an accountant for a small firm.

But Katie had come like an eager spirit ready to burst into mortality much sooner than we'd expected. It was tragic that John didn't live to really know her. The car accident took his life three weeks before Katie's second birthday. But I couldn't think about that. There were too many bitter feelings buried safely in my heart that I wasn't ready to resurrect.

Katie wiggled off my lap when she saw a middle-aged couple walking hand-in-hand down by the street.

"Wait, honey!" I called, but she darted across the gravel drive, around a bramble of wild blackberries, and down to the old ranch-style fence which bordered our yard. I followed Katie's erratic trail of size-5 boot prints left in the scattered remains of snow, avoiding eye contact with the couple. I wasn't ready to meet any neighbors yet. Something had happened to me with John's death. It was like part of me had died with him, and I couldn't seem to revive my former, upbeat self.

Katie waved hello to the strangers like she had to the ice cream man in Mayfield last summer. "I'm Katie! An' that's my new house!"

The dark-haired woman bent to her with a grandmotherly smile. "Well hello, Katie. We're so happy you're going to be our neighbor."

As I slowly approached, the couple greeted me warmly. "Hello! I'm Steve Matthews, and this is my wife Elaine." He had a full head of thick, salt-and-pepper hair, and his eyes were crinkled at the corners from amusement. His wife had an air of unassuming elegance and seemed to glow with an inner light.

"Ashlyn Carter," I said, giving them a brief handshake above the fence.

"It's wonderful to meet you," exclaimed Elaine brightly. "Your parents mentioned you'd be moving into the neighborhood. We just live three houses down"—she pointed down the narrow, country road—"in the brick rambler."

I lifted my gaze to locate their house, but from where we stood, I wasn't sure I could make it out. Most of the homes were tucked uphill from the street, under the shady cover of towering pines and ancient, moss-covered oak trees. The shoulder of the road was nearly nonexistent. Spongy, brown leaves, yellow pine needles, and snow blanketed the wild, grassy patches on the red-clay slopes. Clumps of manzanita hugged most of the property lines, their red stems gnarled like Great-Aunt Susan's fingers.

"When will you be moving in?" Steve asked, pulling my gaze back. "We'd love to help."

Wow. When John and I had moved to Ohio, we had no one to help us move into our first home, a tiny 1950s rental. Yet here stood two strangers offering to help . . . and I wasn't comfortable with the situation in the least. Was it possible to feel utterly lonely but still not welcome others into your life?

I picked at the chipped paint on the fence separating me from the Matthews. "I'm pretty sure we'll have enough help tomorrow—between my parents and sister and my brother's family in Auburn. But thanks for offering."

Just as I spoke, a small splinter embedded itself in my finger. I instinctively jerked my hand back from the weathered wood. It felt like it was bleeding, but I didn't check. Instead, I tucked my finger inside my fist.

Oblivious to my pain, Katie bobbed up and down with the unbridled joy of youth, trying to remain part of the conversation. "You can help me move my bed and my toys tomorrow!"

Oh, Katie. I looked away, a gust of cold wind smacking my face. *How do you explain to a three-year-old what you can't explain to yourself?* I allowed the winter air to fill my lungs before turning back and smiling awkwardly at the Matthews.

"We'll stop by tomorrow to see how you're doing," Steve offered.

"Thank you," I said, masking my negative thoughts with a smile. My finger still stung, and the tips of my ears and nose were ice cold. This was an unusually cold winter for Northern California. Hoping to make my escape, I quickly said, "Well, it's nice to meet you."

"You too," said Elaine with that glow of warmth that mystified me. "We're going to love having you here."

"We'll see you tomorrow," added Steve. "Bye-bye, Katie."

They both waved then continued walking down the road, their clasped hands like permanent, interlocked fixtures. I stared after them for a minute, an enigmatic sensation encompassing me. The light I'd felt in Elaine's company had dispersed too quickly.

"They're nice, huh, Mommy?"

I looked down into Katie's precious, vibrant face and wrapped my arm around her. "Yes, they are, honey."

Thank goodness for the light my daughter brought into my life, especially when I couldn't find my own.

*****

A faint knocking sound woke me, and I resisted groggily. As I opened my eyes, my surroundings transformed from a dismal blur into the clarity of windows with flowery curtains, walls with prom photographs and out-of-date knickknacks. Rubbing my eyes in confusion, I looked around the room. A forest-green *Colfax High Falcons* banner clashed with a tattered Backstreet Boys poster on the mauve walls. My once-favorite Ben Affleck poster hung in all its mouth-watering glory over the bed.

I moaned into my pillow, remembering now. I was in my old bedroom. It was somewhat comforting to wake up in familiar surroundings, but this room epitomized my youthful, girlish past. Not the woman I'd become.

Katie bounded into the room and jumped on the bed. "Hi, Mommy!" she burst with excitement. The bed undulated like a raft on the lake, making my head swim.

"Good morning, sweetheart." I grinned, reaching for her. Katie had a way of scattering sunshine unlike anyone I'd ever known, and I loved her for it.

"We slept at Grandma's house!" Katie sidled up beside me and put her head on my shoulder. "Wake up, Mommy. Grandma made pancakes, an' she made me a Mickey Mouse an' a snowman pancake!"

"She did?" I chuckled softly.

"Uh-huh! Grandma has brown syrup 'cause it's time to eat them. She said I could come in when you're awake now!" Katie's zest for life always made her sentences seem like they had just been through a blender.

"Guess what, Mommy. We're moving today!"

I tried to match her enthusiasm. "We sure are."

At the moment, the only thing I thought my brain could handle was the mindless monotony of solitaire. I wasn't sure why I kept playing it over and over. The virtual game seemed to serve a minor purpose—any round I actually won made me feel like I'd at least achieved something. And hey, temporary satisfaction beat total apathy.

But the shallow success of solitaire wouldn't do today. Duty called. Life beckoned. Somehow I had to find that inner robotic switch that kept me moving. I started singing, "You are my sunshine," Katie's all-time favorite song. She grabbed my hand and joined in, swinging our arms back and forth as we walked down the hall.

I found my mother in the kitchen, serving a breakfast of scrambled eggs, bacon, and blueberry pancakes. *That's my mom for you*, I thought. She'd always been an amazing woman, the ideal for magazine motherhood. I'd always wanted to become like her but had a long way to go.

"Here we are, Grandma!" Katie shouted, causing my ears to ring.

Mom turned from the hot griddle and smiled. "Well look who it is! My sunshine girls." She wiped her hands on a faded, threadbare calico apron and lifted Katie into her arms. Then she smiled fondly at me. "How are you doing, sweetheart?"

"Oh, I'm just raring to go," I joked, swinging my fist up in front of me.

"Oh, honey." Mom surprised me with a sudden surge of compassion. "I know this is hard . . . how you must miss him. But he's watching over you, Ashlyn."

Compressing my lips with a slight nod, I avoided my mother's tender eyes. There was no way I wanted to talk about John right now, to open an anesthetized wound. I helped Katie sit at the table and casually asked, "Where's Megan?"

"I'm right here!" my sister sang, springing around the corner. She held up her cell phone with a cheer. "He's coming today!"

"Who?" I asked, putting a scoop of scrambled eggs on Katie's plate.

"This new guy I want you to meet," she answered, helping herself to a stack of small pancakes.

I shook my head. "Another new guy? Megan, you date more guys in a month than I dated my whole life."

"Hey, I like dating. But seriously, I can't wait for you to meet Ryan. He's completely . . ." She broke off with a dreamy sigh, and I couldn't help laughing. My twenty-two-year-old sister was beautiful, smart, and fun to be with. It was no wonder she was always asked out.

"Pancakes, anyone?" Mom asked from the other side of the kitchen.

"I want nudder one!" Katie said.

After serving Katie and Megan, Mom offered me some, but I held up a hand. "No thanks. I don't eat much in the morning. Besides, I could stand to lose a couple pounds," I muttered, looking down at my tummy.

"Oh, pff, you'd blow away," she said, motioning toward my plate. "Eat."

Well, I wasn't remotely close to my toothpick cheerleading days, but I had to admit I did need to eat. After making an effort to swallow down a few bites of breakfast, I escaped to the bathroom for a shower. But I did something I hadn't done in a long time—really study my reflection in the mirror.

What I saw was disconcerting.

The reflection wasn't the me I knew. It looked like someone else, someone older, with circles under vacant blue eyes. My honey-blonde hair was carelessly pulled into a messy ponytail. The worn-out, gray sweatpants had a hole in one knee. The equally frumpy sweatshirt hung loosely over my figure.

My shoulders sagged, and my eyebrows scrunched together. How long had I looked like this? I really didn't know. All I knew was that, at one time, I'd not only *looked* pretty, but I had *felt* pretty too. Life had a way of taking you places you never planned on, places you didn't necessarily hope to be. I could hardly believe I was a twenty-nine-year-old widow.

Widow! I thought bitterly. I could hardly even choke out the word. Widows were little old ladies people remembered at Christmastime with paper plates full of cookies. They were the ones who always sat together on the side benches in the chapel during sacrament meeting. I wasn't supposed to be a widow. That's not what I'd planned for my life.

Not in the happily-ever-after version.

"It was a clear cold morning I shall never forget . . ."
—James Marshall, Sutter's Mill, 1848

Chapter 2

MEGAN FOLLOWED ME INSIDE THE empty house, still talking about the boys in her singles ward. "Drake is completely adorable, but he's still too chicken to ask me out."

My sister, the dating machine, couldn't get a date with a shy boy. How ridiculous was that?

"Anyway," she went on, grabbing a roll of paper towels, "Ryan moved in around the corner, on Hillsdale. Every girl in the stake has her eye on him." She looked dreamy-eyed about her new target until she suddenly snickered.

"What?" I asked, grabbing a bottle of window cleaner.

"Remember Bethany Albright?"

"Who could forget her?" That girl had wreaked havoc at every birthday party Megan had ever had. Bethany had always bulldozed into conversations for attention and was jealous of any female threat. Mom had always encouraged Megan to be nice, suggesting that "maybe all she needs is for someone to be nice to her." It'd never done any good.

A wicked glint appeared on my sister's face. "Well, guess who wants to swoop in for the kill?"

"Oh boy. No guy is worth having to deal with Bethany!"

"Ryan is."

I stopped my window-cleaning to look at her. "You're that serious about a guy?" Megan's dates didn't usually get that far in her future imaginings.

Her smile slid. "Uh, actually he's known as the guy who avoids marriage like the plague, so nothing serious yet. I think something happened at BYU because he high-tailed it out of Provo a couple years ago and never went back. He's finishing his master's at Davis and interviewing for jobs."

I shook my head and resumed cleaning. "Megan, only *you* could be that motivated over a guy who avoids marriage like the plague!"

"Hey, you never know. I could be the one girl who can change his mind!"

"Megan," I scolded, "what if he did change his mind? Then what would you do?"

"Marry him, I guess. I mean, if Drake never asks me out, then I'll give up on him. Besides, Ryan is looking pretty darn good right now. I just wish I could tell how much he liked me, you know? He loves gold rush history so much . . . maybe if I dressed up as a gold-panning forty-niner, he'd fall for me faster."

"Megan Kennedy, the things you'd do for a guy. You're hopeless!"

Dad poked his head in the door at that moment and added mischievously, "You're telling me . . ."

"Dad!" Megan chucked her wad of paper towels at him and told me, "He only thinks I'm hopeless because I'm not on a mission."

Dad blocked the wad and hurtled it back at Megan, thumping her on the side of the head.

"Hey!"

My parents adored Megan, but they always bugged her about going on a mission. She was just as fickle in *that* department as she was with dating. Most of the time, she acted like she wanted to serve a mission, but then she'd meet a new guy and change her mind. She could be a star in reality TV if they made a show called *Hooked on Dating*.

"The truck's here. Ready to unload the sofa, Megan?" Dad asked.

Megan groaned. "Dad, you're the one who's hopeless!" Another streak of white sailed across the room as he lunged out of the way with a whoop.

Outside, my older brother, Shaun, and his wife, Karen, were just driving up. And much to my surprise, a few others started showing up too, in spite of the chilly weather. The problem was that I didn't feel capable of socializing with them all. I didn't know what to say besides repeating thank you over and over, so I relied on my robot switch for introductions and hovered near my family.

My dad heaved on the U-Haul's back door—making a harsh, grinding metal sound as the door slid up—and the contents of another life were exposed. I had to shove thoughts aside and work. It was the only way to get through this.

Don't think about John. It only brings more bitterness and anguish.

The boxes began to be unloaded. Strangers were handling my things. Someone I recognized from years ago passed by, carrying a box marked *Kitchen*. What was his name . . . Jenson? Brother Jackson, that was it. He was the guy who used to do reckless ATV stunts out in his pasture. Shaun used to tell everyone he'd grow up to be just like Brother Jackson and do stunts for a living.

"Thanks for your help today," I said. He deserved to be treated well regardless of my state of mind. I just couldn't believe how humbling this whole situation was, depending on others.

"You bet. Glad to be here." He marched along full of gusto I could only dream of. He could probably outlast the Energizer bunny.

How could I resent the help of others when I was so needy? People had willingly come, but I barely knew what to say to them. I wasn't merely frustrated with my situation in life, I was frustrated with myself. If only this part of my life could be far behind me. If only I could feel happy again.

"Hey, Ash," called Shaun over the top of a big, wood rocking chair, "where should I put this?"

I blinked at the rocker and forced my brain to think. Our parents had sent John and me the money to get a nice rocking chair when they found out we were expecting Katie. He'd hardly ever used it. The piece of furniture seemed to stare back at me, the knots in the wood like piercing eyes.

"In the back bedroom is fine, Shaun."

My dad walked into the kitchen from the garage carrying a box of my treasured books. "Where would you like these, hon?" he asked cheerily.

"Uh . . . how about in the family room?"

I directed a few more helpers, knowing it would be like this until the last item was removed from the truck—people coming at me from all directions, waiting for me to make decisions. It felt like the inside of my new home, my past, and myself were all being dissected regardless of how the procedure went.

Looking for a quiet place to regroup, I went to Katie's room and found my sister-in-law, Karen, playing dolls with Katie. She stood when I walked in. "How are you doing, Ash? I mean, really?" Her eyes could look right through people because she cared so deeply.

"I'm all right."

"I'm so glad you decided to move back to California," she said, putting her arms around me. "I want you to know that Shaun and I will help you any way we can. We're here for you."

I smiled gratefully, clutching her hand. "Thanks, Karen. I know you are." I felt a trail of tears spill down both my cheeks.

"You're going to make it," she assured me as I wiped my eyes. "I promise."

"Yeah," I said with a weak nod. I wanted to believe her.

She squeezed my arm affectionately before I went back outside to see how things were going. As soon as I stepped into the cold air, I took a long, deep breath. The calming effects it produced settled over me for a moment as I watched the hustle and bustle.

"Ash, he's here!" Megan startled me. She grabbed my hand with a tug. "Come on, I want you to meet him."

I followed her over to where Shaun and Megan stood talking to a tall guy in a Lake Tahoe hoodie. One of my nephews chased his sister around the side of the house and almost ran into the three of them.

"Whoa, careful guys!" my brother scolded.

The Tahoe sweatshirt guy turned laughingly in my direction, and my words froze at the back of my throat, my thoughts coming to a crashing halt. Recognition launched me into immediate panic.

It couldn't be! What is he *doing here?*

Mortification flooded through me, along with memories. My fight-or-flight response kicked in, but I couldn't run anywhere—I lived here! *This* was the Ryan my sister had been talking about?

His eyes lifted to mine, and I forgot how to breathe. As though completely oblivious to my reaction, he extended a hand to me saying, "Hi, I'm Ryan Anderson."

In a pathetic haze, I extended my hand, willing my brain to send communication signals to my mouth. He didn't remember me! A charge of relief coursed through me, but it was quickly replaced by resentment. How could he not remember me? I'd dealt with all that turmoil years ago, and he didn't even *remember* me? How long had it been, eight years? He'd grown up and filled out, but I'd know that face anywhere.

"Ryan, I'd like you to meet my sister, Ashlyn Carter," Megan introduced us excitedly.

He immediately dropped my hand, and I saw the recognition in his wide-eyed stare. "Ashlyn . . . ?" he said almost inaudibly as though testing the sound of my name. So he did remember. His mouth turned up at the corners as he raised one thick, dark eyebrow. "You're . . . ?" He glanced at Megan then back at me.

Megan frowned. "You've already met?"

I tried to reply, but my brain didn't seem to be functioning.

"Uh, a long time ago," Ryan answered, piercing me with his gaze. "When I used to live here."

I gulped down my embarrassment the best I could, hoping the cold air would extinguish my flaming cheeks. Of all the people in the world to show up today, why did it have to be *him*? I thought I'd never have to see this guy again!

"You used to live in Meadow Vista?" Megan exclaimed. "When was this? And where did you live?"

I was rescued from that conversation when Elaine Matthews walked up to see what she could do to help. "Can I help you unpack boxes, Ashlyn, or clean anything?"

"Um, yes, that would be wonderful." *Just get me out of here!*

Shaun headed back to the U-Haul, and I didn't stay long enough to see where Ryan and Megan went. I showed Elaine into the kitchen, and we began unpacking boxes of kitchen items. I was relieved she didn't seem to notice that anything was wrong.

While we chatted, I couldn't help remembering what had happened all those years ago. I was Ryan's math tutor, and he— I closed my eyes, but that didn't make the memories fade. What happened was permanently engraved in my memory, and it practically gave me hot flashes just thinking about it. Why did he come back to Meadow Vista?

I opened my eyes to slice through the taped flaps of a box. As I lifted a dinner plate from the box, my thoughts shifted to the day John and I had picked out the set, just a few weeks before our wedding. I lightly fingered its smooth, shiny rim, remembering the dreams that had accompanied those dishes—family dinners together, starting with two place settings and adding to that over the years as our family grew—birthday parties and family night desserts. The dream was gone.

Elaine began quickly washing the dishes in the sink to remove any dust, and I helped her dry them. "Which cupboard would you like these in?" she asked.

I looked up at the maple cupboards the previous owners had recently installed, my mind glazing over. There weren't any new dreams either. I had no idea how I wanted to organize the cupboards and kitchen, let alone my life. It was beyond me at that moment.

Elaine must have sensed my overwhelmed state because she offered to put them in the cupboard closest to the sink. "You can arrange everything later, the way that works best for you, but they'll be put away for now."

"Thank you, Elaine. That's great." I began unpacking another box, wishing to somehow return her kindness.

Within a few minutes, people I hadn't noticed before trailed through the house with lamps, rugs, bed rails, and boxes. The dissection was in full swing—probing, opening, exposing. It reminded me of giving birth to Katie and having doctors invite medical students—strangers—to examine me in my state of vulnerability. I wanted privacy but needed help.

My dad walked in the front door then, sharing a hearty laugh with a nearly bald-headed elderly gentleman. I glanced up and broke away momentarily from my troubled thoughts when I saw Brother Loveless. I felt a rekindling of former delight as I hurried over to embrace the much-loved bishop of my youth.

"I'm so glad to see you." I smiled.

He looked just the same except the small amount of hair had changed from almost gray to pure white. He wrapped his arm warmly around my shoulder.

"Laurel President Ashlyn Kennedy. Look at you, all grown up! It's so good to have you back in the ward."

"Thank you," I said, squeezing his hand fondly, not minding the use of my maiden name. Kennedy, Carter . . . they were pretty similar. Looking into his kind eyes, I truly felt glad to be back.

Dad asked, "Are you ready for us to set up your bed, Ash? We've got all your bedroom furniture unloaded."

Brother Loveless nodded with a sparkling smile. "Ready and willing."

Having my privacy invaded was difficult enough when the men began to carry my bedroom furniture into my room, but when they returned a few minutes later, juggling the box springs and headboard, Ryan was helping too.

Did he just toss me some kind of look?

I turned away, trying to initiate a forget-about-it plan, but couldn't help stealing a glance at him. He chanced to look back at the same time, his sooty, gray eyes questioning me with a hint of amusement. My cheeks ignited, so I quickly spun away again. By no means did I consider the situation amusing—not in the least! His presence had reopened an embarrassing, *very* closed, chapter of my life.

Ryan grinned, struggling to angle his way around a corner without knocking the bedposts against the walls. "How's it going, ladies?"

"Fantastic!" my sister announced, coming into the room. Well, that was a Megan answer for you. It never ceased to amaze me that *fine* was simply not in her vocabulary. Everyone else in the world said, "Fine," but Megan was always some kind of fabulous. "Let me help you with that," she offered, helping him move down the hallway into the master bedroom.

I whipped my gaze away from them and focused on the boxes sitting on the table, waiting to be unpacked. Shoving the knife through two layers of packing tape, I lifted one of the box flaps and heard jovial voices drifting from my bedroom. Was that my sister's laugh? I slapped the box flaps back down. What was so funny in there? Muffled chitchat was followed by more laughs.

I couldn't stop myself from moving down the hallway toward the bedroom. I couldn't believe this was happening—that he was here in my house! My footsteps faltered when I heard Katie's voice. Actually, the whole neighborhood could probably hear Katie's voice; it was so loud.

"Whatcha doing?" Her elfin voice swooped up and arced back down in a sing-song wave like a hawk's plunge over the Sierras. Katie must have joined her Grandpa. She'd loved tagging along after him the last few days—like she was drawn to a male influence. But it wasn't my dad who answered.

"We're putting your mommy's bed together," Ryan said. His voice was deeply masculine now, which unsettled me. "What's your name?"

"Katie Celeste Carter."

"Well, hello, Katie Celeste Carter. My name is Ryan."

This guy was setting off a jumble of feelings inside me. I'd been living in such a wooden, unemotional state for so long that actually *feeling* was foreign to me. Being detached from the pain, finding safety by emotionally shutting down was all I was used to. And I'd never let anyone in after John died. No one knew what I was really feeling. They thought I was merely grieving.

I need to move. I can't stand here like this.

Like the rescuing angel she truly was, Katie skipped out of the bedroom into the hall, nearly colliding into me.

"Mommy, come quick!" she squealed, grabbing my hand and pulling as hard as she could.

"What, honey? What is it?"

"You gotta see something!" Katie beamed while she tugged. "Close your eyes, an' I'll show you!"

"Okay. Hold on." I lurched into my bedroom.

"Keep closing your eyes!"

"I am." I squinted for her, hoping no one was watching me come in.

"Ta da!" she exclaimed joyfully, jumping up and down.

I opened my eyes and quickly scanned the room. My bed frame was finished and pushed up against one wall, the nightstands on either side. My dad and Brother Loveless stood grinning beside Katie. Megan was putting some things in the closet. Then I saw Ryan. His grin slackened uncertainly when our eyes met. He stood next to my bed, one large hand on the bedpost.

"See! It's your bed, Mommy! Only, it needs the bouncy part."

Shifting my gaze from the long, masculine fingers gripping the bedpost, I forced myself to smile at Katie. "Yeah, that's great, isn't it?"

"Grandpa built it, and *he* built it," she said, pointing to Brother Loveless; then, jumping over to Ryan, she added, "And Rain did too!"

Ryan laughed and scooped Katie up into his arms.

"His name is *Ry-yun*, Katie," Megan corrected laughingly, walking up to them to softly pinch Katie's cheek.

"Hey, that's okay," Ryan said good-naturedly. "With three brothers, I've been called a lot of things."

Did he just glance at me when he said that? I could swear he had, and I wondered what was behind the murky look. How much did he remember about that night anyway?

Right now, he was tugging Katie's pigtail, making her giggle, and I suddenly recognized another meaningful glance my sister was throwing at me. Megan seemed to wordlessly bellow, "Look at him! Have you ever seen anything so magnificent?" All the Megan-style things that could be communicated in that look flashed through my mind. I felt like I was choking.

Catching my gaze, Ryan said, "After we get the mattress on, we can make the bed—if you have any idea where the sheets are."

I barked out a "No!" before adjusting my tone a notch. "Don't worry about that. I'll take care of the sheets later." *Sheesh, I can make my own bed!* I definitely didn't need him touching my sheets.

Ryan crossed his arms against his chest, looking at me pointedly. My face prickled with a bit of shame. What was going on inside my head? Emotions were tumbling out of me before I could make sense of them. *He must think I'm nuts.* He showed up to help someone out, probably not realizing it would be me. I should respond with gratitude.

Operation Forget-about-It.

"I wonder who else wants their bedroom set up?" my dad was saying with a gleam in Katie's direction.

Katie squealed, "Me, Grandpa! Me!" She turned in Ryan's arms to ask, "Will you make my bed too, Rain?"

Ryan chuckled. "Sure. Let's go."

Everyone filed out of the room. Everyone except me. I shoved a hand through my hair and stared at my bed. Now in place, the mattress was faded and worn. There was a bleach spot where Katie had spilled a sippy cup of red juice just before the move. Beside that were several scribbles of artwork done in pen, trailing unevenly down the left side of the mattress.

My heart softened a little. Katie had moved fast that day, before I could get the clean sheets on. But her scribbles were a precious reminder of the gift she was in my life. She was everything to me, and I needed her.

Looking at my bed, I noticed two long depressions on either side of the mattress where John and I had slept. Even though he'd been gone for over a year, the dip in his side—slightly less pronounced than mine—was still visible.

I squeezed my eyes against hot, pooling tears and turned away. Once there had been fairy tales of falling in love, getting married, blissful happily-ever-afters.

Fairy tales don't come true.

"We shall have to await the sunshine; and when will it come?"
–John Muir

Chapter 3

THE LATE-AFTERNOON SUN DID LITTLE to warm up the remaining helpers. The frosty wind whipped up, bringing flurries of snow with it. The truck was completely unloaded, and my parents were returning it to the local rental location in Auburn.

Some ward members, the Jennings, had brought their whole family over to introduce themselves, offering a pot of hot potato soup and a loaf of homemade bread for dinner. Most everyone had gone, but Ryan was hanging around somewhere with Megan. I wished he'd gone home too. He'd won the gold medal in the Non-Family-Member-Who-Helped-the-Longest category. He could leave and spare me the increasing stream of embarrassment I felt around him. If he thought we'd get a chance to talk about the past . . . It wasn't going to happen.

Remembering how cute he used to be as a teenager, I had to admit that, as a full-grown man, he was off the charts. Man, had he filled out! With striking features; a deep, sultry voice; and the whole superhero-buff thing going on. And for some irrational reason it annoyed me all the more.

Alone now in the hall bathroom, I was going through a box of toilet paper and cleaning supplies. I bent down to put it all in the cabinet under the sink when I heard that deep voice behind me.

"Ashlyn?"

Ryan hovered just behind me. I wanted to pretend not to hear and just stay under the sink, but I wasn't exactly in a dignified position. I moved back and glanced up at him briefly, swiping my hair out of my face. Questioning me with the same enigmatic expression as before, he looked as ill at ease as I felt. His eyes searched my face, and I noticed warm flecks in them, catching the light.

"Hmm?" I resumed my mechanical sorting through the box, lifting items out to stare at and put back in the same place. Cold medicine, cosmetics, Q-tips.

Ryan fiddled with the light switch just inside the doorframe. "I, uh . . . I was just . . ."

My hand froze inside the box, the pause hanging in the space between us. Warily, I lifted my gaze to his.

He rubbed a hand across the side of his face and down his jaw. "I know this is awkward."

I fingered a half-empty bag of cotton balls, trying to form a response. He opened his mouth to finish, when Megan bounded up beside him.

"Hey, guys, what's up?" she asked. Megan wasn't just bubbly. She effervesced.

Ryan closed his mouth, giving me an apologetic, half smile.

"The house looks great, Ash," Megan said. "Is there anything else we can do to help?"

"No, things are settling down," I answered with a brush of my hand. "You guys can take off, but thanks."

Megan smiled at me sympathetically. "Anytime."

Ryan lingered. "Can we pick up anything for you at the store?" he asked.

We? He and Megan were already a "we"? I knew my sister worked fast, but . . .

"We're going to Auburn and stopping at Raley's," he was saying. "We promised Katie a little surprise."

"What?" my head shot up. "What surprise?"

Ryan's mouth formed a lop-sided grin. He half whispered, "Is marshmallow cereal a no-no?"

My eyes popped wide. "She asked you for cereal?"

Megan laughed, placing one hand affectionately on Ryan's arm. "I think Katie has a crush on him. She's been talking to him all day, explaining all the benefits of cereal. In detail."

I choked on a half laugh. I could picture Katie doing just such a thing, actually. "Don't feel obligated—"

"I want to," he broke in, "as long as it's okay with you."

Every time he looked at me, it was unsettling. "That's fine," I said barely above a whisper. "Thank you."

Ryan smiled slowly, offering a slight nod. Several things could be behind that look. Would we continue to ignore the fact that an elephant-sized embarrassment danced between us that only the two of us could see?

"Well, should we go?" Megan said brightly, interrupting my thoughts.

Ryan looked at her blankly for a moment before nodding his assent. I saw his hand press lightly against Megan's back as they walked away, leaving me alone in the bathroom with the boxes.

*****

"Mom, I'm sure," I said. "I really do want to stay and get settled."

"But you only have that soup the Jenningses brought for dinner. I could feed you so much better than that."

Oh, Mom. Feeding people *well* was so important to her. I put my arms around her and hugged her tightly. "I love you, Mom. Thank you for taking such good care of Katie and me. You've been wonderful."

"All right, but you call me if you need anything."

I knew she meant well, but I didn't want to be fussed over like a pathetic— Well, maybe I was pathetic right now. But I wouldn't always be. Someday I'd be normal. At least, I hoped.

My dad gave me a bear hug and kissed my cheek. "Let me know if you want me to help you set up the computer."

"Thanks, Dad."

"I'm so glad you're here, honey," he said a bit emotionally. "I don't ever want you to forget that we love you and are here—very close—whenever you need us."

As they left, my mother called out through the muffling snow, "I have an extra gallon of milk at home. One of us will bring it over." She nearly slipped, but my dad steadied her as they cautiously made their way down the driveway to their Honda.

Mom always had Dad to lean on, to rely on. *I'm going to have to do this all alone.*

Katie and I waved to them, and when their car disappeared around the corner, we went back inside and shut the door. Katie ran back to her room, leaving me in the front room alone. Painfully alone. It was the most alone I'd felt since first hearing of John's death. The quiet engulfed me. Would this work, living in Meadow Vista? I had my parents nearby, which was a big plus. Financially I was okay for now because of the life insurance, although it made me feel half guilty to be surviving on it because of my husband's death—the other half felt deserving.

But what was to become of me? Should I go back to work? Would Katie grow up here in this house while I just grew old and alone? Was this all that life had to offer? A broken dream and then . . . nothingness? I looked around at the blank, colorless walls. Was I expected to put up family photos with John in them? I wasn't sure I could handle it. It certainly wouldn't bring me any comfort.

My parents didn't understand, but that wasn't their fault. I'd never let them know that all my naïve hopes for the future had been shattered by cold reality. The Cinderella dream of finding someone *did* happen. From the day I had met John at a UC Davis dance, it was magical. Even though he'd just been baptized and we couldn't be sealed yet, we were so in love that we decided to get married right away.

I remembered my parents' devastated reaction—it was like cutting off their oxygen. But they had agreed to support us if John and I truly felt like it was the right decision. The wedding was all I could have dreamed of, and I couldn't have imagined my happiness ever changing.

But things did change. John worked so hard at his new job that he was hardly ever home. He often missed dinner and was too tired to do anything when he did get back. He wasn't interested in taking the temple prep class either. When I'd pressed him about it, he told me to stop hounding him, that he wasn't ready.

When Katie was born, my dreams rose again. Surely he would love her; we'd talk more and take family walks together, pushing our baby in the new stroller. But John was too busy or rarely ever home to spend time with us. He was never unkind to Katie, but he seemed to think of her more like a pretty figurine that was set aside to look at occasionally.

It had been so devastating to me that I couldn't bear to tell my parents about it. I'd made excuses and let them believe life was great, trying to convince myself more than anyone else. I used to think that perhaps my marriage was fairly normal, what most people experienced . . . that maybe *I* was the one who'd had completely unrealistic expectations. But as we grew more distant with each other, I began to doubt if I wanted to be sealed to John at all.

And all that time, I never knew what was *really* going on . . .

"Mommy?" Katie was beside me again, tugging on my sleeve. I welcomed the interruption of my thoughts.

"Hey, sweetie." I picked her up and held her close. "Are you hungry?"

"Uh-huh."

"Let's get some dinner then."

The potato soup and bread from the neighbors were heavenly, and I was surprised how hungry I was. It was probably from a hard day's work. And Katie—frequently a picky eater—ate even more than usual.

"I'll clean up the dishes, and then we can read some stories."

"Okay, Mommy. Can we read Cinderella?"

Ugh, not the fairy tales . . . "What about Dora the Explorer? You like that one. Or how about the Sesame Street counting book?" I was glad Katie loved books as much as I did, but at this point in my life, I preferred to focus a little more on reality.

"I want those books *and* Cinderella!" Katie declared in her strident voice.

I sighed. "Okay." At least there was some balance in the selection. "I'll help you find the books."

"Rine found them, Mommy!"

"Ryan?" I asked while I rinsed the bowls.

"Yeah, in a box! And he's coming to my birthday party!"

"Oh, really?" I chuckled. Katie's birthday wasn't for another six months.

"Uh-huh. He's my best friend!"

I smiled ruefully as Katie skipped away. I finished rinsing our dinner dishes and put them in the dishwasher. After wiping the countertops, I was ready to go find Katie. Then I noticed the sink faucet was dripping. I lifted the handle up and down a couple times. Drip . . . drip-drip.

Great. Everything was working the day I bought the house. I'd never fixed an appliance in my life. I wasn't handy! Did I have to spend the rest of my life relying on other men to bail me out of every job a husband usually did? I shuddered at the thought. I wanted to be self-contained, independent in my own home. So I would just have to learn things. Tool things—like the difference between a wrench and a screwdriver. Maybe True Value hardware taught classes for people who didn't know one end of a paintbrush from another.

A knock at the door made me jump. Katie zoomed down the hall, yelling, "I get it! I get it!" as she hurdled past.

"Wait, Katie," I called out. "It's nighttime. Mommy needs to help you."

Katie went even faster, trying to beat me. Her momentum almost slammed her right into the door. I let her open it but stood right behind her.

"Hey!" Megan grinned, standing on the porch. She was bundled up in a bright red parka with fluffy white trim on the hood. The only light on the porch was coming from inside the house. Another thing to get—light bulbs for the porch lights.

"What was that whirlwind I heard?" Megan bent down in front of Katie. "Was that you?"

"No, it was Mommy." She grinned.

A deep, male chuckle emerged from the darkness behind Megan. I made a conscious effort not to groan aloud. *Is he here again?*

"Ryan and I brought you some stuff," said Megan, her face aglow.

"Oh." *Great.* "Come on in," I said, holding the door open for them, glad they couldn't read my thoughts.

Ryan's long, easy strides followed Megan's up the steps and out of the cold. His eyes twinkled at me like winter stars in a black heaven. The night's cold radiated off his large frame. Seriously, all he needed was a hammer or shield and he'd fit right in with the Avengers.

I quickly looked away.

"Here's some milk from Mom and Dad," said Megan, handing the container to me. "You know how she is about having enough milk in the house."

Katie jumped up and down in front of Ryan. "Did you get me a s'prise?"

He grinned at Katie with a sparkle in his eyes. "There might be something in here . . ." He rummaged through a brown paper bag. "Let's see. Here's some bread."

Katie stopped jumping. "No, that's not the one."

Ryan's grin angled toward me. "Then we'll just give this to your mommy." He handed me the loaf of bread. In his large hands, the loaf looked like it should have been squashed.

I reached over and took it, avoiding the lively spark in his eyes. "Thank you."

"What else is in there?" Katie asked.

Ryan rummaged some more, producing a few items of no interest to Katie, placing each in my hands. During the whole interchange, I noticed my sister gawking at Ryan with unabashed admiration.

"Hey, what's this?" Ryan finally said shaking something in the bag. "I think we've got something . . ."

Katie began to jump again, her volume way up. "What is it?" she asked, flapping her chubby hands. He pulled out a bag of cereal with multicolored marshmallows, and Katie grabbed the bag, almost popping it open.

"Whoa, hold on there, pumpkin," I said, making a quick move to save the bag.

Ryan did the same and bumped into me. "Oh, sorry," he said, steadying me with one of those big hands on my arm.

I felt the heat of his hand seeping through my sleeve. He looked into my eyes again, questioning me like he had earlier that day. It only lasted an instant, but I felt like I was being sucked into his gaze.

Jerking back, I muttered, "It's fine." After prompting Katie to thank them for the cereal, which she willingly did with added hugs, I retreated to the kitchen to put the groceries away while they talked to her.

What was it about this guy that got to me so thoroughly? I shoved the bread into a cupboard without thinking. Other items followed until I realized that I'd put the milk in there too. I huffed with frustration, yanked the milk container out, and plopped it inside the refrigerator. It banged more loudly than I expected, sloshing the milk inside.

"Hey, Ash," Megan said quietly, suddenly behind me. "You doing okay?" Her perfect features crinkled into a frown.

I turned warily to be sure she was the only one there. Thankfully, Ryan and Katie were around the corner, out of earshot if we whispered.

"Yeah, why?"

Megan shrugged. "I don't know. It's just . . ."

I waited, unwilling to help her out with this particular conversation.

"I know things are tough and all, but . . . you don't seem your old self."

I sighed. "What's my 'old self'? Like when I was some giddy teenager?"

Megan pouted then shook her head. "I just want you to be happy."

Summoning all the sisterly affection trapped deep inside, I placed a hand on Megan's arm and said, "You be happy. Don't worry about me."

Megan glanced over her shoulder then eagerly turned back to me. "What do you think about Ryan? Isn't he great?"

"Oh. Yeah."

"He told me how you used to tutor him when his family lived here, but I don't remember him at all."

I certainly did. I had even babysat Ryan and his brother, Jason, when they were younger. And he was still on my mind as I relived the events of the day—seeing him for the first time in eight years, wondering what he thought of the situation, realizing how very much he'd changed. I didn't think he seemed nearly as affected by the awkwardness as I felt. He'd stayed to help instead of disappearing and now seemed perfectly ready to start something with Megan.

I pictured Ryan helping to set up my bedroom furniture today. His large, thick hand on my bedpost this morning had been a big distraction. I tried to picture my husband's hands instead, but doing that was a huge mistake. It brought to mind John's horrific betrayal.

Megan grasped my clenched fists. "Ashlyn, what's wrong? What happened?"

I pulled myself out of the sinking pit I was in, trying to focus on my sister's face. I needed to breathe, but all I could do was shake my head back and forth.

"Talk to me. Do you want me to stay here with you tonight?"

I shook my head again as Ryan and Katie walked into the kitchen. Apparently sensing he had interrupted something, Ryan looked away abruptly.

"Mommy, can I eat my new cereal in the morning?" Katie asked.

While I answered her, I was aware of Ryan whispering something to Megan about waiting for her in the car. I felt a twinge of guilt. I hadn't made him feel welcome or appreciated—not once today. I felt like I was seriously losing it, but I couldn't explain it to anyone. Shortly after John's funeral, my parents had asked if I wanted to see a counselor . . . Maybe I should have done that after all. It might have helped me cope with what my husband had done. Maybe it wasn't too late to get some help.

I heard the front door close softly. Megan's probing eyes were on me.

"I-I'm just tired, Megan. It's been a long day—Katie and I both need to go to bed. Go ahead. I'll be fine."

She wavered between me and the door.

I added, "I promise."

"Are you sure?"

"I'm sure."

She hugged me good-bye then did the same for Katie. Just before she left, I rushed over and wrapped my arms around her once more. "Megan,

I love you. Thank you for being concerned about me and for everything you and Ryan did today."

She nodded sympathetically. "Love you too."

Later, I helped Katie get into her princess pajamas and say her prayers. We read several bedtime stories before her eyes drooped shut. I kissed her soft cheek, whispering, "I love you," in her ear.

Katie stirred and reached out, half asleep. "Mommy?"

"I'm right here, baby," I said, smoothing a soft curl on her forehead. "I love you."

"Does . . . does . . . Daddy love me?"

Pain. Unbearable pain.

My breath stopped, my chest feeling like it was being ripped apart. "Yes," I managed. "Daddy loves you."

Through my tears, I saw that Katie had fallen back to sleep. I began to sob. My whole body cramped into one big knot, convulsing in anguish for my baby, who was growing up without a daddy. I cried for myself and all that was locked inside me. It had been a while since Katie had asked about John. In that moment of half sleep, she seemed so insecure.

I'd vowed to take care of my little girl and was trying to do my best. Yet in this moment, I wasn't sure. I longed for someone to take care of us both. Of course I had my family. And I knew I should turn to my Savior for comfort. But a surge of anger filled me with more pain and tears. God hadn't taken very good care of me so far. Was he punishing me for choosing to marry someone who couldn't take me to the temple? Was I losing my faith?

I was too weary to make sense of anything more, so I went to bed and tried not to think. As I drifted off to sleep, a pair of unwelcome steel-gray eyes intruded upon my fuzzy thoughts, reviving old memories of a forbidden kiss.

"It feels so old a pain.
I wonder if it hurts to live . . ."
–Emily Dickinson

Chapter 4

A SHRILL RINGING NOISE WOKE me from a restless sleep. I was groggy and disoriented. Reaching over for my cell phone, I vowed to change its harassing ring tone. When I actually did get reception, I should at least have a decent ring tone.

"Hello?" I said, rubbing my eyes; then I realized it was the telephone ringing, not my cell. Our first call on the land line. I lunged even farther for the receiver and finally answered.

My mother's voice was gentle and sweet on the other end. "Good morning, honey. Glad your phone is all hooked up. Did you sleep well?"

If you could call that sleep. I'd definitely had better. "Fine, Mom."

"Did you get the milk last night?"

"I did. Thanks for sending it with Megan."

"Sure. Do you need any help getting Katie ready for church this morning?"

Church. It felt like a load of rocks had just fallen on me. Going to church this early in the morning was really difficult. I wouldn't wish for an afternoon time, but nine was just too hard.

I hadn't told my mother that I'd missed church occasionally since John died. It's not like I was going inactive. Falling apart and crying uncontrollably for three hours in front of people just didn't cut it.

"No," I answered. "We'll meet you there at church."

"Call if you need anything."

I mumbled my thanks and said good-bye. Then I sunk back into bed, where the covers were still warm. I *really* wanted to stay there. My eyes focused on the white, square room. Every day I woke up I would have to face this unasked-for life all over again. It's not like it just happened yesterday—it had been more than a year. Why was I shriveled up, parched, lifeless? I felt like a forgotten piece of toast still stuck in the toaster—cold, crusty, dry. Would I ever be able to move on?

Light footsteps padded into the room. My bed shook as Katie climbed up and snuggled against me. She was quieter than other mornings. It felt nice just to lie with her tucked in my arms.

"Good morning, Katie." I said, stroking her wispy curls.

"Morning, Mommy." Katie looked up, suddenly more energized. "Is it time for breakfast now?"

"What makes you so eager for breakfast this morning?" I wiggled Katie's nose and teased, "You aren't excited about eating something special, are you?"

"Uh-huh!" Katie bobbed her head up and down against me. "I got my cereal!"

We tried to eat quickly—while Katie raved about "Rine" and her cereal—then searched for church clothes. Most things were already on hangers, but a few things, like Katie's church shoes, had to be dug out of a box.

We would only have been a few minutes late, but the drive to Colfax took fifteen minutes. Considering the fact that we might still be in bed, I thought we did pretty well.

Not even trying to locate the bench where my parents sat, I snuck into a space on the back row, Katie in tow, hoping no one would look in our direction during the meeting. Being invisible didn't exactly work out with the typical volume Katie could produce. But it wasn't altogether awful.

It was more disconcerting than anything else. This was a family ward, but *widow* seemed to be stamped in bold letters across my forehead. Was there anyone else in the ward like me? I scanned the chapel, my eyes ending up on a side bench. There were the elderly widows, just like I had remembered. Is that where I belonged?

My eyes wandered to the stand. The bishop wasn't someone I recognized—the program said his last name was Truman—but his counselors on either side were men I knew well. Brother Clark—a stout man, who always appeared to be contemplating something unpleasant—had been our home teacher for many years. On the other side of the bishop sat Brother Wilson—six foot seven inches and so gaunt he resembled a spaghetti noodle. His petite wife and posse of adorable children always sat on the front row in sacrament meeting. Was that another baby in her arms? Wow, did they ever believe in multiplying and replenishing the earth.

I couldn't believe how strange it felt to be back in my home ward. After getting married and moving away—living a new life—it didn't feel quite right to return to the place from where I had started. It was like regressing. Or simply failing. And since things had changed here, there wasn't a true sense of coming "home."

When I noticed Ryan's parents sitting a few rows up, I felt a moment of panic. But I reminded myself that they didn't know what had happened. Unless he'd told them.

I didn't want to think about it.

When sacrament meeting was over, I scouted out my parents, clear up in the front talking to someone. I scooped Katie up and worked my way to the front, occasionally needing to greet those who knew me and wanted to extend a welcome.

The bishop walked in my direction, his thin lips pressed together, his stride purposeful. Did he know about John? Would our bishop in Ohio contact the bishop here to let him know what John had done? I wasn't sure if bishops did that sort of thing, but I didn't want Bishop Truman to reveal something right there in the chapel where people could hear. Thankfully, he only shook my hand with a brief greeting of welcome and moved on. Almost too brief. Brother Loveless would have belted out a warm, friendly greeting the whole congregation could hear.

My parents saw me approaching and waved me over excitedly. "Here are my girls," my dad greeted with the famous smile that my brother had dubbed the Labrador-retriever grin. Turning to a middle-aged man beside them, Dad made an introduction. "Paul Hitch, this is our daughter Ashlyn Carter and her daughter, Katie."

I turned to the man standing beside them—out of courtesy more than interest—and extended my hand. He shook it with prolonged enthusiasm.

"It's really nice to meet you," he said.

I was slightly taken aback. Why was it so nice to meet me? He didn't know me from Eve. "Nice to meet you too," I said, withdrawing my hand before he could pump it any more.

Paul gave Katie a toothy grin, took her chubby hand, and began pumping again. "How are you, little one?"

Katie shrank away from him, hiding her face in my dress.

"Uh . . . she's a little shy," I said, even though it was only a half truth. She took to some people right away.

Paul pulled back and rubbed his thinning hair self-consciously. "I'll walk with you all to Sunday School," he said to the group in general, but

I felt his words were aimed like an arrow—with me as the target. I felt its lance in the pit of my stomach. Why was he looking at me like that? Like he was choosing his favorite flavor of ice cream?

I'm not for sale.

The thought hadn't occurred to me until that moment that someone might be interested in me again someday. It made my head spin, and I panicked. There was no way on earth I wanted to go through dating and marrying again! Besides, he looked much older than me.

My parents appeared perfectly content walking behind us while Paul walked with Katie and me. He played the part of a gentleman, holding the doors and helping me move through the crowded hallway.

"If the singles ward meets for choir practice, we have to battle our way down to our classes," Paul was saying as he collided into someone with an "oomph."

"Rine!" Katie shouted over the noise. Flinging an accusatory scowl at Paul, she cried, "Mommy, he crashed into Rine."

I felt my cheeks redden. Katie was supposedly shy, after all, and had transformed into Volume Child at the sight of Ryan. Paul must have collided into him pretty hard judging from the look on Ryan's face and the way he rubbed his arm. That burlap, sandpapery carpet stuff they put on the walls could inflict road rash, after all.

But when Ryan saw Katie, he grinned at her. "Hey munchkin, did you eat your cereal this morning?"

"Uh-huh." Katie bobbed her curls up and down. "It was yummy."

"Good. Save me some, okay?"

"Okay. You can have breakfast with me tomorrow."

I glanced at Paul wondering if he noticed Katie's obvious lack of shyness toward Ryan. Ryan seemed to notice Paul hovering, and his gaze moved from me to Paul and back. I felt sandwiched between them both, which made the warmth on my cheeks intensify.

"Say good-bye to Ryan, Katie," I said softly.

"I don't want to."

"Don't worry," he told her gently. "I'll see you later. I promise."

Ryan gave me one last look I couldn't define but made my heart skip a beat. Then he moved on to shake hands with my parents, who had fallen behind in the crush. I pressed forward through the migrating crowd until I found the Primary room, where Katie eagerly joined the Sunbeams.

Back out in the hall, I found my parents waiting for me, Paul Hitch standing beside them. In the Sunday School room, I thought he'd at least find his own row to sit on. But he sat right next to me instead. I peeked at Paul's face. He wasn't handsome, but he wasn't ugly either. Somewhere in between. He wasn't stocky or overweight. Neither was he a frail toothpick like Brother Wilson. Just average.

I tried to shift my attention back to the Sunday School teacher. The lesson was on the teachings of Nephi—at least, I thought that was what was being discussed. But Paul seemed to be omnipresent beside me. Had he managed to scoot closer than a folding chair usually allowed, or was I just imagining things?

I could hear him breathing.

How bad would it be if I got up and left? I had to get out of there. I glanced at my parents on the other side of me, completely absorbed in the lesson. How well did they know Paul? Were they hoping I'd hit it off with him, or were they completely unaware of anything going on here?

Paul leaned over to whisper something in my ear, and I jumped. My scriptures slid off my skirt and fell on the floor with a thud. I bent down at the same time as Paul to retrieve them, and our heads whacked together.

Oww! For crying out loud, I can pick up my own scriptures!

"I'm sorry," apologized Paul more jovially than expected. Somehow he managed to slip his arm over the back of my chair to pat my back.

Did he think we'd bonded now that we'd cracked skulls? I leaned forward for a while, away from his hand, trying to focus more on the lesson than how uncomfortable I felt. I wasn't interested in getting to know Paul or any other guy. I never wanted to marry again. After John, I'd never be able to trust a man again.

The clock on the wall ticked slower than it should. Once, the hands even seemed to move backwards. When—quite mercifully—the bell rang, the men stood up to leave for their priesthood meetings. In an effort not to encourage Paul, I turned to talk to my mom instead of looking at him.

His hand tapped on my shoulder in spite of my efforts. "It was nice to meet you, Ashlyn."

I turned around reluctantly. "Nice to meet you too, Paul."

He held his hand out for me to shake. Why was it so hard for me to be nice? *Just shake his hand and be done with it. He's a decent person trying to be polite.* I shook Paul's hand, adding the best smile I could muster. Then he left the room.

Relief Society sisters of varying ages wandered in, the volume increasing with each new addition. An elderly woman in a turquoise polyester dress suit lowered herself gingerly into the chair beside me. She smelled like

Pine-sol and roses. On her lapel, a rhinestone broach sparkled in spite of the fact that several stones were missing.

Ah, yes. Sister what's-her-name, the oldest widow in the ward.

Leaning close, the silver-haired lady winked and said, "Isn't he wonderful?" in what she must have *thought* was a whisper. I was certain the whole room could hear that crackly voice—even above the Relief Society socializing roar. A few heads turned, affirming that assumption.

"Excuse me?" I asked.

"Brother Hitch, such a good man, that's what I say. A widower, you know. Comes from a fine family too. Been in this area since the Gold Rush almost. His children are all musically talented, you know, performing all the time throughout the Sacramento Valley. A real catch."

I blinked. Twice.

But my hesitation was an invitation for another slurry of sentences from the elderly woman about Paul Hitch's amiable qualities—"a true gentleman, that's what I say"; about the problems with our community building—"if they'd listen to me, they'd finish the darned thing"; and about the benefits of psyllium husk for boosting fiber intake—"it's best taken the night before you want your results."

Mom passed me a pink handout. "Are you feeling okay, honey?" she asked, concern in her eyes. "You look a little queasy."

I nodded. "I think I'm just tired."

"Do you think you can make it through Relief Society?"

"I'll survive, Mom."

The elderly sister on my left tapped my arm with a spotted, wrinkled hand. A large turquoise and silver ring weighted down her arthritic, spindly fingers. I turned back to her, praying for the strength to endure her fragmented sentences.

"I forgot to introduce myself, dear. Mary Chatham in the little, white house down by the Morrises' place, with the fake deer in front, though there's more blackberry bushes than anything else these days, which drives me crazy. Just plain difficult to find good help anymore, that's what I say. We were born and raised near here, my husband, Milt, and I. Broke his back riding the propane tank out back for the grandkids. Thinking he's a spring chicken or something, ol' coot."

I couldn't help the smile that was forming on my face. Mary was hilarious. But a gentle, kind sort of hilarious. "I remember you," I said. "I'm Diane's daughter."

"Oh, how nice," said Mary, patting my arm affectionately. Then leaning in front of me, she added with increased volume and its accompanying halitosis, "It's nice to have family visit, isn't it, Diane?"

My mother leaned forward to whisper, "Ashlyn is in the ward now, Mary. She just moved in."

Mary's mouth puckered into a pleased, "Oh."

The room quieted as Sister Flores stood by the lace-covered table, clearing her throat to begin the meeting. Mary must not have realized. Or else she thought she was whispering again. But just at the height of silence, she leaned over and, with a conspiratorial wink, said with the strength of a foghorn, "Well I say you could do much worse than Paul Hitch!"

The silence that followed was deadly. The whole room seemed to undulate in waves of turning heads. I felt my breath being sucked out of my body. My skin became cold and clammy. Up front, Sister Flores paused midsentence for a fraction of a second, her mouth open.

Mom's whisper was more like a hiss. "Mary, she doesn't even know Brother Hitch. They just met today."

Sister Flores redirected everyone's focus as she welcomed us all to Relief Society. But her sympathetic eyes seemed to wander constantly back to me. The announcements were being made, and any second now they'd announce that I'd moved in. All eyes would be back on me. It would have been difficult anyway, but now with Mary Chatham's unfortunate declaration, it would be ten times worse.

I felt like I was going to black out. I needed to escape, to hide somewhere safe. Was I even breathing? Finally, I stood up, excused myself, and fled. I nearly ran down the hall to the restroom. Inside the stall, I leaned against the cold, metal door, sucking in all the air my lungs could hold.

"Ashlyn?"

At the sound of my mother's voice, tears welled up and stung my eyes. I held the next breath.

"Honey, I think I should take you home."

I exhaled shakily inside the stall, my eyes pooling.

In a voice barely above a whisper, Mom added, "I'm worried about you."

I opened the stall door and saw her reflection in the mirror. I felt like the older of the two images. "Mom, I'm sorry. I'm just not handling anything very well." My voice cracked, tears spilling down my cheeks. I covered my face with my hands, wishing I could hide. I didn't want to ruin my mother's Sunday. She didn't deserve having to deal with an emotionally crippled daughter.

But she was instantly at my side, arms around me, soothing with loving words. "It's all right. Everything's going to be okay, Ash. I know it will." She gently stroked my hair. "You'll get through this. It'll take time, but you *will* make it. You have a Father in Heaven watching over you, waiting for you to let Him help you."

She stepped into the stall, pulled some toilet paper off the roll, and handed it to me. Sniffling, I tried to pull myself together, fearing that someone might walk into the bathroom any minute and see me crumbling like a baby. It wasn't like I'd never seen ladies in the restroom with bright-red, watery eyes. But those were probably tears from testimony meeting or something, not because of completely losing it.

"Do you want me to drive you home?" Mom asked.

Yes, I wanted to go home, but I didn't want to leave the bathroom with this red face. "I'll be fine, Mom." I sniffled again, trying to pull myself together. "You can go back to class. But would you mind bringing Katie home for me?"

"Sure." Her worried look remained. She took in a deep breath and patted my arm soothingly. "I picked up a car seat yesterday, so I don't need yours."

I knew she wouldn't leave unless she saw for herself that I was all right. I took a hesitant look in the mirror.

Ughhh! Worse than I thought.

I wiped my mascara smudges and blew my nose. Then with another deep breath, I headed for the bathroom door. My mother followed. I cautiously opened the door and looked down the hallway. All clear.

"I'll see you later, Mom. And thank you," I whispered. Then I dashed toward the blurry, plum-colored foyer and out the glass doors.

"Keep close to Nature's heart . . . and break clear away, once in awhile, and climb a mountain . . . Wash your spirit clean."
–John Muir

Chapter 5

I RACED OUT TO THE parking lot in my heels, hoping I wouldn't trip. Feeling like an utter failure—weak and dysfunctional—I let my tears resurface and cascade down my face. I didn't bother swiping at them. My car was in sight, second level of the terraced parking lot. Just ten more feet. I pulled my keys out of my purse and slipped into the space between my car and a big van.

"Ashlyn," a voice called from somewhere behind me.

Oh no! Please, I've just made it to my car, to safety.

Too bad I didn't have keyless entry. I pretended not to hear, frantically flipping out my key to clumsily shove it into the driver-side door. What was wrong? The lock couldn't be iced over. It never got cold here like it did in Ohio. At least I didn't have to scrape snow off the windows.

Come on, key! Turn!

"I was wondering—" The masculine voice cut off abruptly.

Why can I not escape him? No one in the singles ward should be there right now. What was he doing in the parking lot? I felt Ryan's hand on my shoulder, firm and warm, but I refused to turn around. I wasn't about to give him a close-up of my swollen eyes, runny nose, and red face.

Go away, I mentally hissed.

"Hey . . . what's wrong?" The sudden tender concern in his voice produced a fresh flood of tears. His hand stroked my arm in a comforting gesture.

Oh, please, not sympathy! It always made me cry even more.

I didn't answer. I couldn't.

I felt him reach gently for my keys. "Here, let me help—"

"No!" I burst out, finally getting my keys into the lock. "I don't need your help." In a softer tone, I pleaded, "Just . . . let me go. Please."

He backed away as I opened the car door and slid into the driver's seat.

"Ashlyn, what's wrong?" he asked again, just before I slammed the door shut.

The engine hummed to life, and I backed up, swiping away tears. Only when I had safely backed out did I look in my rearview mirror to see Ryan staring after me, dumbfounded. I guess he'd just been given a glimpse of the psycho sister who'd have to be dealt with as long as he was dating Megan.

Instead of the noisy freeway, I took the long way home, down Placer Hills Road through Eden Valley. I needed the quiet mountains and thick woods, the rust-colored slopes and mist-covered pastures. What was wrong with me? A fresh deluge of tears coursed down my cheeks, so I pulled off to the side of the road under the safe, wintery canopy of moss-covered oak and stately pine trees, shifting into park.

I hadn't cried like this since John died. I'd been making it through each day since then. Of course, some days were better than others, but I hadn't been falling apart as a rule. Why now? Was I so dead inside before that I never felt it?

I didn't know the answers, and I didn't prevent my tears from falling now. I felt so lonely and ashamed of how dependent I'd become. And most of all, I felt guilty for still being angry at John, so angry I couldn't let it go. My parents would be appalled if they knew how angry I was! How ironic that he was the one in heaven while I was sinning with all this anger down here.

I rammed my fist against the steering wheel. *I'm the one who wanted to go through the temple! I'm the one who tried to have a forever family!*

That call to inform me of my husband's death was only the first blow. After the funeral, I'd sat alone on my bed thumbing through John's wallet in an effort to feel close to him. I'd fingered the photos of our engagement, wedding, and new baby . . . removed his driver's license from the stiff plastic covering to smile at his goofy expression . . . taken out the five-dollar bill in the back compartment.

And then I saw it. A note, innocuous at first glance, which shattered my world. Little by little, I discovered more incriminating evidence to piece together the woman's name and hotel accommodations from business trips John had taken that year. Looking back, I realized there had been signs that should have set off alarms in my head, but I'd denied them. I didn't want to discover that kind of truth.

Knowing why I wasn't sealed to my precious little girl now stung bitterly. It was all John's fault! *I'm glad we weren't sealed, John, because I hate you! I hate you!* I wept bitterly against the steering wheel until I could cry no more. Finally, amid the tears, my body wore down, and my anger simmered. My tense muscles settled back against the fabric seat. I was spent. Before exhaustion overtook me, I drove the rest of the way home, crawled in bed and fell asleep.

Sometime later, a noise woke me. It came again, a rhythmic tattoo on the front door, and I figured it must be my parents. I leaped out of bed and darted to the bathroom to wash my face.

"Coming!" I called, making my way to the door. But wait a minute. What if it wasn't them? I couldn't have guests looking like I did! I opened the door a crack.

"Oh, Megan, it's you," I said with relief. But I peered around Megan before letting her in, just to be sure Ryan wasn't hiding out there.

"Hey, Ash," Megan said quietly, taking in my puffy eyes, wrinkled clothes, and tousled hair.

"I, uh . . . guess I fell asleep."

Megan nodded. An awkward moment passed before she said, "I was worried about you."

"Why? Did you see Mom?"

"No."

"Has news spread that I couldn't take Relief Society?" I asked jokingly.

"No, it's not that. I was—what happened in Relief Society?"

I sighed. "I sort of fell apart."

"Oh, Ash, I'm sorry." Megan put her arms around me so tenderly that it felt like she was the adult and I the child in need of comfort.

"What time is it?" I asked.

Megan looked at me in confusion. "About noon. Why?"

I wandered into the kitchen. "Mom and Dad are bringing Katie home from church for m—wait a minute." I spun around to face Megan. "How did you know I was upset?"

Megan's mouth opened but couldn't seem to form any words.

"Did Ryan tell you?"

"He only—"

"So it *was* him!"

"Hey, what's the deal?" Megan asked.

"I don't want him interfering with my problems."

"Ash, he wasn't interfering. He was just concerned about you."

"Why should he be?"

"Oh, come on!" Megan shook her head in disbelief. "Why can't he be concerned? Ryan Anderson is the most decent, caring guy I've ever met. I'm telling you this guy's genuine. He can see you're going through a lot—that things are really tough—and he just wants to help. What's so bad about that?"

I didn't answer because I had no explanation. She was right. Why was I so upset? Was I still being completely irrational?

"Ryan's done nothing wrong," she blustered on, seeing no concession on my part. "And one more thing—I could easily fall for him, so you'll just have to get over it!"

Now red in the face, Megan spun around and marched out the front door.

"Megan, wait!" I called to her. But she strode angrily to her car and slammed the door shut. She shot the car in reverse, almost grazing an unruly manzanita bush, her tires spewing gravel until she got down to the road.

I watched the car disappear around the bend, groaning to myself. How pathetic could I get? It was bad enough to be an emotional basket case, but now I was infecting my family with my problems. This couldn't go on. *I* couldn't go on like this. I had to change . . . but how?

I felt like I was clinging to the last strands of my wellbeing, while hovering over a deep, dark pit. Perhaps I needed to take a leap of faith and jump to solid ground, to rethink my life and move in a new direction. Whatever I was holding onto was not making me happy, not getting me anywhere. I hadn't relied on my Savior like I should have. I'd wandered alone in despair rather than staying on course. How could I find my way?

Heavenly Father, are you even there?

*****

"Megan, can we talk for a minute?" I asked, hoping to make things right with my sister.

Sitting in my parents' downstairs family room on a bulky, green leather sofa—Mom's 1980s tribute to our Irish heritage that she couldn't part with—Megan closed a thick textbook and eyed me doubtfully. "Why?" she asked with a sour expression.

I sat beside my frowning sister. The muffled sounds of Katie and my mother drifted down from upstairs. Katie must be jumping off the sofa again, judging from the constant thuds overhead.

"Because I need to apologize for being kind of . . . out of it, I guess, this afternoon."

"Out of it?" Megan almost shouted. "Are you kidding? You've been far more than out of it, Ash! You're like a—" She broke off abruptly, as though she hadn't meant to say that much.

"I'm like a what?"

"Like a stranger, like I don't even know you!" She crossed her arms in front of her and made a show of studying the coffee table in front of her. She was probably going to say "zombie" or something. It's what I felt like.

"Come on, Megan. Talk to me." She didn't budge, but I continued anyway. "I'm sorry I haven't seemed very . . . normal."

She made an amused grunt while rolling her eyes.

"I don't know what's wrong with me, Megan. I'm just having a really hard time right now."

My sister finally turned to me. "When people are having a hard time, they're supposed to let others help them."

I exhaled. "I'm not very good at that."

"Obviously."

"I'd rather be left alone. Even if I really do need help."

"Does that include Mom and Dad? Does it include Shaun and me?"

"No, of course I appreciate all you guys have done. It's just that . . ."

"You'd rather not accept help."

I gave my sister a sheepish look. "Is that so bad?"

"It is if you are denying people the chance to serve. That's all Ryan wants to do. He told me how much he wanted to do something to help you. It's the kind of guy he is."

I shifted uncomfortably. "It's not his responsibility to help me. It's not like he's my home teacher or anything."

"He *is* your neighbor."

"Yeah, and I used to babysit him!"

My sister wrinkled her nose and brow in revolt. "When he was a kid, maybe! What's the big deal, Ash? Why won't you just let us help you?" Megan's eyes pleaded.

Seeing the earnest look on my sister's face, I realized how much this meant to her. She loved me and Katie and simply wanted to serve us.

I felt a welling up of gratitude for Megan and her goodness. I'd never understood just how difficult it could be to accept help. And the thing was, Megan was including Ryan in all this. Could I handle letting him help as well? Or anyone else for that matter?

I needed to, but choosing to do the right thing wouldn't be easy. I'd have to chip away some of that pride from the emotional block of ice in my heart. At least Katie would be ecstatic if she could see Ryan around the house. So I smiled reluctantly and put my arms around Megan. "Okay."

"Thanks," she said, returning the embrace.

"So"—I nudged her—"you two are together a lot. Any wedding bells ringing yet?"

She pulled back and laughed. "Not even. I might tell Ryan I'm going on a mission just to see if I get a reaction out of him, you know?"

That made me smile. I took my sister's hand. "I love you, Megan."

"Love you too, Ash." She considered me for a moment before asking, "Would it be okay if we came over tomorrow afternoon?"

I let out a shaky sigh. "Tomorrow? What for?"

Megan attempted not to appear exasperated. "I think Ryan picked up some light bulbs for your front porch. He said he'd noticed a few things you might need."

"I can go to the store and get stuff. It's not like I'm an invalid, you know."

"Just let him bring them over. It's not a big deal."

"Aughhh . . ." I moaned in exasperation and jumped up off the sofa. "Fine. Come on over." Walking toward the stairs, I tossed over my shoulder, "Bring the whole ward if it makes you happy—it'll be a party."

Megan laughed, and my smirk turned into more of a smile on the way upstairs.

*****

As I pulled into my driveway later that evening, through a flurry of wet snowflakes, I saw the shimmer of something colorful on the front porch. Katie and I walked over and found a loaf of homemade bread wrapped in pretty, decorated cellophane. It was still warm. A note was attached that read, "Welcome to the neighborhood. We're so glad to have you in our ward." It was from Sister Flores, the Relief Society counselor. That was sweet of her. She really seemed nice in Relief Society that morning.

"What is it, Mommy?" Katie asked, rubbing her eyes.

"It's some yummy bread. Would you like some before bed, little sleepyhead?"

"Uh-huh."

As I turned to go inside the front door, I caught a glimpse of bright green poking out of the ground below me. What was it? I stepped off the porch onto the snow-dusted grass, and there, below the lifeless roses, a tiny cluster of snow drops struggled to rise from the ground.

New life.

I touched the bell-shaped, milky-white petals and was filled with something I hadn't felt for a long time. Something that could only be described as hope.

"I'll tell you how the sun rose a ribbon at a time."
–Emily Dickinson

Chapter 6

WALKING DOWN THE EMPTY CHURCH hallway, my feet almost dragging on the mauve carpet, I wondered why the bishop wanted to speak with me. He sure wasn't as friendly as you'd expect. But when the ward clerk had called to make the appointment, I figured I'd better go.

I sat down on a folding chair outside the bishop's office and stared at the dark wood door. What would Bishop Truman have to say? If my Ohio bishop passed along everything I'd told him about John, this could be a difficult interview. Maybe it was nothing more than getting a calling. If so, I hoped it would be an easy one. Anything but teaching Gospel Doctrine or Relief Society. I couldn't fathom standing up in front of the sisters with Sister Chatham ready to drop potentially disastrous comments. Actually, I couldn't imagine myself in any calling right now. Shouldn't they pick someone more . . . normal? Someone that fit the Mormon ideal? Someone with fewer hang ups?

The door opened, and I sat up a little straighter.

"Sister Carter?" Bishop Truman asked reservedly, stepping out of his office to shake my hand. He looked tired—that heavy kind of tired. But not unkind.

"Hello," I said more serenely than I felt.

"Thanks for coming. Please come in." He held the door open while I slipped past him.

I sat in a chair on the opposite side of the desk from where he sat. Three pens in one corner of the desk were lined up in parallel perfection. A box of Kleenex had been placed on the other corner, its edges square with the desk. Bishop Truman opened a leather organizer, put on his spotless bifocals, and read some notes.

"How are you doing, Sister Carter?" he asked, glancing up over his bifocals.

"I'm fine, thank you." What was written on his notes? How much did he know about me?

"I'd like to thank you for meeting with me today," he said, tapping the tip of his pen on the corner of a piece of paper.

I nodded, suddenly realizing he looked more nervous than I did. The poor man tugged at his collar, wiped a bead of moisture from his face, and then cleared his throat. "I, uh, wanted to talk with you for a few minutes. To get to know you a little better."

I shifted in my chair, focusing on a thin scratch running down his desk. "All right."

He chatted with me for a few minutes about benign topics like Ohio, unpacking, and the weather before getting to more serious matters. "I understand your husband passed away about a year ago." It was more of a question than a statement.

"That's right," I said quietly.

"I'm sorry. It must be difficult in so many ways."

"It is." That was an understatement. But he seemed to understand.

"H-how have you been getting through everything? How do you stay strong?"

Shifting my gaze, I inhaled deeply, feeling thick tightness in my chest. I shook my head. "I just keep moving forward each day, I guess. I live for my daughter."

He nodded and tapped his pen again. "Katie, right?"

"Yes."

"How old is she?"

"Three."

"Mm. That's young."

I nodded.

"How is Katie dealing with her father's death?"

"She has questions, you know, like where he is, if he still loves her. I've tried to talk about it openly whenever she asks something, but I'm not sure how much she understands."

"That makes sense. It's hard for children to grasp the concept of death when they're as young as your daughter." He looked down and fiddled with his pen. I wondered if he was speaking from experience with his own children. I didn't really know anything about him.

His next question surprised me. "How strong would you say your testimony is?"

Oomph. That was a hard one to answer. "I don't know. It's been hard getting to church in the past, but I'm doing better. I'm sure my testimony could be stronger."

"Do you believe in your Savior?"

I gave the question sincere thought. "Y-yes."

"Do you believe that He loves you?"

"I think so."

With a couple more pen taps, he said, "I can assure you that He does. Even when it's hard to feel it, He loves you and is mindful of everything you're going through." He paused to look at his notes again. "Sister Carter, I have a question for you. Do you feel like you'd be willing to accept a calling?"

Here it was, the calling. I was on a ledge and either going to be tipped off or pulled back to safety. He stuck a finger inside his collar and tugged. "As a visiting teaching supervisor?"

I blew out a gust of relief. "I can handle that."

"Wonderful," he frowned at his notes.

Were we done? Should I get up? Bishop Truman looked up like he wanted to say something more, so I remained in my seat. I didn't think it was possible for the man to look any graver, but the way his eyes searched mine astounded me.

"Sister Carter, I want you to know something," he said fervently. "I've been praying for you—to know how to serve you as your bishop, to give you some guidance from the Lord. And I've had the impression to invite you to prepare for the temple."

I felt my eyes literally bug out. *The temple?* I couldn't go to the temple, could I? I thought I had to wait until I got remarried or something.

"We have a temple preparation class beginning soon. It will take place during Sunday School. There are a few people signed up already. Would you be interested?"

"W—yes, I would. It's just—-are you sure I can go to the temple?"

"You can go to receive your own endowment."

"But I can't be sealed to Katie."

"Not yet, but someday that can happen."

A wave of raw emotion washed over me, starting from the tip of my toes, rushing up through my body, and pooling in my eyes.

Apparently dismayed by my tears, Bishop Truman hastily added, "I'm sure you want to be sealed to your daughter, and it's disheartening to think of going without her. Children are sealed to both a mother and a father. But for now, going yourself will be a tremendous blessing to you both. And I promise you, someday, when the time is right, you can be sealed to Katie in an eternal family unit."

His gaze pierced through the puddles in my eyes. His words echoed in my mind and found a place in my heart. And somehow I believed him.

"And here you once again appear . . ."
–Alexander Pushkin

Chapter 7

EARLY ONE MORNING, SEVERAL DAYS later, I awoke to a thin ray of sunlight shining down on my comforter. All traces of snow would vanish soon. Meadow Vista's elevation was just under the snow line, so unless there was a heavy winter, any snow we got never lasted long in the foothills.

While lying there in bed, listening to the drips of snow melting from the roof, I thought about my interview with Bishop Truman. He might not be as personable as Brother Loveless, but he was sincere. I got a calling I knew I could handle and was going to take the temple prep class. I still had a hard time believing it!

I'm going to go to the temple!

I thought about the first time I'd done baptisms for the dead as a Beehive. It used to be a long drive down to the Oakland temple. Now, with the Sacramento temple so close, my parents loved going more frequently.

This move was changing my life in more ways than I could have imagined. Was my heart actually feeling happy?

I acknowledged the delirium and got out of bed. There were so many things that needed to be done today. Might as well get started. I grabbed for the ragged, comfy sweats I usually wore but stopped myself. Instead, I thumbed through my pants and selected a pair of dark jeans. Since my sweatshirt had peanut butter all over one sleeve, I had to dig through a box of clothes to find something else.

Memories flooded back when I uncovered a burgundy sweater I had bought back when John and I were in school. I had hoped he would say I looked "stunning" in it—like he used to. I loved the color and had felt gorgeous in it, even if it was inexpensive.

I considered the sweater for a moment then decided to try it on. It was slightly form-fitting, the fabric gently hugging my torso. Standing in front of my dresser mirror, I studied my appearance. I wondered if my curves were feminine or desirable. Was I pretty? Self-doubt had plagued me alongside rejection, and I didn't know if I could ever be enough for a man.

After showering and tugging on my jeans and the burgundy sweater, I brushed my hair out and went in to check on Katie. Still sound asleep, she looked like a tiny angel. I smiled lovingly down at my little girl and decided to let her sleep a little longer.

While I ate a small breakfast, my sister-in-law, Karen, called to see how we were doing. We had a brief but good conversation that left me feeling like I could handle the day. I began unpacking the rest of my clothes, which smelled slightly musty from being in the boxes. The pile of things that needed to be washed was multiplying.

It wasn't long before my mother showed up. "I wondered if I could help you do a few loads of laundry," she asked.

"Seriously?" I chuckled. "You always know exactly what I need."

"Mother's radar."

Katie shuffled in, awake after hearing her grandma's voice. My mom gave her a big hug. "How's my little angel?"

"I'm not a angel, Grandma." Katie giggled. "I'm a girl."

"Ohhh, I see." My mom smiled. "Well, how would this little girl like some angel pancakes?"

Katie started to say yes but made a sudden beeline for the pantry. "Wait! I'll show you, Gramma!" She pulled out the bag of cereal Ryan had bought for her. "See? I got this!"

"Ooo, sugar bombs," Mom laughed. "Let's find you a bowl."

"Megan and Ryan brought that over for her the other night," I explained, putting the clean kitchen towels away. Mom had rarely allowed sweet cereals at the breakfast table when we were growing up.

She looked up from pouring cereal. "Oh, a little cereal's not going to hurt anyone."

No judgment? My mom was getting soft.

"Ryan sure is a nice young man, don't you think?"

A jolt coursed through me. "Uh . . . sure."

"I remember you'd come home from tutoring those boys so frustrated with their goofing off. It's nice to know they turned out to be so outstanding."

I stopped. "So you really like him?" I hoped my face appeared indifferent.

She smiled meaningfully. "I do." She poured some milk into Katie's bowl.

"Do you think he and Megan might get serious?" I asked.

Mom found a spoon and handed it to Katie. Her expression was contemplative. "You know what, honey? I could only hope so. He'd be wonderful for Megan, but you never know with her." She shook her head and laughed again. "That girl goes through more young men than anyone I know. I'll bet half of them are left with broken hearts, and she doesn't even know it."

I smiled. That was Megan. And yet, it seemed like the two of them could be serious. They were always together, weren't they?

"Mommy?" Katie called.

"Yes?" I walked over to stroke her soft, tousled hair.

"Can Rine come play with me?" she asked, her mouth full of cereal.

I found a napkin and wiped the milk from her mouth. "Well, Ryan and Megan might be coming over later. Would you like me to find a friend for you to play with?"

"Rine *is* my friend." The expression on Katie's face indicated that that info was painfully obvious. *Duh, Mom.*

"I know," I said, unable to hide my amusement, "but wouldn't it be fun to find a little girl your age to play Polly Pockets with?"

Katie stopped munching for a second and shrugged her shoulders, considering the idea.

My mother added, "Lisa Goodwin has two little girls. They live a couple houses down the road. You should give her a call to see if the girls could all play together."

"That's a good idea," I said.

Katie appeared skeptical until an hour later, when two little girls showed up on the doorstep with a pink, sparkly bag full of dolls and colorful rubber clothes. Five-year-old Grace and three-year-old Lily were so excited to play that the girls took no more than ten seconds before they all disappeared down the hall to play in Katie's room.

I thought about the willingness of children to accept each other so easily. *I need to be more like Katie.* I determined that I should be more pleasant when Megan and Ryan came by, more easygoing and sociable. But I was really out of practice.

"Hey, Ash," Mom said. "I was just curious. I mean, you don't have to answer if you don't want to, but I wondered what you thought about Paul Hitch?"

My resolution went on a downward spiral, about to crash and burn, but I pulled out of it just in time. "What do you mean?" I stalled, trying to think of an answer. *Remember: pleasant, easygoing, sociable.*

She cleared her throat. "Oh, you know, did you like him?"

"Uh . . . I don't know. Did you want me to like him?"

Mom folded a towel with great concentration. "Not necessarily. I just noticed his obvious interest in you and wondered—"

"If I might be interested?"

She scrunched her forehead. "I don't know. I might be thinking too far ahead."

Here we go . . . that conversation I never wanted to have.

"You wonder if I'll ever want to get married again."

A pained look crossed my mother's face. "Oh, honey, your dad and I just want you to be happy. We know how much you love John and miss him . . ."

I turned away guiltily.

". . . but if you were to someday find a good man who made you happy . . ."

"Mom, please—"

"Are you worried about being sealed to someone else? Someone besides John?"

I cringed. I *really* didn't want to be discussing this. Preparing to go to the temple for myself was doable. Beyond that was too much for me to handle. My sweet, perfect mother was beginning to upset me.

Noting my distress, she put her arms around me and held tight. "I'm sorry, honey. I shouldn't have said anything. I'm just a mama bear who doesn't want you to think you have to be alone for the rest of your life."

"Mom, I could never think about getting married again," I said, shaking my head distastefully and shuddering at the thought. "There's just . . . no way."

"I know. I'm sorry." She held me in her warm embrace, stroking my hair.

It reminded me of being rocked by her in the big, wooden rocking chair when I was a child, soothing away every trouble with her loving comfort. But even her magical touch couldn't heal my loneliness, hurt, and unanswered questions right now.

"It's okay, Mom. I know you're just trying to look out for me. But I really can't picture myself dating again or ever getting interested in anyone."

I'd never wanted to explore these feelings or this topic in my mind before. There was more to it than the insurance money eventually running out or possible dependence on another man. There was also more to it than dealing with trust issues because of what John had done. Deep down I felt . . . past my prime, discarded, used up. Who would ever be interested in a woman who'd already had a life with another man? Someone with a child.

Someone who couldn't even keep her husband's interest.

I could picture a widower—left with a bunch of children—looking for someone to take the place of his wife and care for his family. Tears quickly pricked my eyes. That was definitely not the picture of happiness I had dreamed for myself.

I took a deep breath and pulled myself together. There were clothes to finish organizing and plenty of odds and ends still waiting to be unpacked from stacks of boxes.

*****

In the late afternoon, Megan and Ryan came by. Katie squealed especially loudly when she heard them come in. She raced to the front room to greet them and was rewarded by Ryan twirling her around in the air. I hugged my sister, trying to focus on my new "be nice" goal amid the commotion.

"Is Mom still here?" Megan asked.

"She went home already," I answered.

Ryan leaned over to put Katie down. His eyes caught mine as he stood back up, and the expression on his face changed. He seemed to be eyeing me in a peculiar way, one that made my middle quiver. I self-consciously smoothed out my sweater, wondering if we'd ever talk about "It."

Then I remembered what I'd said to him in the parking lot on Sunday: *I don't need your help. Just let me go.* I owed him a pretty big apology. I couldn't remember being rude like that to anyone before. If only I could erase that whole scene.

"You ready to put us to work, Ash?" Megan asked eagerly.

"Okay, uh . . ." I stammered, suddenly feeling itchy all over.

Megan angled a severe look at me.

I scratched my arm. "I do need to vacuum . . ."

Ryan stepped toward me. "Can I do that for you?"

I couldn't explain the sensation that fluttered inside me when he spoke. It made me uncomfortable having all that masculine maturity staring at me like that.

"Sure. The vacuum's in the hall closet."

Ryan left, and I felt like I could breathe again.

"Can I help you clean?" Megan asked. "Or is there more unpacking to do?"

"There's a bunch of boxes in the back room I still have to go through. But that's going to be drudgery."

"Hey, I didn't come to be entertained, you know. Is that where I should start?"

I exhaled. "All right. Thanks, Megan, you're the best."

Megan grinned. "What are sisters for, right? And hey," she added with a twinkle, "you'll survive our help. I promise."

I watched her go down the hall. The vacuum hummed to life in Katie's room, so Ryan must have that underway. Then a sudden panic hit me.

Did I leave anything embarrassing lying around my room?

I raced to my bedroom, looking for jeans on the floor, bras lying around, or anything else I wouldn't want Ryan to see. Because he *would* be coming in here. Unless I asked him not to vacuum my room, which I simply didn't have the courage to do.

My bed was haphazardly made, so I quickly redid it. Then I scanned my bathroom. A hairy hairbrush was on the sink, and the towel from my shower was draped over the shower stall. But he wouldn't be coming in here. There was no carpet in here, only the ugly, mottled brown tile. Someday I wanted to replace that. And maybe put in hardwood floors in the kitchen area. But that was too overwhelming to consider yet. Glancing up, I noticed the colorless wall too. The pasty neutral glared at me cadaverously. Maybe I should paint.

I heard Megan calling to me from the back bedroom.

"Coming!" I called back. I found my sister sitting in the middle of a pile of miscellaneous objects. "What's all this?"

Megan laughed. "That's what I want to know. Should I put it all back in the box, or do you want to go through it?"

I found a space to sit down and thumbed through a stack of things: tickets from a 49ers football game, a dusty box of carbon check stubs, and a small envelope of photos. "What on earth?"

I pulled out the old photos—John's parents, his high school graduation picture, several from his childhood, and our engagement photo. I held the last one, studying our faces, remembering the day we took those for the wedding announcement. John had been in a hurry to finish the photo shoot so he could get back to take a test—always rushing off somewhere—and I'd been obliviously happy.

I am not going to cry.

"This must all be John's old stuff. I don't remember packing it."

"You miss him a lot, don't you?" Megan whispered, reaching to squeeze my hand.

I swiped a tear away and sort of nodded. *I miss what never was.*

Megan pantomimed something, mouthing "we need a tissue" to the area behind me. The vacuum stopped. A moment later, I felt a big, warm hand on my back. Ryan leaned over to hand me some tissues. He didn't say anything, but his long fingers on my back moved in gentle comfort, a silent giving.

Then I heard his footsteps as he quietly went back to vacuuming. I appreciated that he hadn't said anything. It was as if he recognized or respected my need for privacy—and yet wanted to show compassion. Was he trying to show me he was good brother-in-law material?

Megan picked up an old engineering textbook. "Maybe we should put this stuff away for now?"

I nodded in agreement. We repacked John's things, and I stood to leave.

"Hey, Ash," Megan said, just as I reached the door, "you look really good today. I like that sweater."

My eyes widened in surprise. "Are you serious?"

"Of course I am. Why wouldn't I be?"

"Well, I was regretting wearing this because it's a little tight."

"What? No, I think you look hot. And that color is definitely you."

With a watery laugh, I thanked her. "I think I might keep you." Without thinking, I added, "Why don't you stay for dinner?"

"Sure. But what about . . ."

"Uh, Ryan can stay too. If he wants."

"Thanks, Ash. You're the best."

Now I had to find something decent to make for dinner and didn't have the slightest idea what to fix. I went to the kitchen to see what I could throw together. At first I didn't see Ryan. Only his lower half was visible—a trim waist and long legs clad in faded blue denim—protruding from under my kitchen sink. What was he doing down there?

Ryan popped his head out from under the sink and gave me a lopsided grin. "I picked up some washers for those valves." He stood up, registered the blank look on my face, and explained, "Uh, for the leaky faucet." He pointed his thumb over his shoulder in the general direction of the sink.

I nodded, clearly skeptical. Ryan turned away, reached for a wrench, and began disassembling the hardware on the sink. My eyes popped open in disbelief. Why did he think he had to fix my sink? I might not have a home teacher yet, but I owned a phonebook with yellow pages. My dad was—well, my dad didn't touch any plumbing system since the 1992 bathroom incident, when my mother declared that the cost of repairing the flood damage was simply not worth it. But there were others who could help. I couldn't decide if I was irked or impressed. This was not the teenager I'd tutored in algebra and physics. I had a guy who looked like Thor or Captain America dismantling my kitchen—and I was definitely staring.

Deciding to ignore the twinge I felt around Ryan and his well-defined biceps, I began opening cupboards in search of something for dinner. There were a couple cans of chili and a box of macaroni and cheese. In the fridge was some leftover stew I'd made and a nearly full jar of peanut butter.

Opting for the stew, I also remembered the loaf of bread from Sister Flores. That would work. But the bread was on the other side of the kitchen. I glanced at Ryan and cautiously stepped around him to reach for the bread sitting on the counter. I began to prepare the food, avoiding bumping into him. Once, I turned around and found his eyes on me. But he quickly turned back to the washer he was replacing, leaving me with my heart in my throat. I continued slicing the loaf of bread.

How did he know what he was doing? He wasn't *that* old. I stopped midslice, my eyes wandering down again, to calculate how old he'd be now. He was four years younger, if I remembered right. That would make him about twenty-five.

A squeaky twisting sound came from behind me, accompanied by a deep grunt. Ryan said, "There, that should do it." He turned on the tap to inspect his work. "Let's see if it drips anymore."

When he pronounced that the leaky faucet looked good, he washed his hands then turned to face me. He scratched a tuft of tousled hair self-consciously. "Ashlyn, I—"

Suddenly, Katie skipped into the kitchen. "Mommy, Mommy! They're eating at our house!" she shouted, cutting off Ryan.

I bit my lip with an awkward look at Ryan. "If they'd like."

The corners of his mouth curved slowly upward. "I'd love to." That warm, penetrating look was on his face again. Was it just me being crazy, or was the adult Ryan Anderson hypnotizing? As an inexperienced and shy twenty-year-old I'd been attracted to him. And he—four years younger— must have been attracted to me as well, otherwise that forbidden kiss would never have happened. But was he as good-looking all grown-up, or could my impressions of his attractiveness be a little skewed given my weak state of mind?

Allowing the subject some consideration, my eyes grazed his strong, clean-shaven chin . . . wandered up to his thick, dark-brown hair. He was tall and well built with firm, broad shoulders. His lips curved with sensual mystery, and his dark, thick eyebrows were more than just striking, they could drive a girl—

Okay, so he's handsome!

The clock on the wall ticked for several seconds while Ryan's eyes held mine. They really were nice eyes . . . the thick, dark lashes made them beautiful. Megan said she had a lot of competition, and there was no doubt in my mind why so many girls were attracted to him.

I blinked several times to clear my head and turned away to find the place mats.

"Can Katie and I set the table?" Ryan asked behind me.

"Yeah, Mommy, I know how."

"Okay, here are four place mats," I told her. Avoiding Ryan's gaze, I said, "The silverware is over here."

He followed me to the drawer. I started to pull it open, but it stuck part way. I yanked on it, causing the silverware to clang around in each compartment. It still wouldn't open. *What's wrong with you?* I silently chastised the drawer. *You just had to embarrass me in front of this guy.* I yanked one more time.

"I think there's something in the way," Ryan said close beside me. He bent down to look inside, wedging his hand into the open space. Katie came as a spectator.

"Oh no," he gasped, speaking to Katie.

"What?" she squealed.

"An alligator's got me!" he cried, pretending his hand was trapped and causing Katie to giggle. "Save me!"

Katie began pulling on his arm with tiny grunts for added effect, her high-pitched laughter filling the entire house. I watched them both in amusement. He certainly had a way with kids.

"Here we go. I'm almost free," he grunted. Then he pulled out a warped, red silly straw and handed it to Katie with a flourish.

"My straw!"

"What's going on in here?" Megan said, coming into the kitchen.

"An alligator eated him!" Katie exclaimed excitedly.

"An alligator, huh?"

Ryan laughed—a deep, mellow laugh that matched his voice.

"Let's do it again!" Katie cried.

I picked her up. "We don't want him to lose his hand, do we? Let's set the table, sweetheart."

Katie pouted and began whining.

"Hey, I can't find the forks, Katie," Ryan said with the silverware drawer pulled out, trying to distract her. "Which ones are they? I need your help."

Katie almost jumped out of my arms to show Ryan the forks. They set the table together, while Megan helped bring the food to the table.

During dinner, I realized I was getting a little more used to Ryan. But there was still that thing in his eyes that made me flutter inside—not to mention our history.

"Ashlyn," he was saying, "this stew is amazing. You always were a fabulous cook."

I nearly choked on a piece of bread. I wasn't expecting either the compliment or the reference to the past. Was that the first time he'd said my name since we'd met? No, he'd said it before. Why did it sound different just now?

"Thanks," I croaked. "So, Megan says you're graduating soon and are interviewing for jobs."

"That's right. I'm going into electrical engineering—"

"Like John," Megan inserted proudly.

"—and I've started interviewing with a few companies."

"Here in California?"

"All over. Some of the better-paying jobs, like one with a division of Boeing, are back East."

I wondered how Megan felt, knowing that her boyfriend might take a demanding job that far away, but I didn't say anything.

"Mommy, let's make some cookies for dessert!" Katie clapped, apparently feeling left out of the conversation.

I tugged one of Katie's ringlets affectionately. Katie loved to be with me in the kitchen, especially if we made cookies together. It was a special time for the two of us, even if we made a huge mess. "I guess we could make cookies," I said.

It turned out to be a fun activity for everyone, scooping cookie dough, snitching little tastes, and enjoying them hot out of the oven with cold milk. Ryan and Megan even did the dishes.

"These are, like, the best cookies I've ever had," Ryan said, reaching for another one.

Megan looked at her watch. "Wow, I didn't realize it was so late. I have an early class tomorrow, so I probably should go soon."

She looked to Ryan as if questioning if he was ready to go too. For a brief moment, I thought a look of disappointment flashed across his face, but it instantly disappeared.

"Yeah, I have some things to take care of for Elder's Quorum. Let me replace the porch light, and then I can drive you home, Megan."

A sudden pounding on the door startled everyone. Katie moved first, while I followed behind, thinking it was probably my parents. They would probably check on me a lot until I was really settled. But my parents didn't pound on doors like that. I opened the door and was completely taken aback to find Paul Hitch holding a bouquet of flowers.

Oh, help! What is he doing here?

"Night's darkness is the bag that bursts with the gold of the dawn."
–Rabindranath Tagore

Chapter 8

PAUL SPREAD HIS LIPS WIDE. "Hello. I brought these for you." He handed me the expensive flowers and added, "As a housewarming present."

With a quick glance over my shoulder, I said, "Thank you, Paul." Less enthusiastically I threw in, "Would you like to come in?"

"Sure," he said eagerly. He stepped inside and looked surprised to see Megan and Ryan. "Oh. I didn't know you had company."

I made the introductions, even though Paul and Ryan had unofficially met in the church hallway incident. I hoped this awkward moment would end as quickly. Megan was throwing all kinds of looks at me with those raised brows and knowing grin. Ryan seemed to be eyeing Paul skeptically. I felt the blood rush to my face and didn't know where to look.

In this company, Paul seemed really old. Ryan and Megan were college-age students, inexperienced in many ways. Team twenty-something. Paul was a well-established older guy, having been through much more in life. Team thirty-something.

So where did that put me? With receding-hairline Paul? At twenty-nine, I felt so old. My UC Davis days were long gone. So much had happened since then—marriage, a baby, a big moveto Ohio, becoming a widow. It was a strange feeling.

"Paul and I were introduced at church on Sunday," I explained.

Paul reached out to shake Ryan's hand. And although both men said, "Nice to meet you," I sensed a note of opposition between them, but it could've just been my imagination.

Paul pointed over his shoulder, saying, "I noticed your porch light is out, Ashlyn. I'd be happy to replace the bulb for you."

Ryan pulled a small pack of light bulbs from his coat pocket. "I've got it covered. I was just heading out there now." His chin jutted up slightly as he left to do the task, his eyebrows angled sharply.

I glanced at Paul. I didn't know how to get rid of him. Megan and Ryan were leaving any minute, and I didn't want to be alone in the house with him. And not just because he was a man. I knew I wouldn't have the slightest thing to say to him.

A squeeze on my leg reminded me that Katie was hanging on to me and had been silent since Paul had walked in. A few painful minutes of small talk passed in slow motion. When Ryan came back in for Megan, the two of them said their good-byes. Ryan looked at his watch and glanced at Paul. Then he turned to me, briefly placing a warm hand on my arm in a friendly gesture. "Thanks again for dinner. Everything was delicious."

"I'll call you, Ash," Megan said with a sly grin.

I nodded. "Thanks for your help."

Don't leave me here with him!

Unaware of my silent plea, Ryan and Megan walked outside.

"Wait," I called out, making my way out to the porch. "Ryan, I . . . thanks for fixing the light."

He paused and turned to face me.

"And the faucet," I added, vaguely realizing I had to look up at him. How tall was he now? "Thanks for all you did."

Megan had already disappeared in the dark thick of trees where his car was parked. Standing there alone, Ryan smiled, a softer look appearing in his eyes. "Thanks for letting me."

He gazed down at me, hands shoved deep in his pockets. The light from the porch created a canvas of light and shadow on his face. Then he scratched his head the way he had earlier.

"By the way," he said quietly, an uncertain smile playing on his lips, "uh, I was going to tell you . . . that's a nice sweater."

He turned away, leaving me alone on the porch, my mouth frozen in a half-open position. My heart felt like it had stopped. My skin felt uncomfortably flushed, electrocuted. That look had been in Ryan's face again when he had complimented me. Just thinking about it sent an inexplicable feeling pulsing through me. It was something new, yet somehow remembered—like having the volume turned on and hearing for the first time in years.

Maybe Ryan was like some guys who complimented people more than others, I reasoned, trying to regain my composure. It didn't mean anything, of course. It was just that I hadn't had a man say anything like that to me for a long time. I wasn't used to the feeling it gave me. Ryan had always been the outgoing, generous type. And as much as I had to admit the pleasure it had given me, the flattery was probably just his way. Most likely another reason so many girls liked him. He was genuine, and girls would certainly respond to that.

But I wasn't just any girl! I was Megan's older sister, his former tutor, and a widow to boot! How long would embarrassment plague me?

I closed the front door and came back inside the house, hoping my discomfiture didn't show. I found Paul sitting on a kitchen chair trying to engage Katie in conversation. Katie warily nodded in response to something he had asked her. When she saw me, Katie ran up, reaching out to be held.

"I think it's about time to get you ready for bed, honey." I picked her up, hoping Paul would take the hint and not stay too long.

He stood up. "Can I put the flowers in a vase for you?"

"I'm not sure I have one, but I can check to see . . ." I started opening kitchen cupboards, knowing I had no idea where anything was yet. "This tall glass should work."

I filled it with water and brought it to the table. Paul eyed the glass disappointedly but unwrapped the flowers and placed them inside. I adjusted a rose, and my hand accidentally brushed against Paul's.

The chilling sensation was nothing like the fluttery shiver I'd felt a moment ago on the porch. This was like the chills accompanying the flu. My hand involuntarily shot back.

"They look beautiful," Paul said, his voice suddenly husky.

Oh no. The husky voice set my comfort meter in the red zone. It implied things. And I wasn't going there!

"Ashlyn, there's something I was wondering . . ."

I swallowed painfully, waiting, willing him not to speak.

"Would you consider having dinner with me?"

At first, my mouth wouldn't open. When it did, nothing came out. My whole body seemed to have congealed.

He spoke again before I could form an intelligible answer. "I know what it feels like to lose your spouse. I thought—well, maybe you could use a friend who understands what you're going through."

A friend? Oh. The idea wasn't too bad, actually. Not that I would have chosen Paul for the task. But if it was just a friend thing . . . I really hadn't been able to talk to anyone who truly knew what I felt. Everyone had been loving and sympathetic, but they didn't fully understand. I wondered if Paul had ever felt angry with his wife. I tried to picture him in a rage.

Yeah, probably not. His wife probably hadn't done anything wrong before she died either. Maybe I was abnormal feeling as angry as I did. So what was I going to do about the dinner thing? As long as there was nothing romantic involved, I might be able to handle it. But I'd need to find a babysitter for Katie. And I wouldn't want to be out late.

Paul waited expectantly for my response. Before I could speak, he chuckled. "You don't have to answer right now. Just think about it. I'll give you a call later."

"Okay," I nodded uncertainly, thankful he hadn't pressured me any more.

"Well, I better go now. Have a nice evening."

"We will. Thank you."

I saw him to the door, and he left with a friendly wave.

*****

The sun was warmer each day, melting away all traces of snow in the foothills but leaving the ski resorts a haven for skiers farther north. Tiny crocus and daffodils were poking above ground in shoots of vivid green. The promise of tulips was yet to come, but my poor roses still appeared lifeless. Even though I couldn't detect it, there had to be some kind of change taking place within the brittle stems. Someday they would bloom again.

Megan called one morning to convince me to head up to Squaw Valley with her that weekend.

"I don't think so," I answered firmly.

"Oh, come on! Think about it. Blue skies, powdery mountains, Lake Tahoe a glittering sapphire below us. Doesn't that entice you?"

"Very poetic." I laughed. "But no."

At one time I would have jumped at the opportunity. But I was a mom now and actually loved being at home with Katie. Besides, I was completely out of practice for the kind of skiing Megan loved. She was a black diamond kind of girl.

"What if we only went up to Soda Springs? You could invite Brother Hitch . . ."

"Knock it off."

"Are you sure there's nothing going on there?"

"Megan."

"Okay, okay. If you change your mind about skiing, let me know."

"I will."

As it turned out, Katie wanted to go outside to play, so I bundled her up. We walked down the road and saw her new friends, Grace and Lily Goodwin. They had a heavy, plastic slide on their small patch of lawn and were making each other laugh by going down backwards.

Katie greeted them at her full-lung capacity, and Lisa, their mother, invited us to come over. "Thanks for letting my girls play with Katie," she said. "They had so much fun."

"Thank you for sending them over. Katie was desperate to have someone to play with."

"I hear you," Lisa laughed, rubbing her protruding belly. "I don't have the energy to play with my girls like I used to. I'm getting too big." She was one of those pregnant ladies who looked like they had a basketball under their shirt—skinny everywhere but the bump.

"So when are you due?" I asked.

"Two months," she answered eagerly, taking a swig of her morning coffee. "Can't wait to have him out."

"A boy then?"

"Yep. My husband's last chance to get his man-child." Her laugh was infectious. "Have a seat."

I sat beside her in the mommy zone—the porch step—while the girls played on the slide. I noticed the crocus bursting with colorful promise near our feet.

"Are you getting settled into your house?" Lisa asked.

"Yes and no. I have some boxes I still need to go through."

"I think everyone I've ever talked to has boxes kicking around with unidentified objects!" Lisa laughed heartily. "I wonder why we hang on to so many things when we should just send it all to the Salvation Army. I mean, if you don't need it or miss it for a couple years, why keep it, right?"

I laughed with her, but I was thinking about the box of John's things. How many more like that were there? After all he'd done, I didn't want to hang on to them. They'd make a great bonfire. But someday Katie might want to have a connection to the father she never knew—in spite of everything. John's parents might want some of his things as well. I should go visit them someday, but I knew they didn't like me. We'd had no contact since the funeral.

A ray of sunlight sprung through the morning sky, warming my cheek. A trail of water trickled away from the house and down toward the road.

I realized that thinking about John didn't hurt as much today. Perhaps the cold iceberg in my heart was thawing out as well.

"Why don't you come inside for lunch?" Lisa invited. "It's only peanut butter and jelly sandwiches, but hey, the girls love it. And anytime I can find something they'll actually eat, it's a good thing." I followed her inside the house. "Is Katie a picky eater?" she asked, leading me to the kitchen.

"Not too bad."

"Ugh, you're so lucky," Lisa sighed dramatically as she pulled a jar of creamy peanut butter out of a cupboard. "I'm so tired of sneaking hidden tidbits of nutrition in their food, trying to disguise stuff only to realize that their food radar already went off."

I laughed. "Do they hide food under their plates?"

"Under plates, in their pockets . . ."

"My brother, Shaun, was famous for doing that."

"Oh, but get this. Sometimes they ask to leave the table to go to the bathroom, like I'm clueless or something, so they can flush their food down the toilet. One day—it was so funny—I was cleaning their bathroom and found carrots and potatoes shoved into a Kleenex box. So I asked the girls, 'How did these vegetables get in here?' and Grace says, 'A robber did it.'"

A squeal of little-girl giggles down the hallway accompanied our own laughter. Lisa called the girls for lunch, and I was surprised at how enjoyable it was to be there, how comfortable I felt with her. She didn't make me feel like a widow; she just made me feel like a friend. I liked that.

After the girls had eaten and played a little longer, Katie and I walked back home. There were two messages waiting on the answering machine. The first was Mom checking up on us. The second was Brother Loveless informing me that he was my new home teacher! And because I was a widow, Sister Loveless would be his companion. I cheered with a happy "Yes!" since I loved them both. My spirits were so lifted that I had a sudden inkling to go for a run with Katie in the jogging stroller.

*****

Megan shoved her cell phone toward my face. "See what you missed?"

I scanned the pictures she'd taken of her ski trip. "Looks like you had fun."

"Oh yeah. You should've come!"

"Some other time."

"Okay, your loss. I better get moving. I don't want to be late for class."

If Megan had stayed in Sacramento, she wouldn't have to deal with the commute to UC Davis. I could imagine how bothersome that would be. Most people had some kind of commute—the trade-off for living up in the woods. If I ever went back to work, would I have a long commute? I wondered if I'd be able to find a job close by. I realized that the idea of working again had penetrated my thoughts.

Is this a prompting? I didn't even know how to tell. I'd been a little out of practice with prayer and having a personal relationship with my Father in Heaven. How did one know if something was just a good idea or actually an inspiration?

But working at this point in my life didn't seem feasible. Maybe when Katie was in school all day I could work it out, but not now. I didn't want to leave her. So it couldn't be a prompting if it didn't even make sense, right? Maybe I'd talk to my dad about it. He was so wise. Brother Loveless was too, for that matter. I could trust anything coming from him.

Just then, Katie came up and tapped my leg. "Mommy."

I wrapped my arms around her and squeezed. "What, sweet girl?"

"My friends have princess beds. With sparkles."

"Oh really?"

"Uh-huh."

"Did you like their room?"

Katie nodded sadly. "I don't have pink."

"I see." Even Katie had noticed the lack of color around here.

"And they have a daddy."

I nodded sadly. I understood what she meant. As young as she was, Katie recognized the feeling a father brought to the Goodwin home, and she wanted a daddy too.

I should find a photo of John holding her and frame it. Surely I could find one decent picture that would work. Then Katie could put the photo on her nightstand where she could see it every day. There wasn't much else I could do about a daddy. But I could do something about the pink princess situation.

"So tell me, what kind of things did the girls' room have that you liked?" I asked, redirecting Katie's focus.

"They had pink beds and pink pillows and pink dolls. And sparkle things."

"Hmm . . . pink and sparkles, huh?"

"Yeah. I like pink and sparkles."

"Yes, you do." I smiled broadly, hugging Katie. "How would you like it if we made you a princess bedroom?"

Katie nearly combusted with excitement. She let out a high-pitched shriek of joy and jumped up and down.

"Maybe we could go to the store tomorrow and find some sparkly pink stuff."

"This gonna be so 'citing of my castle!" Katie sang out as she zoomed around the house, shouting something about marrying the prince.

Now where did all that come from? I didn't want Katie too heavily immersed in a fantasy world, so I'd have to keep this princess thing in check. But somehow it didn't bother me too much today. *I guess a little bit of fun won't do any damage.*

The phone rang, and I was smiling when I answered. When I realized it was Paul, my smile slid.

"Hi there," he said smoothly on the other end of the line. His voice reminded me of Grandma's fudge for some reason—and I wasn't too crazy about fudge. I instantly regretted not checking the caller ID before picking up. But he only mentioned friendship the last time we talked, so I should be able to talk to a friend.

"Hello, Paul."

"I was just calling to say hi."

"Oh. Thanks."

"And I was also wondering if you had a chance to think about going to dinner with me?"

It took me a moment to form an answer. I didn't have any interest in going to dinner with him. But maybe it would be good for me to emerge from my self-imposed seclusion—to come out of hiding, so to speak. Then again, it could be the most miserable thing I'd ever do.

"I guess I could go to dinner with you. Sometime."

"How about Friday night?"

Friday? Sheesh. That seemed so soon. "I don't have a babysitter."

"Oh. What about your parents?"

"They might be able to. I'd have to see."

"Would you like to call me back when you know?"

I sighed. "Sure."

After a few minutes, Paul hung up, and I slumped onto the sofa.

"I don't want to date again," I moaned to myself, rubbing my hands over my eyes. Why did I have to go through this? What did I do to deserve this life?

Then I felt Katie's soft little hands gently stroking my arm. I opened my eyes to see her worried look. "You sick, Mommy?"

I picked her up and rocked her close, loving the way she felt in my arms—like a little piece of heaven I was privileged enough to hold.

"No, I'm not sick, sweetheart."

"You sad?"

There was no way to explain, really. So I nodded.

Katie wrapped her arms around me and kissed my cheek. "That better now?"

"Oh, Katie. I love you so much! You did make me feel better."

"I love you, Mommy."

I continued holding Katie as long as possible, basking in the warmth of her love. There were plenty of other things to be done, but for now this was exactly where I wanted to be. It was exactly what I needed.

"Let us open our leaves like a flower . . ."
–John Keats

Chapter 9

"YOU HAVE A DATE?" MEGAN's outburst was precisely what I'd hoped to avoid, but it wasn't turning out that way. "Are you serious?"

"It's not a date. It's just like . . . a friend thing. His wife died, my husband died. Sort of a group therapy kind of thing." It sounded lame, but I was trying to convince myself that it would be okay.

"Ash, do you even like him?" Her nose scrunched up, and her lips curled down in a way that made the idea seem an impossibility.

I shrugged. "He's nice. But I'm not interested in having a relationship. I mean—"

"I know. You loved John."

I closed my mouth, my sentence unfinished. Feeling a knot in my stomach, I picked at a spot of carpet in Megan's bedroom.

Megan took my hand. "Do you think Brother Hitch understands how you feel?"

I don't even know how I feel. "You make him sound ancient, calling him 'Brother Hitch.'"

"Isn't he old?"

"Not that old!"

"Oh. Well, I can't imagine calling him Paul."

To me, that made sense. Megan was so much younger than Paul, it was like a generation gap. I was somewhere in between.

My mother came in the door holding a plate of brownies. "Hi, girls. Thought you might like some dessert."

"Come on in, Mom."

"What's new? Anything exciting?"

I loved that my mother played the role of comforter and protector but could also fill in as a friend. Megan was waiting expectantly for me to reveal the news, as if it were a bomb about to detonate.

"Paul Hitch asked me to go to dinner."

The plate of brownies tilted precariously. "I see."

Megan sort of tried not to laugh while helping Mom slide the brownies back in place.

"So what did you say?"

"I told him I'd let him know."

"And I said I'd babysit," Megan added resignedly, taking a huge bite of brownie.

"I'd be happy to watch Katie too, of course," Mom said. "It's a courageous step even considering it, Ash. I'm proud of you."

A shaky laugh escaped my lips. "Well, it's not a real date. Paul said he thought I might need a friend, someone to talk to about all I'm going through. Do you really think it would be good for me, Mom? I don't know what to do."

"Honey, you know me—eager beaver to see my kids happily settled. But you're probably the only one who can decide."

"I know," I moaned, sinking my teeth into a brownie.

"But if you think you might enjoy his company, then I think it could be a good thing. Just take things as slow as you want. I'll support you, whatever you decide."

I nodded, still unsure.

"And hey," Megan said between bites, a smear of chocolate dotting her upper lip, "if the date's a total bomb, it's not like you ever have to go out with him again."

Something about her blunt word choice, combined with the chocolate on her lips, made me laugh hard for the first time in ages. And it felt good.

Megan always did have a knack for saying something funny at the right time. Perhaps that was one of the many reasons she was so well liked. A quick scan around her room was proof. Photos of Megan and her friends cluttered her walls and dresser, and in almost all of them, the subjects were laughing. Most of her prom photos were in boxes under her bed, but the evidences of her dating prowess were still plentiful.

I looked for a photo of Ryan amid the others, but I couldn't find one. I wondered how many dates Megan had thought were total "bombs." It was true though. I wouldn't need to worry about going out with Paul ever again if it didn't go well. So maybe that was the answer, just see how it might go.

"I guess I better check where Katie is," I said, realizing the time. "She might be driving Dad crazy."

They followed me to the family room, where Katie sat quietly watching a woodworking show with her Grandpa.

Surprised that my mini tornado wasn't bouncing on the furniture or doing some equally energetic activity, I said, "Hey, Dad. What's your secret? You've got the magic touch."

He looked up, a light in his eyes. "Hey, when you've got it, you've got it." Then he winked at his wife. "Isn't that right, dear?"

Mom shook her head and chuckled at him. I loved the way my parents interacted with one another. Shaun and Karen seemed to be like that. It was the way I'd thought it would be with John. I'd never experience that now.

Would Ryan and Megan be like that? If they got married, would they be blessed with that kind of relationship? Ryan didn't seem like the kind of guy who would cheat on his wife, but there was no guarantee of anything in a relationship. Most likely, Ryan would be perfectly wonderful to Megan. I should be happy for her.

*****

"Will you be good for Grandma and Grandpa, sweetie?"

I knelt beside Katie in my parents' half-lit foyer, trying to reassure her. But it didn't seem to be working. Paul stood behind me, a looming presence.

I can't believe I'm doing this.

I'd convinced myself that by going out with Paul, I'd be moving forward, progressing, moving on. I took a quick glance at him. Everything about him was foreign: the scent of his aftershave, his expensive-looking sweater and leather penny loafers, his hands. He did look nice, and his expression was kind . . . but I wondered how many dates he'd had since his wife had died. He was probably more used to this than I was.

Not that I'd ever be used to dating. Or that I'd ever *want* to be used to dating! Besides, this wasn't a date. Or so I continued telling myself.

"I'll be a good girl," Katie nodded solemnly. Her face scrunched up to ask, "When are you coming back?"

"In a little while. Maybe after your Cinderella movie is over."

Katie shoved her tiny fists onto her hips and scowled as if she'd been told something appalling. "At sixteen o'clock?"

I held back my amusement, knowing this was serious business to my little girl. But I heard Paul's low chuckle behind me. "No, not that late. Only nine o'clock." I stroked Katie's cheek tenderly. "Okay?"

Katie heaved a sigh of frustration. "'Kay."

My mother came into the foyer to pick up Katie. "We're going to have so much fun! How would you like to make cookies with sprinkles on them?"

"What color?"

"I have pink and yellow and green."

A knock thudded on the front door. Paul was standing right in front of the door, so he asked, "Shall I open it?"

Mom said, "Sure, it's probably Ryan. He and Megan are going to dinner."

Paul opened the door. On the other side, Ryan looked up, his casual expression changing when he saw Paul. He stood at the threshold, eyebrows furrowed, not moving.

"Hello," Paul said neutrally.

"Hi." Ryan looked beyond Paul and saw everyone else standing there.

Katie perked up considerably. "It's Ry-yun!"

"Come on in, Ryan," my mom said warmly. "Megan's getting ready. She'll be out in a minute."

Ryan stepped inside and glanced around. In one swift motion, he seemed to assess the way I was dressed, how Katie clung to her grandma, and the way Paul hovered beside me.

Turning to Katie, he asked, "Hey, cutie, been practicing my name?"

Katie giggled. "I 'ready know your name!"

As he chuckled, he caught my eye. His smile creased his cheek adorably. I turned away guiltily for having had the thought.

"Paul and Ashlyn are just leaving for dinner," Mom explained.

"So where are you two eating tonight?" Ryan asked casually, his long fingers shoving the sleeves of his thermal shirt up his solid forearms.

Shifting my wandering eyes over to Paul, I realized that he hadn't mentioned what he had in mind for dinner, so I let him answer.

"I thought we'd try Carpe Vino," Paul answered, taking another step closer to me.

I saw Ryan's eyebrows raise a notch, which made me wonder if it was an expensive restaurant. I wouldn't know; I'd barely dated anyone before I met John.

"What about you?" Paul asked Ryan.

"I don't know for sure. I'll let Megan decide." Ryan rocked back on his heels, avoiding everyone's eyes by focusing on a painting in the entry. Something was definitely up between those two.

Paul placed a hand at my back. "Shall we go then?" he asked, appearing quite at ease.

I nodded, though still apprehensive—especially about leaving Katie. I'd only left her a handful of times before. And I was terribly inexperienced with dating.

Mom reassured me. "We'll be fine. Go ahead and have a nice time."

I looked back to blow Katie a kiss. She reached out to "catch" the kiss in her hand and press it to her cheek. I grinned. My parents had always done that with me when I was growing up, and I had automatically taught Katie. I hoped Katie would pass the little token of affection on to her own children someday.

"Bye, Mommy," Katie's voice was sad.

"Bye, Katie. I love you."

Paul held the front door open for me. I took one last look at Katie, but as I turned to walk outside, my eyes snagged in Ryan's gaze. The expression on his face caught me off guard. It was intense, drawing me in. Something fluttered wildly inside my body while I was locked in his gaze. I pressed a hand instinctively against my midsection.

How does he do that? How did he manage to affect me so intensely? It was completely unexpected and utterly baffling.

The pressure at my back brought me to the realization that Paul was helping me out the door. I stepped outside, and he shut the door. The air was chilly but not cold. Newly emerging daffodils lined the walkway interspersed with short green shoots of future tulips.

Two cars were parked out front. Ryan's old, white sedan was rusting in a few places and had several scratches in the paint. It must have been keyed because an unsightly gray streak extended waist-high along the side of the car. Paul's car, on the other hand, was a small, sporty-looking thing, its glossy black paint gleaming perfectly in the moonlight.

He opened my door and helped me in. I did like the fact that he was a complete gentleman.

When he got in, he asked, "Does Carpe Vino sound good to you? Because Monkey Cat is another option if you prefer."

"Wow, I don't know. I've never been to either. What kind of food do they serve?"

"Well, Carpe Vino has duck, steak, scallops. It's all very nice. Monkey Cat has a little of everything—pasta, seafood, lamb . . ."

"It all sounds good." I laughed nervously.

Before reaching the Southern Pacific Railroad trestle, Paul exited I-80 and headed into historic Old Town Auburn. I could almost hear my grade school teachers chanting, "The oldest gold mining town in the West!"

"I haven't been here for ages," I realized. "Don't you love the old courthouse?"

The historic Placer County courthouse, sitting high atop a hill, was the first thing most people noticed as they came into town. A proud gatekeeper to the town below, the gold-domed building—a combination of classic revival below, with a Renaissance-inspired bell tower crowning the ornate structure—could be seen from the freeway as well as from many vantage points through town.

Paul nodded. "It's impressive. I like the yellowish color."

"Appropriate for gold country, don't you think?"

"Definitely. If you'd like, we can drive past some of the landmarks."

"I'd like that very much." I smiled. I loved Auburn's history and remembered it being one of the subjects I enjoyed most in school.

We drove past the colossal concrete statue of Claud Chana, a tribute to the prospector who discovered gold in the Auburn Ravine just months after the events at Sutter's Mill. I remembered climbing up the kneeling statue to pose with my friends inside his gold pan. The artist who'd sculpted it had done several others down on Auburn Ravine Road—as kids, we'd always referred to them as "the naked statues." My parents avoided driving us past those after Shaun stuck his first camera out the window for some close-ups.

We continued on Lincoln Way past the Queen Anne–style red-and-white firehouse and then the historic post office, famous for being the oldest continually operated post office west of the Mississippi.

"Right across the street here is Carpe Vino." Paul pointed. The rough, red bricks of the old Union Saloon brought to mind the days of rowdy gold miners and bawdy saloons.

Okay. So dinner option number one: a modern-day saloon. This could be interesting.

"I'll drive by Monkey Cat, and then we can decide."

"Okay. Sounds good," I replied, thinking he was right on the same wavelength.

He followed Lincoln up to High Street. A welcome sign to Downtown Auburn greeted us at the town square, where the old-fashioned clock tower was located. It seemed funny to call this "downtown" when it still had the feeling of the old West. My mom always called this section "Old Auburn" and the really old section "Old-Old Auburn."

Paul drove up the other side of Lincoln Way a couple blocks and then pulled into a parking space in front of my favorite building in town—the Auburn Drug Company. Grandma Kennedy used to bring the grandkids here for cherry phosphates at the white marble soda fountain. I wished I could walk in, hear the bells chime on the door, sit on a barstool, and soak up the turn-of-the century atmosphere. What were we doing here?

"Monkey Cat is on the corner," Paul said, pointing three doors down. "We don't have to eat here, I just thought I'd take the parking space since it was so close."

"Let's eat here. This is fine," I said, realizing I actually meant it. Things were fine. I felt different, but it was a decent kind of different. Not exactly comfortable but content.

During dinner, there was little of the awkwardness I'd anticipated. It was fairly expensive after all, but the food was delicious. We talked quite freely but never actually about John or his death. Paul did most of the talking, telling me about his wife, Danielle, and her cancer story. It was terribly sad. His three children had taken it very hard when she died.

"Christopher, my oldest, was in fourth grade at the time. He's in seventh grade now. He seems to be doing all right, but he's such a quiet kid that you never know what he's thinking. Kaden's in fifth grade, and Krista's in third."

I smiled sympathetically, not knowing what to say exactly. Sometimes words were inadequate.

"I'd really like you to meet them," Paul said rather intently. "I know they'll like you."

Whoa. Comfortable just flew out the window. I knew Paul was older than I was, but I didn't realize he was old enough to have kids that age. And he wanted me to meet them? I stared at the ice clanging together in my drink as I swirled my straw. A drip of condensation slid down the side of the glass.

Paul must have noticed my shift in moods because he was quieter on the drive home. When we arrived at my parents' house, he turned off the car and turned toward me.

"Ashlyn," he said quietly, drawing a pattern on the dashboard between us.

Wondering what he was going to say became agonizing. Perhaps my mood shift had pushed him away. Maybe he thought we didn't click enough to go out again. Or he realized how much older he was and didn't want to go out with me again. That was fine with me . . . seriously.

Paul cleared his throat. "I just wanted to tell you that I—" He broke off, appearing to search for the right words.

I felt my nerves getting the best of me. It was suddenly stiflingly hot in the car. I needed some air. But the windows wouldn't work with the car turned off. It would be rude to open the car door. I'd die of suffocation in a minute if I didn't get some air.

"I had a very good time with you tonight. It meant a lot to me."

It wasn't what I'd expected him to say. My throat felt too dry to respond. But I had to say something. "I . . . had a nice time too. Thanks for dinner."

"Can I call you?"

Oh boy. He was nice, and I enjoyed being treated so well, but I didn't feel anything romantic between us. At all. I wasn't ready for that even if I did.

On the other hand, what if he was the right one for me, and I just couldn't see it? What if I pushed him away when I shouldn't? How did you know who the right one was, anyway? I thought John was the right one, but he died before we were sealed and had an affair before that. What about Paul? Were there two "right ones" for some people?

The gushing river of thoughts churned together, and my head hurt trying to stay afloat. Should I agree to let Paul call me? It wouldn't be that big of a deal, would it?

Finally, I said, "Sure."

Paul placed his hand over mine and smiled meaningfully. "Thank you."

It did feel nice and was kind of flattering to have a man interested in me. *But no way am I kissing you, buddy!*

As he walked me to the door, one hand cautiously at my elbow, I noticed the white car in front of the house. Megan and Ryan must be back. But thinking about Ryan in that snug-fitting thermal shirt did strange things to my full stomach, so I focused on the front door.

Paul coughed and tapped the doormat with the tip of his shoe. "I'll give you a call next week if that's all right?"

"Fine." I nodded, clinging to the doorknob in a death grip. "Good night."

I leaned against the door, and it sprang open, making me stagger forward. I hung on, tripped backward, and the door slammed shut. I was spared from further mortification.

Oh, that was impressive.

I rushed inside, slunk against the door, and closed my eyes with a sigh.

"Is that you, Ash?" my mom called from the kitchen.

"Yeah, I'm back."

I went into the kitchen, where Mom and Megan were washing pots and pans.

"How'd it go?" Megan asked cautiously.

I shrugged laughingly. "I guess it was okay."

Mom smiled and raised her eyebrows, waiting for more.

"Dinner was really good." I scanned the room, wondering where Ryan was. Somehow I felt embarrassed discussing my evening with him around. "How did Katie do?"

"She stole Ryan away from me," Megan laughed offhandedly.

"What?"

Mom clarified, "After we made cookies, she started asking for you. When Ryan and Megan got back, she cheered up and hasn't left his side since."

"So where are they?"

Both of them exchanged an amused look. Then Megan said, "You have to go see. It's adorable. Ryan read her a story on the sofa downstairs, and they both fell asleep."

"Oh." I puckered my eyebrows. I wasn't sure how I felt about that.

They waved me off, and I went downstairs. The silent room was dark except for one lamp that cast a hazy, amber glow over the two sleeping figures. Ryan was slumped over on the sofa, one arm protectively around Katie. The storybook was slipping out of his fingers. Katie looked so happy, so peaceful snuggled up to him.

Something stirred inside me. It was unlike anything I recognized— warm, like the glowing embers of a fire on a cool, summer night.

I approached and gently took the book, watching Ryan's long fingers close instinctively against his palm. I stood mesmerized by the scene. It awakened feelings I'd never experienced before. As I watched the two of them, Ryan's deep breathing the only sound in the room, I was filled with an overwhelming sense of trust. It was comfortable to see him with my daughter. There was no feeling of hesitancy.

Picking Katie up without waking her was my biggest concern. I definitely didn't want to wake Ryan. Edging close to them, I was acutely aware of the way his shirt rose and fell with each breath. The soft, well-worn fabric clung to his hero-sized torso.

Leaning forward even closer, I caught the scent of sandalwood, spices, and citrus. Long, dark eyelashes fanned out over his smooth skin. I wished I had eyelashes like that. His lips were slightly parted, allowing each breath an escape as he slept. The curvy shape of his lips was absolutely—

Ashlyn Rose, stop staring at his mouth!

I cautiously slid one hand under Katie, trying not to touch Ryan in any way. They both stirred. Arched over them, I paused, my heart in my throat. If Ryan woke, he might not appreciate seeing me there—practically in his face. I tried again to get hold of Katie.

He mumbled something softly, and I froze in place.

His eyes drooped open slightly, his free hand unexpectedly lifted to my face. "Hi," he whispered, gently stroking my cheek with his thumb in a tender caress. His eyes closed again, his hand falling back to his lap.

I couldn't move. I couldn't breathe.

I stood transfixed by the slight upward curve of his mouth. The feel of his fingers still lingered on my skin, shocking my senses, burning me. My heart raced wildly. He must have thought I was Megan! He couldn't have thought it was me. Maybe he was dreaming. I didn't know, but the warmth of his touch had felt . . . indescribable.

If only I could be loved that way again, tenderly touched as Ryan had done in that simple gesture. I wanted to feel it again but knew I wouldn't. Not from him, not from John. I didn't have a husband to love me anymore. I was alone in the world.

Getting a better hold on Katie, I lifted and carried her away, leaving Ryan behind, hopefully still asleep.

"Cute, weren't they?" Megan asked when I made it upstairs.

"Uh . . . yeah, they were."

"Let me help you out to your car, honey," Mom said, grabbing the bag of Katie's things. "Do you want Dad to carry Katie for you?"

"That's okay, I'm used to it," I answered ruefully. "Uh, Megan, he's still asleep down there."

"Who, Dad?"

"No, Ryan."

"Oh, okay." She flipped a hand over in the air. "If he doesn't come up in a minute, I'll go wake him."

I thought my sister seemed a little unconcerned about her date but didn't press the issue. I put Katie in the car, thanked my parents for watching her, and headed home.

Later that night, lying in bed all alone, I stared at the ceiling. I couldn't help remembering the sensation of gentle fingers brushing my cheek. My hand reached out to the other side of the bed and found emptiness.

"While new emotions, like strange barges, make
Along vein-channels their disturbing course . . ."
–Ella Wheeler Wilcox

Chapter 10

THE FOLLOWING WEEK, KATIE REMINDED me that there were no sparkles and pink things in her bedroom, so we drove to a few stores looking for ideas. Katie seemed most enamored with princesses and fairies—all the fairytale stuff.

It didn't exactly thrill me at first. Yet seeing Katie's eyes light up as she felt fluffy pink pillows or saw glittery room decorations, it was worth it to make her so happy. Not wanting to spend too much money, I was relieved to find several things at discounted prices.

Paint was another story. There was no way I would walk into a home improvement store without my dad to help. I didn't have a clue how to select a paint color. What were you supposed to do with those little paper rectangles they had organized in every color in the universe? I could picture myself looking like a complete idiot to everyone in the store by asking ridiculous questions that probably had obvious answers to everyone else. But I could learn. Everyone had to start somewhere.

"I'll ask Grandpa if he could help us paint your room, okay, Katie?"

"Okay."

Then I remembered Brother Loveless was my home teacher. People were supposed to ask their home teachers for help. It just didn't feel right to ask for *that* much help. Painting a room seemed like an immense undertaking that would require far too much service of anyone. Maybe I could ask him to do something smaller. Like . . . what? Repaint everything I ruined?

The next evening, after cleaning up our small dinner, Katie and I went over to my parents' house for dessert. Mom had made a huge carrot cake with real cream cheese frosting to share with everyone. But as soon as I walked in the door, the voices coming from the family room made me realize that my mother's version of "everyone" included Ryan and his parents.

I couldn't avoid this guy if I tried!

And now I had to face Brother and Sister Anderson as well. I couldn't escape because Katie had already raced up to her grandpa for a hug. They all knew I'd be coming around the corner any second. And I couldn't be mad at my mom—Diane Kennedy couldn't help inviting people over. She'd been doing it since the beginning of time.

The problem was facing Ryan after what had happened the night he fell asleep next to Katie. Did he realize what he had done, or did he think it was Megan he'd touched? My heart whirled erratically inside my chest just remembering the way it had felt: sweet, tender, caressing—

Picturing a needle scratching across a vinyl record, I brought that thread of thought to a halt. Anyway, how was I supposed to act around him? I could pretend like nothing had happened. We'd become experts at that by now. Then I could watch his behavior around me to gauge what my response should be. Maybe he'd been so tired that night that he didn't remember.

Please, don't remember.

As I came into the room, my dad stood up to welcome me. "Here she is!" he said, extending his arms.

"It's so good to see you again," Valerie Anderson said, standing to give me a hug. "It's been a long time, hasn't it?"

"Yes, it has."

Her husband, Joe, also stood to extend a greeting. Every eye in the room was on me, reminding me of the reason I never took drama. I wouldn't have felt any more conspicuous if they had each pulled out theatre binoculars and aimed them at me. I felt a rush of heat spreading across my cheeks.

"Come have a seat, honey," my dad said, indicating the spot on the country blue, floral sofa where he'd been sitting. I sat down between my parents, taking a quick sweep of the room. Joe and Valerie were on my left, Ryan on the right. Megan and Katie sat on the hearth of the fireplace, directly across from me.

Through the large window, Lake Combie was visible through dense pine and oak, a smooth, green emerald below. I'd loved growing up on the lake. When summer came, I'd finally be able to take Katie out in the boat, a dream I had tucked away for the future. And at that moment, I'd have done anything to be down there instead of up here in the house!

"So, do you feel like you're all moved in now?" Valerie asked pleasantly.

I smiled and cleared my throat. "More or less. There's always something else to do, but I'm getting there."

"When you get there, let me know how you did it"—Joe laughed heartily—"because I don't think we'll ever arrive! Every home we've lived in has needed repairs or improvements. When we get to the point where we think we're settled in Meadow Vista again, the deer will eat every living thing in our yard to remind us who's boss. It keeps us on our toes, I guess."

I nodded with a smile. The deer were permanent residents in the area, and my family had years of experience dealing with them. My parents had fenced in a small garden on the side of the hill, hoping to keep them out, but it was only a partially successful venture.

Still not having summoned the courage to glance at Ryan, I kept him just beyond my peripheral vision. But I could almost feel his eyes on me. His dark, leather shoes were a stark contrast against the buff-colored carpet. His long, lean legs stretched out in front of him. I was aware of every movement they made. Did he ever let his parents know about what happened between us? I wouldn't think so, and besides, they didn't act like anything out of the ordinary had ever happened.

Conversation safely continued, mainly between the two sets of parents. They began with the subject of houses, progressing to jobs and grand-children. Megan was playing rock-paper-scissors with Katie, half listening.

What was Ryan doing? Curiosity triumphed over timidity. I took a quick glance at him, and my heart nearly stopped. He'd been staring right at me before abruptly turning his head. I should be used to the strange effect Ryan had on me, but I stared back at him, dumbfounded, waiting for my heart to calm down. He knew I'd seen him staring at me, if the ruddy tinge on his cheeks was any indication.

"So, Megan," Valerie was saying, "tell us about the project you're cooking up for your sister."

Megan's head shot up as fast as mine turned.

"What project?" we asked simultaneously.

"You mentioned getting the singles ward together. For a service project?" she prompted.

Megan inhaled sharply. "Ah, yeah . . . that project." Turning to me, she cautiously explained, "I was thinking, Ash, that a few of our friends could come over to do a little spring yard work for you." She turned to Ryan for support.

He finally turned his gaze to me. Full on. The expression in his eyes lanced through me. "I think it would be a great service project for everyone. We'd really like to come."

"Thanks for the offer," I answered, feeling strangely threatened, "but I'm not sure that'll work for me right now."

He wasn't so easily put off. "We could paint your fence, clean up the tree branches . . . anything you'd like. You'd be doing us a favor too."

"How would that be doing you a favor?" I asked, instantly wishing I could take back my words. I hadn't meant to sound impolite; it just came out that way.

Every head present seemed to swing from me to Ryan and back like they were watching a tennis match. Back and forth, the ball was now in Ryan's court.

"We've been looking for a service project that—"

"I'm not a service project," I volleyed, realizing my words hadn't improved in politeness.

Megan seared me with a warning glance. The Andersons seemed to be holding their breaths. Dad had his mouth open, probably about to say something.

Then my sweet mother came to referee. "This is a tough situation, isn't it, Ash? With things that need to be done but not wanting to appear helpless." She put her arm around me. "You are a strong, independent woman."

Yeah, you tell 'em, Mom! I don't need their help.

"But you need their help."

"Wha . . . ?" I wheezed.

"I think inviting them over is a wonderful idea, for both you and them. They're looking for a way to serve, and it'll be a blessing to you by doing so."

I resumed breathing. Of course my mother was right, darn it all! As much as I hated to admit it, I knew I really did need help. I just wasn't ready. Sure, I'd already told Megan that she and Ryan could come over, but when I'd jokingly told Megan to bring her whole ward, I didn't think she'd really do it!

What would it be like to have a herd of young single adults fixing up my yard? There was plenty of work to be done outside. When would I ever find time to do it all myself? Even with my family's help, it would take a while. Fixing up the inside of my home was daunting enough. I knew I needed help with the yard.

I'd glued on my coat of pride and worn it so long that now it was hard to pry off. But I was realizing the need to try. "You're right, Mom. It would be"—I swallowed hard—"great."

*****

I take it back! I don't want everyone's help!

I panicked at the sight in my front window—a mob of young single adults approaching my house. A few weeks after agreeing to get help, I was getting ambushed. I didn't feel ready for them, but there was no turning back.

Megan jogged up to the front porch, ahead of everyone else. I might have stood frozen by the door, but my three-year-old tornado ripped through the house to answer it.

Katie jumped into Megan's arms and then looked beyond her. "Where's Ry-yun?"

"He's coming. Hey, Ash." She smiled. "We're all here."

"Hi, Megan. I was—" I broke off when a girl stepped out of an Audi wearing designer jeans that looked like they'd been spray painted on her. Even her top was molded to her curves. Her eyes were rimmed with enough eyeliner for a theatrical production. And she was stunning.

Megan turned around to follow my gaze.

"Who's that?" I whispered.

"Bethany," Megan answered, swiveling her eyes in disgust.

I did a double take. I would never have connected her to the troublemaker I remembered from years ago. This girl looked like she'd just stepped out of the pages of *Cosmopolitan*—and knew it, too, judging by the way she strutted her stuff.

Katie suddenly squealed, "Hi, Ryan," and jumped down to see her buddy as he walked up to the porch.

"Hey, how's my girl?" Ryan scooped Katie up. As he stood, his eyes met mine, and his cheeks seemed to flush. "Hello."

I felt an unexpected flutter in my chest when he spoke to me. "Hi," I said.

That crazy, unexplainable zinging sensation I got around him wasn't getting any better. He held my gaze, an uncertain smile on his lips, until Bethany walked gracefully up to Ryan, eyeing Katie warily.

"Wow, Ryan" she gushed, managing to drape a slender arm over his shoulder, "you're totally good with children."

Ryan chuckled good-naturedly. "Who wouldn't be with this little pumpkin?" He ruffled Katie's hair, making her giggle.

"I'm not a pumpkin, silly."

I could have sworn Bethany snorted distastefully at Katie but couldn't be sure. The quiver of Bethany's eyelash extensions had suddenly engrossed me. The girl looked like she was covered in extensions—hair, nails, chest. Where did she get the money for her beauty regimen and upgrades?

As another carload of people drove up the gravel driveway and parked, my attention shifted to their youthful faces. They got out of the vehicle and tromped up to the porch, all radiating enthusiasm for the service project. I invited them all into the garage, where Ryan began making the introductions.

Casually putting his hand on my upper arm, he said, "This is Ashlyn Carter and her daughter, Katie."

He was several inches taller than I was. Standing beside him reminded me of the way it felt standing next to John—protected and worth protecting. I liked that feeling . . . far too much. What was wrong with me?

Don't blush in front of these people.

There were five guys and four girls. I was introduced to the famous Drake, who was too shy to ask Megan out. He was tall and skinny with black-rimmed glasses. In a cute, slightly nerdy sort of way, he thanked me for letting them come. I didn't think he had anything over Ryan, but Megan liked every guy she came in contact with.

A short, curvaceous girl named Erin squeezed my hand in a bone-crushing handshake, informing me that they were all there to work hard. "So go ahead and put us all to work, Sister Carter!"

Being called "Sister Carter" instead of Ashlyn made me feel ancient next to their lush youth. Bethany apparently hadn't deemed it necessary to give me any particular notice up to that point, but seeing Ryan at my side, she tilted her face, eyes narrowed, sizing me up with displeasure. Feeling like an amoebic specimen under scrutiny in a biology lab, I could imagine all my visible flaws. And I could've sworn Bethany smothered some laughter—not the friendly kind either.

Ryan's hand on my arm slipped away, and I was left feeling strangely bereft. I watched him explain how they'd be helping today. He was confident and energetic, a true leader, with a way about him that drew people in. I noticed the faces of the other girls riveted to Ryan's. They were pretty girls and all probably secretly crushing on him.

Ryan chuckled about something, and I had to look away. His smile was upsetting my equilibrium. I still didn't know if he realized he'd touched my face the other night, but seeing the captivating shape of his lips reminded me all too clearly.

Everyone laughed at something Ryan said, and I glanced back.

Did he just wink at me? I missed the gist of the conversation. But if Ryan had winked at me, he didn't wink so everyone would notice. It appeared that it was only meant for me—a private, shared moment between us which made me feel weak inside.

I couldn't explain the effect he had on me. I could handle him when he was younger, but this was ridiculous. He probably affected everyone that way now. How could he *not* with looks like that? Anyone would think they were attracted to him, but I had to get this under control. I would not repeat past mistakes. And Megan had been going out with Ryan longer than any of the other guys she dated before. If she was finally serious about someone, I wasn't about to do *anything* that would mess it up for her!

"We'll split up into two groups," Ryan was saying. "Who wants to paint the picket fence?"

Several hands went up. Bethany's most definitely did not. She was examining the rhinestones embedded in her fingernail and the way they sparkled in the sun.

Ryan handed out the paintbrushes and paint my father had brought over earlier. Those who were left were assigned to rake soggy leaves that had fallen last year and gather the tree branches scattered messily across the yard. Ryan began aerating the small patch of lawn, amazing me yet again with his adeptness in so many areas.

Back inside the house, I could see everyone from my kitchen window, noticing their energy, youth, and vitality. One girl with silky, long brown hair—and a figure to die for—was in constant motion: paint, flirt, laugh . . . paint, flirt, laugh . . . She was unbelievable!

Did I ever act like that when I was younger?

Another girl was giving Katie piggyback rides up and down the yard to keep her away from the wet paint. It made me tired just looking at them. Then my eyes came across Ryan, who was talking to Drake. Drake said something that must have been funny, and Ryan playfully slugged him in return.

Hearing a lonely chuckle escape my lips—the only sound in the kitchen—brought my attention to the obvious separation between me and those outside. I was not part of that playful banter. I was alone, isolated, different.

Forcing myself to walk away, I gathered a load of laundry to put in the washing machine. I wasn't so sure I was cut out for the whole homemaking role. And now, without a husband to help me with the house, I really would need to learn to accept help. I thought about Megan's friends and everything they were doing outside. It wasn't exactly easy having them here, but I was grateful for what they would accomplish.

"Hey, Ash?" Megan's voice called from the front of the house.

"Yeah? I'm back here. In the laundry room."

Megan's footsteps stomped through the house before her angry face appeared inside the laundry room doorway. "Hi," she growled.

"Hi." I raised my eyebrows expectantly, knowing my sister was going to blow. "How's it going?"

"I'm going to scream, Ash!"

Amusement sparked inside my chest. "What's wrong?"

Megan huffed loudly before mouthing "Beth-a-nee" in disgust.

"What's she doing?" I asked, fishing a sock out of the dryer.

"Nothing! That's what she's doing! She's fawning all over Ryan, doing absolutely nothing to help out there."

"Ahh," I said, stifling a smirk.

Megan gave me a rattled look. "Ash, she's driving me crazy!"

"I believe you."

"I mean, why come if you're not going to do anything, right?"

"Right."

"But she's determined to get Ryan."

"You don't just 'get' someone."

"Exactly. But don't tell her that. She had a revelation or something that he was The One."

"What?" I finally laughed outright. "Are you serious?"

"I'm serious. She was talking about her so-called spiritual experience recently."

Just then, the object of our conversation called out a shrill "Hello-o? Is anyone here?"

Megan pressed her forehead against the laundry room door and muttered something unintelligible under her breath.

Rumpling Megan's hair, I walked past her. "Coming!" I found Bethany in the kitchen, peeking inside a cupboard. "Can I help you?"

Bethany spun around, her hair flipping into her eyes. "Oh, well, I came inside to get some water. For the guys. They look thirsty." Her perfectly painted acrylic nails stroked the hair out of her eyes and off her sticky lip gloss.

"All right," I said, looking behind me to see if Megan had followed but finding no sign of her. "The cups are over here, Bethany."

I filled a glass pitcher of ice water and set it on the kitchen table. Bethany filled a single cup and proceeded outside, leaving the pitcher and stack of cups on the table. I shoved a hand against my hip and stared after her in bemusement. *I guess "the guys" translates to "Ryan."*

Megan cautiously walked up. "What's she doing?"

"Providing refreshment to the thirsty," I answered, biting my lip.

"Oh. Well, I guess that's . . . decent," Megan stated grudgingly.

I looked down at the pitcher and cups. "There's just one problem—she forgot the refreshment."

Megan snorted, and neither of us could hold back a hint of laughter.

"Maybe we should help her out," she suggested, lifting the pitcher.

"Good idea."

I took the cups and followed Megan outside. We walked across the yard to the larger group painting the fence. Katie sat nearby, watching them. A good deal of giggling and flirting appeared to be taking place, yet they had managed to paint quite a big section of the fence.

Megan asked, "Anyone thirsty?"

Hearing several grunts of agreement, we passed out cups of water, seeing neither Bethany nor Ryan.

"Thanks, Sister Carter," Drake said, scooting his glasses up the sweaty ridge of his nose. "We're about half done. Does it look all right to you?"

"Yeah, it looks so much better than it did. You're all doing a great job." The painted part of the fence was shiny white, a stark contrast to the grayed, weather-beaten section. When they finished it would make such a difference on how my yard looked.

After satiating everyone's thirst, I took the pitcher and cups back into the house. Megan remained outside to help finish the painting. I glanced behind me, wondering where Ryan and Bethany were, but I still couldn't see them anywhere.

Inside the house, separated from the youthful display, I washed the dishes in the sink, thinking about all the single adults out there. I wondered if many went to Sierra College or if they were going to UC Davis. How many had graduated and were working? If I were to go back to work, would I be abandoning Katie? Was working what I really wanted to do? Was it the best thing for us?

I washed all the cups and then the glass pitcher in the sudsy water, considering my life. My finger trailed down the grooves in the glass. Aunt Louise had given the pitcher to John and me for our wedding. It was such a beautiful gift, a symbol of all the hopes I'd had for a beautiful future.

Something caught my eye out the window. I looked up from the suds and saw Ryan and Bethany in a fairly intense conversation outside, out near the propane tank on the side of the property. Bethany moved in closer to Ryan, running her hand up his arm. I felt the pitcher slip out of my grasp. My right hand shot out to catch it, but the handle struck the side of the sink, shattering the glass.

"No!" I wailed faintly. Glass slivers and fragments fell in the sudsy water and behind the faucets. My beautiful wedding present was ruined!

I reached cautiously into the water to unplug the sink and felt a large piece of glass. I lifted it out to throw the piece away, waiting for the water to drain away before cleaning up the rest of the glass. With a paper towel, I scooped around the sink, fishing for any remaining shards.

A circle of crimson spread across the paper towel before I realized I'd been cut.

Uh oh. I didn't even know if I had any Band-Aids. At least it wasn't a big cut. It should stop bleeding in a second. I threw away the paper towel holding the glass pieces and washed my hands, looking for the cut where I felt a small prick of pain. As soon as I turned off the water and reached for a clean paper towel, I saw blood dripping into the sink.

Great. It wasn't a small cut after all. A flap of skin on the underside of my thumb was oozing blood down my hand. I pressed the paper towel against the wound to stop the bleeding. It was beginning to hurt now.

I heard the front door open.

"Megan, is that you?" I called out, wondering why I felt a little woozy. I'd never had a problem with the sight of blood before.

"No, it's me," I heard Ryan grumble. "I wanted to see if—" His words came to a halt when he came into the kitchen and saw my white face and blood all over the paper towel I'd clamped to my hand. "What happened?"

My knees became rubbery, and I grabbed for the counter.

"Whoa!" Ryan raced to my side, wrapping an arm around me for support. "Here we go. Let me help you to a chair."

"I'm fine. Really."

I tried to pull away, but his arms held fast. He grabbed the roll of paper towels then led me over to the chair at the head of the kitchen table. Lowering me down cautiously and reaching for my hand, he said, "Let me see."

His fingers gently lifted mine away from the bloody wound. Sucking in his breath, he softly said, "Ouch." After inspecting it briefly, he folded two paper towels into a pad and pressed them against the gash. "Keep the pressure on it for a sec."

"I'm fine. Don't worry about it."

He took the soiled paper towel to the garbage can. Coming back to sit in front of me on another chair, he took my hand in his again, turning it palm up, to see if the blood had stopped.

"You don't have to do that," I said, feeling considerably flustered . . . not just from the cut, but from his close proximity and the gentle, warm touch of his fingers on my skin. His knees pressed against mine as he leaned forward to check my hand.

He looked up, concern furrowing his thick eyebrows. "So what happened?"

"I dropped a glass pitcher in the sink."

From where I sat, I could see the broken remains on the countertop. It would have to be thrown away. My pitcher that had once been so pretty would now have to be discarded. It was useless, just like I felt.

Ryan saw a tear slide down my cheek. "Hey, it's okay," he rubbed my forearm consolingly with his free hand. "Do you have any Band-Aids? You're going to need something on this."

"I don't know. I'll go look." I practically rocket-launched off the chair to escape his nearness and almost stumbled, but he jumped up and caught me.

"Ashlyn, sit down," he said softly. "Please. I'll find them for you."

"I don't even know if I have any, let alone where they'd be."

"You know what? We've got plenty at my house. I'll go down there and be right back." He leaned over me again, placing both hands on my shoulders. "Just stay here, all right?"

I nodded in agreement. The pressure of Ryan's hands on my shoulders increased. I didn't dare look up at him. If I did, my face would be inches away from his. I couldn't take this nearness. If Megan walked in, she'd tell in an instant what was happening to me.

How could I be so affected by him? Where was my animosity toward the person who'd tainted my tutoring career? Nothing made sense, and my head was getting fuzzy. As soon as Ryan was gone, I got up to look for the broom. I didn't know if any glass got on the floor, but I would need to sweep just in case. I didn't want anyone else getting hurt.

Megan came inside—Katie close at her heels—and started fussing over me like a mother hen. "Hey, Ryan told me what happened. Sit down, Ash. Forget the glass. I'll take care of it."

"I'm okay, Megan."

"Mommy, how did you get hurted?"

"I dropped something that broke. Stay on the sofa over there, Katie, in case there's any glass on the floor."

"Okay," Katie whimpered.

Before long, there was a light knock at the door. Ryan came in, calling, "I'm back."

Katie ripped around the corner and dive-bombed his legs, wrapping them in her tiny arms. "Ry-yun, Ry-yun! Mommy got hurted."

He stroked Katie's soft, blonde curls. "I know she did. Look what I brought." Showing her the small, white box, he asked, "Do you know what these are?"

Katie's eyes bulged wide with instant delight. "Band-Aids!" Grabbing the box, she spun around. "Mommy, look! It's Band-Aids! I'll find a good one for you."

"All right."

Trying to find any remaining broken glass, I awkwardly attempted to sweep the floor. I avoided Ryan's gaze, conscious that I hadn't remained sitting as he'd suggested and conscious of the effect he had on me.

"Thanks for getting those, Ryan," Megan said. Then pointing her thumb over her shoulder and rolling her eyes, she hissed, "She won't stop sweeping."

Like I couldn't hear her! Ryan's lips turned upward before he walked over to me. My sweeping faltered as I finally looked at him.

"Did it stop bleeding?" he asked.

"Yeah, it's fine," I said, looking down at my hand. Before I realized, he had the broom in his hand.

Megan called, "Ash, come here. Katie picked out a pink neon Band-Aid for you."

"Okay." I glanced at Ryan again. "Thanks for getting them."

He grinned. "Sorry about the colors. I grabbed the first box I saw." Then he nudged me. "Go get fixed up. I'll be outside if you need anything."

Megan took my hand to unwrap the makeshift paper towel bandage and position a Band-Aid over the cut. I was vaguely aware that Megan and Katie were talking while my eyes trailed Ryan as he walked away.

Chapter 11

How DID IT GET TO be Sunday again? It seemed like there were more Sundays in a week than other days. Maybe the other days of the week blurred together, and Sunday stood out more. But over time, I was starting to feel like Katie and I belonged in the ward, and I was eager for the temple prep class, which would be starting next week.

A rhythmic flow of water through the rain gutters indicated that it was, or had been, raining. Would my roses be in bloom next month, or did I have to wait longer? I wished they could bloom sooner but knew they weren't ready yet. Some things took time.

Sunday. I sighed. Would Paul be breathing down my neck again, probing for an answer about going out with him? In some ways it would be nice to get out again, but I wasn't sure if I was up to another date. He was sending signals, and I kept avoiding him.

I rolled out of bed, realizing that it was getting a little easier to face each day. A small step, but a step nonetheless. I got Katie up, and we ate a hurried breakfast before getting dressed. When we arrived for sacrament meeting, the rain had diminished to a mere drizzle. And we were only eight minutes late. Sitting on a bench with my parents, I felt pretty good about my achievement.

When it was time for the hallway crush afterward, Katie's Primary teacher came to take her to sharing time. My parents followed them, but I chose the opposite hallway. I'd been able to avoid Paul the last few Sundays this way. Walking down this less-crowded hallway toward Sunday School, I felt victorious again—until accidentally brushing shoulders with someone. A large, warm hand captured mine, and my heart jolted inside my chest.

Please don't be Paul.

I looked up and saw that it was Ryan.

"Hi," he said softly. He looked taller in his charcoal suit. It did wonders for those striking, steel-gray eyes. His tie was a gorgeous blend of smoky blues and greens. The suit material covered his broad shoulders in absolute perfection. "How's the cut?" he asked, lifting my hand to see.

I was painfully aware of the touch of his hand on mine. His thumb stroked the sensitive flesh of my palm next to the bandage. Something was different today, something I couldn't quite put a finger on. He didn't seem any younger than I was. He was just a guy standing beside me. We were simply two people in the hallway—with something unquestionably humming in the air between us.

That heated look was in his eyes. Only this time it was more vibrant, a living entity that arced from Ryan and flowed right through me. My heart responded emphatically.

That's when I knew. It was undeniable, as real as him standing there. I knew what my heart was feeling. It made no sense and didn't matter if it was right or wrong—it existed. There was no denying it, however embarrassing it was to admit. I couldn't even allow my mind to express it in words.

He can never know! Not ever.

Did he recognize what was happening? I couldn't encourage it. He couldn't find out how he affected me. Megan couldn't find out. I wouldn't hurt her for anything! And I had good reason to dislike him anyway. Sixteen-year-old boys should not make a pass at their twenty-year-old math tutors!

I was twenty years old and inexperienced back then. I was so shy with boys, but with Ryan and his little brother, Jason, I'd felt comfortable, and I gained more self-confidence with all the time I spent in their home, first babysitting and then tutoring as they grew older. When Brother Anderson accepted a new job in Arizona, I was between quarters at school. I helped them pack and clean. There was only a month's warning before they'd move, and it was hard on all of us. We were so close that the thought of saying good-bye really hurt.

The week before they moved, my friendship with Ryan rapidly progressed to something more confusing. I rationalized that holding his hand one night when we were alone was okay because he needed some comfort. But it escalated from there and, yes, I did kiss him back . . .

Someone turned a corner in the hallway and was approaching us. I started to pull my hand away, but Ryan didn't let go. His eyes held mine in their magnetic grasp. I tugged again, and he allowed my fingers to slip away from his. But he didn't move away. He didn't say anything either. He just held me captive for a moment longer by the intensity of his magnetic eyes.

I cleared my throat. "I have to go now."

His eyes squinted slightly, as though analyzing or questioning me. Perhaps he was just as confused as I was about what was happening between us.

"I'll be seeing you," he stated before walking away.

I'll be seeing you. Was that a promise? If so, I needed to do something to discourage him. I pulled from my memory an image of the scrawny little deacon I'd done algebra with when I was sixteen. The age gap had been huge back then. It would help to dwell on that.

I walked into Sunday School and sat down next to my parents. A short visual sweep of the room provided no sign of Paul Hitch—yet. That was good. I replayed what had just happened in the hallway with Ryan and got flushed remembering the feeling of his thumb rubbing the center of my palm. I hadn't been touched like that for a long time. It made me feel weak all over.

Don't be an idiot! I was just lonely and missed being loved. I missed that even when John was alive because he was never home.

But even as I pushed the thoughts away, something stirred inside, awakening dormant emotions. My frozen heart seemed to be reviving, renewing the awareness of feelings that had been dead. I wasn't sure I was ready to feel again. Definitely not to feel something for the wrong person! And my sweet sister's boyfriend was unquestionably the wrong person.

So why did the sight of him make me fluttery inside? Why did the touch of his hand cause me to go weak from head to toe?

I caught myself and shook my head. *Stop it!* I was not going to be interested in him or anyone else. If I ever *were* to think about caring for someone again, that someone would have to be—

Suddenly, Paul Hitch stood above me, extending a hand for me to shake. "Good morning, Ashlyn."

"Good morning," I said unevenly, shaking his hand.

He scanned the row where I sat and, finding it full, moved on with a wave and found a seat in the next row in front of me.

He'd have to be . . . what? Honest, kind, caring. He'd need to have the means to take care of Katie and me. He'd have to put his family before work. He'd have to love Katie. But who could truly love little Katie as his own? How many men would want someone else's child? I couldn't imagine that very many would. This figurative man I was concocting, who'd have to possess all the right qualities, would still need one more thing. I couldn't just remarry because I found someone with all the right stuff. I'd want to be attracted to him. I'd want to be in love with him. But I'd have to be able trust him.

And the likelihood of that happening again was slim. I'd already been through that.

I can't do it again.

I won't.

*****

Springtime in Northern California was a magnificent thing to see, and this year was no exception. As the days passed, wild grasses turned a vivid, almost unearthly green, making the rolling hills a brilliant emerald landscape. Wildflowers burst from the sleepy ground, baby birds sang, little critters ventured outside, azaleas and lilacs bloomed. Eventually the local fruit orchards would become a cloud of pink blossoms. One of my favorite spring sights in California were the hillsides bursting with orange poppies, creating a sea of orange interspersed with shoots of purple lupine.

Today, I sat on the living room carpet, a handful of plastic packages, instructions, parts, and pieces spread out in front of me. Playing with a doll, Katie looked over to ask, "You almost done, Mommy?"

Feeling like pulling my hair out for being so inept, I sighed heavily. "Nope, Mommy is *not* almost done."

"How come?"

"Because I'm trying to figure this out, and it doesn't make an ounce of sense," I answered vaguely, picking up the instructions again. The box for the princess dollhouse claimed it could be assembled with ease in a few short minutes.

Assembled with ease, my foot!

I flipped the instructions over. Chinese characters covered the page.

"What's it say on the paper?" Katie asked encouragingly.

"I don't know."

"You're 'posed to read it."

I tossed the instructions down and went back to the pieces spread out on the floor. *This big piece looks like it goes in here . . . but, ughh, it doesn't fit.*

Surely Disney wouldn't endorse a build-it-yourself-in-thirty-minutes dollhouse if it wasn't possible to build? Come on, there was a woman right there on the box, grinning from ear to ear as she effortlessly built the darned thing. So why couldn't I figure it out?

I sighed. Okay, maybe this was a job for my home teacher.

A knock on the door sent Katie running and me gaping. Holy cow! Was it really Brother Loveless? Talk about being inspired. And what a relief, not to have to deal with—

Nope. It wasn't my home teacher. Megan and Ryan walked inside, both peering down at the mess. No one in my family could believe she was still dating the same guy. It had to be a world record.

"Whatcha doing, sis?" Megan asked, snickering.

Megan knew better than anyone about my nonexistent handy skills. Since the day back in junior high school when I had decided to "redesign" her bed—causing Megan to crash to the floor in the middle of the night and have night terrors for the next two weeks—it had become a private joke between us.

I focused on Megan, commanding my eyes not to notice the gray-blue shirt Ryan was wearing or the way his arms and broad shoulders stretched the material in all the right ways. I refused to notice those strong hands tucked inside his jean pockets or the masculine way he stood there, just inside the door. It wasn't right to ogle a man several years younger than you—who also happened to be your sister's boyfriend. I knew what betrayal felt like, and I wouldn't be the cause of it.

Pretending I didn't notice Ryan, keeping my attention riveted to Megan, I could still feel the scorching heat of his gaze. Did he have any idea what he did to me? If he found out, maybe he'd be disgusted with me and never want to come back. *Hmmm . . . there's an idea.* Momentarily, I pictured throwing myself at the poor guy, just to get rid of him, and almost laughed. *I don't think so.*

"Uh . . . I was just trying to put Katie's dollhouse together," I said. "I'm not doing a very good job." I wasn't doing a very good job with a lot of things.

"So I see," she said playfully. "Mom sent us over with a casserole and milk."

"Oh, thanks. You can put them on the counter."

"Look guys!" Katie jumped over the crumpled instructions and lifted a bright pink piece of wood with rose decals all over it. "See? It's gonna be a princess house!"

"Wow, aren't you lucky," Megan said. I smirked at her.

"A princess dollhouse for a little princess," Ryan added, grinning at Katie. "Can I see?"

Katie bobbed her head up and down, thrilled with the attention she was getting. Ryan sat on the floor beside Katie, only glancing at me once. But that's all it took. In that one glance, he managed to set my heart pounding and make my cheeks flush with riotous warmth that radiated down to my throat.

This insanity had to stop! Maybe I should go out with Paul again. I didn't know anyone else my age who was single. Didn't Shaun and Karen say they knew someone? I needed to get my head screwed on in the right direction! I had to figure things out . . . with someone appropriate. Disjointed thoughts clanged discordantly inside my head: maybe I'd end up getting married again. I never thought I'd be this desperate. He was so perfect it was ridiculous.

"So what do we have here?" Ryan asked, picking up the piece I'd been trying to shove in place.

Megan walked into the kitchen to put the food away, tossing a "good luck" over her shoulder. I picked up the instructions, embarrassed at how crumpled I'd made them.

"I don't know. It's all Chinese to me."

Ryan scooted over, leaning into my shoulder to see the instructions. I felt the warmth of his breath on my skin, and all my muscles tensed. I must not respond! I had to steel myself against what was imagined, what I was only longing for. It wasn't real.

His hand reached around me for the instructions. "What's on the other side?"

I let him flip it over and said, "More Chinese."

He chuckled. The throaty sound was intoxicating. I glanced up, and his eyes met and held mine. They spoke to me with sooty heat. He seemed to study me so thoroughly, so deeply, that I felt exposed. Light poured through my body . . . wakening, warming, calling. If this wasn't real, then what was it? His gaze slipped down to my cheek, over to my mouth, and quickly back to my eyes. I knew he was remembering what happened eight years ago. For a brief moment, we were both transfixed in a silent storm.

"Ryan, can you fix it?" Katie's voice jolted me from my thoughts.

I practically leapt off the floor, bumping into Ryan, who had bolted as well. He steadied me with one arm as we mumbled, "Sorry," at the same time. But he yanked his arm away.

Megan came back into the room, oblivious to the electric tension. "Hey, it's nice and warm outside, Ash. We should take Katie to the park. She'd love it there."

Katie bounced around the room like a rubber bouncy ball gone wild. "Yeah, I want to go to the park! Please, Mommy? Let's go to the park!"

"Okay, that sounds like a good idea. I'll deal with this thing later."

Ryan cleared his throat. "I can put it together if you'd like. It shouldn't take too long."

I didn't dare glance at him, focusing instead on the mess on the floor. "Uh, sure. That would be great. I'll go get Katie a sweater."

I fled from the room, feeling Ryan's gaze following me. I opened Katie's closet and stared blindly at the clothes. I had only agreed to go to the park to be away from him. If Ryan planned on coming, I'd have to back out. I didn't think I could be around him another minute without making a fool of myself. Maybe they could take Katie while I stayed at home. I could tell them I didn't feel well. That was completely true. I was weak and breathless, my heart palpitating recklessly.

When he had gazed at me just then, I was reminded of how it had felt falling in love with John. I remembered the way John had held me in his arms the night he proposed. Even though we weren't going to be married in the temple, we were so happy and so in love. I remembered our wedding night and how perfectly he had loved me. Waking up the next morning beside my husband had been one of the sweetest moments of my life.

A painful, wrenching sob escaped my lips, and I realized that the clothes in the closet had blurred from my tears. I hadn't even realized I was crying.

Oh, John . . . why?

As my sobbing increased, I realized I didn't truly hate my dead husband. I'd loved him; I really had! I'd loved that man with all my heart and soul! What had gone wrong? Was I a bad wife? Was I not woman enough for him? I'd never know now because he was gone—forever gone. I'd almost rather have had him alive and unfaithful than dead. Maybe we could have worked out our problems, given time. In death, he was completely lost to me.

I'd been abandoned, permanently—fused to a life where I had to get up in the morning as a functioning parent while I ached inside. I had no husband to love me, to hold me, to cherish me. How I needed it again!

I need someone by my side. I want to be loved.

The sound of my sobbing was heart-wrenching even to me. Pain washed over me. How could I ever forgive John for his betrayal? It had to be time to forgive him, but I didn't know how. I had to forgive John for letting me down in so many ways—not being ready for the temple, leaving me alone so often, not being more of a father to Katie, being unfaithful, for dying.

Megan's arm was suddenly around my shoulders, rocking me back and forth like a baby. "Shh . . . it's okay, Ash. Don't cry. It's going to be okay," she soothed lovingly, over and over. "What is it? What happened?"

I wasn't able to answer. My hands shook at my side. She pulled me away from Katie's closet and helped me to my bedroom. "Here, sit down on your bed, Ash." Megan handed me a box of tissues and then rocked me some more. "Do you want to talk about anything?"

"No," I cried, overcome by another wave of tears.

"It's okay. Why don't I take Katie for a walk and give you some time alone? Is that okay with you?"

I nodded, drawing in a ragged breath, then continued to sob.

"Here. Lay down for a bit. Ryan's going to stay to build the dollhouse, and I'll be back in a little while. Everything's going to be okay, Ash. I promise."

Megan tucked a blanket around me then left, allowing me to come to terms with some of the things I had shoved away inside for too long. I cried for a long time. Afterward, I almost felt cleansed of harbored hate and pain. It lingered, but I felt renewed, ready to live again, ready to be happy again.

I almost felt free.

"O, follow, leaping blood,
The season's lure!"
–Lord Alfred Tennyson

Chapter 12

THE HOUSE WAS PEACEFUL WHEN I woke up. I glanced at the clock and
saw that I'd been asleep for a good half hour, so I got up. After splashing
my face with cool water, I patted it dry and left my room, wondering if
anyone was here. I found Ryan on the floor, the dollhouse almost finished.

"That's not fair," I smiled ruefully.

Bewilderment etched in the creases of his forehead when he looked
up.

"You're almost done."

"Oh." He smiled with a tinge of embarrassment.

"Looks great." I sat on the floor so the dollhouse was between us.
"Katie's going to love this."

He didn't answer. He looked at me as though contemplating whether
or not to speak. It made my stomach clamp into a big knot.

"Do you need help?" I asked warily.

"I do actually. This section here needs two people to get this board
positioned right."

"Okay. Show me what to do." I grabbed the piece he had pointed to,
but he touched my hand.

"Ash." His voice was low.

I looked up uncertainly.

"I was wondering if . . . we could talk?"

I opened my mouth to say no. I was embarrassed about falling apart
earlier and didn't feel like talking yet—especially about our past. "I don't
think—"

"Please?" he asked softly, giving my hand a slight squeeze.

I set down the piece I'd held, and the stillness of the house surrounded us. The refrigerator hummed gently in the kitchen; outside, a woodpecker tapped in quick bursts against a tree.

Ryan leaned forward, resting his arms against his legs. He tapped his fingers together, looking as if he were struggling to find words. I waited for him to speak first, having no words of my own. Too many memories burned through my mind.

He tilted his head. "I don't even know where we should start."

"How about: *what were you thinking!*"

"What I was thinking when—now or a long time ago?"

"Eight years ago would be a good start."

"The kiss?"

"Yeah."

He sighed heavily. "It's been a long time. I've had a lot of time to think about—"

"*You* have? I'm the one who had to deal with the shame! Why did you do it?"

"Shame?" he asked incredulously. "Ashlyn, there wasn't anything to feel ashamed about. It was an innocent kiss."

"You came on to your tutor!"

He raised his eyebrows. "As I remember, you kissed me back."

Oh, heck. He remembered that part. I pressed a hand to my forehead. "You shouldn't have kissed me, Ryan. It ruined everything."

He picked up a set of screws and started working again. "I wanted you to know how I felt about you."

"Ryan, your move to Arizona was confusing everything—"

He shook his head in protest. "It wasn't just that. Could you hold this piece in place for me? Thanks. The truth is . . . I had a crush on you for years."

"But—" It was that kiss. It wasn't a mere brush of lips—I mean, it was a *kiss* kiss, full, intense, and . . . incredible. "I was four years older than you!"

"It's not that big a difference," he tried to say, but I could only see my guilt. I should have known better. I should have been more responsible. I'd aimed so much anger at Ryan, but inside I knew I was just as much at fault.

"Yes, it is." There was a big difference between a responsible twenty-year-old and a sixteen-year-old, no matter how mature he was. I was in college! He was a junior in high school! How embarrassing was that? My mortification was the reason I'd kept it a secret, locked away in a mental compartment that had to be sealed. I didn't want my parents to know how badly I'd botched my tutoring job. Nor did I want Ryan's parents to find out, for obvious reasons.

And yet the secrecy felt wrong, so I suffered from all kinds of guilt—guilt that it happened, guilt that I didn't tell anyone. I felt like such a bad person, but once they moved away, I felt free to put it all behind me and move on with new resolve not to flub up my life. Of course, I never officially tutored anyone again.

"I'm sorry, Ashlyn. I never wanted you to be upset." Then he growled, "All I do is upset you." Seeing my expression of surprise, he added, "Every time I'm over here, I manage to upset you somehow. I've never wanted to do anything more than help."

"I know." While I helped him finish the dollhouse, I looked down at the wedding ring on my ring finger. It made me realize I still had it on. Was I supposed to wear it forever, or should I take it off?

"Ash, I don't know what happened to make you cry earlier," Ryan said, "but if I said or did something . . ."

"It wasn't you, Ryan," I finally said, forcing the words out just above a whisper. He looked up again, meeting my hesitant gaze. I pulled a strand of hair behind my ear. "I haven't been coping with life very well."

"Oh, come on. You're doing great."

"No, I'm not."

"You have to be a strong person to do all you do. Buying a home, moving here, raising Katie . . . I think you're incredible, Ashlyn."

I bit my lip, feeling the hint of a smile lurking at the corners of my mouth. "You're going to make me cry again," I warned.

Ryan groaned and laughed all at the same time. "Please don't cry!" He leaned in to touch my elbow. "It's the truth, Ashlyn. You're an amazing woman and a great mom. You're courageous and so good."

"Thanks, Ryan. But I'm a basket case. Losing my husband has been—" I shook my head, finding no words to describe all I'd been through.

He swallowed. "I can't imagine."

"But I realized something."

He nodded, his expression open for whatever I had to say.

"I'm sure it sounds horrible. I mean, it *is* horrible. I doubt there are very many people who've felt the way I have. No one in my family even knows how I've really been feeling. I haven't told them. So I don't have a clue why I'd start telling you—" I broke off my babbling, a burst of panic filling my heart. *Zip it, girl, and start backpedaling!*

"Hey," Ryan reached out to touch my hand, a gesture of comfort and reassurance. "You can tell me anything. Even if I'm dating Megan, you and I are still friends, aren't we?"

Friends. *Were* we still friends? He could end up being my brother-in-law, which made our relationship all the more confusing. Seeing the earnestness of his expression, I felt drawn to his sincerity, but I'd never voiced the awful feelings that were lodged in my heart. I realized that I didn't want Ryan to think badly of me. Well, any more than he already did. I had acted kind of psycho lately. Once the words were out they couldn't be retracted.

"Ash, is this about your husband?"

I looked up at him in surprise then nodded. "The thing is I've been so angry." I sucked in a breath as heat and pain seared through my chest. The words gushed out from deep inside. "I've been angry with him, and I despise some of the things he did. But I realized that I really did love him." I gulped down a sob, pressing my hands to my face, but I wasn't able to stop the tears.

I felt Ryan scoot over to my side, tentatively resting his hand on my shoulder. "I've done it again, haven't I?"

I shook my head and mopped the moisture from my face. I had to let him know it wasn't his fault I was crying, but the words weren't coming.

With eyes full of concern, he asked, "Do you want me to leave you alone? I'll go if you want me to. I just don't know if I should leave you . . . or hold you."

Needing that tenderness, I turned and buried my face against the warmth of his shoulder. It was all Ryan needed to tuck me into his arms. I felt his hand press against the top of my head and his fingers hesitantly stroke down my hair. He let me work through the emotion until I was ready to talk again. In the silence, late-afternoon sun filtered through the window, creating a golden dust trail that looked like glitter floating down. A warm and peaceful orange glow filled the room.

It was a moment so tender, so perfect, that words would have been an intrusion. We sat together quietly, and I wished I could capture that moment like a photograph and relive that feeling whenever I needed it. I hadn't felt that peaceful in a really long time.

A thunderous knock on the front door startled us both.

"I'll get it," I whispered.

Ryan nodded but reached a hand gently to my cheek to brush away a lingering trail of moisture with his fingertips. Looking into the dark gray depths of his eyes, I could have lived in that moment forever.

When the second round of knocking came, I hopped up to open the door. Brother Loveless, my old bishop and new home teacher, stood there with a plate of cookies that his wife must have baked, a big smile on his face.

"Hello, Bishop. Come in."

"Oh thanks, but I can't stay. I just wanted to bring by some cookies for you and—" His smile faltered as he noticed my blotchy face and then saw Ryan walking up behind us. "Well hello, Brother Anderson." His greeting sounded like a question.

Ryan reached around me to shake his hand. "Hello, Brother Loveless. Good to see you."

I suddenly saw the situation in a different light. Brother Loveless wouldn't come inside unless his wife were with him because I was alone—a young widow. Yet I was here alone with Ryan—not the greatest impression to give. Of course, nothing happened that I couldn't tell Megan. But it still felt awkward.

"Good to see you too." He handed me the plate of cookies, glancing at Ryan.

Brother Loveless considered us both before a light of understanding changed his expression. "Ashlyn, didn't you used to tutor Ryan—or maybe it was Jared—when the Andersons used to live here?"

Grateful for his memory, I smiled. "I did. I helped them both with math."

"That's right," said Brother Loveless.

No one seemed to have anything to say after that. It was a relief to see Megan and Katie coming up the driveway, back from their walk.

Brother Loveless greeted them with his usual charm before he had to leave. Then the rest of us came inside to see Katie's reaction to the finished doll house.

"Mommy, my dolls can play inside there!"

"They can, sweetheart. You'll have to thank Ryan for finishing it." I turned to my sister. "And thanks for the rescue, Megan." I gave her a big hug.

"No problem. Are you feeling better?"

"I am, thanks," I said, glancing at Ryan. "Hey, are you hungry? I've got some snacks."

"No," Megan shook her head. "I've got to go anyway. But I'm sure this munchkin wants some. She kept asking if I had food in my purse."

"Katie!" I laughed, but she didn't pay me any attention. She and her imagination were busy at work.

As Ryan and Megan were leaving a few minutes later, he touched my elbow, ever so gently and softly said, "See you later."

My stomach went weak. I tried to smile casually and appear like I wasn't affected by him but wasn't sure I was pulling it off. *What is happening to me? I can't do this.*

From the porch, Katie and I watched the two of them straddle a sleek, black motorcycle. I didn't even know Ryan had one. At that moment, he seemed stronger and more confident than I'd ever realized. As he pulled out of my driveway, he turned to look back at the house with a wave, making my stomach clench and a flush of warmth course through my body.

Heaven help me.

*****

Less than an hour later, the phone rang. Katie grabbed it with an eager, "Hello?"

I watched her grin turn to a giggle as she held out the receiver. "It's Ryan talking!"

I quickly took the receiver. "Hello?"

"Hi, Ashlyn. It's Ryan."

The sound of his voice sent ridiculous flutters through me. I took a deep breath to settle my nerves. "Hi."

"Did I leave my cell phone over there?"

I glanced over to where we had sat on the floor. "I don't think so. Did you lose it?"

"I don't know. I can't find it," he said.

"I don't think it's here . . . wait a sec . . . no, I don't see it."

"That's okay. I must have misplaced it."

"I'll call if I find it," I told him.

"Thanks."

I couldn't think of anything more to say. "Thanks for talking with me."

"You're welcome." He paused before adding, "We didn't really finish. I wanted to stay but thought I should leave when Brother Loveless came."

I was grateful he couldn't see my lips curve upward. "I know."

He gave a shaky laugh. "Wouldn't want him to get the wrong idea."

"Right."

Awkward . . .

I was relieved when Ryan blurted out, "Do you mind if I ask you something?"

My first reaction was wariness. But he'd earned my trust. "What?"

"You said you hated your husband."

"Yeah, but it's complicated. I was angry with him for dying and leaving me all alone. It's—there were other things too. I know it sounds selfish and doesn't make any sense, but—"

"Ash, it's okay. I'm not judging you. I was going to tell you that my aunt felt the same way when my uncle died. She was burning mad at him for dying."

"Really?"

"Yeah, but I know how much she loved him underneath all that anger."

I did love John and would have loved him forever if he had been faithful.

"Do you think you'll ever get married again?" he asked.

"No! Well, not anytime soon, anyway. Why?"

"No reason. My aunt never did. I guess you're dating Paul Hitch, right?"

"I'm not dating him. We went out that once. And it wasn't a date either. Not exactly."

"Oh. What was it?"

"Just dinner. As friends."

Ryan was quiet for a moment. I felt compelled to explain, but it didn't make sense why I should have to.

"Ashlyn, you still consider *me* a friend, don't you?"

My stomach flip-flopped. "I think so." I heard his sigh and was a little confused. "Why do you ask?"

"I guess . . . well, I was wondering. You don't have to, but I thought we could take Katie somewhere fun where you and I could talk. As friends."

I didn't know if my eyes were bugging out or not, but my heart hammered uncomfortably in my chest, and it was difficult to breathe in. "You're asking me out?"

My word, what have I done?

"No!" he laughed nervously. "No, no, I'm just saying we didn't get to finish talking, so I thought we could take Katie somewhere fun where we could talk. We could even do some gold panning down on the American River."

"Oh." I was an idiot. He'd never ask me out. I was just an old friend. "Yeah, I bet she'd love that."

Katie would definitely love doing something with Ryan, but I'd want to talk to Megan first, to see if she could come too. Having her there would be good. There was no point telling her that my wacky heart had been responding to Ryan because that whole piece wasn't going anywhere. At all. Period. If she came along, then we'd go.

I pictured a day spent with Ryan, watching Katie play, and felt the same warm longing I'd felt when John was alive. That's how the shattered dream went—the cute family having fun together. Ryan had offered a small portion of the dream, but it wasn't the same. John was the man I was supposed to do those things with. Ryan was just a friend.

But for now, maybe that would be okay. Going to the park with Ryan and Megan sounded really nice. I wouldn't worry anymore about the unsettling effect Ryan had on me. He was only offering his friendship, and friendship was a good thing.

Chapter 13

"Hi, Megan."

"Hey, what's up, Ash?" Megan's voice rushed over the phone.

"Did Ryan talk to you about . . . ?" I hesitated. Would she resent my spending time with him?

"About gold panning?" she filled in.

Releasing a deep breath, I said, "Yeah."

"It would be a blast, don't you think?" Megan sounded winded, as though she was dashing all over the house trying to get ready for something. That was pretty normal for her.

"Katie would love it. Will you come too?" I asked.

"Sure." I heard Megan reach with a grunt for something she must have dropped. "When did you guys plan to go?"

"Ryan was talking about Saturday afternoon."

"Ooo, sorry. Can't."

"You have something then?"

"Yeah, but you and Ryan can go, right?"

"You'd be okay with that?"

"Sure. Why wouldn't I be?"

Talk about confidence. No, I simply wasn't a threat to her.

"Hey, Ash," Megan interjected, "I'm going to have to go. Sorry. I'm going out in a few minutes, and I can't find my shoes."

"What?"

"I've got a date, and I'm not dressed!" she panted.

"Who are you going out with?"

"His name is Jared. He's a friend of mine."

"But—what about Ryan?" I never did understand my sister's dating habits, but I thought she was crazy about him!

"It's fine. We go out with other people."

"Wait, I thought you've been dating only Ryan for the last two months!"

"I was, mostly."

"Did something happen between you two?"

"No, not exactly. It's just that Ryan's a little . . . I don't know. When we first started dating, we both agreed that it was okay to go out with other people because neither one of us is looking for a serious relationship. Remember I told you he avoids marriage like the plague?"

"Yeah."

"Well, the problem is the more I'm around him, the more I like him. I think I might actually be falling for him."

"Oh, Megan." My heart sank for her, but it was also palpitating strangely. "Maybe you should tell him how you feel."

"I don't know," she grunted. "I'm not going to mope at home over Ryan when I could at least be out with my other friends."

"Megan!" I chided. "How are you ever going to get married if you keep going out with every single male on the planet?"

"I don't know. Ahh! Gotta go!"

"Tell Ryan how you feel," I called out before she could hang up.

"Maybe. Love you!"

"Love you too. Have fun."

"I will." Megan laughed and hung up.

Holy guacamole. My sister was a man-eater. But I could tell she was covering up her hurt over Ryan. If only I could do something for her. I wanted to help. My ridiculous attraction to Ryan was nothing—my sister was everything. I could cook up something. Perhaps when we went down to the river . . .

*****

On Saturday, the sun was out, and I knew the area down by the American River would probably be full of activity. Getting Katie's pants and shoes on was a nightmare. I made the mistake of telling her about the trip *before* getting dressed, so Katie was all but bouncing off the walls. My ears were still ringing from all her squeals.

I'd been working hard on my tactics for the day. I'd practiced and pep-talked myself into believing that any attraction I'd felt for Ryan was insignificant, inappropriate, and immaterial. I was over it. Megan loved this guy, and I would do everything in my power to help them get together. It was a perfectly simple plan.

After grabbing a beach bag full of towels, snacks, and drinks, I took Katie outside to wait on the porch for Ryan. The sun felt warm, and the day was beautiful. Tulips were blooming now in reds, pinks, and yellows. The neighborhood trees were showing off their new spring colors.

"That pink popcorn tastes like strawberries," Katie said, pointing her finger across the street at a blossoming almond tree.

"It does?" I laughed. "What does the white popcorn taste like?"

Katie tilted her head back to study the white blossoms on the apricot tree in our yard. "I think it tastes like marshmallows."

"Mmm. Sounds yummy." I said, hoping the blossoms didn't suffer a sudden freeze, or everyone would lose their fruit. "Hey, there's Ryan."

He rode up the gravel drive on his motorcycle, parking under the trees. I scooped up our things while Katie shrieked and ran down to fling herself in his arms. I'd have to watch that daughter of mine! Thank goodness Ryan didn't mind her exuberance. In fact, he was holding Katie quite tenderly. If he became Katie's uncle, she'd be so lucky!

I smiled when he walked up. "Good morning."

Ryan grinned, his whole face lighting up, and *wham*! The crazy, all-encompassing feeling hit me full force. One smile, that's all it took. My pep-talks had done nothing! I was in serious trouble.

"Good morning," he said. "Are you fine ladies ready for an adventure?"

Katie jumped up and down. "Uh-huh! And I got a babing suit, see?" She lifted up her Rapunzel t-shirt to show off her pink, Lycra-covered belly.

"I see that!" Ryan said, squatting down in front of her, one hand behind his back. "And guess what I brought you?"

"What?" she eagerly cried.

"This," he said, holding up a bright-yellow plastic shovel. "Now you can help me dig for treasure!"

"Yeah!" Katie took the shovel and hugged Ryan. "This is going to be so 'citing!"

Ryan laughed and turned to me. "Ready?"

I nodded with a smile. "That was so nice of you. Thank you."

"Oh, I couldn't wait to give it to her. We're going to have fun, huh, Katie?"

Ryan held the door of my car for me while I buckled Katie, then he opened the driver-side door to help me in. I watched him go around and get in on the other side, wondering two things. The first was when he'd found time to get a toy for Katie. It was such a thoughtful thing to do, and I knew he'd been busy. The second thing I wondered was when he'd become so irresistible? I didn't get it. A few weeks ago, he didn't look this good and suddenly he's Mr.—

Oh. My. Gosh. All he did was sit down and shut the door, and my heart was racing.

Knock it off! Think Megan . . . think Megan.

"You look nice," Ryan said.

Flustered, I choked and laughed at the same time. Like that comment made things any easier! His lips curved upward, and his beautiful teeth flashed, making me lose my concentration, and I almost had to swerve around a cluster of mailboxes at the end of the lane.

"Whoa!" he laughed.

"Sorry about that. I don't know what's wrong with me." I checked the rearview mirror, relieved to see all the mailboxes with their bright orange newspaper slots for the Sacramento Bee still in place. I kept an iron grip on the steering wheel the rest of the way.

"Megan's the good driver," I said stupidly.

He nodded vaguely in response to the lame information. I'd have to think of something more intelligent than that if I wanted to help my sister out.

We drove through Auburn and from there on Historic Highway 49 just past the confluence of the North and Middle Forks of the American River where the Foresthill Bridge towered majestically over the canyon. Katie saw her first glimpse of the river and shook her car seat with anticipation. I felt the same way. I had fond memories of coming to the Auburn State Recreational Area when I was younger, but I'd never been gold panning before. The thought of sharing this experience with Katie sent a rush of happiness through me like a burst of adrenaline.

Ryan pointed to the road up ahead. "If we park up here on the right, we can take the trail down to the water."

I pulled over and parked. When Ryan and I were both out of the car, Katie called, "Come get me!" from her car seat in the back.

"I've gotcha," I said, unbuckling her. "Now stay right next to me so you're safe, okay?"

She gave me a hurried "okay" before trying to take off.

"Katie, wait!" I yelled, chasing after her. I didn't want her to fall over the edge of the ravine down to the gravel below, and the road we were on was just as dangerous.

"I'll get her," Ryan said, taking off just behind her. When he caught up with Katie—tossing her over his shoulder like a sack of potatoes—I breathed a sigh of relief.

"Look what I found," Ryan said with a wink at me. "It's a pink, fluffy duck that wants to see the water. And it giggles whenever I poke her. See?" He tickled Katie, who squealed with laughter as he set her down.

I knelt in front of her. "Katie, you can't run off like that, okay? It's not safe. You need to hold Mommy's or Ryan's hand so you don't fall and get hurt."

Katie stuck her bottom lip out.

"Do you understand?"

"But I won't fall down," Katie insisted. "I'm big."

"I know you are, but big girls can still hold their mommy's hand."

"Hey, Katie," Ryan said, "if you grab both our hands we can do one-two-three-jump."

Liking the idea, Katie took our hands, and we swung her between us as we made our way down a worn dirt path to the river. The spring grass was green, and we heard birds chirping and even saw a family of quail in the chaparral. By the river, Ryan found a shady spot, where we put our things. We were on a gravel bed, and ten feet away, the narrow curve of the river flowed briskly over granite boulders.

Katie looked up above us and exclaimed, "There's a road in the sky!"

"That's the Foresthill Bridge up there," I explained. "It lets cars and trucks get from that side of the hill to this side."

"So the cars gots to drive up there and not crash in the water," she concluded.

I glanced at Ryan with a smile, and he grinned back. "That's right, honey. You're so smart."

Ryan opened his backpack and took out a small camp chair and some equipment. Then he handed Katie a large, green plastic bowl. "Here, pumpkin. This pan is for you. Let's go to the water, and I'll show you how to find some gold."

Down at the water's edge, Ryan sat on a rock with his feet in the water and poked around, shifting large rocks in the water. I let Katie splash around in the water and throw rocks while he worked. She didn't seem to mind how cold the water was from the spring run-off. When Ryan had gathered a hefty pile of muddy and rocky debris, he began to explain the process of placer mining and how to pan for gold. Katie and I watched him swirl the pan under the water, shaking the dirt and rock around to let objects with a higher density—like gold—sink down to the bottom. Then the water would rinse away lighter rocks and other deposits.

"It takes a while, and you've got to be patient," he said. "But you can end up with some good color."

"I wanna do it!" Katie said, grabbing her pan and shovel.

"Okay, take your dirt and put it into your green bowl," he said.

I did the same thing, and for several minutes we sat swirling and shaking, then letting lighter materials rinse away in the current. Katie mimicked us for a few seconds before coming up with more interesting ways to use her big green bowl and shovel. She was in heaven, and it made me happy just to watch her.

"When you finally start to see black sand, you're going to want to watch for color. There's not much left after that."

Ryan swirled his pan around to show us the small amount of black sand remaining in the left ridge of his pan. As he swirled water around, I saw a tiny fleck of bright yellow appear on one side.

"Hey we've got some color!" he shouted.

"No way," I gasped.

"I know! I didn't think we'd get any the first try today." He swirled the water again. "Look at that!"

Katie leaned over the bowl, her head touching Ryan's. "Is that a treasure, Ryan?"

"It sure is!"

I watched in amazement as he took Katie on his lap and let her touch the tiny pieces of gold. How did he do it? How did he learn to be so good with kids? I felt gladness and heartbreak all at the same time, knowing that Katie was having such fun with Ryan but would never have that chance with her daddy.

We stayed by the water for two full hours before we decided to head back, but Katie still didn't want to leave and started to cry when we packed up.

Ryan bent down and whispered something in her ear, which made Katie's eyes widen and her bottom lip slip back in place. "Okay," she said with a watery smile.

I questioned him with a curious glance, so he stood and leaned in to say under his breath, "I promised an ice cream cone if she's good." His lips curved up in that particularly irresistible way that was a mixture of sensuous and adorable. This time the *wham* came with such force that my face flooded with heat. I had to whip around so he wouldn't see my reaction.

"Ash, what is it?" He touched my arm, trying to turn me toward him. "You don't want her to have the ice cream?"

"No, no. That was really nice."

"But it wasn't my place?"

"No, it's just that . . . you're so good to us," I finished quickly. "Don't be sorry."

He touched my arm, and I was captured by the tender light in his eyes. A host of thoughts seemed to flash across Ryan's face, his expression changing from concern to warmth. I was trying with all my might to resist him, but he was unknowingly making it worse.

When a splash of cold water hit us, we both turned to see Katie kicking water with her shoe.

"Hey, who's getting us wet?" Ryan warned, as he stomped over to her.

Katie let out a piercing shriek as he chased her down and splashed her back.

We gathered our things and walked up the trail to the car. When we got back to Meadow Vista, Ryan bought a box of ice cream sandwiches at Holiday's, the town market, for us to share. Katie managed to get her clothes, face, hair, and car seat covered in chocolate. She looked like a mud wrestler.

"You've got to have a picture of this." Ryan chuckled as I drove up my driveway. "She's totally covered."

I took one look at her and shook my head in dismay. "She's going straight into the tub! It's everywhere."

"I'll help her inside. But seriously, go get your camera."

I laughingly ran into the house and brought back my digital camera just as Ryan was carrying Katie up the steps to the porch. I took a couple quick pictures but decided to zoom in better on their faces. Katie was giggling, her white teeth contrasting with the brown chocolate smears all over her face. Adjusting the zoom, I focused on Ryan's face. His eyes sparkled with delight over my messy munchkin. His affection for Katie warmed my heart. And his smile took my breath away.

When Ryan turned to look at the camera, I snapped the picture. The image that appeared on the small screen was perfect. Amazing. I quickly turned the camera off, making the screen go blank before he could see. Could he tell what I'd done?

Ryan set Katie down on the porch. "Did you get a good one?" he asked.

I felt my cheeks flush. "Yeah," I answered guiltily, putting the camera back in its case. "A couple good ones. Katie, it's time to say good-bye to Ryan and thank him for the fun day."

"Thank you, Ryan."

"You're welcome sweetheart." He kissed the top of Katie's head then turned to me. "I hope you both had a good time."

"We had a great time. Thank you so much."

"You're welcome." He took a step closer. "Maybe we can do it again sometime?"

I nodded. "Sure."

He stood in front of me, not moving away. I wondered what he was thinking. Then I noticed a smudge of Katie's ice cream on his cheek.

"Uh, you have a little bit of ice cream here . . ." Without thinking, I reached up to wipe the smudge of chocolate off his cheek.

Ryan self-consciously lifted a hand to his face, intending to wipe it away as well, but his fingers brushed against mine. He stopped to look at me, and I found I couldn't breathe. My heart thumped erratically. Then, a gradual look of amusement lit his eyes. Ryan leaned in close to my ear and whispered, "So do you." He brushed his thumb across my cheek, so tenderly it almost hurt; then he turned to walk away.

Staring at his retreating image, I realized my lower lip had drooped open, my heart beating ten times too fast.

Ryan swung around, that laid-back grin creasing his cheek, to wave at me. "I'll call you."

"But every house where Love abides, / And Friendship is a guest,
Is surely home, and home-sweet-home: / For there the heart can rest."
–Henry Van Dyke

Chapter 14

LISA GOODWIN CAME OVER FOR lunch a few days later with her girls. That's when I asked her to help me with the pink sparkle project—Katie's bedroom.

"Piece of cake," Lisa said enthusiastically. "Besides, I love spending other people's money!"

I laughed. "Katie will be so happy to get her room finished. I'm hopeless." Taking a bite of my chicken salad sandwich, I continued, "You should have seen me trying to put together her dollhouse."

The second I said it, I wished I hadn't. Remembering the way Ryan had sat beside me, wreaking havoc on my senses would only make me blush. In some ways, I almost wanted to mention Ryan to Lisa. An impartial point of view would be helpful as I talked things through and tried to make sense of the crazy way I'd been feeling. And the confusing way he'd said good-bye on my porch.

"Looks like you did a good enough job to me," Lisa said, taking a look at Katie in the family room playing in front of the dollhouse with Grace and Lily.

"Well, I ended up getting help."

"So what do you want to do in here?" Lisa waved a hand in front of her to indicate the kitchen area.

I glanced vacantly at the plain walls. "No idea."

"Oh, come on. What colors do you like? Are you a traditional kind of girl? Do you like the retro look? Cottage?"

"I don't know."

Lisa gave me a look full of mock horror, which made me laugh.

"I'm serious! I have no clue. But I like the color yellow."

"Okay, that's a start. However pathetic."

"Hey!"

Laughing, Lisa said, "Just kidding. We can work with yellow. Let's go to the store and see what you're drawn to. It would be fun."

I glanced at her basketball belly. "You feel up to that?"

She patted the roundness. "Absolutely. This guy doesn't stop me from shopping."

"I thought the doctor told you to take it easy."

"Decorating *is* taking it easy."

I laughed, thinking how grateful I was for this new friendship. Lisa was full of energy and enthusiasm, and it seemed to be rubbing off on me. "Okay, let's do it. When would be good for you?"

"Depends. If we take the girls, then whenever. If you don't want to drag them out shopping, I'll have to arrange for my sister to watch them."

"Let's just take them. Katie's a pretty good shopper."

"Do you have time right now? There's this cute shop in Auburn I'd love to take you to. It's where I found a bunch of stuff for our house."

Twenty minutes later, Lisa, the girls, and I walked into a small store, where I was able to point out several things I liked.

It wasn't long before Lisa summarized, "So you're sort of a sophisticated, country-type girl. With a touch of traditional."

"Whatever that means." I laughed. "Should I buy anything, Decorating Diva?"

"Not unless there's something you're dying to have. We can keep looking around to get more ideas for the rest of the house. But for now, I'd suggest sticking to the pink sparkle project."

"Sounds good to focus on one thing. Sometimes it feels like I have so many people coming over to help that I don't even know what to do with them."

"Like who?" Lisa asked incredulously. "I'd do anything for a drop of help!"

"Oh, family, church, my sister and her boyfriend, Ryan Anderson."

At the mention of Ryan's name, Lisa's eyes widened. "Your sister's going out with *him*?"

"Yeah, why? You know him?"

"Mormon, right? I know who he is, and holy Hannah." Lisa's eyes rolled back dreamily. "Is that guy the most gorgeous thing that ever walked the earth or what?"

I opted for staring rather than answering.

"Seriously, I think I'd pass out if he showed up on my doorstep wanting to help. If I wasn't a married woman, I'd pass out on purpose, just to fall into his buff arms."

"Lisa!"

"I know, I know. I'm naughty—even if I am kidding. But the guy is hot!"

I sputtered with embarrassment.

"Sorry, Ashlyn. Didn't mean to make you uncomfortable. It's a talent I have—saying crazy things I shouldn't."

I shook my head. "You're okay, Lisa. I sort of know what you mean." *About Ryan, that is. He's beyond adorable, but I wouldn't admit it.*

I turned around to check on Katie, sure that my face had become even redder. I liked Lisa and didn't mind her outspoken ways. She was genuine. It's just that I hadn't untangled my chaotic tangle of feelings for Ryan. And Lisa's words had felt terribly . . . well, accurate.

"Mommy, come here!" Katie sang out excitedly, interrupting my thoughts. "Come see!"

Grace had discovered a bedroom display that would be any little girl's fantasy. Katie showed me a beautiful canopy bed draped in white tulle. Fluffy pillows in coordinating pink prints adorned the top. "And look at this," she said, pulling my hand over to the nightstand, where a grouping of porcelain dolls sat beside a miniature tea set.

"That's cute, isn't it sweetheart?"

"Uh-huh. Can I have a tea set Mommy?"

I looked for a price tag under the teacups and was pleasantly surprised how inexpensive the set was. I ended up purchasing several items from the pink set including a throw rug and a wall hanging of the word *princess* in fancy lettering.

Lisa suggested we stop off at Home Depot to look at paint samples. With her help, I selected "Rosy Outlook" for Katie's bedroom, as well as the supplies to do the job. I just hoped we'd have a rosy outlook once the light-pink color covered the walls.

"And you promise you'll help me?" I was practically begging, but I didn't care. There was no way I could tackle the job without help.

"I promise!" she said, laughing away my worry. "Trust me; it's going to look great."

"You're a lifesaver, you know."

"I know," she flung back playfully.

Feeling so grateful for Lisa's friendship, I said, "Let me watch your girls so you and Tim can go out. I want to do something in return."

Lisa's expression was comical. "Free babysitting? Are you serious?"

"Of course."

"You don't have to ask me twice."

"Good. How about this Friday?"

"You got it!"

*****

"Okay, so you line up the tape like this," Lisa said, sprawled awkwardly over the top of the ladder, showing me how to tape off the ceiling and door casing with blue painter's tape. Her basketball belly threw her off balance. "Then follow the edge and press it down."

"Lisa, I don't want you going into labor on the ladder."

"Don't worry about me. I do everything when I'm pregnant."

"I am not delivering your baby on the floor, you know."

"Relax," she laughed.

Katie bristled when she walked in and saw the blue stripes all over her room. "Hey! That's not pink!"

"Don't worry," I said. "We take all the blue tape off when the painting is done."

"Princesses don't like that color, Mommy!" Katie said before marching out of the room to play Barbies with Grace and Lily in the family room.

Lisa chuckled as she stepped to the floor and rubbed her back. "My girls did the exact same thing. You'd have thought I was planning a bedroom full of fire engines, cowboys, and sports rolled into one heinous affront to femininity."

I laughed so much around Lisa, I surprised myself. She was an amazing blessing and helped make life fun without even trying. It made me want to be more like her.

And as I finished taping off the last section of the room, I realized that I'd changed considerably since moving here. Changed for the better. And it felt good to be progressing. I felt like a success. I'd actually made a big dent in this project and knew that with help, I'd be able to bring the rest of my home to life as well.

*****

Brother Loveless and his wife came by the next evening for a home teaching visit. I remembered that before, as my bishop, he'd been concerned about me marrying John outside the temple. But seeing how determined I'd been to get married, he'd suggested reading material and ideas to help us set goals for the temple in a year.

I wondered how he felt now, knowing how badly it all turned out. Probably somewhere along the lines of, "I told you so," but he was far too kind to say it. Of course, no one knew John had been unfaithful. When I finally summoned the courage to reveal that tidbit of information, it would prove humiliating. How could a sane woman not figure that out sooner? I should have known—or at least suspected!

Brother Loveless read a quote from the *Ensign* which made me think about all the choices I'd made. Was it wrong for me to have married John? If I could go back in time, would I choose differently? Maybe, but not if it meant I wouldn't have Katie. I couldn't imagine my life without her. The thing was I still believed that John had truly loved me in the beginning. I would never know all the answers to fill in the blanks. Did I do something to make him unhappy? What should I have done differently? I felt so stupid remembering the way his sexy co-worker showed up to the graveside service bawling her head off—and me thinking it was a little weird. Days later, after I found her love note in John's wallet, I confronted her about it.

Worst day of my life.

She admitted—almost defiantly—that they'd been having an affair. She gave me enough proof to verify that it was true, and my world crumbled all over again.

"You know, Ashlyn," Brother Loveless's voice broke into my tortured thoughts, "as you start a new life here, Sister Loveless and I just want you to know that we're here for you if you ever need us."

"I know," I said sincerely, "and I'm so grateful to you both for that."

"Have you thought about your plans for the future?" Sister Loveless asked. "Like working or putting Katie in preschool?"

"I have wondered about those things. I could probably find a good job in town, but leaving Katie would be hard."

"That's one of those decisions most moms have to face at some point," she said. "Our daughter Anne had to pray like crazy last year to figure out the very same thing."

"What did she decide?" I asked, hoping to find inspiration through someone else.

Sister Loveless sighed. "To stay at home with her two boys. It was hard because her husband has been in and out of work, and they really needed the money. But they both felt at peace about it."

I nodded, not sure I felt any less confused.

Brother Loveless added, "But what's right for one may not be right for another. You'll get the right answer for you and Katie. And who knows," he chuckled lightly, "in time you might marry and not have to worry about working again."

My hand shot out. "I'm definitely not ready for that!"

Sister Loveless nodded and smiled gently, almost painfully.

"It might be a while before that seems like an option," Brother Loveless said.

But I shook my head. "I'm not interested in dating *or* getting married again."

He rubbed his nose and humorously added, "Well, I have to say, the fellows you meet might have other ideas."

"You're a beautiful young woman," Sister Loveless agreed. "I couldn't blame anyone who wanted to share their life with you."

I mumbled my embarrassed thanks, feeling undeserving of the praise. John didn't share hardly a bit of his life with me. But boy did he ever "share" it with Miss Cry-Her-Pants-Off.

Brother Loveless brushed at something on the arm of the sofa. "And if you ever need a listening ear, we are both here for you. We both care about you and Katie and want to help in any way we can."

"I appreciate that very much."

When they left a few minutes later, I stared at the closed door for over a minute. It was true what they had said earlier about praying. I'd thought a little about working again but hadn't prayed about it. So I'd try that. But there was no way I'd be praying about who to marry. I didn't want any answers in that area.

"Face to face, silent, drawing nigh and nigher . . ."
—Elizabeth Barrett Browning

Chapter 15

A COLD TRAIL OF PAINT oozed over my hand, threatening to drip on the plastic tarp covering the floor.

"Aaakkh." I transferred the saturated roller brush to my left hand so I could wipe my right hand with a damp rag draped on the ladder. "Lisa, what have you gotten me into?" I muttered to my absent friend.

I was so worried last night when she'd called to tell me there had been some pregnancy complications and that the doctor had put her on bed rest until the baby came.

"I'm so sorry!" she'd told me. "I really wanted to help you."

I was far more concerned about the health of both Lisa and the baby, worried that she'd overdone it helping me. But she'd assured me that she needed bed rest with both of her girls, so it was normal for her.

"Is there something I can do for you?" I had asked.

"Yes, get painting! I can coach you over the phone."

I'd laughed until I realized she was serious.

"You can do it, Ashlyn," she coaxed. "I promise."

So a bedside crash course on painting and a hefty amount of coercing got me on this ladder today, dripping paint everywhere. Now I felt as sticky and mucked up as the Tootsie Pop Katie got stuck in her hair last week. At least she was being good in the other room, watching a Dora DVD, instead of getting into the paint.

Look at me! I'm getting paint on everything! A splat on the plastic tarp indicated another drip.

"Hey," a deep voice said behind me.

Startled, I twisted around too quickly and nearly lost my balance on the ladder. A man's firm grip on my legs steadied me. "Oh, Ryan! It's you."

"Sorry. I didn't mean to scare you. I thought you heard me come in."

"That's okay," I said, looking down at him, the roller hovering precariously above his head.

"Katie told me you were back here."

I was acutely aware of his hands on my legs but realized that he was grinning up at me, eyes lit with amusement. "What?" I demanded.

"Nothing," he chuckled. Releasing my legs, Ryan backed up. "Carry on."

I gave him a wary look then turned to slop a crooked W on the wall like Lisa had coached me. A sniff behind me alerted me to the fact that he was trying to suppress his laughter but not succeeding. He could hardly contain it.

"What are you laughing at?" I cried out indignantly, my smile lessening the indignant effect. I already knew I looked ridiculous, pretending to know how to paint a wall.

His hand, in a loose fist, covered his mouth, as if to hide his mirth. "It's just that . . ." He vaguely waved a finger in my direction.

I looked down at my paint-splattered clothes and arms. "I know. I'm getting it all over me."

He nodded. "Yep. *All* over." His eyes trailed down my jeans then swept quickly back up to my face.

"These were old. I was going to get rid of them anyway."

He just nodded, that silly grin still there, so I turned my back to him again, dipped the roller brush in the pan, and slopped more paint on the wall.

"Can I help?" he said behind me.

"And get yourself messed up like me?"

"I don't mind. These are old clothes."

I glanced down at his blue T-shirt and faded jeans. Wow. Muscular, fit, and good-looking. He radiated masculinity like the Brawny paper towel dude. And then there was the thing he did with his hair. I could stare at him for a long time and still be fascinated. Was it normal for a woman my age to think he was that manly? Shouldn't he seem sort of . . . youthful to me? Not as desirable as an older man would seem?

I must be defective, then, because he's looking completely desirable.

I couldn't let him see it. Quickly, I turned back to my work again and dragged the brush down the wall in long vertical strokes, evening out the section I'd just painted. Lisa had warned me about drips: "They're worse than dried boogers on the wall, 'cause they don't wash off!" I wasn't about to let that happen if I could help it.

"Don't you have job interviews today?" I asked Ryan over my shoulder, hoping I was smoothing every possible drip.

"I'm finished for today," he said. "So what do you say? Are you going to let me help?"

"Hey, if you want to paint, I'm not going to stop you. I doubt I'm doing this right in the first place."

"It looks great to me."

Ryan found the brush Lisa had been using the other day and dipped it into the can of paint. Over my shoulder, I watched him skillfully cut in around the door frame, swathing the wall along the taped-off edges.

"Ryan." He turned around expectantly. "Look. I don't want you to feel obligated or anything to help me. I'm sure you have better things to be doing than—"

"Hey," he stopped me. Walking over to the ladder, he stepped up the first rung, holding on with one hand, so we were almost face to face. He finished softly, "I want to help, okay? I like being here with you and Katie."

But you should be other places. On a date with my sister or something, not wasting your time here with us. I couldn't quite say the words with him so close, driving all sense into oblivion, but my eyes must have reflected my doubts because he added, "I'm serious, Ashlyn."

I bit my lip, clinging to my sanity.

"Besides," he continued, a twinkle in his eye, "where else would I get to see someone cover themselves in paint? It's kind of . . . cute."

My eyebrows jerked up in shock. "Are you flirting with me?"

Ryan chuckled, inching up until we were eye to eye. "What makes you think I'd do that?"

A thrill of electricity coursed through me, from the top of my head to the tip of my toes. My eyes bugged out. "Ryan Anderson, stop it!"

"Why?" His lazy smile and drooped eyelashes were making me crazy.

"Well, because!" I spluttered then pointed a finger in the air. "One, you're dating my sister. Two, you can't go around flirting with older women."

"I think I've done that before." Ryan's eyebrows quirked up and down roguishly like the villain of a melodrama. "Successfully, I might add."

I felt my cheeks flame but rolled my eyes at him. He just grinned all the more. I decided he was far too comfortable with our renewed status as friends. I sure hadn't tried hard enough to conceal my attraction or to discourage him from getting too friendly!

"Ryan, don't."

His eyes pierced me with a look so intense I might have collapsed if it hadn't been for the ladder. He leaned in closer. "I have to."

"What are you talking about?"

He pointed his index finger at me. "*You* are way too serious! When you're getting teased, you smile. So, being the good friend that I am, I'm taking care of you."

"You're ridiculous." I laughed.

"That's what I want to see . . ."

His eyes slowly traced my entire face in a way that was almost tangible. It made my knees to go weak. It was thrilling and terrible, wonderful and disastrous, all at the same time. I wanted him to stay yet needed him to move. It was heavenly torture, weakening me beyond belief. The fingers of his free hand leisurely encircled my wrist. That single action made me feel like I'd melt right there on the ladder.

"Mommy, can I get on the ladder too?" Katie shouted as she burst into the bedroom.

I was so caught off guard that I slipped. Ryan grabbed me around the waist and leaned in, the pressure of his body steadying me.

"No, honey," I said shakily, my free hand pushing against his solid chest. "I think we're done with the ladder for now." I looked pointedly at Ryan.

With a knowing smile, he dropped his arm from my waist and stepped down. But his eyes held mine as I followed him down the ladder.

"Ryan, my room is getting pink!" Katie squealed excitedly, completely unaware that her mommy's face was eleven shades pinker than the walls.

"Do you like it?" Ryan asked, turning distractedly to Katie.

"Uh-huh!" Katie cried. "It's gonna be a princess room."

He went down on one knee in front of her. "That's because *you* are a princess." Katie beamed at Ryan before flinging her arms around him in the tightest hug she could give. "Oh, Katie," he said softly, wrapping his arms around her, "you're so precious."

My heart quickened at the sight.

"Wait a minute," Katie said, pulling back to make a stop sign with her hand. "I got a good idea. How 'bout you can give me a piggyback ride?"

"Hmm," he said, rubbing his chin. "That is a good idea. Hop on."

"Okay!" she yelled gleefully, climbing onto his back.

When Ryan had her positioned securely, he turned to smile self-consciously at me. "Be right back."

Equally exasperated as amazed with him, I spun back to finish the last of the painting. Working on a new section of wall, I thought about what Ryan had said. Was I really that serious? I'd come a long way from the lifeless state I used to be in. But the effects of being frozen and lifeless seemed to have confused my heart as well as my mind. My poor heart was thawing out, but it was beating for the wrong person. I couldn't let that happen. It wasn't real; it was an illusion that had formed in my weakened state.

A knock at the door resulted in a Katie-style shriek and rapid footsteps through the house. I wondered who it could be. Hopefully not Brother Loveless checking up on me with Ryan here again. He'd definitely get the wrong idea. Setting the brush down, I wiped my hands on the wet rag and went to see who had come over. It sounded like girls' voices. Turning a corner, I saw my sister standing uneasily next to Bethany Albright.

"Hi," I greeted them, wondering what cataclysm would've brought the two of them together.

Both girls said hello, each with a dozen messages shooting from their expressions. What was going on? Megan didn't look happy at all. Even with the smile, I could tell something had upset her. And Bethany seemed to be masking triumph with her feminine innocence act. I noticed the way she fondled a set of bracelets, which had more "bling" than a diamond tiara. Thanks to Lisa's instruction, I determined that Bethany's lip gloss could rival the sheen of any high-gloss paint.

"What's up?" Ryan asked the two of them, just as I was about to ask the same question. I avoided the side glance he darted me.

Bethany charged like an aggressive viper. "Megan and I ran into each other, and we both wanted to help with the decorating. Didn't we?" She seemed to challenge Megan with a sharp glance. Her bracelets rattled.

I almost chuckled when I saw Megan's eyes bulge in silent disagreement. Bethany must have heard that Ryan might be here and weaseled her way over with Megan.

"I'm really good with interior design," Bethany explained. "It's my major. But you already knew that, Ryan, didn't you?" She smiled coyly, having managed to slither up beside him rather quickly.

Ryan nodded. "I did."

Megan, who hadn't even spoken yet, came up with a wry grin. "Hey, Ash, you could see if Bethany has any suggestions for some of these rooms."

I didn't get a chance to speak before Bethany plunged into a profusion of decorating ideas. "I see Luxe Living or Hollywood Regency in here, black lacquer furniture with an accent wall in icy blue. Like ice. Cold. Blue, y'know? With metallic accents." She swung her hips around provocatively. "This sofa would have to go of course."

Excuse me?

Bethany continued with visions of velvet, crystal chandeliers, and statues. What she described as "an eclectic mix of old-fashioned extravagance and contemporary minimalism" sounded like over-the-top glitz and glamour to me. Basically hideous. I might not know a whole lot about decorating, but I knew I wouldn't like her taste! I also knew I didn't like the way Bethany kept looking down her nose at me like I was an inferior specimen of woman/homemaker. I looked a mess from painting, but come on. Really?

"That sounds interesting, Bethany," I said. "I'll probably just do one room at a time, so I don't think I'm up for that much decorating yet. But thanks for your ideas."

I returned Megan's smirk with a get-you-later look of my own.

"Hey, Ryan," Bethany gushed, "how about going out for frozen yogurt? I'm dying for a Tropical Rhapsody!"

And there you go, folks, the real reason she's here. So much for decorating.

Ryan quavered for an answer. But Katie bubbled, "I like yogurt too!"

Bethany laughed patronizingly at her but frowned at me. She slinked over to link arms with Ryan and Megan. "I meant the three of us." Then she babbled on for several minutes about things only the three of them would know anything about. I was now superfluous in my own home and could have booted a certain someone out the front door.

"So what do you say, guys?" Bethany asked in her sugary voice. "Tropical Rhapsody?"

"Maybe another time, Bethany," Ryan answered, turning to Megan for further appeal, as though it was hopeless to get through to Bethany. "I'm going to finish painting in Katie's room."

"Sounds fun. Can we help?" Megan asked, angling a look at Bethany.

"Sure," I said. "Come on back and see what we've done so far." Then, gesturing to Bethany, I welcomed her as well, even though I hoped she'd leave.

Megan praised me when she saw how much had been done in Katie's room. "This is going to be princess heaven! I love it."

Bethany shrugged, making an ambiguous nasal sound and rattled her blingy bracelets. She wandered out of the room into the hallway, scrutinizing every invisible detail of the colorless, undecorated walls. Then she flipped on the light in the hall bathroom.

I heard a mumbled, "Oof, this needs help."

Now I was seriously going to kick her out! Outdated or not, I loved my new house.

I marched up behind Bethany and demanded, "What does my bathroom need—in your opinion?"

She stuttered for a moment. Then her smooth, calm façade slipped into place. "Without question, I'd say copper."

"Copper?"

"Absolutely. Copper is what it's all about these days. To achieve any kind of sophistication, you need copper. And I'd paint the walls in a medium turquoise." Tapping a long-nailed finger against her pouty lips, she examined the rubber ducky shower curtain. "And I'd replace this." She fingered one edge between thumb and forefinger as though it were covered in mold.

"I just bought that. I wasn't really going for sophistication since Katie is three."

Bethany spun around like she'd forgotten she wasn't alone. "Oh, yeah, no it's uh . . ." Rather than finish, she opted for escape. "What other rooms are you doing?"

"That's it," I said with as much finality as possible.

"Oh, wow!" she exclaimed, eyeballing her expensive watch. "I just remembered I have to meet someone at the country club. Don't want to keep the rich and famous waiting!"

Oh, brother. Megan and I said our good-byes inside, but Ryan courteously walked Bethany out to her car, leaving us behind.

"Ash!" Megan hissed as soon as the door shut, motioning rapidly down to Katie's bedroom. "Get over here!"

Puzzled, I walked up to Megan. "What?" I whispered. "Bethany?"

"No, you!"

"Me? What did I do?" I thought I'd handled things pretty well.

"You've got paint on your rear end! Right here." She smacked the spot for emphasis.

I paled instantly. "Are you serious?" I twisted around awkwardly, trying to check the damage. Sure enough, a large splotch was on my back pocket.

"It looks like a hand print!" Megan snickered.

"Oh, great," I moaned. "Did everyone see it?"

"Well, pffsh, I don't know. It's kinda noticeable."

I moaned again. "I can't believe what a mess I'm making."

"It's just a suggestion, but you might want to change before Ryan—"

"Before I what?" Ryan asked, appearing inside the doorframe.

Both our heads spun in his direction.

"Are you two talking about me?" A spark of mischief flickered in his eyes.

Megan laughed outright. I scowled at her.

"What's going on?" he asked, a slow smile lifting the corners of his mouth.

"Nothing," I stated, leaning back against the ladder.

Ryan's gaze swept from Megan to me before realization sank in. "Megan, you didn't tell her about—" He broke off, a faint tinge of color on his cheeks.

"I *had* to tell her," Megan said, trying to justify herself. "I can't let my big sister go around with a handprint painted smack dab on her—"

"Okay! Thank you, Megan!" I interrupted sarcastically. Then to Ryan I asked, "Is that what you were laughing about earlier?"

Ryan shifted his feet and scratched the side of his face. "No. The paint was everywhere, not just on your . . . not just there." He looked like he was trying really hard to be serious.

After having already dealt with Bethany, I wasn't entirely amused.

"Ashlyn, don't worry about it," he said, plopping an arm around my shoulders. "Come on, we'll help you finish painting."

"Yeah, no worries. Right, Ash?" Megan inserted with a guilty sparkle in her eyes.

"All right," I said, "let's do this. But if I catch either one of you laughing behind my back, you're toast."

Ryan grinned and drew a cross over his heart. "I promise."

"Yeah," Megan added, "he'd never make you the butt of a joke."

"Ha. Ha. Very funny."

"So, Ash," Megan said over her shoulder, "have you ever told Ryan about your famous cinnamon buns?"

I gave her a withering look. I was used to my sister's playful banter. But while we worked, I caught Ryan stealing a look at me several times and felt like I had a neon sign on my backside.

"Thou art to me a delicious torment."
–Ralph Waldo Emerson

Chapter 16

JUST BEFORE KATIE'S ROOM WAS completely finished, Megan's friend sent her a text message about a study group.

"Hey, Ash, I'm going to have to go," she said. "We're meeting at Jana's house at five. We've got a brutal exam coming up next week, and I need to study."

"No problem. Thanks for all your help, Megan."

"Sure. I just feel bad leaving you to clean everything up."

As he was removing a strip of blue tape off a wall, Ryan spoke up. "I'll help with all that. Want a ride over to Jana's house?"

Megan shook her head. "I'm going to run home to change and then go over. Thanks anyway."

I hugged my sister, wishing she would have accepted Ryan's offer. "Happy studying."

"Gee, thanks. Nothing like spending hours and hours discussing DNA."

"Ew. I could never hack your biology major, Megan."

"Says the professional accountant."

Ryan stopped pulling tape off the wall and turned to me. "You're an accountant?"

I wasn't sure why I suddenly felt flustered. "I used to be."

The smile that broke out on his face gave me goose bumps. "I knew you'd do something with all those math skills."

"She was always the smart one in the family," Megan agreed.

I laughed. "Oh, right. You're the one with a scholarship."

"Whatever. Hey, I've got to go, guys. See you soon." Megan waved, adding a kiss on Katie's cheek, and then left in a flurry.

Ryan turned, tilted his head thoughtfully to one side, and studied me. "What?" I asked warily. His expression was so serious.

"I was just wondering."

"Wondering what?"

"Where you went to school before . . . everything."

John. He was trying to ask about my life without hurting me. I nodded, helping him out. "I was at UC Davis. That's where I met John my junior year. We got married and then graduated the year after that."

Crumpling a wad of paint-streaked tape into a big ball, Ryan asked softly, "And then you moved to Ohio?"

I nodded again.

"How did he . . ." he started to ask, rotating the tape ball around in his hands. When he looked back up, his eyes locked with mine. "How did he die?"

It must have taken some courage for him to ask that question. How many people could ask someone how his or her spouse died? I could actually handle this side of him easier than the flirting. He seemed to want to know not just out of curiosity but something more. Like he wanted to know *me*, to know what I'd been through and to help somehow. Kindness and strength were natural to him.

I drew in a long breath and finally managed to answer. "It was a car accident. A drunk driver crossed the median and hit him head on. It was ten days before Katie's second birthday."

He stood there, silently, as though trying to express without words how sorry he was for what I'd been through. In his eyes I saw pain, compassion, reaching out, finding a way to my heart. Closing the distance between us, he wrapped me in his arms with overwhelming gentleness. The thing that was most surprising was that I didn't cry as he held me. I felt his comfort, freely given, healing my wounds. Warmth filled my heart, melting away my loneliness. My arms went around him, holding fast to that warmth, needing it close.

Something had changed between us. There was something different, something new. Ryan's hands pressed tenderly against my back. The burdens I'd been carrying for more than a year finally seemed lighter under the healing force of his compassion.

Pulling back, he placed his hands on my arms. "Ashlyn, I'm so sorry."

I nodded, understanding what was implied so earnestly in his words. He was sorry for all I had been through, sorry he had asked about it, sorry he had ever upset me. I nodded and smiled up at him, loving this friendship; I really did. I just knew it couldn't possibly last. How long we stood this way, I couldn't have guessed, but eventually I realized that Katie was pulling on the hem of my shirt.

"Mommy?" she whispered carefully, sensing the quiet of the moment. "I gotta go potty."

I pulled back with a smile, my amusement intermingled with embarrassment. Ryan dropped one arm down to ruffle Katie's hair, keeping the other around me. He seemed as reluctant to break apart as I was.

"Do you need me to help you?" I asked Katie.

Katie shook her head. "No, I can do it all by myself." She turned and pranced down the hallway, leaving the two of us alone again.

I laughed slightly in a nervous puff of air. "Sorry about that."

"Don't be sorry. It was an important announcement to Katie." I genuinely laughed then, and Ryan explained, "My nieces and nephews make similar announcements at the choicest of moments. Baptisms, soccer games, birthday parties—you name it, they've done it."

Ryan's grin trapped me. Realizing that I was staring, I looked away. But he caught my hand before I could turn away.

"Wait."

I felt like the oxygen in the room had all been sucked away. The feel of his hand holding mine was heavenly, but I feared it at the same time. Holding my breath, I waited for him to speak.

"Can I come over tomorrow?" he asked.

I opened my mouth but couldn't seem to say anything.

"Please?" Ryan's hand increased its pressure. "I could help you paint another room or do yard work, whatever you need."

I closed my eyes for a moment, turning away. I felt Ryan drawing me back.

"What is it, Ashlyn?"

I reluctantly opened my eyes. "It's just—I don't get it."

"What do you mean?" he asked, wrinkling his brow. "What don't you get?"

"Why you spend so much time here."

Ryan's eyes filled with tenderness. He hesitantly raised a hand to my cheek. "Because I do."

"That's not a reason, Ryan!" I flared, snapping my head back as if I'd been stung. "I mean, what's going on here? I'm a widow with a three-year-old daughter. You . . . you're twenty-five, I assume—"

"A proverbial menace to society, I know."

"—but you're dating my little sister, and I don't even know who else. There's probably a ton of girls Megan's age dying to go out with you—which is what you *should* be doing, seeing as how most guys your age are trying to get married—so why waste your time here when you could be other places? Should be other places!"

At first I thought he might start laughing at my overly drawn-out speech, but his eyes narrowed, and his lower jaw moved forward. I must have finally struck a chord with him.

"I'm taking care of it," he growled, more than a tad on the defensive.

"Taking care of what?"

"The trying-to-get-married bit. I'm working on it."

"You're not working on it! You're doing the same thing Megan does—going out with everyone in the universe so you never have to settle down!"

He clamped his lips shut, flaring his nostrils. "Look. If I choose to spend my time helping someone out, it's because I want to do that instead of . . . whatever else you think I should or shouldn't be doing!"

"Ryan—"

"Do you want my help tomorrow or not?" he barked, crossing his arms over his broad chest. "I can get here by two."

Grunting, I shook my head and flung my hands up in the air. "I'm not a charity case!"

"Duly noted. I'll be sure not to act charitable."

"And I don't want you feeling sorry for me!"

"I get it, Ashlyn," he growled. "I get it."

Augh! He was impossible! What a dumb idea, coming over here. If he didn't have the sense to hang out with Megan and stay away from the psycho den, then he deserved what he got!

I watched him plod to the front door, stopping before his hand reached the doorknob to whip back. "Are you even going to be here at two?"

"I don't know."

His head moved up and down, like he had me figured out and wasn't pleased. "I thought we were friends, Ashlyn."

Friends. Always that word slashing through my confused brain. *Friends. Friends. Friends.*

"It's not that, Ryan—"

"Hey, I know when I'm not wanted."

"That's not true!"

He'd opened the door and was stepping outside. I rushed up behind him and reached for his arm. "Wait."

He turned to face me, slapping one hand on the doorframe, waiting for me to explain myself. With me one step above him, we were almost eye to eye again, just like we'd been on the ladder. My hand was still on his arm, and I could feel the tightness and warmth of his skin. He slapped his other hand on the doorframe, leaning toward me.

"What?" he asked quietly, intently.

I do want you to come. Say it.

One of his eyebrows arched up—and they were such great eyebrows. My best friends in high school used to make fun of me for saying that eyebrows could be sexy. But some guys had a certain thing going on with their eyebrows, and Ryan was definitely one of them. A hint of shadow along his jawbone gave him a rugged appearance. His lips curved ever so slightly as though he resisted smiling but couldn't help it. I caught a hint of citrus and sandalwood and felt weak in the knees.

"I want . . ."

He tilted his head, still questioning me.

"I want you to come, Ryan. Katie loves having you around, and you've been such a great help."

His expression softened. "And?"

"What do you mean, 'And'?"

"Are those the only reasons you want me to come?"

"No. Yes. What's wrong with those reasons?" I took a deep breath. I must have been exasperated beyond reason, otherwise I never would have blurted out, "And what the heck are you wearing?"

Oh crud, did I just ask that?

Ryan blinked at me. "Huh?"

"Never mind. It's just your aftershave or something that's . . ."

A look of stunned hurt crossed his face, and he backed up a step. "I'm sorry."

"No, no, it's . . . you shouldn't wear that around girls. It's asking for trouble."

Ryan sort of coughed and choked at the same time, darting a look that questioned my sanity.

I moaned and smacked a hand to my forehead. "Never mind, I didn't mean to say—"

"What *are* you saying? That I smell good or bad?"

"No! You smell good." Without thinking, I muttered, "Too good."

He did his eyebrow thing again. A spark flared in his eyes, its warmth transferring to my face.

I gulped. "Uh, could we just rewind this whole conversation to when you said you'd be here at two tomorrow? I'll just say, 'That's great,' and we can end the discussion."

The flame hadn't simmered yet as he studied me. "Okay." Ryan shook his head like he'd just stepped off a roller coaster. His lips slowly curved halfway upward in a way that could endanger my heart rate. "See you tomorrow at two, then?"

"Okay."

Leaning in, he let his long fingers brushed over my arm. His lips moved as if to say something, but only his eyes engaged me in silent conversation. I couldn't look away from him. The flare in his eyes continued to burn across my cheeks, my jaw, and down to my chin, anywhere I was touched by his glance. I couldn't seem to stop from studying every facet of his firm, shapely mouth, wondering what his lips would feel like if I were to trace them with the tip of my finger.

They'd be soft . . . unbearably soft.

How could I be so attracted to him? How did he do it? How did he make me feel like I was someone else? Someone who could feel and love.

This couldn't be real. It wasn't real! It was a postcard of paradise. I could see the tropical waters, lapping over warm, white sand, inviting me in. But I wasn't actually there. It merely reminded me that I *had* been there once.

"Bye, Ashlyn." Ryan turned and walked away, leaving me bereft of warmth, real or imagined.

"What heart shall touch thy heart? what hand thy hand?"
–Christina Georgina Rossetti

Chapter 17

I AWOKE FROM A FITFUL sleep, having dreamt of the summer I'd attempted to body surf down in L.A. Not the most successful thing I'd ever done, to say the least. There'd been bruises to deal with afterward. Waking up, I could almost feel bruises resulting from the dream.

I needed to put on some upbeat music. Looking through my meager stash of CDs, I thumbed past collections from Shania Twain, The Cranberries, and Michael Bublé. Then, with a little laugh, I pulled out an ancient Backstreet Boys album. "Yeah, I want it that way," I sang out in a cheesy voice.

Making breakfast to the harmonizing male voices put me in a much better mood and brought Katie padding into the kitchen, wiping the sleep from her eyes.

"What is this music, Mommy?" she asked sleepily.

I grinned and picked her up. "Something I used to listen to. Do you like it?"

"M-hm," Katie mumbled unenthusiastically. "Can I have my cereal for breakfast?"

"Sure. Have a seat right over here next to me, okay?"

I had Katie point out letters of the alphabet on the cereal bag in between bites of cereal. It was always so fun to work with my daughter. She seemed particularly bright to me, but I'd heard that most parents felt that way about their first child. Still, Katie was pretty amazing in many ways.

After breakfast, Shaun and Karen surprised us by stopping by for a visit.

"Hey, you guys. Come on in. What's up?"

"Does something have to be up for us to stop by to see you?" Shaun teased.

"Of course not. I'm just surprised to see you."

"He doesn't have to go in to work today," Karen said, nudging her husband.

"But I do have to work on her honey-do list. Karen's a slave driver."

My sweet sister-in-law poked Shaun in the ribs playfully.

I smiled until Karen suddenly blurted out, "Ash, we have a friend we'd like you to meet."

I could only stare at them with a glazed expression. They'd caught me off guard before dropping that one!

"I know what you're thinking," Shaun quickly said, "but this is someone special. He's a single guy in our ward, never been married—"

"And really handsome," Karen finished for him. "He's one of the most spiritual guys I know. He teaches our Gospel Doctrine class."

"Look, guys, I know you mean well, but I'm not interested."

"Mom told us you were going out with people," Shaun reminded.

I sighed again loudly. "I'm not going out with anyone."

"Can we just introduce you to him?" Karen pleaded. "His name is Matt Daniels. We could have you both over for Sunday dessert or something. I know he'd really like to meet you."

"How do you know that?" I asked.

Shaun and Karen exchanged a guilty look. "We already told him about you," Karen said.

I groaned. "Why?" I stomped one foot.

My brother bristled a little. "Matt's been looking for the right woman to marry for a long time, Ash. He deserves the chance to at least meet you."

"Hey, don't put a guilt trip on me for some stranger's inability to get married. It's not my fault."

"We know that," Karen intervened, her gentleness calming things down. "We love you, Ashlyn, and since we think so highly of Matt, we just wanted to introduce you, that's all. There's no pressure."

I nodded, exhaling deeply. Karen had always had that soothing touch with people. But I wasn't about to dive into the dating game that easily. I'd drown before I'd ever get used to the waters. On the other hand, it was the perfect solution for dealing with Ryan. Going out with this Matt would be something real, not vague or imagined. It wasn't already stamped and sealed with the expectation of "friend" all over it. I needed to get away from Ryan before his closeness drove me mad.

"Let me think about it, okay?"

"That's fine," Karen smiled, as though I had willingly accepted. Maybe in her mind, thinking about it was as good as a yes.

"How old is he, anyway?" I asked. If the guy was as old as Paul was, there'd be no way. "And what's he like?"

Karen grinned, resembling the famous Cheshire cat. "He's cute. Really cute. I think he's about your age, wouldn't you say Shaun?"

"Yeah, early thirties maybe. He runs his own construction company, and I think he's into camping and fishing. Trust us, Ash. Matt would fit right in with the family. He's a great guy."

"He even sings and plays the piano," Karen added.

"A veritable paragon," I threw in.

"Oh, come on, Ash," my brother whined. "Give him a chance."

"Okay, look. I'll agree to meet him if it's totally casual."

"Done," said Shaun. He and Karen looked at each other like they'd just pulled off the deal of the century.

I shook my head at them. "You guys are terrible. You think I'll end up falling for this guy, that we'll be married within a month and indebted to you both for the rest of our lives!"

Shaun let out a hoot of laughter.

Karen giggled. "Close. But seriously, we'll just have you over for dessert, and it'll be no big deal. If you don't hit it off, you can use Katie's bedtime as an excuse to leave."

"Okay," I mumbled, wondering if this could work. Would it help me stop thinking about a guy who'd never be more than a friend?

*****

After a rigorous workout video and a quick shower, I zipped over to check the clock. It was almost two. Ryan would be here any minute.

A flutter of butterflies burst through me. Would he still be upset about yesterday? It would almost be better that way rather than the tenderness that made my heart flip-flop.

I will not be affected, I told myself. You couldn't trust anyone who was a flirt.

"Hey, Katie," I said, trying to calm my nerves, "Ryan will be here in a few minutes."

Sitting on the floor close by, Katie dropped all her Barbie dolls, leapt up, and ran to the front window. "I can't see him. Where is he?"

"I think he's on his way. Keep watching for him."

I quickly tidied up, wishing the crazy pounding of my heart would go away.

He's Megan's boyfriend. Megan's way-too-young-for-me boyfriend.

Ten minutes passed. Katie pressed her nose against the window, her warm breath making vaporous images appear and disappear on the glass.

Fifteen minutes passed.

"He's not coming," Katie said, echoing my thoughts exactly.

I might have made him pretty mad. Was I was so mean he didn't want to come back? Wrapping my arms around Katie, I felt my daughter's disappointment tangling with my own, intertwining and spreading into a gnarled mass of hurt and regret.

It shouldn't be like this. He didn't need to mean this much to us. Sure Katie adored him, but children could make fast friends. And I had been annoyed with him most of the time, so why should I feel even a drop of disappointment if he didn't come?

But if I'd admit it to myself, I *had* wanted to see him. I'd looked forward to it. I enjoyed his company more than I'd realized. Whenever he'd been there, I had felt more alive, like I was emerging from hibernation. Something deep inside wanted more.

I took a dejected Katie into the kitchen and made her a "toasty" with an extra special surprise: chocolate chips. Watching her get peanut butter and chocolate smeared on her upper lip made me chuckle lightheartedly. Would John have thought she was as adorable as I did? Or would her messes and noise annoy him?

The unexpected ring of my phone startled me. "Hello?"

"Hi, Ashlyn," Ryan's voice warmed me from head to toe. "I'm sorry I'm late. I'm stuck in a traffic jam. It looks like there was a big accident up ahead."

"Oh." Relief swept over me. "I'm glad to hear that."

"You're glad I'm in a traffic jam? Or glad there was an accident?"

"No! Sorry, that's not what I meant. I just thought . . . well, that maybe you didn't want to come over after all. You know, after yesterday."

Ryan's soft laughter swirled through me. "And miss out on all the fireballs you hurl at me?"

"Ryan—"

"I'll be there as soon as I can, okay?"

My heart was beating unsteadily. Pressing one hand against my chest, trying to slow the racing emotions, I breathed a hesitant, "Okay."

"I'll see you. Oh, and Ashlyn?" he asked suddenly, his voice a little deeper.

"Yeah?"

"I'm not mad about yesterday."

I was grateful he wasn't there to see my reaction. "That's good," I almost whispered, my voice unsteady.

There was a pause before he said good-bye and hung up. I was momentarily assaulted by emotions, warm and pleasurable, wild and electric. What in heaven's name was I going to do? I better tell Karen to schedule dessert with their friend Matt ASAP.

"Mommy, you gots to put the phone on your ear to talk," Katie said knowledgeably, having come up beside me.

I looked down at the phone clutched against my chest. "Oh. I'm all done talking, sweetie. That was Ryan. He's coming in a few more minutes."

"Yay! I gonna show him my princess music!" Katie darted down the hallway to her room, singing an off-tune melody from *The Little Mermaid*.

I set the phone down and rushed back to my bedroom. Standing in front of the mirror, I scrutinized my appearance, deciding it was imperative that I change. Three tops later, I added a little more make-up and pulled my hair out of its ponytail, letting it fall loosely around my shoulders. I had no idea why I was doing this. It was completely irrational and nonsensical.

He's not coming for you! I told my reflection. I figured that eventually I'd recover from this psycho phase I was obviously going through. As long as I played it safe and didn't let anything slip out. Ryan couldn't ever find out about this. I'd be mortified all over again if he did. And as for Megan? I dreaded the thought.

When the doorbell rang later, my heart nearly burst through my rib cage.

Come on. Get it under control!

I opened the door one second before Katie reached it. Paul Hitch stood awkwardly on the porch with a bouquet of red roses.

"It's not Ryan!" Katie stated disappointedly.

"No." Paul's gaze shifted from Katie to me. "Were you expecting someone else?"

"Uh, just Ryan Anderson, our neighbor."

Paul nodded guardedly, leaning back on his heels. "These are for you," he said, holding out the roses. This time the flowers were arranged in a pretty glass vase.

"Oh. Thanks." Why did he bring me roses? Was that supposed to mean he was serious? Taking the bouquet, I asked, "Do you want to come in?"

Paul's expression brightened. "I'd love to."

Oh great. As he stepped inside, I quickly scanned the road for any sign of Ryan. Maybe Paul would be gone by the time he got here . . . if I could cut this visit short.

"So, I was wondering if you'd like to go out again."

My heart sank. Paul was nice. He was a good person. There just wasn't anything there—no spark, no attraction, nothing. But maybe he'd be the kind of husband and father John never was. Maybe he'd spend time with Katie and me, maybe he'd make us feel loved and important. He'd certainly showered me with flowers in a short amount of time. He was a good man. What if he was exactly what I needed? And how could I know?

"I'm not sure, Paul," I said honestly.

"Oh."

"I had a nice time going to dinner with you; it's just that I'm still not all that comfortable with the whole dating thing."

Paul nodded and shoved his hands into his pockets glumly. I felt terrible. My grandmother would have called me a scoundrel if she were still alive. I didn't want to hurt Paul. He didn't deserve that. He was a good guy. But if I continued going out with him, he'd think I felt more for him than I did. It would be less painful to let him down now than to prolong the inevitable.

"Maybe some other time," Paul said quietly.

"Sure," I said kindly.

Through the awkwardness, a little voice inside my head kept badgering, *What if he's the right one for you?* What if he was everything that Katie and I needed? I'd never know because I was pushing him away.

A knock at the door made me nearly drop the vase of flowers. *Murphy's Law for you!* Ryan had arrived at the most awkward moment possible.

Katie charged to the door and let Ryan inside. "He's here, Mommy! Ryan's here!" If her voice didn't shatter the windows, it certainly rattled my nerves.

Ryan's easy grin faded the moment he saw Paul and the expensive flowers. "Hi," he said with a question in his tone.

I smiled a greeting to Ryan, watching Katie jump into his arms.

"Hello again," Paul said, his chin angled upward. Then he finagled a step closer to me.

Following an awkward silence, I felt Paul's hand at the small of my back. "Oh, Ashlyn, before I forget . . . I brought something for Katie too." He pulled a dainty crystal bracelet out of his pocket for me to see and then handed it to Katie, still perched in Ryan's arms.

"Wow. That's so nice, Paul. What do you say, sweetheart?"

Katie thanked Paul and pulled the stretchy bracelet over her hand. "It's pretty, huh, Ryan?"

Shoving a hand through his hair, Ryan compressed his lips together before muttering, "Yeah. Real pretty." He gave me a puzzled look. "Am I interrupting anything? Because I can go . . ."

I felt the blood rush across my cheeks. "No!" I said a little too quickly. "Not at all." Turning to Paul, I explained, "Ryan's been helping paint and fix up the house."

Paul nodded to me slowly, his eyes sweeping to Ryan and back. "I'd be happy to stay and help too."

Awwww . . . Can this get any worse?

"There's no need to stay," Ryan said, coming forward. "I'm sure you must be busy, and I've got plenty of time today."

"No, no. I'm not busy at all. What can I do to help, Ashlyn?"

"Um, I don't know . . ." I thought frantically. What was I going to do with two guys butting heads over who got to do what? This was ridiculous! I should send them both packing, but I didn't have the guts to do it. Besides, I could seriously use the help.

"We could tape off the kitchen," I suggested. "Then it would be ready to paint."

I grabbed a roll of blue painter's tape from the kitchen counter. When I turned around, Paul and Ryan stood facing each other like two basketball centers at opening tip-off. I thought about tossing the tape in the air between them and letting them both have at it.

It must be a guy thing. They couldn't be rivaling over me, as flattering as that sounded. Paul and Ryan seemed to have developed some sort of male antagonism from the moment they'd met. I didn't get it.

The three of us washed and taped off the kitchen walls. But the tension in the air was as thick as Katie's homemade playdough. When Paul finally admitted he needed to get home, I could have collapsed on the sofa in relief. But he dragged out his good-bye for several minutes.

"Well, I guess I'll be going now," he finally said, eyeing Ryan pointedly, as though waiting for him to say the same.

"Thanks again, Paul," I said. "I really appreciate your help."

"Sure. I'd be happy to come again. Anytime."

Ryan reached out to shake Paul's hand. It looked like they both squeezed pretty hard. Forget basketball! This was like watching two bucks duking it out on Animal Planet.

"See you later," Ryan said mildly.

In my mind, I could hear an imaginary narrator explaining the animal antics in a deep, distinguished monotone: *The challenging male retreats, relinquishing the territory to the triumphant, dominant male.* How did Ryan become the dominant male? Paul was older, had more experience, and was well established.

Paul made his way to the front door but turned back. "I'll see you later, Ashlyn." He was sending signals that I didn't want to acknowledge. I didn't feel attracted to him. But he was good and kind, so I smiled and thanked him again for coming.

Once he drove off, Ryan casually asked, "So, you two are seeing each other now?"

I angled him a stern look. "No, Ryan."

His eyebrows arched up. "No?"

"No," I said firmly, wondering if I should bring up the male antics I'd just witnessed or let it drop.

He leaned against the kitchen table, almost sitting on it, studying me closely. "When a guy spends that kind of money on flowers and presents, he's got to be pretty serious."

I picked a rose out of the bouquet and inhaled its sweet fragrance. It was lovely. But I would've rather admired my own roses out front, instead of these from Paul.

"He did ask me out again," I finally admitted.

Ryan nodded expectantly, crossing his arms over his chest. I could tell he was waiting for me to add more detail to that statement by the way his eyes asked, "And . . . ?"

"I'm . . . I don't know if I want to date *anyone.*" I pushed the rose back into the vase, feeling the leaves and stem scratch against the others. "I mean, look at Katie over there, playing with that bracelet. She needs a daddy to love her and spoil her and teach her. She needs a daddy just to be with her. But for her to have a daddy, I have to start dating. And I don't want to do that. So you tell me, am I being selfish?"

"You're not selfish, Ashlyn, not in the least." Ryan said quietly, moving directly in front of me. He lifted a hand to my elbow, adding soothingly, "It's okay to take care of yourself too."

Something in his deep voice distracted me. It made me forget what was troubling me and notice the muscle in his jaw that seemed to clench and unclench as he spoke. I noticed two freckles on his neck, just below his jaw. His skin right there was paler than the skin on his face. It looked like it would be soft. I had to stop myself from imagining my fingers touching the spot.

I swallowed and looked up into his eyes. They seemed to pull me in. Topaz flecks colored the gray irises exotically. And in combination with his dark lashes, the effect was mesmerizing.

He lifted a finger to a strand of my hair, brushing it back away from my face. "Ashlyn, do you have any idea how beautiful you are?"

His words hit like a bucket of chipped ice, cold and sharp. "Stop that!" I cried, pushing him away. Katie's head whipped up, startled by my sudden flare of emotion. "Stop doing that to me!"

Ryan's hands shot up in the air. "Doing what?"

"Saying stuff like that. Flirting with me."

"I wasn't flirting with—"

"You were too! How do you think Megan would feel if she knew you were flirting?"

"I didn't—" he started to reply, looked down for a moment, and then seemed to shift his response. "I didn't mean to."

"It was flirting, Ryan! And you should have the decency not to do stuff like that to a married woman!"

The words were out before I could think what they meant. Why did I say that? Is that what I considered myself? Still married to John?

"Ashlyn, I'm sorry," Ryan said just above a whisper. And then, as though comprehension finally hit, he mumbled almost inaudibly, "Married woman . . . ?"

"I don't know why I said that." I whipped around, unable to face him, and went to a cupboard for a glass. "I guess I forget sometimes. I mean, I was married one day, lost my husband the next, and suddenly I'm not married anymore. But it still feels like I'm supposed to be married." I filled the glass with water from the kitchen sink and stared out the window, my back to him.

Ryan came up behind me, close enough that I could feel his warmth. He didn't touch me, yet I felt completely encompassed by his presence.

"Hey, it's okay," he whispered behind my ear. His breath sent shivers across my shoulder and down my arm. "I imagine it *would* feel that way, being sealed to him."

"What?" I asked, tossing a glance over my shoulder.

"Sealed. You know, for time and all eternity? So you really are still—"

I abruptly dumped the untouched water into the sink, set the glass on the counter, and turned around to face him. "We weren't sealed."

Ryan's head jerked back a notch as he stared at me blankly. Belatedly, I realized that he stood much closer than I'd thought. His shirtfront brushed against mine. Our feet would get tangled if I were to move. I tilted my head back so I could look him in the eye. But being this close made me feel almost as woozy as when I'd cut my hand.

"You didn't get married in the temple?"

I shook my head, braced for his reaction. His eyebrows furrowed.

"We weren't ready. He was a convert, so we got married and planned to be sealed a year later." My mouth turned down disappointedly. "But it never happened."

Ryan exhaled heavily and placed both hands on my upper arms. "Ashlyn, please forgive me for hurting you. I didn't mean to. You've been through so much, the last thing I'd ever want to do is hurt you." His hands moved to my shoulders protectively. "When I said you were beautiful, it was . . . I don't know, the first thing—the only thing—in my mind, and it just came out. But I meant it sincerely. I'm amazed at how beautiful you are. Inside and out." He tilted my face up, compassion in his eyes and in his touch. "Forgive me? Please?"

I nodded, feeling my cheek brushing against the warmth of his hand. "It's okay, Ryan."

He raised his other hand to stroke my hair and shook his head in wonder as though I truly was amazing in his eyes. I'd never felt this way before, not with anyone. Not even with my own husband. It was such a powerful feeling that I couldn't have moved away. I wanted to be there, I wanted his touch.

When his arms tenderly surrounded me, I gave in. I stepped into the embrace, wrapping my arms around his solid back. As he held me against his taller frame, I could feel his heartbeat through the fabric of our clothes, steady and strong. Vaguely, I wondered why Katie hadn't interrupted before now. But I was thankful to have this moment, wanting it to last.

I know he's much younger than I am. I know nothing will come of this. But for now, I need this—I want this.

Ryan pulled back slightly, severing our close contact, and for a second, I thought he would pull away altogether. Instead, he brushed his knuckles lightly along the edge of my face and down my jawline. It was a faint caress, but my senses were working overtime, causing my skin to burn where he'd touched me.

Drawing back to stare down at me pensively, he seemed to be contemplating saying something. In the end, he finally said, "I think I better go now."

My heart was beating so fast, I was worried he'd notice. "Thank you, Ryan," I whispered.

His mouth turned up at one corner. "For what?"

I shook my head, not finding the right words. "For your kindness. For being my friend."

His lips curved upwards into a lopsided grin as he touched my arm. "I'll always be your friend, Ash." Turning around, Ryan saw Katie come into the room and went over to scoop her up over his shoulder with a flourish. Her gleeful squeals filled the room.

"I think I'll take this sack of potatoes home with me," he said.

"I'm not a sack; I'm a girl!"

Pulling her back down, he looked Katie over from head to toe. "Hey, you *are* a girl. Where did the potatoes go?" He poked her tummy. "Any in there? Or over here?"

Giggling as he tickled her, Katie seemed so happy with Ryan that it filled me with an even greater measure of warmth, deep and reviving. When Ryan walked outside to leave, Katie followed at his heels like a devoted cocker spaniel.

"Don't leave, Ryan," she pleaded. "You gotta stay here."

Squatting down to talk to her, he said, "I have to go to my house now, Katie."

"Why?"

"Well, because that's where I live. It's where I eat and sleep."

Katie wrinkled up her face in confusion. "But you can eat here."

Ryan laughed, gently tugging one of her springy curls.

I inserted, "Uh, you're welcome to stay for dinner."

He laughed even harder seeing the look on my face. "Nothing like being forced into inviting someone to dinner, huh?"

"And sleep here with us!" Katie added emphatically.

Ryan shook his head. "I can't sleep here, Katie."

"Uh-huh, Mommy has a big bed."

I spluttered, exchanging a brief, overheated glance with Ryan.

"Oh," his voice quivered ever so slightly, "that's very generous Katie, but I have to sleep in my bed." His gray eyes swept over me, and I could only hope my face wasn't flaming.

This was out of control. Things had gone way too far. How would I ever tell Megan now? Ryan left with a reassuring wink and a squeeze on my arm, waving good-bye to Katie as he walked down the driveway.

"It was a little budding rose, / Round like a fairy globe,
And shyly did its leaves unclose / Hid in their mossy robe . . ."
–Emily Bronte

Chapter 18

"Guess what?" Karen's voice bounced with excitement over the phone.

"What?" I asked warily, sinking down on the sofa to talk.

"Dessert with Matt is going to be this Saturday," she sing-songed, opera-like.

"This Saturday?" I exclaimed. "So soon?"

"Soon? Are you kidding? We've given you a couple weeks to get used to the idea."

"It wasn't long enough." I'd actually forgotten all about it.

"Oh, come on. You're going to love this guy, I promise."

I was tempted to push the red button on my cell phone to end the conversation. Karen would think we'd lost the connection or that my batteries had died. But my sister-in-law was kindness personified and didn't deserve that. And perhaps this Matt could be the one to break the ridiculous feelings I had every time Ryan came near.

"I don't know, Karen." I half laughed, half groaned. Why did I ever agree to meet this Matt guy?

"It'll be fun, Ash! Seriously. He's completely easygoing and will put you at ease the minute you meet."

"What if he doesn't like me?"

"Not possible. You're the kind of person everyone loves."

"What if I don't like him?"

"Again, not possible. He's the kind of *guy* everyone loves."

"Karen . . ."

My sister-in-law was always generous with her praise. She couldn't help it. She imagined everyone else in the world as wonderful as she was.

"Look, what if you're perfect together?" she continued. "You'll never know if you don't come."

I supposed she was right and groaned resignedly. "What do you want me to bring?"

"Your cheerful attitude," she lectured playfully. "That's all."

I laughed. "Okay. I'll do it for you."

"When you meet Matt, you'll know you did it for *you*, not for me. He's great."

"We'll see."

"He is. He's attractive and funny. And he's down to earth, you know? Just an all-over nice guy."

"I'm sure he is. It's just the fact that he's been purposely singled out for me that's nerve-racking."

"Do you have something pretty to wear, Ash?"

"Yeah, I've got a pair of sweats—"

"Don't you dare!"

I laughed. "Hey, they're all broken in and soft, with just the right amount of holes."

"Ugh! Let me take you shopping, my treat. I'll even cut and color your hair."

"You need to have a girl to spoil."

"Well I only have boys, so until then, let me spoil you. We'll have a blast."

I laughed but added more seriously, "Karen, what did I ever do to deserve a sister-in-law like you? You're so good to me."

"Oh, stop," Karen scoffed. I could hear her embarrassment. Shaun had married the kind of woman who avoided praise but deserved every bit of it.

"I'm serious," I told her. "I think you're an angel. Thank you for everything you do for me."

Karen murmured, "You're welcome," before plunging into the details of a full-blown shopping extravaganza and makeover.

*****

I was about to hang my new hummingbird feeder from an old, rusted hook on the porch when Bethany gunned up my gravel driveway. I set the bright-red feeder down on a small table, watching her Lexus lurch to a stop in front of my garage door. For a moment, I actually contemplated hiding, but reason kicked in. I couldn't help wondering what misfortune had brought her here.

In black skinny jeans, she wobbled precariously on ultra-high wedges over the gravel, her arms flailing for balance. But it was the saccharine expression on her face that got my attention.

"Hello, Bethany," I said warily. "What's up?"

She steadied herself, adjusting her perfect blonde waves, and clomped up the steps of the porch. "Hey!" she gushed sweetly. "How's it going?"

Warning signals went off in my head. Bethany Albright with a sudden urge to be my BFF? I had no idea what she was up to. "I'm fine, and you?"

Her eyes narrowed, but her smile sugared up a notch. "Oh, great. Really great." It was weird the way she barely made eye contact with me. Instead, her eyes shifted between my front yard and the patio chairs.

"Would you like to sit down?" I asked, indicating the chair closest to her.

"Uh, sure." She wiped a long-nailed finger along the edge of the chair to unsubtly check for dirt before sitting down. Her skinny jeans looked like they'd split their seams. I waited for her to indicate a reason for her visit, but she didn't seem to be in any hurry. "Nice day, huh?" she said, observing the clear, blue sky overhead.

"Yeah." I really didn't have all day to gab about the weather. Katie would be up from her nap soon, and I liked to get as much done while she slept as possible. "So what's up, Bethany?"

"Hmm?" she asked, whipping her head back to me. "Oh, I just thought it would be nice for the two of us to, you know . . . talk."

"Okay. What would you like to talk about?"

She casually tapped her acrylic nails on the arm of the patio chair. "Well, I was hoping I could confide in you about something. My friends are all so young. But you . . . you're *so* much older and more mature. I'm sure you're the perfect person to confide in."

"All right . . ."

"You see, no one knows this, but I'm actually sort of"—she paused dramatically—"engaged."

"Really?"

"Yes, but promise not to say a word to anyone. Ryan and I haven't announced it yet."

"Who?"

She blinked innocently. "Ryan. Ryan Anderson." When I only stared at her, she giggled. "We've never let anyone know."

"Really." What did she think this was, *Sense and Sensibility*? She could play Miss Lucy Steele all she wanted, but I wasn't playing Elinor Dashwood.

She shrugged coquettishly. "I think a fall wedding would be nice, don't you? We want to find a nice house, of course," she prattled, glancing distastefully at my house. "I have so many decorating plans for our dream home. Ryan loves my ideas." She giggled. "I know how to make things look"—she raised her eyebrows at Katie's dirty toys nearby—"classy."

I'd had enough of this. Standing up, I said, "Well, good luck with that, Bethany. I think Katie's waking up, so I better go in now."

She stood too, smiling, and wagged a finger at me. "Okay, but don't forget you promised not to say a word about it."

"Look, Bethany, I didn't promise you anything. I don't know what games you're playing, but they won't work on me." I moved toward my front door. "If you were engaged to Ryan, then he would have mentioned it to Megan, don't you think? Seeing as how he's dating her?"

Her expression hardened. "No. We date other people because neither of us is ready for marriage yet. But I can assure you, I'm the one he'll marry someday."

"Okay." *Whatever.* Was she delusional?

"I know he's way too young for someone like you, but don't you find it hard being around him?"

"What do you mean?"

"Well, he's always over here helping, and I've been worried about you. Having to deal with someone that good-looking who's so out of reach."

I'll just bet you've been worried. I couldn't believe Bethany was doing this. It was ridiculous, pathetic, and so not worth my time. "Well, thanks for your concern, but I'm fine. I've got to go now, but I'll see you later."

All her smiles vanished, and she hurled one last venomous shot. "I've seen the way you look at him."

I froze. She'd found the one thing to say that could lance right through me. I stood immobile, one hand on the doorknob. *I've seen the way you look at him.* Words to expose, wound, and humiliate.

"I'm only trying to prevent you from making a bigger fool of yourself," she said. "Especially when he accepts the job offer with Boeing out in

Virginia. Oh, you hadn't heard? Yeah. Leaving Meadow Vista and moving on to bigger and better things, I guess."

Ryan had a job offer in Virginia? He'd never said anything about it. "Yeah, I guess," I said, giving her a small wave before walking inside and closing the door.

It wasn't until she'd driven away that I sank to the floor in defeat.

This was bad. Really bad. Had she really seen something in the way I looked at Ryan? Or was she just making it up? Would he really move away, or was she making that up as well? Either way, I'd just been given a crucial wakeup call.

*****

I sat in my car outside Shaun and Karen's house. The sun was setting over the pine-covered mountains in the rearview mirror. I smoothed out my brand-new skirt and checked the way-too-expensive ruffled blouse Karen had insisted on. I had to admit she was right; they did make me look good. She'd even convinced me to get these new strappy sandals as well. The golden highlights in my hair made my wispy, long layers glow. From head to toe, I felt like a new woman.

"Heck, I even painted my toenails," I muttered. But did I feel like I could go in there and meet this guy? "Not even close," I told my rearview-mirror image. But at least I was in an acceptable place doing something appropriate.

A sleek, black car drove past, and a pain shot through my chest. What if that was him? I didn't want him to drive up and see me hiding in my car.

The black car continued down the street. *Phew.* I took one last look in the rearview mirror. There was only a sliver of sun above the mountain. The clouds in the sky were turning from pink and orange to lavender and blue. If only I could peacefully sit and watch the sunset . . .

Quickly, I checked my make-up and teeth and ran a hand through my hair one more time. "Okay, if I hate him, I'll leave. I feel sick anyway."

I opened the car door and stepped outside. The air was actually warm tonight. I walked up to the front porch of the two-story home, trying to calm my nerves. That's when I noticed.

Rosebuds.

I could hardly believe it. Karen's rose bushes were budding! I remembered the day before moving into our home, wondering what color the roses in front of my house would be. It had been a cold winter day. A lot had happened since then. I'd been perfectly aware that spring had come, but could I have missed seeing newly emerging buds on my own roses?

Suddenly, I couldn't wait to get home. I wanted to check my rose bushes. But first I had to face this nightmare blind-date thing. I resented feeling like a guinea pig for Shaun and Karen's matchmaking scheme, but I also had to admit it might be good for me.

Oh, John, what am I doing?

Karen popped out of the front door, startling me with an excited greeting. "Whoa, look at you!"

"Hi, Karen," I said, my nerves going spastic.

"Come on inside," she hissed excitedly, waving her hand back and forth. "Matt's here!"

With a strangled moan, I stepped inside, smelling the decadent sweetness of chocolate in the air. My eyes swept the front room for a glimpse of the male guinea pig. Would he be tall? Short? Friendly? Shy? How would I feel around him? Would this become something more than a date? Would Matt be able to break the spell Ryan had on me? I wasn't looking to marry the guy; I just wanted him to make me forget Ryan.

"The guys are out on the deck. Come on back, and I'll introduce you."

I grabbed Karen's arm. "Wait!"

Karen stopped. "What? What is it?"

"I don't know . . ."

"Ashlyn, there's nothing to worry about. You look fantastic, and Matt's going to think you're gorgeous. He's completely laid back and really fun. It's going to be great, you'll see."

"Okay," I said, taking a deep breath. "But I feel kind of sick."

"You're just nervous. Once you meet him, you'll feel good. Reeeeally good." Karen giggled.

I gave her a mocking glance. But as soon as I stepped out on the deck to meet Matt, I was pleasantly surprised. He was fine. Great actually—tall, curly-blonde, and good-looking.

Shaun stepped forward. "Matt, I'd like you to meet my sister Ashlyn."

Matt stuck out his hand and grinned. "It's nice to finally meet you."

"Finally? How long have they been torturing you?" I asked.

Matt laughed, his perfect, white teeth the highlight of a great smile. He had to be on intimate terms with his bleach trays.

"For a few weeks. How about you?"

"About the same."

"But, hey"—he leaned in conspiratorially, as if Shaun and Karen couldn't hear—"we get an awesome dessert out of it, eh?"

This time I laughed. "You've got that right!"

Karen had set up a fabulous chocolate fountain with strawberries, bananas, marshmallows, and pretzels for dipping. We ate and talked outside, laughter frequently permeating our conversation. I could hardly believe how easy it was to talk to Matt.

"So, you have a little girl I understand?" he asked.

"Yeah, her name is Katie."

He nodded. "How old is she?"

"Three. She's funny, sweet, and mischievous all at once." I couldn't help laughing a little just thinking about Katie.

"Is she into all the princess stuff like my nieces are?" Matt asked.

"Definitely. Although she's rambunctious enough she might end up in sports. She's quite a character."

"I'd like to meet her." He laughed. "She sounds like a lot of fun."

I could like this guy, I thought, watching Matt dip a marshmallow into the chocolate.

"Want some more?" he asked.

"No, thanks, I've eaten enough chocolate for a week." I laughed.

"Aw, come on. You've got to live a little."

Live a little. Yeah, that's it, exactly. I felt like I was living again. And it felt good.

"I take it you're an expert on living it up?" I asked playfully.

"Uh, actually I work at the office all day and come home to my dog, Pete."

"Does Pete liven things up any?"

"Heck yeah. When the neighbors let out their cat, he's a maniac."

Yeah, I could really like this guy. And I never thought about Ryan the whole evening. Well, for a moment one stray thought had wandered into my mind, but I promptly shoved it aside. I was determined to think only about tonight and giving Matt a fair chance.

About an hour and a half later, when I decided I should be getting back to Katie, Matt walked me out to my car. The old streetlight blinked over the sidewalk, and a cluster of gnats fluttered in the shaft of light.

"Thanks for coming tonight," he said. "It was good to meet you. Shaun and Karen have been talking about you for a while, and none of their praise was mislaid."

"Thanks, Matt. It was nice to meet you too."

"I had a lot of fun."

I nodded. "Me too, actually."

He laughed. "You sound surprised."

"Yeah, I am. Oh, sorry! No offense to you at all. It's just that—"

"Hey, no worries. I felt the same way. Getting set up is a bit . . ." He trailed off, searching for the right word.

"Terrifying?" I suggested.

He laughed again. "Yeah. No offense intended."

"None taken." I smiled.

"Would you like to go to dinner with me sometime?"

I didn't have any hesitation. "Sure."

"Great. I'll give you a call."

We said our good-byes, and I drove home feeling quite comfortable with the way things had turned out that evening. When I got home, I walked around the house to the front and peered at the rose bushes in the lamplight. I had to look carefully, but sure enough, there they were— delicate green buds with a burst of yellow showing through.

"There are a hundred places where I fear
To go—so with his memory they brim."
–Edna St. Vincent Millay

Chapter 19

I DRIED MY CLEANED PAINTBRUSH on a rag and turned to look out the window again. Ryan and Katie were still dancing around outside on the front lawn. I let out a puff of laughter at his goofball antics with my three-year-old. But I also felt a sharp prick of concern as I watched them. John had barely spent any time with Katie before he died. Ryan had probably done more with her than John ever had. And hovering in my mind was an ever-increasing apprehension about Katie's attachment to him.

Not to mention my own difficulty trying to—

"Cute, aren't they," Megan said behind me.

I whipped around at the sound of her voice, altering my expression to something more indifferent. "Finished already?"

"Yep, bathroom's done," she said. "Come see."

I followed her with a backward glance at the window then quickly reminded myself about my third date with Matt on Friday. I'd been doing a good job of avoiding Ryan, but when he showed up unexpectedly like today, I got a little rattled. I had to take extra care to be indifferent.

Megan and Ryan had come today to paint Katie's bathroom. They helped me choose a light shade of yellow that made the rubber ducky shower curtain pop with cheerful color. Ryan and Katie had gone outside with popsicles to celebrate the accomplishment while Megan did a few touch-ups and I cleaned the roller.

"I love it," I said, peering into the sunny bathroom. "It looks great."

I saw Megan's ready nod in the bathroom mirror but noticed something in her eyes that made me turn around. "Hey, are you okay?" I asked, taking her arm. It was faint, but there was definitely something melancholy in her expression. I thought I'd noticed it when she first arrived, but I wasn't sure earlier.

"Yeah, I'm fine," she said. But her tone didn't seem to match.

"Megan, you can talk to me," I reminded, placing a hand on her arm. "What's wrong?"

She shrugged and shook her head. "Nothing. Just life."

"Anything you want to talk about?"

She gave me a strange look I didn't recognize then bit her bottom lip. "Ryan and I are . . ."

With the long pause, I found myself anxious for her to finish. "You're what?" I softly asked.

She released a gloomy sigh. "We're not dating anymore."

"What? Megan, what happened?" My first thought was that Bethany had done something. But I was a little confused. She and Ryan had come over together with no indication of trouble. And Megan was crazy about him! Ryan Anderson was perfect in every way; he was everything she could ever want. Maybe he'd avoided marriage in the past, but I figured that if the right girl came along . . .

"We talked last night," she began slowly, "and I don't know. He still wants us to be friends, but . . ."

"Oh, Megan," I groaned, putting my arms around her. "I'm so sorry." I brought my hands to her cheeks. "Are you okay? I know how you feel about him."

She turned her head, saying, "I'll be fine," with an attempt at a smile.

"What were his reasons? Did you guys fight about something?"

"No, no. It's nothing like that. It's just . . ."

Megan shrugged and walked away with a wave of her hand. I might have thought she was being flippant if I hadn't also caught her swiping a tear away. I wasn't sure if she was slashing the conversation or if she still wanted to talk about it, so I followed quietly, wondering how to help or what to say. My poor sister had to be hurting much more than she was letting on.

Seeing me behind her, she said, "Don't worry about me, Ash. I'll get over it. You know me; I never stay with one guy for—"

She crumbled into a puddle of tears and sobs on the floor. I held her close, feeling the sudden trail of warm tears on my own cheeks. Why was I crumbling too?

Megan sobbed through watery phrases that were only partially understandable, expressing her confusion and pain. "What's w-wrong with me, Ash?"

"Nothing is wrong with you!" I cried. "Did Ryan say something?"

"No. He was as kind as always. I must be defective!" She broke into a fresh deluge.

I cradled and soothed, but inside an emotional turmoil was brewing. What if this was my fault? Ryan had been flirting with me lately, and I—I had to be honest with myself, I'd gotten sucked in. What if my behavior had confused him into thinking there was something more than the friend-thing between us? What if I was responsible for my sister's heartbreak? I needed space. Time to think.

I have to get away from here.

It was the first thought that came to me, and the more I considered it—the need to get away—the more it made sense. I should go somewhere I could think straight and get a grip on this thing that had laced itself around my heart and tugged against common sense. Surely Ryan needed time away from me too. He probably wasn't thinking clearly either. Breaking things off with Megan seemed a bit crazy to me, especially if he expected her to remain "friends" like it didn't hurt. If I were to look deep inside myself, I'd probably find more to the Ryan situation than just our age difference and the conflict with Megan, but I didn't want to go there. I didn't want to face it. It made me almost panic.

My aunt Linda had been asking me to come visit. Maybe I should take her up on the offer. Fair Oaks was less than an hour away, and I loved being around her and Uncle Rob. There was no guarantee I could fix things, but if there was a chance that going down there for a week would help, then I'd do it.

That's when I remembered John's parents. They lived down in that area too, in Folsom. We hadn't seen them since moving back to California. Granted, they didn't like me for some reason I'd never figured out, but Katie should visit her Carter grandparents.

"Ash, I'm going to go home, okay?" Megan finally said. "I don't want him to see me like this."

"Okay. What do you want me to do?"

"Tell him I forgot I had to be somewhere," she said, wiping wet mascara from under her eyes. "It's not a total lie."

I hugged my sister, wishing I had the power to take away her pain. "You can go out through the garage," I suggested. "I'll get Ryan and Katie to come inside."

Megan hugged me before quickly slipping away. When Ryan brought Katie inside, she wanted to show me one of their funny dances, but I had to wash her popsicle-stained face and change her top first.

When she was all cleaned up, Katie ran to her room to grab her CD player.

"We gots to have music!" she declared.

"Well all right then," I answered with a little laugh as we returned to the kitchen where Ryan waited.

"Where's Megan?" Ryan asked when I returned with a cleaned-up Katie.

"Oh, she said she had to be somewhere."

"Was she okay?" he asked. It was nice to hear the concern in his voice.

I didn't want to lie to him, but Megan wouldn't want me to say anything about her crying. "Yeah," was my quick reply before turning to Katie. "Hey, pumpkin, do you want to show me your dance now?"

"Yes! C'mon, Ryan, let's do the funny one!"

"The 'Sack of Potatoes' dance? Oh, and it sounds like we'll be dancing to *Little Mermaid* music," he said, giving me a wink. "Perfect choice." He took Katie's outstretched hands and moved her around in a series of goofy flips over his shoulder and back down to the floor.

She laughed in her signature high-pitched voice.

"Hey, come join us," Ryan said with a grin, tilting his head in a beckoning gesture that would have made a younger woman melt on the spot. Not me. I couldn't melt anymore.

"That's okay," I answered. "It takes two to tango, not three."

"Come on, we're not doing the tango. We need three people for this dance anyway; don't we, Katie?"

Katie started jumping and cried, "Yeah! Try it Mommy. It's fun!"

Ryan danced Katie around the room, managing to get closer and closer to me until he finally grabbed one of my hands, pulling me into the dance. It was more like ring-around-the-rosies than dancing. We swung our arms up in the air and back down again, completely at home with our silliness.

"Ryan, show Mommy how you spin me 'round and 'round!"

"Okay," he said, releasing my hand. "Hold on tight, pumpkin. Ready?"

"Uh-huh!"

Ryan spun Katie around in a circle, faster and faster, until her feet left the floor and she was squealing in the air with delight.

"Now you try, Mommy!"

"No, I'm good." I laughed.

Katie couldn't imagine anyone not wanting to spin. "You dis can try it," she patted my leg encouragingly.

"I'll show you how to spin your Mommy," Ryan said, setting Katie on the sofa. "Watch this."

Before I could move, he took me into his arms, flashed me a grin, and then spun us around like ballroom dancers. There was nothing romantic about the setting, but I felt warmth filling me from within. It was a glowing ember that caught fire and spread throughout my body.

Resist him.

Ryan's hand shifted against my back before he spun me away from him. Then, with a gentle tug, he spun me back into his arms, encircling me from behind. Katie clapped, but my attention was entirely focused on Ryan—the way his arms wrapped me in their strength, the way he moved to the music . . . the way he hadn't let me go.

Man, was he a good dancer!

Katie leapt back over, anxious not to be excluded. Ryan took her dimpled hand, and we did another spinning version of ring-around-the-rosies.

Dancing in the living room with my little girl was part of the fairy tale of happily-ever-afters. We were living part of that dream. It could have been this way with John—it should have been! At this moment, nothing could be more perfect than seeing little Katie so full of joy. And it wouldn't have happened without Ryan.

The problem was that I needed it to be like that with someone else, like Matt. I wondered how long it would take to feel that kind of closeness with him.

"So how was your date with the new guy?" Ryan asked, right in sync with my thoughts.

I came to an abrupt stop, stepping back. "Fine."

"Fine?" he asked, raising an eyebrow. "Is that a good-fine or a bad-fine?"

"It's a none-of-your-business-fine." I smirked.

"Okay, okay. I get it. What's another safe topic?"

"I'm going to go down to Folsom for a few days."

"You are?" he asked with surprise. "When did you decide to go?"

"Recently."

He eyed me closely. "What's in Folsom?"

I cleared my throat and looked over at Katie. She'd plopped down on the sofa in a tired heap. "John's parents live there."

"Oh." Ryan glanced at Katie before turning back to me questioningly.

I wandered into the kitchen, and he followed.

"Is this the first time you'll have seen them since the funeral?"

I released the breath of air I'd been holding. "It is."

"You don't seem all that excited."

"Yeah, well, things are a tad hairy between me and my in-laws. They don't like me for some reason. I don't know if they blame me for taking John away from them, or resent the fact that we moved to Ohio." I shrugged. "They've hardly spoken to me since John died. It's like they think his death was my fault."

"That's crazy. It was an accident."

"I know, but when you're grieving, you don't always think rationally." I quickly thought back to the way I'd treated Ryan on several occasions. "Remember how psycho I used to be?"

"You weren't psycho." He chuckled growing serious. "Are they going to be decent to you and Katie?"

"We'll be fine." I nodded. He was concerned about us. It was sweet.

Ryan's eyes dropped to the invisible line his toe drew on the floor. "So, when will you leave?"

"I don't know for sure. Maybe this weekend."

His head shot up. "So soon?"

"Yeah, I think so."

"Does Katie know?"

I shook my head. "Not yet." *Not since I thought of it five minutes ago.*

"How long will you be gone?"

"I don't know. Maybe a week or so. We'll see."

Ryan's eyebrows furrowed. "I'm going to miss you."

I looked away, unable to say what I felt in my heart. I knew I'd miss him too. It was exactly why I needed to do this in the first place.

"Ash?"

I turned back to him, shaking away my thoughts. "Hmm?"

"I was wondering—would you like me to paint in here while you're gone?"

His words took me by surprise. "You don't have to do that."

"No, I'd like to do it. We're so close to being finished with all the painting."

"I don't want you to feel obligated—"

"Trust me, I don't feel obligated."

"—and Lisa Goodwin did promise to help me after she has the baby."

"Which isn't even due for three more weeks," he pointed out. "Let me do it. You picked out some colors you liked, right?"

"Sort of." I grabbed a pile of paint color samples from the counter and thumbed through them. "I like some of these, but you and Megan are better at this than me."

"We could pick one out for you," he teased.

But it was a brilliant idea. If Ryan and Megan had to collaborate and spend time together on a big project like that, the likelihood of them getting back together was much greater.

"You really want to do this?" I asked, not wanting to take advantage of his generosity.

"Yeah, I do."

"Are you sure?"

"Completely."

"All right. Hold on, and I'll get you a spare key." I ran to my bedroom, where I'd hidden an extra house key, and brought it back to Ryan. "Here you go. But remember I don't expect it. Painting can wait if you and Megan are doing something else."

Like "working on it."

"I'd rather come get it done. I like to see things through to the end."

I probably looked at him a little funny, but I couldn't help thinking his words didn't match his behavior when it came to the whole commitment issue. As far as I knew, he'd never seen a relationship through to the end. He'd done a heck of a lot of starting but no finishing in that arena, and in my opinion, it was because he couldn't stop flirting. Flirtation after marriage could lead all the way to infidelity. I wasn't about to relive that all over again. If I ever *were* to marry again, it would be to someone I knew would be completely faithful. Putting some distance between me and this guy with whom I had no future was vital. There'd be no finish to this story, no happy ending.

I knew it.

He knew it.

And the very pain I felt was a huge indicator that things had gone too far already. Going away was definitely the right thing to do.

Megan should know there was something happening between me and Ryan, but I didn't know how to tell her. As long as it remained unspoken and undefined, it seemed less of a reality. But Bethany could ruin everything if she wanted to.

*****

I tossed a large suitcase into the trunk and looked up at the clear, blue sky. It was almost May and perfect weather for a vacation. Aunt Linda and Uncle Rob were ecstatic when I'd asked if Katie and I could visit. And Folsom was only a few minutes away from where they lived, so I could see Gary and Helen Carter. I sure hoped that everything would go well, not so much for me but for Katie. She'd probably need a connection to her father as she grew older, and I wanted her to feel comfortable with her paternal grandparents.

As we drove southwest on I-80, we left the deeply forested foothills to descend into the sunshine-drenched California hills. They were a vibrant green right now from winter and spring rains. California poppies colored many sections, waving in a sea of orange. But soon the grasses would dry and turn golden yellow. That's when they'd appear like Sting's famous "fields of gold."

I'd thrown together that suitcase so quickly that I wasn't sure I'd tossed in everything. But it didn't matter, really. I could buy whatever we forgot. I just needed to be away from Meadow Vista for a while.

"You are my sunshine," Katie sang sweetly off-tune from her car seat in back. "My sunshine."

I joined in. "You make me happy when skies are gray . . ." Katie *was* my sunshine. "Are you excited to see the chickens I told you about?"

"Uh-huh! Can I pet them?"

"I don't think you'll want to pet them. But they're fun to watch."

Fair Oaks, where my aunt and uncle lived, was well known for its chickens, which roamed the village and roosted in parks. They sauntered around the small-town streets like they owned the place, being fed by shop-keepers and locals.

I exited the freeway in Roseville and continued south through Citrus Heights on Sunrise Boulevard. Everything was so alive here compared to Meadow Vista. Every corner was a nucleus of activity—restaurants, shops, gas stations. And it was much warmer too, which made my anticipation of kayaking soar. Linda and Rob used to take Shaun, Megan, me, and our cousins out on Lake Natoma many lazy summers ago. Those were some of the best summer memories I had, splashing each other with cold river water as we baked under the July or August sun.

"Hey, there's the Sunrise Mall," I said aloud. It had been a while since I'd shopped there. I laughed to myself, remembering how I'd spotted a cute boy at a kiosk in the mall when I was fourteen, but I didn't have the courage to talk to him. It seemed like a lifetime ago.

Leaving the busy roads of Citrus Heights to drive into Fair Oaks was like driving back in time a few decades. I wasn't sure why the town center was called "the Village," but the name fit perfectly.

"Look, Katie, there're some chickens!" I pointed off to our left where a cocky, plump hen scuttled across the street ahead of another cluster of chickens. She looked like an anxious tour guide trying to direct her wayward group to safety. All cars stopped to give them the right of way.

"Mommy, a chicken went into that store!" Katie cried out, twisting in her car seat to get a better view.

"They do that here. Those silly chickens."

"Yeah, they're silly!" Katie giggled.

I turned onto a narrow road that led me through rolling hills to my aunt and uncle's pale-yellow craftsman bungalow. "We're here, Katie!"

Katie wiggled restlessly in her car seat until I unbuckled her. "Who lives here?" she asked, apparently not remembering my earlier explanations.

"Aunt Linda and Uncle Rob. I used to come here all the time when I was young. We're going to stay here for a few days. Won't that be fun?"

Katie wasn't sure, but she was glad to hop out of the car. I held her hand as we walked past rhododendron and azalea bushes, a grapefruit tree, and a healthy row of daisies. Everything looked the same as the last time I'd been there. My aunt and uncle had lived there for as long as I could remember, and I loved the place.

Katie saw the doorbell and charged up the porch to ring it five times before I was able to catch her.

"We only need to ring once, honey."

The front door opened, and we were gathered into arms with delight. "Oh, how we've missed you!" my aunt said. "Katie, I'm Auntie Linda, and this is Uncle Rob. We're so excited to have you stay with us!"

"Thank you," I said, instantly feeling how right this decision had been. I could find laughter and family ties here, far from the confusion I'd been experiencing recently.

"Come on in, and we'll have some lemonade."

Their home was full of light from all the windows. The décor was modern and airy, something so different from my parents' house, but I loved the feeling. Fair Oaks was an artsy town, with small galleries and shops catering to specific interests, and over the years my aunt had purchased some striking pieces—like the mottled green-and-blue glass vase strategically placed to catch beams of brilliant light each morning. In the pristine white kitchen, we sat at the bar and sipped lemonade, talking of old times.

"Remember the first time we kayaked down to Folsom Prison?" my uncle reminisced, his tummy quivering with mirth.

"Yes." I laughed. "Didn't Shaun think we'd all get shot and dragged in as inmates?"

"Yep," he chortled. "Poor kid. I've never seen anyone paddle so fast"— his belly laughs prevented him from breathing, so he could hardly speak— "hightailing it out of there." He flapped his arms like an old-fashioned egg beater, making his thick hair bob up and down. It cracked me up more than the memories. That was the thing about Uncle Rob. He made everyone laugh just by almost passing out trying to tell a story. "Ah, those were good times."

"Can I get you anything to eat?" Linda asked.

"Oh no, we're fine," I assured her. "We had lunch on the way."

"I hope you don't mind, but I thought we'd walk to the bistro for dinner tonight," she said.

"Sounds delicious." I knew she didn't used to like cooking, and apparently things hadn't changed.

After a relaxing afternoon, we walked over to The Village Bistro, a tiny restaurant in a pink-stucco, historic building. We ate on the sidewalk out front, where we could watch couples, bicyclists, and chickens wander along.

"This is to die for," I said, dreamily taking a bite of Chicken Piccata, a temperate breeze fluffing my hair.

"You should taste their portabella-and-eggplant sandwich," Rob said, wiping his mouth. "Talk about to die for."

"We'll come back for lunch one day," said Linda. "There's so much to do while you're here; I hope we can cram it all in!"

"You don't have to do anything special for me—"

"Nonsense! I can hardly wait for all the fun!"

I laughed, amazed at my aunt's zest for life. "Well, I would like to drive to the temple grounds." My temple prep teacher had suggested I walk the grounds while I was down here.

"Perfect," said Linda. "What day should we go?"

"Any day that works for you."

"Okay. We could bike the trails down by the river. Oh, and we also want to take you to a concert in the park Thursday evening. Those are fun. And you still plan to do some kayaking, right?"

"I'd love to, if you don't mind helping me with Katie."

Linda clapped her hands. "Katie and I will have so much fun! We have a life jacket her size, and she can splash around while you and Rob are out on the water. We'll have a picnic and everything!"

This was amazing. There was no doubt about it—coming here was definitely the right thing to do. Being with Linda and Rob was sure to be a blast with all the activities they had planned. Just being around them made me feel good.

Then there was the most important thing of all—down here I was sure to forget a certain self-proclaimed, twenty-five-year-old menace to society.

*****

After several days of being pampered, I came to a clear-cut conclusion: I was crazy. While kayaking from Negro Bar under the Folsom Bridges, drifting above massive boulders under the water's surface, all I could think about was Ryan. *He would love it here on the water. We'd have so much fun together.* I pictured him smiling at me from a kayak, mischievously knocking his paddle in the water to splash me. I imagined him exploring the water's edge with Katie, pointing out ducks, geese, and herons.

While window shopping on Sutter Street in historic Folsom, I couldn't keep Ryan from popping into my mind. *He'd love to show me the museum in the old Wells Fargo assay building.* I could hear his voice telling the history of the Pony Express stop and bank for the gold mines of the California Mother Lode.

One evening, Katie and I walked with Linda from her house over Red Bridge to watch the sunset. She pointed out the gnarled, exposed roots of great oak trees hanging over the cliff, high above the water. We saw a teenage group of daredevils jump from the bridge, shouting victoriously afterward from the water below. Down on the American River Bike Trail, people strolled or biked, enjoying the evening breeze. From our spot on the bridge, we gazed at the pink-and-orange fusion in the sky as the sun went down. A couple walked past hand in hand, and I felt swirls of longing coursing through my chest.

It was ridiculous. Either I was crazy, or I wasn't trying hard enough. But each time I tried to picture John in each of those places, the fleeting images were hazy. I probably hadn't been around Matt long enough to allow his face to wander through scenes of my imagination. It might come in time.

If there was one place I shouldn't be able to think about Ryan, it would be at John's parents' house. I was taking Katie to see them today and was filled with dread. Gary and Helen had lived in Folsom all their married life in a 1960s rambler on Mormon Street—until John got baptized and married me. John said it was a coincidence that they moved around the corner from St. John the Baptist Catholic church, but I always wondered. They'd never said anything openly about our religion, but I always felt an underlying current of opposition. Maybe it was because he was an only child and they resented him leaving their life for one of his own. Then again, maybe it was just me they didn't like.

When I pulled up in front of their house, I hesitated. The sidewalk was threaded with cracks. Several overgrown bushes blocked a chunk of the house from my view. One isolated palm tree jutted skyward at the corner of the yard. Everything seemed run-down and uninviting.

I took a deep breath. *I can do this.*

Katie made an attempt for the doorbell, but I caught her before she could ring six or seven times. I didn't think they'd appreciate that. Helen answered sedately, looking down at Katie.

"Hello. Please come in."

Katie looked up at her uncertainly. "Are you my udder grandma?"

Helen looked like she would faint. Her lips trembled as she clutched the doorknob. "I am."

Katie stared, and I had to nudge her forward. "Let's go inside, honey," I said, ushering her into the foyer, praying this get-together wouldn't be a disaster.

"Have a seat in here," Helen said, one arm flowing toward a brown room.

She'd changed since I saw her last. She looked old, feeble, tired. I felt an unexpected swell of compassion for her. This poor woman lost her only child and must still mourn his death. Seeing us must have been painful too.

Maybe I shouldn't have come.

"Thank you for coming," she whispered, in contradiction to my thoughts. "I'll be right back with Gary."

Katie sat on my lap, looking around the room cautiously. The furniture was worn and outdated. As I looked around, I couldn't see anything newer than the clock on the wall. Had they come on hard times? Had John known about it?

Gary followed Helen into the room, and I stood to shake his hand. I hardly knew these people. I'd only met them a few times before my wedding. I knew so little about them. Would they want to be part of our lives now that John had died? Just because they agreed to have us over didn't necessarily mean they wanted to continue the relationship.

We talked awkwardly for a few minutes before Gary looked right at Katie. "Why don't you come over here and give me hug?" he asked gruffly.

Katie glanced at me for assurance then walked over and hugged them both. She was so pure, so angelic. I could swear their hearts melted the moment they felt her loving arms around them. Maybe this was more for them than I'd realized. I'd been so concerned about Katie growing up not knowing John's family that I hadn't thought about what they needed.

They brought out some photos of John that I'd never seen before and let Katie have one that was framed.

"We want you to keep this, Katie, to remember your father," Gary said. "He was a good son."

Helen swiped a tear away, her lips pressed tightly together as though she were afraid she'd come apart. My heart softened at that moment. They had no idea that John had done something wrong, and my previous need to enlighten them about it vanished. It wouldn't make me feel any better to tell on him and would only blight their cherished memories.

I realized that preparing for the temple was changing me, helping me see into the hearts of these people. Our visit didn't last more than an hour, but I felt like it accomplished something important. A step, maybe. I felt bad for John's parents. They were truly struggling over the loss of their only child. And from little things they said, it was apparent they were struggling financially as well.

Had John ever mentioned wanting to help them out? Could that have been one of the reasons he worked so hard? I didn't have answers, and I didn't know that I ever would. But I believed that I could try to heal the gap between us with Katie's sweet influence.

*****

Linda bribed me to stay longer with peanut butter cup cupcakes. I don't know who she got to cook those babies, but they were to die for. Seriously. She pulled them out for dessert one night and promised if we stayed another week, she could get more where those came from. Argh, she was good.

We had picnics and went shopping. My wild cousins came into town, livening things up with all their children. The day we were to leave, I was worn out. By the time we said our heartfelt good-byes and drove away, it was later at night than I'd planned.

When I finally got off the freeway and drove into the quiet dark of Meadow Vista, Katie was sound asleep, exhausted by all the activity. As I got closer to home, it struck me how dim it was in the forest this far away from the city lights. In my headlights, I spotted a group of deer silently grazing on the side of the road. In my rearview mirror, nothing was visible but thick, black night. Sweet, peaceful town . . . It was good to be home.

But I'd rather have come back before dark. I didn't like coming home to a dark, empty house all alone. I pulled into the garage, weary from driving, but left the garage door up for the time being. Knowing how noisy its motor was, I didn't want to risk waking Katie. I unbuckled her and lifted her into my arms, hoping she'd stay asleep so I could put her right in bed. I only knocked one empty box onto the garage floor, but she didn't stir, thank goodness. She seemed to be completely zonked out. I fumbled for my keys and made it up the steps to the kitchen, almost bumping her shoes on the doorjamb.

At last in her room, I laid Katie in bed and slipped off her shoes, gazing at her pure innocence in the moonlight. I was so lucky to be this beautiful little girl's mommy! I tucked her in with a kiss on her downy cheek. When she didn't stir, I couldn't resist a few more.

As I left her room, closing the door most of the way behind me, the darkness of the house made me feel insecure and vulnerable, so I flipped on a hall lamp and went back to shut the garage door. Perched on the top step, I reached around the wall for the switch when I heard an eerie, muffled noise and caught the tic of something in the dark.

Instantly, I was zapped by cold fear.

Something was out there. I could sense it. The hairs on my arm stood on end, and I stopped breathing.

There was the noise! Frozen to the spot, I listened apprehensively, my eyes darting around the garage. Then I peered sightlessly into night's thick darkness beyond the light. Something or some*one* was out there; I was sure of it.

"In the sweet dim light of the falling night
She found him at her side."
–Ella Wheeler Wilcox

Chapter 20

THERE IT WAS AGAIN. FOOTSTEPS! Creeping closer.

My heart constricted, and a scream congealed in my throat.

This was my worst nightmare. I was a woman alone, with no weapon, no knowledge of self-defense—I didn't even have a can of mace. I heard a whimper and realized it was my own voice. Knowing I had to keep a clear head, I grabbed the first thing I saw within reach—a garden spade. I had no idea what I'd do with it, but I clutched it as though my life depended on it. My heart raced inside my chest—my fearful imagination raced just as madly.

"Who's there?" I choked out, realizing the words were barely audible. I took a step forward, every muscle in my body tense . . . then another step to the edge of the light, the border between safety and dark. Was that someone running along my property line?

"Ashlyn?" I heard just behind me.

I screamed, hunching over in terror. Someone grabbed my arm, and I came unglued, thrashing with the garden spade and screaming my lungs out.

"Ash! Ouch! It's me!" the voice said. "It's Ryan."

His words didn't register at first.

"It's okay," he soothed, trying to put his arms around me as I attempted another wallop. "No one's going to hurt you."

It was his calm voice that got through to me, and I sagged against him, crying in relief.

"Shhh, it's okay," he whispered, pressing his face against the hair covering my eyes. "I've got you. Everything's okay."

I clamped onto his shirt, half ready to clobber him, half wanting to hang on for dear life. "You scared me half to death!"

"I'm sorry. I saw the lights on and wanted to check to see who was here." His hands on my back circled in a calming rhythm.

"There's someone out there, Ryan!" I said, wiping my face with the sleeve of my cardigan. "I saw him over there."

"It was probably a group of deer. I saw some run off when I came up."

"Are you sure?"

"I can go check it out—"

"No," I cried, clutching onto him before he moved away. "Don't go. Please."

Ryan nodded. "Let's go inside where it's warm. You're shivering."

I hadn't realized I was trembling. It was much cooler than Fair Oaks up here in the mountains, but that wasn't the only thing making me shake. Ryan kept an arm around me as I shut the garage door, and we went inside.

As soon as I walked into the kitchen and turned on the light, I came to my senses. I began an embarrassed apology, but Ryan took my arm with a gentle "Shh." He turned me around in front of him, gently saying, "Look up." I tried to ignore the sweet shudder of response that assaulted my senses as he covered me from behind like a warm blanket. I looked around the kitchen, finally realizing it had been painted a beautiful moss color that I loved. I sucked in my breath incredulously. "Did you . . . ?"

"Yeah," he whispered over my shoulder. His arms slid around my waist, pressing me snugly against him. "Do you like it?" His voice caressed my ear, and my knees became weak.

A rush of familiar longings flowed through me. I knew what I was feeling—it was there, alive and undeniable. I felt more for him now than I'd ever felt before leaving!

I was in so much trouble.

What had happened to me? What was I going to do? How could I possibly hide this intensity of emotion from him?

I can't!

It was so strong that it could burst from inside me. "I love it, Ryan," I whispered back, tilting my head toward his. As I did, his nose brushed against my cheek, soft and smooth, causing my heart to thump faster inside my chest. Something was happening that went beyond anything that had happened before. His warm hands at my waist increased their pressure, and then he was turning me toward him. My hands ended up on his chest.

Under my palms, I felt every breath he took, felt each beat of his heart. My eyes traveled to the pulse in his throat then lingered on the scar on his neck.

When our eyes met, I felt it like an electric current racing through my body.

Roughly, he breathed my name, "Ashlyn . . ." In his voice I heard desperation mingle with anticipation. His hands moved from my back to glide slowly up my arms until they reached my face. He never took his eyes from mine. And suddenly his lips were on mine in the kind of kiss you only dream of. His lips demanded a response. His hands were on my face, in my hair, stroking my neck, while I struggled for air. His lips only released mine long enough to breathe my name, over and over.

His warm breath against my skin and the sound of my name on his lips transformed me. My senses were awakened and new. I was like a flower opening to the warmth, and Ryan was the sun. His lips breathed new life into me. I was completely alive and wanting to feel.

His hands dove into my hair, moved down my neck, and gripped my shoulders. Responding to him more than was safe, I began kissing him back with a desperation that surprised us both. I melted into him. There was nothing dead inside me now. I was alive and wanting to experience everything! Hands, lips, skin. Our kiss ignited to volatile proportions, and I thought we'd combust.

When he suddenly pulled away, breath ragged and heavy, I opened my eyes, realizing what had just happened. I stared at him in shock, my breath coming in heavy gulps. Ryan stared back at me, absolutely stunned.

Oh, dear heavens! What have I done?

I covered my face in humiliation then fled down the hallway.

Ryan called, "Wait, don't go!"

He ran after me, but I swung my bedroom door shut, wishing he couldn't hear my muffled crying on the other side of the door.

"Ash, open the door." He twisted the door handle even though he knew I'd locked it. Knocking softly, he called, "Let me talk to you."

"Go away."

He groaned against the wood, knowing I could hear him, even though I refused to answer. He said something to himself, but I didn't try to make it out. Huddled on the floor with my legs drawn up to my chest, I hid my face against my knees, unable to hide from the shame enveloping me.

How did that just happen? I was scared, and then suddenly I was all over him! My mortification was all-encompassing.

Still quietly pleading, Ryan called out, "Ash, let me in. Please?"

I leaned against the door, feeling the vibration of his knocking against my back. I didn't answer but heard him clunk his forehead against the door.

"It was my fault," his voice was muffled. "I shouldn't have touched you like that. You were scared, and I wanted to comfort you. I don't know what came over me. I—" A sudden thump on the door jolted through me. "Okay, you know what? I *do* know what came over me, and I'll just say it. I'm crazy about you. I can't stop thinking about you—not ever. I was going nuts while you were away. I dream about you; all I want to do is be with you, to be near you. I want to be part of your life."

I sniffled and pressed a hand against my chest. My heart ached for the words he spoke. But how could they be true? I swiped tears from my eyes. Could he actually feel that way? Or was he just as confused as I was, misinterpreting everything that had been happening between us?

"Stop saying things like that, Ryan."

"What, the truth?" he raised his voice in frustration. "It is how I feel!"

"Then stop feeling that way! It's not helping anything."

"Like I could stop the way I feel about you!"

I rocked the back of my head against the door in pain. How did it get this far?

"Come on, Ashlyn. I'm pouring out my whole soul here—to a door. Come out and talk to me."

After a heavy sigh, I stood up and opened the bedroom door partway. Ryan looked up, bracing himself against the doorframe. His eyes became unbearably tender when he saw the tears in my eyes. There was a pink blotch on his forehead where he must have been pressing it against the door. I saw the tender concern in his eyes, willing me to trust him. He reached out to place a gentle hand on my arm, drawing me out beside him.

"Come here," he said quietly. Ryan drew me closer, enfolding me in his comforting arms.

Being held like that made me feel like I was precious to him. It was warmth and tenderness, a feeling of complete security. But it was so much more. I couldn't have stopped my arms going around him if I had tried. I fit so perfectly against him, the way my hands fit my favorite pair of gloves. He smelled clean and masculine, like a new bar of soap. His shoulders were so broad that I felt like I could disappear in the embrace. I felt his heart beating in tune with my own, with my cheek against his chest.

Oh, Ryan . . .

He pressed a kiss into my hair, one on my forehead, another by my teary eyes.

"Ryan," I whispered, "we can't do this—" There was nothing I wanted more right then than to dive into his kiss, to love him in return without hesitation. But I knew I had to stop this. I felt responsible. This was my home, and I was old enough to know better.

With a sudden rush of sanity, I pulled away, pushing my hands against his chest. "Ryan, please. We have to stop."

"I don't want to let you go," he said.

"This is—it's ridiculous for us to be together, on so many levels!"

"It's not ridiculous."

"What about Megan?"

"She knows how I feel about you."

My eyes popped wide open in dismay. "You broke her heart because of me?" I'd raised my voice too loud and was sure it would have woken Katie, but I continued in a whisper-hiss, "That's so wrong!"

"Ash," he lowered his voice, "Megan and I were never dating seriously. We had fun together, but neither of us was looking for a serious relationship."

"That's not how Megan explained things. She was hurt."

He looked at me in bewilderment, raking a hand through his hair. "Wait, I thought—"

I didn't let him finish but plunged right on. "Besides, I'm so much older than you are."

"Does that change the way you feel about me?" he asked.

I was going to crumble. "There is no way I feel about you," I lied.

"That's not true. The way you kissed me just now—"

"Should never have happened!" I was on the verge of tears again.

Part of me wanted to let him be right and give in to these feelings. How would it be to love someone again? To feel like I was really living life? I'd gone through that once before, but loving John had cost me. I'd lost nearly everything when he died, even more when I learned of his infidelity. Loving someone posed risks I wasn't prepared to take again. The emotional tug-of-war raged within me, both sides equally strong, and no conceivable solution.

I pushed my hands into the hair above my forehead to combat the pounding in my head. "I was trying so hard to fight this," I thought to myself but realized I'd said it aloud.

"I know. I've never been so confused in all my life. But Ashlyn, I'm crazy about you." Brushing a thumb across my chin, he asked, "Do you care about me, even a little?" He sounded vulnerable and endearingly sweet.

I wanted to wrap my arms around him, tell him I did care. That he made my heart thump so loudly the answer should be obvious. Even now, my heart was beating overtime, almost hurting my chest.

Yes, I cared. But I shouldn't. It wasn't right. What would everyone think of me? It was too painfully embarrassing to even go there. *I can't believe how I came on to him*, I thought again shamefully. *I practically attacked him in my own home, unleashing so much passion on the poor, innocent guy.* I could die of embarrassment! Where did all that steam come from, anyway? Is that how dormant tulips felt each spring? A sort of give-me-liberty-or-give-me-death kind of passion and energy that gave them the life to burst from the ground to their full glory?

Whatever the case, I'd certainly done a number on Ryan that he wouldn't soon forget.

Realizing I still hadn't answered Ryan's question, I cleared my throat and stalled again. "Ryan, we need to forget this ever happened. No, stop—just hear me out. I'm a little nuts right now and not thinking clearly. This is all a mistake. A really big mistake. Combining the volatile elements of a crazy, lonely widow with an irresistible, good-looking guy somehow caused a chemical reaction that blew up. I'm so sorry. It never should have happened. I was out of my mind to kiss you like that. I could die of embarrassment!" His suppressed grin didn't help either. "Can we just forget that happened? Please?"

"Actually, that's not the kind of kiss you forget about."

"Come on, Ryan. It's important. Forget that happened. And we really shouldn't see each other anymore," I added, pulling away.

I saw the hurt in his eyes as he shook his head in disbelief. I was bluntly pushing him away, but I had to. Everything inside me screamed against us being together.

"No way." He smiled sadly. "I don't make promises I can't keep." A new light glinted in his eyes. "Especially not if you think I'm irresistible."

"What?" I asked in my exasperation. He was *not* cooperating!

"You said it," he said, planting a hand innocently against his chest. "An irresistible, good-looking guy? That's a start anyway."

Glancing heavenward, I sighed. "Ryan . . ."

"What, my *kulta*?" he asked, in that deep voice that turned my insides to mush.

"What does that mean?"

He gave me a no-big-deal brush of his hand. "It's Finnish. It doesn't really have an exact translation."

"Is that where you went on your mission? Finland?" For a brief moment, I was transported back to the time he used to talk about a mission and the countries he was interested in seeing someday.

"Yeah."

It was a long time ago, a time that had separated us.

I glanced down the hall. "I have to check on Katie, okay?"

"Okay," he said, unmoving.

We continued to stand there in the hallway, locked in each other's gaze. "I need to go," I said pleadingly, willing him to release me. "I'm going to check on Katie."

"Can I help?" he asked doubtfully, as if knowing the answer but willing to give it a shot anyway.

"That's not a good idea." Both of us together in the dark of Katie's bedroom? Uh-uh.

He looked down and tapped his shoe on the floor. When he glanced back up, I could have melted in the sooty warmth of his eyes. "Okay, I'll go," he said. "But promise me we'll talk about this—tomorrow."

He wouldn't agree with me about this right now. Tomorrow, when he had time to come to his senses, would be a better time to talk. "I promise." He still gazed at me longingly. If he didn't go, I'd crumble into a million pieces. My heart would give in to him. And that couldn't happen.

I swallowed, feeling a painful lump in my throat. *Be strong. Fight this.* As perfect and thoughtful and caring as he was, he wasn't meant for me.

"I told her all my heart . . ."
—William Blake

Chapter 21

A PHONE WAS RINGING. I groggily opened my eyes and realized I'd way overslept. A moment of panic hit me right in the gut. I needed to check the caller ID.

I'm not ready to talk to you, Ryan.

Another ring. I lunged onto my side, swinging an arm to grab the phone. It was blurry. I rubbed my eyes and tried to focus on the tiny letters on the screen.

Matt Daniels.

The call would go to voice mail any second. Did I want to pick up? Matt was nice. Completely comfortable. *I guess I could talk to him.* After yesterday's tumultuous, wildly unsettling goings on, a little steady peace sounded rather good. Matt would deliver that, I thought.

"Hello?"

"Hi, it's Matt. I just wondered if you might be interested in going out to dinner tomorrow night."

No nonsense, straightforward, non-confusing Matt. I knew I could talk to him. I wasn't sure I felt like a date after what happened last night. Should I let him know what happened with Ryan? No, that was dumb. I believed in being honest, but I didn't see any need for him to know.

"That sounds fine. I'll have to find someone to watch Katie for me."

"She can come too. We'll have fun."

"Really? You'd be okay with that?"

"Yeah, sure."

Wow. What a nice guy. When I hung up, I actually felt great—the best I'd felt in a really long time. And maybe this was what I needed. Maybe being with Matt was going to be the answer I'd been seeking.

After getting Katie up and ready for the day, we decided to go for a morning walk to see the Whitmores' horses down the road. When I opened the front door, something flickered down by my feet.

Katie rushed out to pick up a bright red gift bag stuffed with white tissue paper. "What is it, Mommy?"

"I have no idea."

Peeking inside the bag, I found an assortment of Hershey Kisses. A note had been written on a piece of cardstock with masculine, boxy letters.

Dear Ashlyn,

I'm sorry I upset you last night. Please forgive me for that. But nothing in the world compares to your kisses.

Love, Ryan.

My heart flip-flopped as a wave of heat washed over me. The bag of kisses dropped out of my hands when I clamped a hand to my breast. I read the note three or four more times, wondering how in heaven's name things had escalated this far.

See, this is exactly what I'm talking about—this breath-stopping, mind-racing whamming of my heart is not going to get me any sanity. It's exactly why I should go out with Matt.

Ryan had even put "love" on the closing. How was I supposed to handle that? One part of me was so in love with this man I could hardly stand it. The other part of me put up an impenetrable wall of defense with all kinds of reasons swirling through my brain. I didn't want to analyze which were valid and which weren't, I just felt everything in my head form a thick wall against everything in my heart.

"Can I have some candy?" Katie asked hopefully, opening the gift bag I'd dropped.

I brought myself back from muddled thoughts. "How about after lunch, okay, honey?"

"But wait," Katie said, holding her little hand up to stop me. "I got a idea. I can have one-two candies, and you can have some after lunch. Huh, Mommy?"

I grabbed her around the waist and turned her over to kiss those sweet cheeks until she giggled like crazy. "You think that's a good idea, do you?" I laughed and kissed her once more. "I love you, Katie girl!"

Thinking I'd agreed to her plan, she gleefully pulled a handful of kisses out of the bag, dropping several on the carpet.

"Hold on there, munchkin. How about one now and two after lunch?"

She'd already popped a chocolate in her mouth, so I gathered the rest and tossed the bag back inside the house. I didn't want to see it for a while. I took Katie's hand, and we walked down the road. The air was clean; a light breeze played with my hair. Blossoms of all kinds bloomed in the neighbors' yards.

"Guess what?"

"What?"

"We get to go to dinner tomorrow night with a friend."

"Are Grace and Lily coming?"

"No. I meant another friend named Matt. I met him at Uncle Shaun's house. He's going to take us to a restaurant."

"Why?"

"Well, to be nice."

"Is Ryan coming?"

I tried to keep my cool. "No, Ryan is *not* coming."

"But I want a friend to come too."

"Matt wants to be your friend too."

Katie scowled. "I want Ryan."

"We'll see Ryan another day," I said firmly, steering us toward the neighbor's horses. Katie continued to pout, but I was determined to smile and enjoy the walk. "Look over there in the trees. Do you see the deer?"

Her pout turned to interest. "Are those the baby deers, and that's the mommy deer?"

"I think so."

The deer looked up to see us walk by and then calmly resumed foraging. Not wanting to think about the deer last night, I moved us forward. We found the horses clipping off the short grass in their field. I told Katie if she was quiet, they might come over to see us. She was excited when they trotted in our direction and stuck their fuzzy noses over the fence. After spending several minutes petting the horses, we continued on our walk, turning onto my parents' quiet lane.

Recognizing where we were, Katie cried, "Let's go see Grandma and Grandpa!"

I knew they would welcome us with homemade cookies and milk or anything else Mom had whipped up. There was always something simmering on the stove or baking in the oven, and with us now living in town, she'd make the most of it.

Before I could stop her, Katie darted up the porch and rang the doorbell at least five times.

"Katie! Just once, honey. Remember, I told you we only ring the doorbell one time."

My mom opened the door before Katie had a chance to give me her classic frown and angry eyebrows routine.

"Grandma!" Katie shot into her arms in pure delight.

"What a nice surprise!" my mom said. "Come on in. I just made cinnamon bread."

"We were taking a walk and decided to stop by."

"I'm glad you did."

"Grandma, we saw some deers!"

"You did? Come tell me about it."

We went into the kitchen, where my mother was able to pamper us with her good cooking and kindness. My dad took Katie outside when she got restless. Mom and I kept talking about everything, from the possibility of my going back to work to finding a preschool for Katie. But throughout our conversation, my predicament with Ryan lurked in the front of my mind.

"I want to be like you and Grandma," I said. "You both had college degrees, had wonderful marriages, raised your families, cook like nobody's business . . . and to top it all off, you grow camellias!"

"Camellias?" she bubbled with amusement. "What's so important about camellias?"

"Real women grow huge bushes of camellias in their front yards, don't they?"

"Oh, for heaven's sake . . ."

We laughed together, and I marveled at how good it was to live close to my mother again. I'd missed her in Ohio—much more than I'd realized. We continued talking about life and motherhood, and in her gentle way, she tried to build me up to feeling like I was doing a better job than I'd ever take credit for.

"Thanks, Mom. I love you."

She put her arms around me. "I love you too, honey. And you know what I'm thinking? A girl's night out is in order. What do you say?"

"Sure, when?"

"How about this Friday?"

"Oh. Actually I have plans."

"You do?" Her eyes gleamed. Mom simply couldn't disguise her obvious euphoria over the fact that I'd had two dates with an eligible bachelor recently.

"Matt asked me to go to dinner with him again." When I saw her elation, I shook my head and let out an embarrassed laugh. "It's just dinner, Mom, not a wedding rehearsal."

"I know." She laughed guiltily. "I'm just happy for you. He must be a special person."

I nodded casually. "Matt's a nice guy. He's comfortable to be with."

"I've been praying you'd be able to do this, to be able to move forward and meet someone."

"We've only gone out twice."

"I know, but this is a big step for you. It's a new beginning." Her expression became tender as she reached for my hand. "I think John would be glad for you."

My whole body seemed to sink with the weight of her words. "Mom, about John . . . I think you should know something." I paused, knowing I had to finish. This was an issue that had been festering inside me, gnawing its way to the surface. I had to tell her at some point. I couldn't hide the truth forever. I wanted to be open with my parents about my relationship with John, but it was admitting defeat, revealing my failure compared to her success.

"What is it, honey?"

I squeezed her hand tighter. "John was . . . well, he worked a lot."

Mom nodded sympathetically. "I know. He was a hard worker."

"Yes. He was," I affirmed with a rock-solid nod.

Her forehead creased in uncertainty. "What is it, Ashlyn?"

"There's something I've never told anyone." I glanced around the room as though checking for privacy, even though I knew no one else was inside.

She searched my face, waiting for me to continue. I knew I could confide in her—that wasn't the issue. I had complete trust in my mother. The problem was having her know in the first place. *She* was the one I didn't want to disappoint. I'd always dreamed of following in her footsteps, carrying on the legacy of great women before her. Women who had the adoration of their husbands and children, women who did things right and were a success. I didn't want to be the genealogy greatness wrecker.

"John did work hard," I started to explain, "but he worked so hard he was never home. Work was all he was interested in."

Her face clouded over. "Ash . . ."

"It's true, Mom. John was a good man, but Katie and I didn't fit into his life. There were a lot of things that didn't fit into his life, like being together, going to church, or preparing to go to the temple. He was too consumed with work. I hardly ever saw him once we moved to Ohio. He barely held Katie more than a handful of times. I could never understand why. Why he would put work before us! I tried to do everything to make him happy, to encourage him and love him. I promise, Mom. I tried so hard to be what he wanted. I really tried!"

"Shhh. Oh, Ashlyn," she crooned. "What a burden you've had to carry. I'm so sorry! I had no idea." She gripped both of my arms and leaned forward so we were eye to eye. "But I want you to listen very carefully to what I have to say. You are not to blame for anyone else's actions. John's choices are not your fault. It's harrowing enough that you had to lose your husband in a car accident, that you had to bury your own husband! Don't add guilt to your suffering."

"But I'm the one who married him! I'm the one who settled on getting married outside the temple, and now I'm not sealed to my own flesh and blood!"

Wiping a tear from my face, she said, "You were counseled to get married rather than wait, remember?" The words made me stop my train of thought. "Brother Loveless felt that under the circumstances, it was better to get married rather than face temptation while waiting."

"I guess he did say that."

She nodded wisely. "Have you been dealing with a lot of anger toward John?"

I nodded remorsefully. "How did you know?"

"It's normal for people to feel angry with a loved one for dying. It's part of the grieving process." She must have read that coping book I never finished.

"You're so calm, Mom. I doubt you could ever imagine the anger I've felt!"

She glanced out the window at my dad in wry amusement. He was unsuccessfully trying to hoist Katie into the old tire swing roped to a crooked oak tree out back. "I get angry."

"I bet Dad never made you *that* angry."

"Are you kidding?" She laughed. "That man can make me madder than a hornet!"

"I've never seen you and Dad fight," I half-accused.

"Well, we have! We just try not to do it front of anyone."

"Really?" I shook my head in disbelief. I'd never seen it. Neither had Shaun and Megan—we'd all had that discussion before.

"Our marriage works because we put God first and ask for his help to work out all our differences. And we *do* have them."

I looked at my mom in wonder. "I've been holding so many feelings in, thinking I could never live up to your example. I haven't told you so many things because I didn't want to disappoint you. I don't know how I managed to bring it up with Ryan the other day, but something slipped out—" I muttered to myself just thinking about him.

"Who?"

"Uh, Ryan. Anderson."

Mom wrinkled her brow in confusion. "I think you lost me. What does he have to do with this?"

Oh dear. I looked behind me, wishing for an escape. I picked at a fingernail and shook my head in futility. "Ryan comes over to help out a lot, and we've been together so much . . ."

A light of speculation flickered in her eyes. It made my heart sink.

"We're just friends," I said hastily. "I know he loves Katie and spending time with us, but . . ." A betraying wave of heat flushed my cheeks while my heart palpitated recklessly. "Oh, Mom," I groaned, turning to her in desperation. "Something happened, and I don't know what to do!"

Her eyebrows remained arched, her lips parted. She covered my hand with hers. "What happened, honey?"

"He saw us getting back last night and was checking to be sure it was us—that everything was okay, you know. We were talking, and he showed me the wall he painted while we were in Fair Oaks, and suddenly there was this kiss"—she inhaled quickly, but I plunged on—"I don't know how it got to that point; it just happened."

My mom stared at me. She didn't even blink.

"How could I have done this to Megan?" I cried, still feeling the shock of it all.

Still absorbing the information, she finally asked, "Do you have feelings for him?"

A nervous whiffle of air escaped my lips. "I—no, it's . . ." *How do I answer this?* "I do care about him. I mean, he's been over so much helping me with the house and spending time with us that . . . I don't know.

I probably developed a stupid crush on him. How ridiculous is that! A nearly thirty-year-old woman with a crush on a twenty-five-year-old guy! You know how I've been coping lately, Mom. Like a crazy woman, so it'll pass, won't it? Please tell me it will pass."

"It might," she said.

"It might? What do you mean?"

"Well . . .'"

"You think it might not?" My heart lurched at the thought.

Mom sighed. "Honey, I don't know what you feel for Ryan or what he feels for you. It's something you'll both have to work through."

"I don't want to work through anything with him! He drives me crazy!"

Her lips curved upward as she angled a look at me.

"What?" I demanded.

"I can't imagine Ryan Anderson driving anyone crazy," she chuckled.

"Yeah, but he does. He drives me so crazy I can't even think straight when he's around. He makes me—" I broke off, not finishing the thought.

"Feel?" she suggested. Quite accurately too.

I had to nod in defeat. "He makes me feel things I shouldn't."

Mom wrapped her arms around me in a soothing rocking motion. "It's a good thing for you to feel again, Ashlyn. You don't want to be trapped in a lifeless state of existence. So if Ryan is the one who has brought feeling back to your life, it's okay. It doesn't have to mean more than that."

"So . . . what are you saying?"

She tilted her head in contemplation. "I'm not saying anything necessarily, just that it's good for you to get beyond the lifeless world you were in. I hated to see you like that. What about Megan? Does she know?"

"No!"

Her forehead wrinkled. "Are you going to tell her?"

"Mom, what am I going to say? Love ya, sis, but I kissed your boyfriend? I mean, she's already upset that Ryan only wants them to be friends. He told me they were never seriously dating, but I *know* Megan was serious about him! Now, what I've got to tell her is going to kill her!"

"She'll survive, Ashlyn. Megan's a strong girl, and she loves you. It'll hurt, but she needs to know."

"I can't do it."

"Yes, you can. You don't want her to find out another way, do you?"

I sighed. "No. You're right as always. How did you get to be so wise?"

"They say 'wise *old* owl.' Count the number of candles on my birthday cake sometime."

It wasn't until Katie and I started walking back home that I realized I never even mentioned the worst—John's affair. That night I took off my wedding ring and studied my bare finger. Finally, I set the ring inside a box and placed it in the bottom drawer of my dresser.

*****

My cell phone vibrated erratically on the kitchen counter. Surprised a call got through, I finished pouring milk over Katie's afternoon bowl of cereal and grabbed the phone.

"Hello?"

"Ashlyn, it's me, Ryan."

Yeah, I knew from the first syllable. His voice was a gong to my senses.

"Hi." My nerves vibrated through my body like my phone had on the counter.

"Hi." I heard him exhale shakily. "I was wondering if I could come over so we can have that talk?"

Feeling a sinking motion inside my body, I gathered the courage to answer. "I guess so."

"Is now a good time?"

Better to get this over with. "It's fine."

"Okay. I'll be there in a few minutes."

I quickly finished my lunch and had just cleaned the counters off when Ryan knocked at the door. Katie bounded off her stool, sending her spoon flailing off the counter to nick the barstool and clatter to the floor. It wouldn't have surprised me if the entire cereal bowl had exploded from her energy.

Ryan came inside, hands in his pockets. "Hi, Katie girl." He bent down to hug her, then turned to me and smiled awkwardly. "Hi."

"Hi," I answered back. We looked at each other, so many things unspoken between us but undeniably felt. "Come in," I finally said.

To release myself from his gaze, I turned to Katie. "Sweetie, would you like to watch a movie in my room?"

"I want Cinderella."

"Okay." I glanced at Ryan. "I'll be right back," I told him, feeling more nervous now that he was here. I followed Katie back to my room, where I set up her movie, then returned to where Ryan sat on the sofa.

"We probably have about fifteen minutes before she comes back," I said, sitting next to him.

"So talk fast?" He let out a nervous puff of amusement.

I shrugged with a hesitant smile. "Probably."

"Well then, here goes." He took a breath. "Ashlyn, I've been doing a lot of thinking since—you know, what happened . . ."

Oh good. He's come to his senses. I hope he realizes that what happened was just one of those crazy, emotional, can't-explain-why-it-happened-it-just-did kind of moments. Then we can forget it and move on.

". . . and I really think . . ."

He'll move on, anyway. It might take me a while to stop thinking about him. He's infused himself into my life. Not to mention Katie's. How did he become so intertwined in our thoughts and emotions?

"Well, I think we should go out. On a date."

Body slam. "What?"

Ryan's lips turned upward as he took both my hands. He looked like he was about to burst. "I really want to go out with you."

My heart began to race at a sprinter's pace, my eyes bulging wide open. "Go out with me?"

"Yes." He grinned.

"No!" I almost yelled.

One of his dark brows arched up in question.

"We can't! No, that's a terrible idea."

"I think it's a great idea. In fact, there's nothing I'd like more."

"Ryan, please"—I couldn't take this accelerated heart rate—"let's be reasonable."

"I *am* being reasonable. Look, I'm just as confused about this as you are. But regardless, even if nothing had happened, I'd want to go out with you." He took my hand in his. "I think you're one of the most beautiful, intriguing, caring women I've ever met." His thumb drew languid circles over my knuckles. "I love spending time with you. I want to do a lot more of it."

I shivered at his touch. Withdrawing my hand, I shook my head emphatically. *No.*

"Just one date? Please?"

"We can't, Ryan."

"Are you still concerned about the difference in our ages?"

"Definitely. But it's not just that."

"Then what? Is it because I'm not employed yet? Because I have some good offers."

"That's only part of it." I didn't know how to explain. "It's complicated."

"Forget complicated, Ash. Just go to dinner with me."

"I can't."

"Yes, you can."

"No."

"Just once?"

I shook my head again.

Ryan dropped his head to his hands and sighed heavily then looked up again. "You are one determined woman, you know that?"

"I'm sorry, Ryan. I don't want to hurt you, but . . ."

"Okay, so what if it's not a date? What if I want to take you somewhere, to show you some of my favorite places? Would you agree to that?"

"Like where?" I couldn't help myself from asking.

Me and my blasted curiosity.

"There's the Empire Mine in Grass Valley, walking the hills of Nevada City, the Yuba River . . ." He presented each location like items to select from a menu.

It sounded like something I'd love doing with him, but I shook my head again. "We can't do that." I would not allow myself to get close to a serial dater and flirt. I knew all too well where that could lead. I wasn't sure I could ever trust anyone with my heart again.

"What if we chose one of those? One day. There wouldn't be any pressure for anything more. Think of it as meeting a friend one day. Or charity—think of it as serving an individual that needs someone to talk to. At lunchtime. I guess if your friend needs to do a lot of talking, it would involve dinner too."

I laughed, wanting to say yes. But the rational side of my brain forbade it.

Ryan was quiet while he rubbed one of his knuckles. Maybe I'd gotten through to him. "Come on, Ash," he persisted quietly.

"Ryan, look, I have—"

"Mommm-me, the movie's not working!" Katie called from my room.

"Be right there!" I called over my shoulder. I swung back and finished lamely, "It's not going to work, Ryan."

He heaved a sigh of frustration then reluctantly stood. I stood so that we faced each other, our emotions running high. My gaze washed over his thick, tousled hair, the planes of his face, and the curve of his lips. His expressive gray eyes seemed to convey everything in his heart.

Taking a step forward, he reached for me and leaned in. It took all my willpower to place a hand on his chest to stop his kiss. "Ryan, no."

"I can't kiss you good-bye?"

"You have to promise never to kiss me again!"

His eyes darkened. "I'm not going to do that!"

"Please, Ryan," I pleaded. "We can't let this happen anymore. Promise me."

Unyielding, he shook his head. "I'm not going to promise."

I was beginning to feel frantic. "You *cannot kiss me* again."

Ryan spun away and growled in frustration, running a hand through his hair. "All right, I won't kiss you," he conceded at last. But he tacked on a provision. "Until you ask me to."

I considered that with a degree of skepticism. "I'm not going to ask, you know."

His lips scrunched up, and one eye narrowed. "Then stop looking so dang tempting."

I turned away in embarrassment and saw Katie stomping down the hallway with the DVD inserted over one tiny finger. She heaved a sigh of disgust and planted the other little fist on her side. "It's scratched!"

"Come here, honey." I reached out to pick her up. "I'll help you in a sec, but first can you say good-bye to Ryan?"

"Ryan can fix it."

Ryan grinned. "I better let your mommy do that, Katie."

"But I want you to," she said.

"Oh, sweetie," he said, stroking her cheek, "I have to go home now. But I'll come see you again soon, okay?"

"Okay," she pouted.

To me, Ryan said, "We'll talk later?"

I nodded but had no intention of making that happen. Something inside me insisted that this had to be good-bye. I wasn't sure what that something was; I just knew how compelling it was.

Ryan started for the door, glancing back once to say, "Just so you know, Ashlyn, I don't give up without a fight."

Chapter 22

THREE DAYS WENT BY WITHOUT seeing Ryan. But he called several times, trying to ask me out like it was a game between us. And he drove me crazy with more colorful gift bags on the porch. A red bag he filled with heart-shaped candies and several red paint samples with names like "Berry Passion," "Lips of Wine," and "Forbidden Red." A green gift bag showed up with a plush leprechaun holding a sign that said, "Kiss me, I'm Irish."

Friday morning, when Bishop and Sister Loveless came home teaching, they brought in a bright yellow bag from the porch.

"This was outside," Sister Loveless explained when I opened the door.

I had to stifle my amusement when I took it from her and invited them both inside. I put the gift bag on the floor to open later. It was crazy, but I couldn't wait to see what Ryan had put in this one. He'd been so creative in his attempts to sway me.

"Ooo, what are you coloring there?" Sister Loveless asked Katie, who sat on the floor with a box of crayons and new coloring book.

"A princess."

I knew she wouldn't listen to the message they had brought if she was in a pink coloring world, but at least she'd be quiet.

"So how have you been?" Brother Loveless asked.

That's when I noticed his look of fatherly concern. His bushy gray eyebrows were wrinkled, his lips turned down in contemplation. Sister Loveless had a similar expression, which she tried to mask with cheerfulness.

"Good. We're both doing fine," I answered.

"Anything new or changed since our last visit?" Sister Loveless asked. Then craning her neck around she added, "Have you been painting?"

"Yes." I was pleased she'd noticed the moss-green color in the kitchen.

"It's a lovely color. I really like it."

"And Katie, would you like to tell them what color your room was painted?" I asked.

She looked up long enough to say, "Pink," before giving the coloring page her studious attention.

"It looks like you've made great progress on the house," said Brother Loveless.

Before I could answer, Sister Loveless added, "We've noticed Ryan Anderson coming and going a few times when we've driven by. Is he . . ." a question hung in the air, "over here a lot?"

Katie suddenly looked up, her pink crayon hovering, to add in her loudest voice, "Ryan likes my Mommy."

Both sets of Loveless eyebrows shot up like rockets on the Fourth of July. I whipped my head around to Katie, doing the same. When did she get so smart? Were things that obvious?

"Oh." Sister Loveless faltered, turning to me for clarification.

I had to think fast. "He's our friend, isn't he Katie?"

She bobbed her head up and down. The Lovelesses seemed a little less shocked, but with the way I was sweating, I wasn't sure if I really pulled it off.

Brother Loveless leaned forward and put his hands out in front of him, fingertips pressed tightly together—the same way he used to preach a lesson to the youth. "So have you already started that temple prep class?"

"Yes, last week actually. I'm so excited about it."

"If you'd like, we can prepare home teaching messages about the temple."

"That sounds great. I'm eager to learn as much as I can."

He gave me a rascally grin. "Maybe we'll plan a message about dating again." He chuckled, probably remembering how opposed I was to the idea before.

I rolled my eyes and shook my head with a laugh. "You're incorrigible. But I've already taken the plunge. I have a date tonight."

Sister Loveless cried, "Oh, that's wonderful! I hope he treats you like a queen." She patted her husband's knee and gave him the most radiant, loving look that made him draw her close. The love he returned to his wife in his eyes really affected me.

That was what I wanted. Right there. Could I ever find that for myself, or was it only something a privileged few experienced in this life?

*****

With my date tonight, Katie in tow, I couldn't have Ryan invading my every thought anymore. Or Katie's, for that matter. And the only chance of that happening was if I severed our friendship. I didn't know how I could do that, but maybe it needed to be done. I wasn't sure why this date seemed to matter so much, why I felt like it had to go well or everything would fall apart. It's not like I was desperate.

So why did I feel this strange urgency for everything to work out with Matt? He was charming and funny, not to mention his good character—as harped on repeatedly by Shaun and Karen. Putting all my expectations on Matt and my date with him that night might not be logical, but that's how I felt. Something else was closing in on me, threatening to engulf me with its strength.

Would Matt like Katie? Would our threesome tonight have the same comfortable feeling I'd had with him when we met? Would everything click, or would it be a disaster? What if he was the right one for us? If I was actually going to give in to the notion of getting married again, it had better happen fast. I couldn't stand the thought of dating a lot of men. It would be way too hard on Katie. And plain torture for me.

Please let Katie be good tonight, I thought prayerfully. I needed her to be on her best behavior. An unbidden thought flashed through my mind: *That was never an issue with Ryan.* It had never mattered how Katie behaved with Ryan, good or bad, because he had such a way with her. He always seemed to know what to say or do with her.

I shook my head, squeezing the thoughts from my mind. That made no difference! All that mattered at the moment was how Matt and Katie got along.

And whomever I ended up marrying would have to think of Katie as more than just part of a package deal. He'd have to love her and love being around her—enough to want her to be his forever. Because this time I wouldn't settle for anything less.

Obviously, I felt bad for John. If I married someone in the temple and Katie was adopted and sealed to us, John would miss out on those eternal blessings. Part of me wanted to shout out, "You had plenty of chances, and you blew it, mister!" The other part ached for him. Would he get another chance someday?

I had no idea how the legalities regarding adoptions and sealings worked, and just thinking about it made my head hurt. *Enough. One thing at a time.* And right now, it was time to prep Katie on manners and behavior. We'd need it tonight.

Matt showed up for our date, his curly blonde hair looking adorable. It almost had the same bounce as Katie's hair. They'd look good together, like a real family.

"You must be Katie," Matt grinned down at my deceptively serene daughter. "I brought you something." He pulled a daisy out of the bouquet he was carrying and handed it to Katie. She took the knobby stem and shoved her nose up against the yellow center.

"Eew! It's stinky!" She giggled.

My hand flew up to my troubled brow. "Katie, just say thank you." I looked apologetically at Matt.

He laughed good-heartedly. "She's got expensive taste, I guess. I'll remember to get something that smells really good next time, Katie."

Next time? At least he hadn't already silently vowed never to step foot over here again.

"Sorry, Matt."

"No, no. It's fine. Shall we go?"

Katie stepped up right beside Matt and tugged on his arm. "I'm coming too."

Tilting his head down to her, Matt said, "Yes, you are. Would you like to leave the stinky flower here or bring it with you?"

Katie laughed as if it was the funniest joke she'd ever heard. "Bring it!"

I put the flowers he gave me into Paul's vase—with a twinge of guilt—then smiled. "Ready."

"Okay, then!" He grinned. "Let's go."

Matt carried Katie's car seat to his car but allowed me to fasten it in and tug the seatbelt securely around Katie. Then he held the door for me as I got in the front.

He's very good-natured. Even with Katie. That was a potential disaster that he'd handled well. So far, not a complete train wreck. As we drove, Katie started waving her flower while singing her ABCs. I almost stopped her, but Matt joined in, making me laugh.

Yeah, this is what I'm talking about. Comfortable. I didn't need a "wham" to the heart right now.

Matt drove to Auburn, where he pulled into a small parking lot for a Thai food restaurant. Surprised, I hoped Katie would at least eat rice, if nothing else. How many things on the menu would she freak out about?

"This place is really good," Matt said. "Have you been here before?"

"No, but I like trying new things." *Katie's another story, but oh well.*

A tangy, Oriental aroma tantalized us as we made our way up the front steps to the door. Inside, Matt found a petite woman speaking to someone in another language.

"Three, please," he said when she greeted him.

Katie found a gilded statue of a woman adorned in traditional Thai clothing and colorful jewels. Before Katie's astute hands had the chance to pry any off, I reminded her, "Just look; don't touch."

"But she has beautiful sparkles on!"

Matt snickered. "Ah, don't tell me—you want some jewels too?" Then to me he whispered, "See what I mean about expensive tastes?"

I opened my mouth to reply then promptly closed it. He didn't mean that unkindly; he was just trying to have fun with Katie. Trying to put us at ease with his jovial manner.

We were soon seated and given menus to look over. Matt eagerly recommended his favorite curry dishes.

"What would Katie like?" he asked.

"She'll probably stick with rice. And if I'm lucky, she might eat a few pieces of chicken."

"Picky eater?" He smiled.

"Sort of. But not too bad. So tell me more about your family, Matt."

"Well, there are six sisters and me."

"Six!"

"Yeah. I'm smack in the middle—and was my whole life. In the middle of girl drama and girl paraphernalia." He laughed aloud. "It was insane at times. My mom says it's the reason I never got married."

Alarms went off in my head before he continued. "She thinks I was traumatized and never want to raise girls. She's joking, of course. I love my sisters. And I'd love to raise girls." The alarms turned off, and he added somewhat awkwardly, "Boys too," turning a bit red.

Okay, that was cute.

The waiter, an elderly Asian gentleman, took our order and brought Katie a small cup of water with a straw.

"That'll put her in seventh heaven," I said, pointing a thumb at my daughter. "She loves straws."

We barely had time to finish our small talk before the food arrived. The distinctive aromas of coconut milk, peanuts, and lemongrass mingled in aromatic perfection. The Mussaman curry was so good that even Katie asked for more.

And I found that Matt was just as easy to converse with as he'd been before. The evening turned out great. Matt never tried to touch me. I never had to worry about him trying to kiss me. He was a perfect gentleman. Totally comfortable.

Just what I wanted, I thought as I said good-bye at the doorstep.

"Thanks, Matt. I really enjoyed dinner."

"Me too." He put his hands in his pockets and rocked on his heels. "We should do it again."

"I'd like that." I waited expectantly for an offer.

A fly buzzed past my right ear, swooped into a giant U-turn and landed on the post behind Matt's head. It looked like it was staring right at me with its bulbous black eyes.

"Would you like to go somewhere, maybe next Saturday?"

So it was a vague offer, but it was something.

"Sure, I'd love to," I said, trying not to look at the fly. "Maybe I can have my mom watch Katie."

"Okay," he nodded, still rocking on his heels. "Six thirty work for you?"

"I think that should be fine."

The fly didn't move. It just sat there, above his head, doing nothing. *Dumb fly.*

"Okay," he grinned. "See you then."

I smiled in confusion, waving to him as he left.

After getting Katie to bed, I sat on the edge of my bed. The date was exactly what I had hoped for. Katie wasn't too bad. The food was good. We had a good time talking. He didn't try to kiss me or hold my hand. So why did I feel slightly . . . empty?

What could I possibly be missing?

*****

The question entered my mind again during my temple preparation class on Sunday. I loved that class. I loved the lessons and was eager to learn everything I needed to enter the temple. So far we'd studied the plan of salvation and basic principles of the gospel. I felt the Spirit's influence in my life, helping to change my heart. I was becoming new, whole.

So what was it that was missing from my life? I couldn't quite put my finger on it. But as I contemplated the things needed for exaltation, I thought about my parents, their marriage and deep love for one another. Would I ever have those blessings in my life? I knew I didn't need to have it all immediately, but I realized I did *want* those blessings someday.

My thoughts drifted to Ryan, who now lived up to the title of "menace." His crusade for getting me to go out with him was still going strong. He was imaginative too. I smiled to myself when I remembered the hunk of fool's gold he'd left on the porch weighing down a sign that read, "No fooling. Find real gold with me!" He'd outlined a day trip of panning for gold on the Yuba River and exploring the old mining town of Nevada City. I had a *really* hard time saying no to that one.

"Sister Carter?"

I snapped my head up and brought myself to the present. Temple prep class. Bishop Truman visiting. Blessings of the temple. Closing prayer. People leaving.

"Yes?"

It was the bishop, and he was frowning with concern. "Is anything wrong?"

I hopped out of my chair. "No, I'm fine!"

"I just thought maybe you had a question about the lesson?"

"Oh. No, not really."

My mom's words came to mind. *"Anyone can talk with you and give his or her own advice, but your bishop is inspired to help those he has stewardship over."* I didn't want to ask to speak to him just so I could spill my whole love life. People didn't do that sort of thing, did they? I mean, talk about embarrassing!

Bishop Truman shook my hand and began to walk out of the small classroom. I watched him go, unable to stop him. He didn't want to talk with me about the stuff going on in my head. He had better things to do, bigger things to worry about.

Give him a chance. Mom's voice echoed in my mind.

I went after him. "Uh, Bishop Truman?" I called. When he turned around, I said, "Would it be possible to talk with you for a few minutes?"

"Sure. I believe I have time right after church."

"That works. Thank you."

I found my parents and asked them if they'd take Katie home with them so I could talk with the bishop.

"No problem at all," my dad said, giving me a fatherly squeeze. "When you're done, come over for Sunday dinner."

When church was over, I walked down to the bishop's office. The ward clerk was busy on the computer, and Brother Wilson was taking tithing envelopes from several people. I waited until the bishop appeared and invited me into his office.

When I sat down and he shut the door, something interesting happened. I felt a blanket of peace drape over me. I still saw the parallel perfection of his desk supplies. He still tugged at his collar and reached for his notes. But this time *I* was different. Somehow, at that moment, I knew this man was called of God. He wasn't gregarious or flashy, but when I looked into his eyes, I saw Christlike love. I felt safe.

"Sister Carter, how can I help you?"

I took courage and began. "As I've been learning about the temple, I keep thinking about eternity and exaltation. My parents have everything. I want to have a forever family of my own, but I'm so confused about my life—should I get a job, should I get married again . . .

"I mean, how are you supposed to figure out who you're supposed to be with for the rest of eternity? I was counseled to marry my husband, a brand-new convert, but he died before we made it to the temple. So now what do I do? I didn't think I'd ever want to get married again, but I've gone out a couple times, and maybe I will someday, but I don't know what I'm doing."

Bishop Truman tapped his pen a few times. "I don't know what I'm doing half the time either. But I do know one thing—that you have a Father in Heaven and a Savior who know you and love you. They know the righteous desires of your heart, and they want you to be happy."

I nodded, wanting him to continue.

"If you are prayerful, you'll be guided in all these things because they are important to you. Heavenly Father will guide you to the right man at the right time."

I told him a little about Paul and Matt. "They are both nice men and financially secure, but . . ."

"No sparks flying?"

I lifted my eyebrows.

He explained, "When two people talk about becoming one, it's a physical, spiritual, and emotional union. They need to be attracted to one another physically, spiritually, and emotionally. Being financially secure is a bonus but certainly not essential."

"The only person I'm attracted to is . . . wrong."

"Wrong?"

He waited for me to continue, and I ended up telling him about Ryan—the way he made me feel, the way he loved Katie. "I'm ashamed to feel this way about a guy who's so much younger than I am."

"Four years isn't too big of a difference. Is there possibly something else that's holding you back?"

"He's interviewing for jobs all over the country. Who knows where he'll decide to go." Then I bitterly added, "He won't stick around for long."

He looked at me in a way that reached deep into my heart. "Sister Carter, was your husband faithful to you?"

That's when I lost it. I sobbed out my story, using every last tissue on his desk. He listened and gently consoled me while I got it all out. When the burden I'd been holding inside was completely released, I was wiped out, but it felt good to finally let go.

"It's not going to be easy to trust again," Bishop Truman explained. "Trust is earned. So it's understandable for you to feel reluctant with another relationship."

I nodded tearfully, waiting for him to continue.

"Ryan might have commitment issues and not want to settle down. But it's also possible that when the right woman comes along, he'll change his mind."

Oh. Did that mean . . . ?

"You said he's asked you on a date?" he asked.

"Several times."

"What would happen if you gave him a chance?"

I was too surprised to find words. I gaped helplessly.

"You'll never know what might happen unless you do," he continued. "Just let things happen as they happen. Eventually, you'll know what direction you're both headed."

"Really?" I felt lighter all of a sudden.

"Accepting a date is taking one step forward. It's not entrusting your whole life to him; it's just giving him some of your time. Then you can see what comes of it."

Could I allow myself the possibility? I felt a smile coming on and couldn't help but think that my life was teetering over the edge of a precipice. I could fall one way or the other and truly hoped I'd land in the right place.

Bishop Truman actually grinned back. "Go on a date. See what happens."

*****

"Mom, what should I do? You've got to help me here!"

She laughed outright while wiping the counters in her kitchen. "Just call him."

"I can't call him," I wailed, forehead pressed against a cabinet. "After I refused him so many times, he's finally stopped trying. The worst part is that I still haven't talked to Megan!"

"Uh, honey," my mom said, glancing out the kitchen window, "I think you're about to."

I almost broke a soup tureen when I shot across the room in a panic. "No! Is she here?"

"Get it over with, Ash. You'll feel a whole lot better if you do."

"Mom!" What could I possible say that wouldn't hurt my sister? What would she think of me and this whole ridiculous situation?

"Hello, everyone!" Megan sang as she came into the kitchen.

My mom greeted her warmly, but my mouth had gone dry. "Come on in and have some banana bread."

Megan dropped her purse on the counter and reached for a piece. "Mmm, ith good," she said over a mouthful.

I was about to excuse myself, chase down Katie, and race home, but my mom was busily finding out about Megan's day. Afterwards, she gave me a purposeful glance and said, "I have a batch of laundry that needs to get in the dryer. I'll be back, but you two stay and talk."

Mom! How could she do that to me?

"Talk about what?" asked Megan through another bite of banana bread.

"Uh, I kind of need to talk to you," I squeaked, wishing the floor would open up and swallow me whole.

"About what?" she repeated.

I turned to my mom for support, but she'd already hightailed it out of the room, leaving me to face things once and for all. My fingers were shaking. "About . . . Ryan."

"Oh," she grunted unhappily before walking over to the fridge. "What about him?"

"Well, you know that we were friends a long time ago, right?"

"Yeah . . . ?" She carried out the word apprehensively, a gallon of milk in hand.

"He's done a lot to help me with my house."

"I know. Remember how you didn't want his help at first?"

"Yeah. But the thing is . . ." I watched her pour a glass of milk, take a sip, and set the cup down. "Dang it, this isn't fair."

"What are you talking about?" she demanded, sitting on a stool.

I sat on the stool next to her. "I like him." There. It was painful to get the words out, but at least they were out.

She tilted her head and gaped at me. "Wh-what are you—are you telling me . . . ?"

I nodded while biting my finger.

"Are you serious?" She laughed incredulously then stopped. "You're not serious."

I dropped my head onto the palms of my hands, cringing.

"Oh. My. Gosh. Ashlyn, spill it!" she demanded. "How did I miss this?"

"I've tried so hard to ignore my feelings, Megan. You've got to believe me. I knew how much you cared about Ryan, and I wasn't about to mess that up. But he and I . . . we sort of have a history." I quickly glanced behind me, but no one was there to hear. I cleared my throat and tried again. "We used to spend a lot of time together when I tutored Ryan and his brother. But he was only four years younger than me, so we were more like friends in a way. But when they had to move, it was really hard. The night before he left, Ryan held my hand. But then"—I dropped voice to a whisper—"he kissed me, and I didn't push him away and—"

"How old were you?" Megan's whole face manifested her shock.

"He was sixteen, and I was twenty. I had so little experience with boys at that point in my life. But after it happened, I was totally ashamed. So mortified that I ran home, never saw him again, and never told another living soul until now."

"I can't believe this," she said, shaking her head like she was faint.

"Do you hate me?" I groaned.

"Yes!"

Then I groaned even more. "I didn't want this to happen, Megan."

"I can't believe this. I always thought Ryan was perfect," she mused, "for *me*."

"I know. I'm so sorry."

"I guess that explains a lot though."

"Like what?"

"Things he'd say. Now I can see what he was trying to tell me, but I couldn't see it before. I'm such an idiot."

"You are not."

"So are you guys . . . like . . . ?" She gestured for me to fill in the blank.

"I don't know *what* we are."

Megan's nostrils flared. "He's going to hurt you, Ashlyn. I mean, this really hurts what you're telling me, but you're my sister, and I care about you. You want to find someone who isn't afraid to get married and have a family, and Ryan is definitely not that kind of guy! Knife. Stabbing. Pain. Mark my words. Ryan Anderson will do nothing but break your heart!"

*****

There he was—down the hall, heading my way!

He didn't see us yet in the after-church crush. Katie would go nuts in my arms when she saw him. She'd missed him and couldn't understand why he hadn't been around as much lately. Any second she'd blow our cover behind Brother Wilson. Okay, it wasn't much of a "cover" since he was as thin as a spaghetti noodle, but—

Ryan looked up. Our eyes met over the crowd, and I felt a butterfly party go off inside my chest. What should I say?

Oh, help! Why was I so nervous?

He walked toward us looking like some kind of superhero again. I couldn't believe what this guy did to me. Katie jumped down to dive-bomb his legs. His eyes dropped away from mine as he scooped her up and closed the distance between us.

"Hello, Ashlyn."

Hearing his deep voice made me feel like I'd crumble. "Hi."

He said nothing and yet everything, all in unspoken messages zipping and colliding between us like atoms out of control. I knew I'd never felt this around Matt. This time it wasn't a mere "wham." It was so much more. Small talk was unnecessary. We both knew what was going on here. I knew what he wanted.

"I'll go out with you," I whispered.

His stunned expression surely had to be a reflection of my own. "What did you just say?"

I looked down the hallway in one direction then the other. It was clearing out as people went home, but there were still those who hung around to talk. They had to be staring at us—I could feel it. "I, uh—"

"Ryan, wanna see my picture?" Katie interrupted, shoving a crayon-scribbled picture between our faces.

"Wow, that's beautiful, Katie," he said, glancing meaningfully at me around her head.

Elderly Sister Chatham walked up in her turquoise suit. She slugged Ryan in the side with her vinyl purse and whisper-shouted to me with a wink, "He's a winner, I'd say!" Then she knowingly marched down the hallway.

I sniffled my amusement. Our private moment had gone very public, but Ryan didn't seem to mind. He kissed Katie's cheek then asked me, "Would you mind repeating that thing you just said before we were interrupted? Because it kind of sounded like, 'I'll go out with you.'"

I nodded, trying not to smile too idiotically. "That's what I said."

"Are you serious?"

I nodded, completely unsure of what I was doing. I was thrilled at the idea yet terrified of hurting Megan more.

"You'll actually go out with me?" Ryan asked doubtfully.

"One date," I said, not expecting that much of anything could come of it.

"You'd better call 911," he said. "I think I'm having a heart attack."

Chapter 23

I STOOD IN FRONT OF the bathroom mirror brushing my hair, admiring the subtle highlights Karen had given me. I loved the wispy layers too. I felt feminine and beautiful. So different from the person I'd been before moving into this house. I'd lost weight too. Though it pained me to remember the old me—lifeless and gray—it did help me realize just how far I'd come. At that moment, I definitely felt alive, especially while my heart thumped in anticipation for this date.

Getting into a new pair of capris and a great top I'd found on clearance, I thought about the differences between the single co-ed I had been years ago and the woman I was now. Would Ryan see what I saw? That I didn't have the same cute little body I used to have? After having a baby, my hips had gained more womanly curves. It was one thing John had actually noticed and appreciated. What did Ryan see when he looked at me?

When he showed up ten minutes later on his motorcycle, wearing a black leather jacket, I gawked through the front window. I couldn't help it; the guy was smoking hot. Faded blue jeans defined his long legs, and when he pulled off his helmet, his hair got rakishly mussed. I felt an unexpected rush. As I went outside to greet him, my palms became sweaty, my heartbeat quickened.

"Hi," he grinned, sending another fluttery wave throughout my body. He got off his bike and walked up to me.

"Hi."

"I can't believe you said yes, that we're doing this."

"Me either." I glanced down the street self-consciously.

"Feel like going for a ride?"

My throat felt dry. "On your motorcycle?"

"Yeah. Is that okay? You're not afraid of motorcycles, are you?"

"No, not at all." I grinned. "I used to go with Shaun anytime he'd take me when he got his first bike."

"Awesome. We're going on an adventure."

I followed him to the back of his bike, where he grabbed an extra helmet for me. "This is for you."

"Thanks," I said, squashing the helmet over my hair. He helped by tucking in my hair and smoothing it down. He seemed to enjoying touching my hair, taking care of me. He stood so close I could smell the fresh scent lingering from his shower. It was clean like an ocean breeze.

He looked me over and gently laughed.

"What? Are you making fun of me?"

"Nope. You just look cute in a helmet."

Cute wasn't too bad, I decided. He showed me where to mount his bike and familiarized me with the foot pegs and hot exhaust pipe. I loved that he was concerned for my comfort and safety.

"You can hold on right here to this passenger bar, or you can put your arms around my waist." His eyes sparkled with mischief. "I like the latter option."

I laughed but said, "You *will* remember your promise?"

He raised a hand in the air. "I've got it covered."

No kiss.

He swung one leg over the motorcycle seat then turned to offer his arm so I could swing up behind him. When he had his helmet on, he called out, "How does it feel back there?"

"Great."

"Ready to go?"

I wrapped my arms around his waist, his leather jacket cool against my hands. "Ready."

He patted my hands at his waist in approval then started the engine. Excitement flowed through me, the same feeling you get riding a roller coaster for the first time. Shaun had taught me how to avoid knocking helmets, how to look over his shoulder in a turn, and how to move with the driver. But that was my brother. I'd never thought twice about putting my arms around him. But holding Ryan this closely, moving in unison with him was an entirely different feeling. I tried to keep in sync with him, to move as he moved, to sway with him at each turn. I enjoyed the feeling of speed mixed with the security of holding him tightly.

"Doing okay back there?" he asked when we came to a traffic light.

"Yep!" I shouted over the rumble of the engine.

I felt, more than heard, his chuckle under the weight of his jacket. He patted my hand again, letting his fingers linger on mine. When the light changed, he let go, leaving the cool air to replace the warmth of his hand.

He drove north on woodsy back roads up to Colfax, before pulling over at a small gravel pull-out. He turned slightly to face me. "Are you comfortable on these roads? They wind around a bit."

"As long as we don't drive off any cliffs or into a ditch, I'm fine."

He grinned back. "Warm enough?"

I gave him a thumbs up.

"Tap me on my right shoulder if you feel like stopping for any reason."

Ryan's consideration was impressive. Shaun had never been this solicitous when I'd ridden with him. He tugged my arms tighter around him, like a reverse hug, before setting off again. We breezed through historic Colfax, where reminders of the days of old railroads and mining were well-preserved. We continued onto the Colfax Highway, a curvy, forested road in the heart of gold country. The verdant grasses were beginning to change to dry yellows, soon to be like waves of gold under the evergreen forest.

When he pulled off at a rustic bar and grill called The Red Frog, I wasn't sure why we'd stopped. "Are we going in for a beer?" I joked.

"Not unless you want to."

"Mm, I'll pass, just this once."

Ryan laughed and extended his arm to help me get off. "You've seen Cape Horn from here, right?"

Wrinkling my forehead, I tried to remember. "I think so."

I leaned on his arm for balance and swung my leg over the motorcycle. Then he got off and removed his helmet. When I pulled the helmet off my head, all my hair tumbled down, making me think I looked like Medusa—until I saw the intensity on Ryan's face. His expression made me feel like one of those lanky models in black leather removing her helmet in slow motion, hair billowing out of the helmet to fall softly around her shoulders.

"You can read the marker about it over here," he said distractedly, reaching for my helmet.

"So this is one of the places you wanted to show me?" I asked, trying to sound unaffected by his penetrating gaze.

"One of many," he answered. Instead of moving forward, he remained where he was, eyes wandering from my hair down to my shoes. A tingling sensation hummed through me.

Avoiding him, I wandered over to the bronze plaque that explained how Chinese laborers in the 1800s were lowered over the cliffs in wicker bosun's chairs to blast a rail bed in the steep rock for the Transcontinental Railroad.

"No one knows how much of the legend is true, but supposedly a lot of workers fell to their deaths in the process."

I cringed at the thought. We went to the overlook and saw a spectacular panorama of the forested Sierras and the North Fork of the American River snaking through the canyon over a thousand feet below.

"That rounded knob over there is Cape Horn. Can you see the rails along the—hey there's Amtrak! Perfect timing." Ryan put his arm around my shoulders as we watched the sleek passenger train swoosh along the cliff edge.

"You like trains, don't you." I was stating the obvious. He looked like a little kid in a toy store picking out his first train set.

"Oh, yeah. There's history and excitement and the sounds and . . . arghh! I get a little carried away." He grinned sheepishly.

"No, it's actually kinda cute."

"Hmm. You like me then?"

I playfully shoved his arm, but he caught me around the waist and pulled me against his chest. His expression softened. The longing on Ryan's face was transparent, creating emotions that I'd willed to be dormant. His eyes captured mine with their gray intensity. I saw his Adam's apple move up and down as he swallowed. A bird overhead let out a sharp squawk, and suddenly the moment was over—like he'd forgotten himself, and now he was back.

"Ready for the next stop?" he asked in a raspy voice.

"Sure," I said.

We got back on the motorcycle and continued west, through dry, forested hills. We passed ranches lined with white fences, small fruit orchards, and turn-offs to outlying wineries. When we reached the Empire Mine, Ryan pulled into a space in the parking lot. He took a small, rolled-up blanket and a bag out of the small compartment at the back of his bike and started humming a tune I quickly recognized.

"Neil Young?" I asked with a smile.

He looked up, surprised and a little self-conscious. "Yeah. Being here with you makes me think of it."

I nodded in agreement. "One of my favorites. What's this?" I asked, pointing to the bag he held.

"Lunch." He grinned. "Come on." He gestured forward.

I moved in step beside him and felt his hand at the small of my back. I followed Ryan to a picnic area, but instead of taking one of the picnic benches, he wandered under the shady canopy of trees to a spot under a tall pine tree. He spread the blanket out over rust-colored pine needles behind a tangled clump of bushes.

He took my hand and helped me sit down. "Comfortable?"

"Yeah, it's great."

"Good," he said, pleased.

From the bag he'd brought, he pulled out a box of crackers, a small hunk of cheese, and some apples, setting them between the two of us. Plastic cups and Martinelli's apple cider followed.

"Wow, aren't you fancy?"

"Not as fancy as that Brazilian place Brother Hitch took you to, I know."

"Ryan, I didn't mean that. I love this." I spread my hands around me. "All of it. I think this is perfect."

Ryan picked up an apple, tossed it in the air, and caught it. "Do you like your apple peeled or with the skin on?" he asked.

"Peels on."

He cut the apple and sliced the cheese, then arranged them on a paper plate. "So how was Katie when you had to leave her?"

"She was fine. Mad she couldn't come, but fine. As soon as my dad offered to give her a piggyback ride, she forgot all about me. That's how I escaped."

Laughingly, Ryan said, "I remember pouring on the water works when I couldn't go somewhere. I hated getting left behind."

"But I think she needs to learn that we don't always get what we want."

"I agree with you. My parents taught us all that we had to work hard for things we wanted but that sometimes we had to do without—and that was okay."

"You don't think you were ever spoiled?" I teased.

He looked at me pointedly then laughed. "Maybe a little, but I did my fair share around the house."

He took off his leather jacket and leaned back on one arm to stretch out beside me. "Thank you for coming with me," he said intently, his eyes penetrating straight through me. "I'm glad you came."

I dropped my gaze to the blanket, where a small bug was making its way over a fuzzy fold. A gust of air whipped through my hair. "Me too."

"I know you've got a lot of other guys wanting to go out with you, so thanks for coming with me."

"Ryan, it's not like I've got guys lined up to take me out."

"Yeah, they are. I heard you're going out with some new guy, not to mention Brother Hitch—who, incidentally, is too old for you." I laughed outright, but he continued, "I bet there are plenty of others. Any guy who sees you is going to want to take you out."

I dismissed that with a shake of my head then turned the conversation right back at him. "What about you? I hear you've gone out with every girl in the singles ward."

Ryan looked away, obviously self-conscious. He started to say something, stopped, and looked down, absentmindedly rolling a cracker crumb along the edge of the blanket until it fell off and disappeared in the dirt. "I have to date different people if I have any hope of finding the right person for me," he said.

Or he could be avoiding marriage altogether if he was having too much fun going out all the time. Maybe his motto was "No commitment, all fun." Did he get bored going out with the same person? Not a good sign if you were looking for the completely devoted type. Was that John's problem? Actually, my husband had been completely devoted—to work, not me.

When we finished our lunch, Ryan showed me around the state park museum, where we saw several displays and a scale model of the underground workings of the mine. There were samples of ore and minerals in another room. Outside, he pointed out the remains of the stamp mill, and we wandered through the courtyard full of old, rusted mining equipment: ore cars, an ore crusher, the steam donkey, and a Pelton wheel.

"Did you have a fourth-grade field trip here?" I asked.

"I wish! We didn't live close enough back then."

"I remember thinking we'd be going miles underground and get buried alive. I was scared to death."

He laughed. "What about now? Feel up to seeing the mineshaft?"

"Of course. We're only allowed a little ways down, right?"

"Yep."

He grabbed my hand and eagerly led the way through a marked door into the cool, dark entrance of the mine. We went down a flight of cement stairs to a dimly lit landing where we could look down the incredibly steep slope of the mineshaft.

"This is the 'man skip' that miners rode on," Ryan said, pointing to a rickety wood contraption on the rail system. "Going down the incline shaft was like riding an out-of-control roller coaster down a steep drop at six hundred feet per minute. They stuck the new guys in front in case they lost their breakfast."

"Yuck."

"Yeah." He squeezed my hand, reminding me that he still held it. "These skips here went down to the 4,600 foot incline level, but the lowest part of the entire mine went clear down to the 11,000 foot incline level."

"Eleven thousand feet down?" I asked in amazement.

"Down the incline. Straight up and down that was about a mile underground."

"Wow." I had to smile over Ryan's passion for the facts and history of the Empire Mine. He absolutely loved every detail.

Next, we wandered through the sprawling gardens of the cottage-style mansion where the mine owner, William Bourn, had lived in the 1800s. What a contrast to the dirty, rough life of the miners—who were only allowed in the gardens once a year for the miner's picnic, Ryan explained. The English rose gardens contained hundreds of bushes in over fifty varieties. It would be spectacular when they were all in bloom. A worn brick pathway, crafted in a bordered herringbone pattern, lined the lush gardens closer to the cottage. The brick pathway led down a few steps to beautiful sitting areas and a multilevel waterway that cascaded into a reflecting pool. On the side of the cottage, two circular fountains sprayed elegant arches of water into the sunlight. Rhododendrons, azaleas, and draping greenery blended like a painting.

"It's so beautiful here!" I exclaimed. "It's been so long since I was here; I didn't remember it having such gorgeous grounds."

"People actually do weddings here."

I angled a sharp glance at Ryan, but he was looking off toward the cottage.

"Did you know the rock on this cottage is the mine's yard waste?" he asked, pointing to the rough, gray stones.

"Are you serious?"

"Yeah. And the red-brick trim is clinker brick—bricks that used to get thrown out for being crooked or the wrong color."

"I love the way the cottage looks with the two colors. This whole place is perfect for photos."

He turned back to me, warmth from his gaze seeping through me. "You know what? *You* are more beautiful than the gardens. I have to take your picture right now." He pulled his cell phone out of his pocket, unaware of my thudding heart.

"I'm not photogenic, Ryan." I laughed. "You don't want to do that."

But he'd already snapped one. Then another.

"See," he said, flipping the image around for me to see. "Beautiful."

I shook my head. "You always make people feel good about themselves."

He captured my hand, letting his fingers slide between mine, and led me to a concrete garden bench. "You should always feel good about yourself, Ash. You're amazing."

Sitting together, we seemed connected by more than just our hands. His heart touched mine; it beat in tune with mine. He lifted our joined hands in front of us, turning them over and then back.

"I like your hands," he said, stroking my knuckles. "They fit perfectly in mine."

I squeezed his hand affectionately. Then he brought my hand up to his face, trailing my fingers down his cheek, brushing them along his mouth.

"Ryan . . ." I found it suddenly difficult to breathe. "You promised."

"I'm not breaking my promise," he said softly, roving my fingers against his bottom lip, a twinkle in his eye. "I'm just holding your hand." He smiled that boyish, endearing smile.

I tugged my fingers away from his face but still held his hand. Would it be such a bad thing to allow myself to love him? Everything inside me resisted. I couldn't rip out my newly mending heart and offer it to him, knowing there was a chance he might toss it right back.

But I could belong to him. My heart did a somersault at the thought. Katie would have the best daddy a little girl could hope for. I briefly closed my eyes and listened to a jay squawk a shrill call to another bird. A gentle breeze fluttered through the branches and leaves overhead and ruffled the edges of our blanket. But Ryan didn't seem to notice. He was playing with a loose strand of my hair.

Maybe he *did* know what he was doing to me. Maybe it was completely transparent to him how I wanted his touch . . . while fearing it at the same time.

"Ashlyn." The throaty change in his voice made my heart respond. "Relax. You're safe with me."

My resolve was weakening like a well-worn cloth. I was ready to release the tattered threads of reason that I clung to. "I'm not safe! We should only stay as friends."

"Why? What is the real reason you're holding on to?"

"I can't follow my heart if it leads to a dead end with you. I can't do that to Katie or to myself."

"A dead end?"

"I heard you have a job offer back East?"

Ryan frowned. "I do. It's a killer job offer, actually. The one I was really hoping for."

"Back East. That brings us to your issue with commitment."

He squinted into the blue sky overhead, making me wonder where his thoughts had taken him or if he would share them with me. Finally, he turned back and took me completely by surprise. "I didn't always have commitment issues. I was engaged once."

I never would have expected him to say that. "When?"

"Right after my mission. I was at BYU." He leaned down to pick a blade of grass and started tearing it in little pieces. "Her name was Amy."

"What happened?"

He frowned and tugged another piece of grass from the ground. "She was wonderful, everything I could have hoped for," he said. "We got engaged and were perfectly happy planning our wedding. But I kept getting this feeling, an awful feeling that wouldn't go away. I didn't know what it was, and it scared me. I loved her and had felt right about marrying her, so it didn't make any sense why these feelings were hitting me."

"Did she know about it?"

"No, I didn't tell her. I didn't want to hurt her or make her worry. It was supposed to be the happiest time of her life, and I didn't want to ruin it. I still planned to marry her and believed that everything was going to be okay."

"But it didn't?"

He shook his head. "I decided to pray like I'd never prayed before. The impression I had was to really put my Father in Heaven first in my life, before my own righteous desires, and even before Amy. It was hard to let go of what I wanted, but when I did, I knew that He had a different plan for me. I had to break my fiancée's heart, the worst thing I've ever had to do."

"I'm sorry, Ryan. That's awful."

With a heavy sigh, Ryan leaned forward to rest his arms on his knees. "Knowing I was the one responsible for her suffering was the worst part."

I could almost feel the pain that Ryan and Amy might have felt. "So you came back home and transferred to UC Davis?"

He nodded. "Eventually I started dating again, but I was still afraid to get serious with anyone. I still tried to put God first, but He wasn't sending me any thumbs up for the girls I met."

"There must have been several who could have been serious about you. You never felt right about any of them?"

"I dated a lot but never got very close to anyone. It never seemed right."

He became quiet for a moment, and I took the opportunity to study him. There wasn't a part of this man I didn't adore, but now that I understood his past, I worried all the more that we should only be friends.

"We should go," I said.

"Why?"

"After what you told me . . ."

"Wait. You didn't hear the rest of the story."

"Okay. What's the rest of the story?" My curiosity was piqued.

He breathed in deeply. "One day, I was outside in the freezing cold, you see, wondering where my life was going. I was getting discouraged and losing hope. That's the day I looked up . . . and saw *you* again."

"Oh, Ryan." I pressed my face against his shoulder, so confused.

"I'm not going to hurt you, Ash."

"John promised he'd never hurt me."

"He didn't die intending to hurt you."

"No, but nothing lasts. *You* could—" I bit off the dreadful words.

Understanding filled his eyes. "Is that what this is about?" He took one of my hands and stroked my fingers. "Anyone could die; that's true. But taking a chance on loving them is worth the risk."

"You can't know that either. You haven't lost someone like I did."

Ryan sighed. "You're right. I haven't. But would you rather go through the rest of your life completely alone rather than risk losing someone you loved?"

I squeezed my eyes shut, my chest hurting with each breath I took. "I don't know."

"I know how much you love Katie. She's worth everything to you."

He was right. Having Katie was worth everything I had been through. I'd never go back in time and undo my marriage to John, not if it meant I'd lose Katie too. But with Ryan, everything was different.

"Ashlyn, I'm so in love with you," Ryan said in a raspy voice. "I think I always have been."

I felt a tear slip down my skin and soak into the fuzzy warmth of his shirt. "Ryan," I whispered. He was precious to me and so giving of himself—his deepest self. I couldn't trample on that. "I don't want to hurt you."

"Then kiss me and end this madness," he said in an attempt at lightness, but his voice was thick with emotion. He put an arm around me and pressed his forehead against mine. If the pulse at his neck was any indication, his heart was beating just as fast as mine was. The pressure of his hands increased, but he didn't move otherwise. His eyes were pleading with me, and moisture pooled in my eyes.

"Are you crying?" Ryan asked tenderly. He wiped the shiny trail of moisture from my face then brushed the corner of my eye, where another tear threatened to escape. "What is it?"

I wanted to say *I love you*, but I wasn't ready to give my heart away when his future was so uncertain. If he took that job, our relationship would be severed. "What are we going to do?" I asked.

"I don't know."

The trees creaked high above us, and a ray of sun filtered through the trees and washed over us.

*****

Later, when Ryan dropped me off to pick up Katie, he didn't get off the motorcycle right away. I watched him become silent, studying the crack on his handle bars. I wondered if he was having any regrets. Our relationship had drastically changed in twenty-four hours!

I bit the inside of my lip, not sure if I should walk to the doorstep by myself or wait for him. I began to turn away, but his arm shot out to stop me.

"Wait," he implored. Then, before I could think, the space between us was obliterated as he pulled me into his arms. His hands were in my hair and at the back of my neck, willing me closer. "I wish you didn't have to go in now," he groaned.

"I know," I murmured.

"I don't want this day to end. Will you spend the day with me tomorrow?"

"Doing what?" I asked.

"Let's take Katie out on the lake and have a picnic."

Thinking about all the reasons I should probably do something else, I gnawed on my bottom lip. Then I grinned. "That sounds so fun."

After Katie was tucked in bed for the night, I took a long, hot bubble bath and contemplated my life. When I got into bed, I snuggled down into the smooth sheets and was startled by my cell phone suddenly vibrating on the nightstand.

It was Ryan's number, so I answered.

"Hi," came that deep voice that made me melt. "I just wanted to hear your voice before I fall asleep."

I covered my face with one hand, cuddling into my pillow. Could this be happening to me? If I wasn't completely melted before, I was now. "We can't wait to see you tomorrow," I told him, thinking about Katie's excitement over going out on the lake.

"Ash?"

"Hmm?

I heard him breathe in and then sigh. "Good night."

"Ever drifting down the stream—
Lingering in the golden gleam—"
–Lewis Carroll

Chapter 24

"RYAN, ARE YOU SURE ABOUT this?" I asked at the edge of the wooden dock, clutching Katie's life jacket so tightly my knuckles poked out.

"I'm positive," he said, leaning over the edge of the boat to help us in. "You can trust me."

Katie wiggled in my grasp, trying to inch closer to Ryan and the promised boat ride. "Can I get in now?" she asked excitedly.

"Here we go, pumpkin," Ryan called, reaching for her. "Give me your hand, and I'll help you in."

Straddling Katie, I wriggled us closer to the edge. Katie shot forward, completely trusting Ryan. It was endearing how much my daughter adored him. Ryan confidently scooped Katie up and sat her down in one of the middle seats. Then he turned to flash me a gorgeous smile.

"Your turn, cutie."

I blushed and grinned at the same time, placing my hand into his as he helped me into the boat. Before I could sit down, Ryan had me locked against his solid chest. "Wow, you smell good," he said close to my ear. He fingered a wisp of my hair. "I'm so glad we're doing this," he added in a voice that could melt every last glacier in the Sierras.

"Boating with Katie?" I glanced uncertainly at my live-wired daughter.

"Boating with Katie, being together, you and me . . . all of it."

I tucked the wayward strand of hair behind my ear and sat down. I'd been nervous to show up in a bathing suit today. Granted, I had on a cover-up that hung at mid-thigh, so I wasn't exactly naked. But it was still discomfiting. I'd grown up on the lake, practically living in a swimsuit during the summer. There had always been parties and ward activities on Lake Combie. In those days, I'd never thought twice about swimming or water skiing in front of a crowd. But this was different. Somehow having Ryan see me was a much bigger deal. It mattered now.

Sitting beside Katie, I watched Ryan maneuver the boat away from the dock. Katie giggled with delight.

"This is so uh-citing! Huh, Mommy!"

I laughed. "It sure is!"

Over the hum of the engine, Ryan called out, "Do you have any preference which way we go?"

I shook my head. "Down near the dam is always fun," I suggested.

"To the dam it is, then."

I loved the carefree, tousled way his hair looked today. He looked fantastic in that thin, white T-shirt. A well-used pair of Tevas were strapped to his feet. And his charcoal board shorts were just plain hot.

Out of the no-wake zone of the cove, in the open, emerald water, he asked Katie if she was ready to go fast.

"Uh-huh!"

"Okay, hold on tight!" he warned before shifting to a higher speed.

Katie screamed with delight over the roar of the engine. I had never seen such an enormous grin on a child before. It made my heart swell with irrepressible joy. To me, this was the fullest possible moment of living! All my senses were alive. The warmth of the sun enveloped us, splattering its winking brilliance across the lake. The occasional spray of water was cool and refreshing. The wind whipped across our faces and messed up our hair. Best of all was the three of us together.

Ryan's gaze locked for a moment with mine, his eyes sending silent messages that were quite transparent. My heart flipped over recklessly. His lopsided grin with crinkles at the corner of his eyes seemed to say something my heart agreed with.

Ryan slowed the boat as we wandered the lake, catching glimpses of homes tucked in the cover of steep, forested hills—new mansions in some areas, older homes in others. We passed wake-boarders, skiers, and a few cruising around on jet skis, but for the most part, the lake was quiet, a Northern Californian paradise.

Katie got on her knees to look down into the water. "Ryan, are we going to find a gold treasure in there?"

"Not in this water, Katie," he said. "But if you look around really carefully, you'll find some gold." Katie gave him a hopeful glance, and he said, "Look at your mommy's hair in the sunshine."

Katie giggled, and I blushed. She continued to look down at the water when she suddenly yelped. "Ryan, I saw a shark over there!"

"You did?" he asked, putting the boat in neutral to pick her up.

"Sweetie, I don't think there are any sharks in this lake," I said, exchanging an amused glance with Ryan. "They live in the ocean."

Katie looked to Ryan for confirmation, as if her mother's word wasn't enough. "Sharks hate this lake," he agreed, flicking his hand up. "They only like the ocean."

She thought for a moment then asked, "Are there fishies in there?"

"Lots of them." He nodded. "Want to go fishing with me one day?"

"No. I don't like fish sticks," Katie declared, scrunching her nose.

Ryan laughed and gave her a squeeze. "I don't like fish sticks either. But when I catch a fish and cook it, it's delicious."

"Eeew, yuck! Mommy, he ate a fish!" She giggled, convinced that was the silliest thing she'd ever heard. I was sure she was picturing a live, flopping fish being swallowed whole.

"I guess we'll have to show this girl what fried fish tastes like." Ryan grinned.

"As long as I'm not cooking," I said apologetically. "I'm not the greatest cook in the world."

I wondered what he'd make of that news, but all he did was shrug and say, "No problem. I'll do the honors."

"How do you know . . ." I shook my head in disbelief. "Is there anything you can't do?"

"What are you talking about?" he asked, plopping down beside me, setting Katie on his lap. He put an arm around my shoulders, drawing me closer.

"Every time I turn around, you're showing me another amazing skill—fixing faucets, first aid, painting, cooking fish . . ."

"Oh, come on."

"It's true," I said, absentmindedly fingering the T-shirt on his upper arm. It was warm from the sun. "You're amazing." Ryan's eyes followed my fingers until I realized what I was doing. I yanked my hand back in embarrassment; my eyes flew to his.

"It's okay, Ash," he said quietly, obviously affected, the way his voice caught. "You can touch me." Something electric hummed between us, an unspoken understanding so strong that if Katie weren't with us, I could only imagine how things might have progressed.

After giving me a look full of longing, Ryan stood up. "So who's up for swimming?"

"Me!" Katie answered, raising her hand above her life jacket. "I want to go at the swimming pool!"

"Swimming pool?" Ryan said in mock dismay. "We get to go swimming right here in the lake, pumpkin."

"But there's fishies in there," Katie said warily. "They eat me."

"I'll take us back to the dock. The fish, uh, don't swim over there." Ryan looked to me to make sure the white lie was okay, raising his shoulders and putting his hand palm up.

On a truth scale of one to ten, he might be at a two, but I nodded to him with a smile and stroked Katie's curls. "I swam in this lake when I was a little girl, Katie. See the dock up ahead?" Ryan had turned back into the cove and was slowly approaching his family's shoreline. "It's safe to swim there."

"Did a fish eat you when you were little?"

"Nope."

Ryan turned off the engine, and we drifted up against the dock. Ryan hopped out to secure the boat. "Here we are!" he said. "Ready for a swim, Katie?"

Katie nodded uncertainly. I picked her up and handed her over to Ryan. Then he helped me out of the boat, allowing his fingers to linger on mine. He pulled off his T-shirt in one swift motion, revealing his beautifully defined arms and chest. "Watch me, Katie," he shouted before jumping into the water. His splash shot a cold spray of water across us. Katie ran to the edge of the dock to watch Ryan surface.

"Whoo!" he yelled, slicking his wet hair back. "It feels great. Hop in!"

Katie almost jumped in before I remembered to take her Velcro sandals off. "I'm going to do one-two-three-jump, 'kay?"

"Okay, I'll catch you," Ryan called, swimming nearer.

Katie jumped to Ryan, and her shriek of happiness brought a harsh, scolding cry from a flock of Stellar's Jays in the pines. When her life jacket pulled Katie to the surface, she gasped and swiped the water from her eyes. Then she clutched onto Ryan's neck, peering warily into the water.

"You're safe, pumpkin. I've got you," Ryan said, wiping his eyes. Katie's splash had caught him right in the face, but it didn't seem to faze him.

"Mommy, I'm swimming!" Katie cried ecstatically. "You jump in too!"

"Why don't I sit here so I can watch you guys?" I suggested.

"No. You gots to jump in. You can do it, Mommy. It's safe, huh, Ryan?"

Ryan's eyes met mine. "Yep, it's safe."

Yeah, but jumping in means stripping off the cover-up. I'd inspected myself in a bathing suit for a good fifteen minutes this morning in the mirror. I had to admit, those workouts were paying off. But still . . .

"Want me to catch you?" Ryan playfully teased with an undercurrent of warmth that produced a streak of crimson across my cheeks.

"I've got it, thanks," I answered, pulling the terrycloth cover-up over my head. I couldn't bring myself to look up, to see him watch me. I tossed the wadded-up fabric across the dock and hopped into the lake, going under the cool water and resurfacing with a grin. "It does feel great."

"Good job, Mommy."

Ryan chuckled meaningfully. "Yeah, very good job."

I felt my cheeks growing an even more ridiculous shade of red, so I dived under water and came up right beside Katie, who giggled with delight.

"You can swim!"

I nodded and tugged on Katie's toes. I felt Ryan put an arm around my waist, tugging me closer to him. "I learned to swim when I was a little girl, just like you. Want to try?"

"Okay," Katie said.

"I'll give you a push to your mom," Ryan suggested. "And then you kick those little alligator legs until you reach her."

Katie's laughter was infectious. "I don't have alligator legs, silly."

"I mean kick those little chicken legs," Ryan teased, his white teeth glistening in the sunshine. His hand squeezed mine under the water before trailing away as he backed up a few feet.

Katie splashed back and forth between us, arms flailing and legs kicking, until she grew tired. Then we hopped back onto the warm dock to eat our snacks. While taking a few bites of sandwich, Ryan angled several looks at me.

"What?" I asked.

"Nothing," he answered but then added, "Well, there is something I wanted to ask you."

"Okay," I said before biting into a crisp, juicy apple.

He finished his sandwich and gave me one more mysterious look before saying, "Would you come with me to the single adult party this weekend?"

I angled my face and squinted piercingly.

"I'd really like it if you came. It's a barbecue at the Albrights'." He leaned back on his arms, waiting for my response. The sunlight played across his broad chest, his hair dripping water down his neck.

"Ryan, that would hurt my sister. She really had feelings for you, and seeing us show up together would be too hard on her."

"Then I think we should sit down and tell her how we feel."

"I don't know."

"Megan and I are comfortable with each other. It'll be fine," he tried to reassure me. Then, he turned to Katie. "What do you think, pumpkin? Do you think your Mommy would like to go to a party with me?"

"Does it have balloons?" Katie asked.

"No, I don't think there'll be any balloons."

"Oh," she said, deflated.

"Is it okay with you if I take her to the party?" he asked. It was a sweet gesture to ask Katie's permission. Very endearing.

"Yeah. I can play at Grandpa's house."

Ryan swung back to me, grinning. "Is that cute, or what?"

I couldn't keep my eyes off him. "Very."

"So what do you say, is it a date?"

"Maybe."

"All that glisters is not gold;
Often have you heard that told: . . ."
–William Shakespeare

Chapter 25

WINCHESTER WAS SYNONYMOUS WITH WEALTH, a tribute to travertine and timbers. Subzero and concrete drives, opulent golf courses, mansions, luxury. There were some old-timers who didn't think the community belonged in Meadow Vista. Bethany Albright's family must have disagreed.

As Ryan pulled in to the circular drive in front of a sprawling estate, I gasped. "Are you serious? This is where they live now?" Most of the homes in the neighborhood were stunning, but this one demanded a bit of drool.

"I'm serious." Ryan chuckled, shaking his head. "Hard to believe, isn't it?"

"It's monstrous!"

Turning the engine off, he smiled knowingly. "You don't like it?"

"Like it? It's . . . it's so . . ."

"Big?"

"Yeah."

The two-story mansion had rock, stucco, and wood accents all in woodsy earth tones. A fountain marked the entrance to the enormous porch. I took note of the yard boasting granite boulders, large pine trees, and many varieties of shrubs. With no lawn, it appeared natural in a professional-landscape-architect-was-here kind of way.

Ryan walked around the car to get my door. Slipping one arm around me, he drew me close and whispered against my hair, "Don't wander away from me tonight."

"Why?"

"Um, I kind of want you all to myself."

"Then why did we come?" I hissed. I still didn't think I should have agreed to this, even after talking with Megan. My sister promised that it wouldn't be awkward, but how could it not be? I didn't want to be at this party any more than I wanted a root canal, but Ryan needed to be there.

"Duty. Trust me, I'd rather be somewhere else with you."

"Then let's get out of here!"

"I wish." He chuckled before nuzzling me behind the ear.

We walked up the front steps, and I rang the bell.

"We could doorbell ditch," Ryan suggested, swinging his gaze back to his car. "They'd never know it was us—"

With a clomp of stilettos, the door opened. "Hello, Ryan!" Bethany whined in a nasally sweet voice.

What in tarnation was she wearing? Was that a dress or a bikini with fringe? She actually wore stuff like that in front of her parents? Apparently they never got the memo on modesty.

When she finally realized I was present, Bethany winced, but she recovered quickly with a syrupy voice. "Come on in! Glad you could make it," she sing-songed.

Ha! Like she was glad. Every glance in my direction was a carefully aimed lance. Obviously, she couldn't fathom how I could even dare to show up for the party.

"We're all back in the game room," Bethany said with a casual flick of her fingers. Spotting the way Ryan's hand rested at my back, she spun around and ba-da-boomed her way ahead of us.

We passed the curved staircase and an extravagant kitchen down to a massive family room that opened onto a covered patio overlooking the golf course. Several people stood with cue sticks around a carved mahogany pool table. French doors were opened so guests could mingle either indoors or out. The lavish buffet on the patio looked like someone was practicing for a wedding reception. Little glass dishes. Puffs of cream-filled treats. The young adults were engaged in their usual multitasking activities—eat-flirt-mingle. Megan and Drake were the first to come over to say hello.

"What's up, dude?" Drake mock-slugged Ryan; then he smiled and held out a hand to me. "Sister Ca—uh, Ashlyn."

Ouch. Well, he'd tried, anyway. One day he's respectfully serving the widow, the next, having to party with her. I didn't blame him for being a little uncertain. I knew the feeling. Heck, I should be crowned Queen of Uncertain tonight. It was only Ryan's nearness that kept me from bolting.

While the guys were talking, Megan asked under her breath, "Glad you came?"

"Don't know yet," I whispered back.

She leaned in closer to me saying, "Be careful," thrusting her wrist at me in a covert, knife-jabbing motion.

I elbowed her in return.

"Would you like some lemonade?" Ryan asked me, unaware of the exchange.

"Sounds perfect," I said.

He led the way through the French doors out to the patio buffet, greeting a group and introducing me as they brushed by. He filled a cup and offered it to me before filling one for himself. "Check out these chocolate things," he said, reaching for a decadent pastry and popping it into his mouth. "Holy cow," he mumbled, trying to keep his mouth closed. "You've got to try one."

"That good, huh?" I nearly laughed. I fingered one of the chocolaty confections before taking a bite. My eyes widened in amazement before I stuffed the rest in my mouth. "Wow. Who made them?"

"I think Bethany's mom is a gourmet cook or something. I'm pretty sure she did all this." He pointed out the crystal beverage cooler and swoops of pale tulle surrounding exotic-looking hors d'oeuvres and desserts.

I caught the eye of a heavy-set girl sitting in one corner of the patio with a plate of goodies. I smiled—and much to my relief, she smiled back. After selecting a few treats, Ryan suggested we walk downstairs to the lower patio, where a waterfall bubbled over granite slabs and pooled at the bottom. The pine trees surrounding the patio framed velvety-green views of the golf course. The smell of freshly cut grass drifted over.

"This is gorgeous," I said, sitting back against a granite boulder that was part of a retaining wall.

"Think you'd like a place like this?" Ryan teased, but a strange undertone seeped into his words.

I shrugged. "I've always loved my parents' home on the lake, old rusty bits and all. It's outdated, but I think it's perfect."

Ryan's smile warmed me more than the sunlight overhead. I knew how much he loved old things as well, but I also wondered if he worried about measuring up financially. I didn't want him to think I was the kind of woman who expected a rapid rise of wealth to satisfy a certain lifestyle.

A boisterous cluster of people descended the steps down to the lower patio, so instead of trying to have a private conversation, we mingled. And it was actually fun. Ryan had a way of never neglecting me, including me in conversation. He had a way of expressing himself without saying a word—the extra pressure of his thumb along the ridge of my fingers, a brush of his hand along my spine, or a speaking glance.

A cackle of laughter overhead alerted me to the sneer lingering on Bethany's face up on the balcony. *Really? Are we still in junior high?* The look Bethany gave me spoke volumes. There was confusion and questioning, irritation and resentment. Everyone else had been accepting so far. What was Bethany's problem? Did she honestly think her so-called revelation about Ryan was valid? That he was her only marriage option? I couldn't help but feel some sympathy for Bethany. She might really be hurting.

"Did you guys hear the news?" Drake called out over the railing upstairs, getting the attention of everyone below. "Jen and Joseph are engaged!"

A cheer rose up at the news. I didn't know who the couple was, but from snippets of the ensuing conversation, it sounded like the engagement was a long time in coming. Everyone seemed to have an amusing anecdote to add.

But Ryan looked decidedly uncomfortable with the topic, which made me uncomfortable. We hadn't talked about our relationship yet. It was still tender, like the delicate wildflowers sprouting up across the Sierras. A few meaningful looks were aimed at the two of us, the obvious question every-one wanted to ask left unspoken.

At the first break in the conversation, Ryan turned to me. "I'm a little thirsty. Want some more lemonade?"

"Yes, please."

He took my cup and headed up the steps to the buffet table. I wasn't sure if I should follow him or stay where I was. Maybe he needed to get away for a couple minutes. It was understandable. I decided to go upstairs as well but gave Ryan some space by wandering into the game room. I found an Egyptian-looking side chair to sit in, but it was stiff and made my back arch funny. I crossed my legs and nearly fell out of the chair.

Okay, maybe I'll go find a bathroom.

Seeing two girls I recognized from the service project, I approached them. "Do you know where the bathroom is?"

The taller one giggled. "Yeah, it's down the hallway here on the right."

"Thanks."

"Sure. And check out the mirror while you're in there." She laughed again.

I wondered what that was about, but as soon as I stepped into the bathroom and switched on the light, I figured it out.

Copper. Everywhere. The sink was a hammered copper vessel, and above it, funky copper fixtures poked grotesquely out of the tile. Hammered copper switch plates and copper tiles adorned the walls, but the pièce de résistance was the bathroom mirror. A large, zigzag-shaped shard of mirror was surrounded by a mosaic of copper tiles intermingled with shiny copper pennies. *Holy copper, Batman.*

Our rubber ducky shower curtain must have seemed beyond cheap to Bethany after this. My eye caught something in the lower right-hand corner of the mirror-thing. What was that? Peering closer, I made out the tiny script that read, "Designed by Bethany."

Ah. Now I got it. No wonder Bethany was touting the merits of copper. Somehow she'd come up with this . . . uh, *objet d'art*. To be fair, I stood back and scrutinized it a little more objectively. It was colorful. Original. Dynamic, in an electrocuted sort of way. Flipping the light off, I backed out of the bathroom with one last look at the mirror and bumped right into Bethany.

"Oh, sorry!" I cried, guilt spreading through my veins as though Bethany could read my thoughts about the whole copper overload.

Bethany skewered me with a rigid, arctic glare.

"You have a beautiful home," I said, almost afraid to be in the hallway alone with her.

"Don't even—" she bit off whatever she was about to say and compressed her lips into a tight line. "You think I don't see through this?"

I jerked my head back in surprise. "What?"

"It's not going to work, you know."

"What's not going to work, Bethany? What are you talking about?"

She shook her head in disgust, crossing her arms into a knot. "I'm talking about the way you waltzed into my home with Ryan. You're making a fool of yourself, you know, showing up here with him."

I felt the blood drain from my face. I hadn't expected anything this vicious. I'd had an overdose of doubts and fears about coming with Ryan. But I thought it had been going pretty well up until now.

"Bethany, I—"

"How old are you anyway?"

My eyes bugged out. "Does it matter that much to you?"

"Ryan should be with other girls. He *deserves* to be with someone younger, without the burden of kids."

Now that hurt. Katie could be a pill at times but not a burden, and for Bethany to say anything against my own daughter made my Hades head-flame explode. I sucked in a stream of air, trying to calm down. "You know what, Bethany? It's none of your business."

"If you think about it, the best thing you can do is walk away before he does. And you know he's going to."

I glanced down the hallway then gently lowered my voice. "Bethany, look, if you have feelings for Ryan, I'm very sorry. But—"

Bethany's anger gave way to pain. "You have no idea what I feel for him!" she seethed, her eyes pooling over. "Or for how long!"

"I'm sorry I've hurt you, Bethany." I extended a hand for comfort, but she swatted it away.

"Leave me alone!" she cried, pushing into the bathroom and thumping the door closed.

I shut my eyes in disbelief, Bethany's harsh words echoing inside my head.

You're making a fool of yourself.

He deserves to be with someone younger.

The kindest thing you can do for him is walk away.

Yep. It wasn't like they were new thoughts. I'd muddled over the same things for a long time. Was I making a fool of myself? I definitely felt foolish after talking to Bethany. I thought about Paul and Ryan and their male antics at my house. At least they'd been civilized. Their animosity never came to anything more than nonverbal antagonism. Bethany and I had exchanged words, leaving Bethany crying in the bathroom. So yeah, I felt like a fool.

I shuffled down the hallway with a troubled heart. Ryan had always made me feel that the difference in our ages was insignificant, that he wanted nothing more than to be with me. He loved me. I didn't doubt that. I'd always felt like he deserved someone younger. I didn't plan on falling in love with him, but I had—and hard.

I had no idea what he'd do about a job, but surely he wouldn't accept something far away from Katie and me? Something amazing was happening between us, and I doubted he'd just walk away from that before we had a chance to figure it out. Sure, it was awkward for us both to be standing there with everyone blabbing on and on about marriage. But we weren't ready yet to talk about our own future.

I'd have to leave Bethany's anger behind me. I was strong enough to not let that girl destroy me. Love was stronger than hate and disappointment.

I made my way back to the game room. Not seeing Ryan, I continued out to the buffet table but still found no sign of him. Where had he gone?

I peeked over the edge to the patio downstairs but didn't see him, so I sat down to wait. Like a wallflower.

Good grief. One of the reasons people got married was to eradicate the dreaded wallflower situation. I thought I'd taken care of that. *Man, never become a widow,* I silently admonished all the girls there. *It stinks.*

I stood again, ready to force myself to mingle while I tried to find Ryan. I needed that cup of lemonade, so I wandered back outside to the upper patio, where all the refreshments were. While filling a cup, I thought I heard Ryan's voice. I looked up but realized the sound was coming from below. Maybe he was on the lower patio.

"So what's the deal with you and the sexy widow?" another male voice down there said.

I froze, my cup halfway up to my lips. Widow? They were talking about *me?*

Ryan's voice said, "Can't stay to chat Josh."

"Ha!" the other guy laughed smugly. "Avoiding me proves my point. Are you finally ditchin' the single life?"

"Nope."

"Oh, come on, dude. It's pretty obvious."

"Josh, we're just friends. Nothing serious, so lay off."

"I hear she has a kid. A whole package," the guy taunted.

"Like I said, we're just friends." Ryan's voice was getting edgy.

"Rumor has it you accepted the job in Virginia."

"Yeah, what about it?"

"I guess you'll be ditching everyone here then?"

I didn't hear Ryan's response over the sudden clamor coming from the group at the pool table. I didn't stay to hear any more, though I was sorely tempted to march downstairs and slug the jerk downstairs. *Nice package?* How dare he call us a package! Did Ryan actually say he had accepted that job? I was so mad I almost squashed my cup of lemonade. Why didn't he tell me? If he'd made the decision about something this important, wouldn't he have told me? Katie and I were the ones who'd be affected by his choice the most. We deserved to know. *We're just friends. Nothing serious,* he'd said. I didn't believe that, but at the same time I wasn't sure what to think.

Maybe he still worried about making a commitment to someone after what he and his fiancée went through. I didn't know, but I sure wasn't going to find any answers standing there, abandoned, in the middle of a party. Walking through the house, I saw Bethany glowering at me, and I decided I'd had enough. I was ready to leave. If I couldn't find Ryan, I'd take off on foot, but I didn't want to stay another minute as the abandoned date, the gossip topic, or the shooting target.

I'd probably been foolish to think Ryan and I could take one day at a time. Did he think I'd be happy to fall in love with him for however long it lasted and when it was over just move on? Is this what he'd done to all the other girls he'd dated—sucked every living heartbeat out of them until *he* felt like moving on because commitment wasn't in his plans?

Maybe I was overthinking and getting myself all worked up, but my heart still stung inside my chest. I needed to talk with Ryan, but I'd have to wait until we were alone. If only I had my own car, I'd take off and let him fend for himself. He could go kill as much summertime as he wanted in this horrible place. We could always talk later.

"Hi, I'm Julie!" a brunette said, trying to engage me in conversation. The girl's energy ricocheted between us.

"Ashlyn," I responded, wishing I didn't have to make small talk at the moment.

"Nice party, huh?"

Oh yeah, real nice.

"Though your eyes with tears were blind . . ."
–George William Russell

Chapter 26

"Ash, what's wrong?" Ryan called, jogging up to me from the Albrights' front porch. "Where have you been?"

"Where have *I* been?" I challenged. "Where have *you* been?"

"Looking for you! I've been trying to find you for twenty minutes!"

I started walking toward his car. "That's what I was doing. Can we please go now?"

"Is everything okay? Are you not feeling well?" He put his arm around me in concern.

"I'm not sick; I just need to go."

"Okay. That's fine."

Once we left, I was glad to finally be back on our sleepy, small-town Meadow Vista Road where I felt more comfortable. But I wasn't sure where to begin. My mind blurred with images and thoughts all competing for recognition.

"I think we need to talk," I said.

"What is it, Ash?" He tried to keep his eyes on the road but kept sending flashes of worry my way. "Talk to me." His warm fingers reached over to curve around my knotted hands.

We turned onto the narrow road that led to my parents' house. The moon was just coming up over the pine trees. A high-pitched chorus of frogs warbled somewhere outside in the darkness.

"I have to ask you something, Ryan, and I need you to answer honestly."

"Sure." Sensing we were about to have a serious discussion, he drove the rest of the way without talking. The silence hung in the air between us.

In front of my parents' house, he turned off the engine and turned in his seat to face me, a look of worry marring his handsome features. "What's going on, kulta?" He leaned over to take my hand in his.

I turned to face him, tilting my head against the back of my seat. My heart was tender. I could pretend like I didn't hear that conversation and push my worries aside. It wasn't necessary to bring it up right now, was it? Maybe it should wait.

I briefly closed my eyes and listened to a coyote howl a mournful cry in the distance. But I knew I couldn't move forward without knowing where I was headed. "What are we doing, Ryan?" I mumbled vaguely. Being more direct seemed beyond me at the moment.

His forehead puckered. "What do you mean?"

"You and me," I said, pointing a hand back and forth between us. "What are we doing? What is this?"

"A date? Spending time together?"

That wasn't the impression he'd given at the party. "Yeah, I know. It's just that . . . I'm a little confused."

"About what?" He was troubled now.

"Us."

"You mean you're confused about our relationship?"

"Yeah. Like where are we headed?"

He quickly looked away, looking decidedly uncomfortable. He drove his fingers through his hair, making it stick up all over. "I thought we felt the same way about each other and want to be together. That's what we're doing, isn't it?"

"But for how long?"

His chin jerked back slightly. "What do you mean? As long as we want it to be, right?"

"Not if you're moving to Virginia!"

He appeared shocked. "How—"

"I overheard your conversation at the party, Ryan."

His eyes narrowed. "What conversation?"

"The one where you told some guy that there's nothing between us and that you'll be ditching us all."

"You mean Josh? That guy's a freak! I wouldn't tell him what I ate for breakfast, let alone anything personal."

"So you just made that up?"

"I was protecting *you* back there! I didn't want you to be uncomfortable with all that talk of marriage."

"*Me*? I thought *you* were the one who was uncomfortable. Did you really accept the job in Virginia?"

He exhaled forcefully.

This was a big one. Everything was hanging on this answer.

"I *did* accept it, but—"

I dropped my jaw and stared open-eyed in disbelief. "Then what we have"—I motioned between us—"means nothing to you."

"Whoa, slow down! How can you say that?"

"Because it wasn't important enough to tell me! How many people know?"

"I've really only told my parents. I wanted to talk to you about it, but I didn't think we were ready for such a big discussion."

I turned away, not wanting to hear any more. "I should never have let things go this far."

"Come on; that's not true!"

"Ryan, our relationship doesn't have a future, does it?"

"Ashlyn, please don't do this." His voice rose a notch.

"I have to, Ryan." I spun back to him. "I don't want to hurt you, but I'm also not going to let you hurt me or Katie. So I think we should end this now if—" I shook my head, squeezed my eyes shut.

"Don't say it. Why do you want to rush this any faster than we need to? Just because I have a job in Virginia doesn't mean we have to end everything."

"Do you ever plan on getting married?"

He whipped away from me in frustration, thumping his hand against the steering wheel. "Why does everyone *do* that? The second you show interest in someone, they grill you about marriage! Of course I *plan* on it someday . . ."

"Well, how can you possibly succeed if you can't commit yourself to anyone? You're always running away!"

"Maybe this *is* what I want!" he said. "Right here, with you and Katie."

"Ryan, you can't have us!"

"Why not?" he demanded, raking a hand through his hair.

"Because you plan on leaving us! How do you think this affects Katie? If she starts believing you're a permanent part of her life, and then suddenly"—I snapped my fingers—"you're gone . . . you'll be leaving behind more than one broken heart. She's already forgotten John yet still asks if her daddy loves her. I don't want her being hurt anymore."

"Okay, stop," Ryan gulped, bolting from the car. He darted around the front of the car and opened my door. "Come here," he ordered, taking my hand to help me out. He led me to a stand of trees where my parents had put in a bench. "Sit down, all right?"

He stood over me, propping a foot on the edge of the bench next to my legs. He shook his head wearily, making a nervous laugh. "I'm not exactly ready for this conversation tonight, but . . . Okay, first of all, you know I love Katie, and I'd never do anything to hurt either of you, right?"

I drew in a breath of courage to look up at him. "Not intentionally. But we shouldn't pretend like this is going somewhere it isn't."

"I'm not pretending. I know what I feel. We just need some time."

"But if we're just prolonging a doomed relationship—"

"We don't have a doomed relationship, Ashlyn! It's incredible!"

"Yeah, it is," I said softly. "But it won't be incredible the day you suddenly say, 'So long, I'm out of here.'"

"I'd never act like that!" he snapped, pushing away from the bench. "And I never will! You know me better than that." He paced around. "Ugh, this is not the way this conversation is supposed to be. Everything is all messed up now!"

I started to stand, but he instantly stuck his hand out. "Wait, sit down! I have something to ask you."

"Stop ordering me around!" I countered, standing anyway and crossing my arms.

How did we end up yelling at each other? If things were confusing before, they were nothing compared to the direction our conversation had taken. What the heck was happening between us? There was something pressing in on me that almost felt like panic.

Ryan pinched the bridge between his eyes.

"What were you going to ask me?" I asked.

"Well, you didn't give me a chance to get this right," Ryan snapped. "And I wanted it to be perfect!"

A lance might have ripped into my chest, with the devastating implication of his words. I gaped at him wide-mouthed. "Don't!" I gasped, clutching a hand to my chest.

"I want to ask you to—"

"Stop it!" I cried. "Whatever you're doing, just stop!"

"Whatever I'm doing?" He raked his hands through his hair again, still pacing. "What I'm trying to do is ask you to marry me in spite of the fact that we're yelling at each other, my speech isn't prepared, everything is wrong at the moment, and I don't have your ring!"

"No!" Now my stomach had a stabbing pain. "Why are you doing this?" I sobbed.

He groaned and reached for me. "Because I love you, Ashlyn Carter."

"You don't want to marry me. What kind of games are you playing?" My mind was reeling. Nothing made sense.

"This isn't a game, Ash. It's a complete *disaster*—I have to admit—but it's not a game. Will you marry me?"

"No! You just threw that out in the heat of the moment." I was shaking now.

"No, I didn't! I love you and want to marry you! I just wasn't ready to ask tonight!"

"I don't believe you." I couldn't stop shaking my head in disbelief. This wasn't what I wanted! I couldn't do it! It was all wrong.

"What are you scared of, Ash?"

"I'm not scared!" I cried, at a complete loss to all reason.

"Then say you'll marry me. You are the one I want to spend the rest of my life with."

"No! I can't!" I took off running down the back slope, not even sure what I was running from. What was I doing? Ryan was everything to me, everything to Katie too. So where did this panic come from? I'd never felt such fear as I did at that moment. I thought I'd wanted a commitment from Ryan but assumed he wasn't willing to give one. But *he* wasn't the one bolting—*I* was!

I have to protect us! The words repeated over and over in my mind. I had to protect Katie. I had to protect my heart.

"Ashlyn," he called, catching up to me near the edge of the still lake. "Wait!" He grasped my arms, trying to coax me closer. "What's going on? I don't understand."

"Let go, Ryan! Just leave me alone!"

"But Ash—"

"Please! I need to be alone for a while." In my mind, it would be a very long while. I felt nothing but finality between us, and it was killing me.

Still, he didn't give up. "I know you love me as much as I love you. Why are you rejecting me?"

I shook my head repeatedly, seeing all the reasons in my mind.

"Did your husband hurt you?"

"Don't do that!"

"Don't do what? Be honest? Tell me why you won't marry me."

"Because!" I finally cried, "I'm not woman enough!"

There it was. I just revealed one of the most private corners of my soul to him! Ryan looked so stunned, I couldn't even tell if he was breathing. My embarrassment came in a blood-rush to the cheeks. I spun away to lean against the bright-green moss covering the trunk of an old tree and stared out at the lake.

"Not woman enough?" Ryan said incredulously, coming to my side. "What could possibly make you say such a thing?"

"I was *dumped* for some stupid, sexy, bombshell coworker!" I fired off. "I couldn't even keep my husband's attention for two lousy years!"

At first he was silent. Then I heard him growl, "Scumbag!" as he kicked a fallen tree branch all the way out onto the water. He paced angrily before storming back to me. "You don't actually believe that do you?"

"I know what happened before, and it'll happen again! You like flirting! And if you take that Boeing job, you'll be working long hours away from home and never see us. Eventually you'll notice everyone younger and sexier, and you won't want me either!"

The hurt in Ryan's eyes was more wounding than the thought of not seeing him again. His disbelief pierced through me. "You don't mean that."

"Yes, I do."

He dropped his voice to an eerie composure. "Then you're right. We have no future. If you don't believe in me or trust me better than that, then we have nothing!"

I held my hand up like a shield, unable to bear any more and too choked up to speak.

Ryan bit the inside of his mouth, his lips compressed into a hard line. "I am not your dead husband, Ashlyn." He backed away from me in the darkening thicket, his anger and disbelief clearly visible. As he left me there alone, frogs chanted their lonely nighttime cry, trees rustled and swayed in the slight breeze while my heart shattered for the second time in my life.

*****

In a shaft of sunlight pouring through the seams of the tree branches, I knelt on the ground with a trowel in hand. I was determined to clear a small section of wild brush and ferns in my front yard so I could plant some camellias—incompetence be hanged! For some reason the task seemed vital, so I kept tugging and clipping, but it was proving to be more difficult than I'd anticipated.

"Can I dig too?" Katie asked, wiggling into position beside me.

"Sure. Where are your new pink digging tools?"

Both my grandma and my mom had grown camellias in their yards for as long as I could remember, and I was determined to follow suit. I wanted to become whatever it was I should become, and for some reason, I randomly zeroed in on camellias.

Katie hopped off for her tools, singing her ABCs, causing me to chuckle. It felt good. I hadn't been myself for ten days—as long as it had been since I last saw Ryan. After our blow-up, we decided to give each other some space. In my head, I was sure that was best, but my heart hadn't caught up yet. He'd flown to Virginia to sign his life away, and I knew it was all over between us.

And yet I missed him. I still loved him. The feelings were always there, in everything I saw or did or touched. I had his image burned in my memory—that scar on his chin, the shape of his hands, and the way his hair got lighter in the sunlight. I could see him with Katie, so loving and patient. He was respectful to everyone he talked to, and he was so hard working. But that hard-working trait was an issue for me if it took priority over family. In my mind, that's what he'd done.

But if I ever thought about Ryan's proposal for more than a second, I had an instant, unexplainable onslaught of panic. How could I get over my trust/self-worth issues? When would I be able to tell my parents about John's infidelity?

"Look at these roses," I said aloud, sitting back on my heels to admire them. They were blooming en masse in a variety of yellows—sunny lemon to pink-tipped gold. It was truly spectacular. How could I feel down when there was such beauty as this! I had a good life. I had so many blessings, especially knowing that soon I could go to the temple for the first time.

I wanted to be happy. We'd had a Relief Society lesson on happiness recently where Sister Jones said you should fake it. At first I'd thought she was nuts, but the more I thought about it, I understood what she was trying to say. Happiness was a choice. So if you chose to be happy— or faked it by smiling and pretending you were happy—then eventually you'd get to the point where you *did* feel happy.

I leaned forward again and tugged a gnarly tangle of brush away, leaving a bald spot of dirt. Katie rushed up with her new plastic trowel and shoved it into the ground.

"This is fun!" she cried, launching a dirt clump into the air.

I knew her play clothes would be a casualty of the red clay, but at this point it didn't matter. She was happy for the moment, instead of wondering why Ryan didn't bring the digging toys over himself. It was thoughtful of him to bring her a gift, but she couldn't understand why he'd left it on the porch instead of giving it to her in person. She wanted to see him, and I couldn't blame her. I knew how she felt.

Wiping a bead of sweat from my dirty brow, I heard the phone ring inside. I groaned, wishing we had better cell phone service. By the time I made it to the phone, I heard someone leaving a message.

"Hello?" I said, picking up. "I'm here."

"Hi. It's Matt."

"Oh, hi. Sorry, I was outside."

"No problem. How's it going?"

What should I tell him? *Great, oh and by the way, I fell in love with another guy since I saw you last, but we're not exactly together because while I thought he had commitment issues it turned out that I was the one with the real issues, so now I'm not sure where he and I stand or what to do about you?*

"I'm fine," I decided on. "How are things for you?"

"Fine. I was calling to see if you'd like to go for a drive with me this Saturday. I was thinking the two of us could have a picnic down along the American River."

The two of us, meaning no Katie. I'd been praying so hard lately to be able to figure my life out and know what I should be doing. I'd prayed that my heart could heal from everything it had gone through. Was being with Matt the direction I should follow? I liked him. He was kind, easygoing, funny, enjoyable to be around. I'd heard Ryan describe the difference between fool's gold and real gold. I wondered if it applied to people. If it did, who or what or where was my real gold?

"A drive sounds nice, Matt."

"Great," he said. "I'll pick you up at ten."

We talked for a few minutes about nothing really significant before saying good-bye. I returned to my digging and found Katie covered from head to toe in dirt.

"What happened to you?" I asked, seeing reddish-brown clumps tumble out of her hair and off her shoulders.

Katie's head whipped up guiltily, her eyes wide in concern. "I'm planting."

"Oh? What are you planting?" I asked, sitting beside her to brush off some of the dirt, wishing I had my camera.

"Me."

I laughed. "You? Are you a Katie plant?"

She laughed at me and joined in the hilarity.

"Stay right here, and let me get my camera, okay? I've got to take a picture of my special plant."

*****

After planting the camellia bush, we got cleaned up so we could visit Lisa and see her brand-new baby, Ryker Cole Goodwin.

"I want to hold the present!" Katie said, grabbing hold of the blue bag stuffed with blue-striped tissue paper.

"Be careful. We don't want the baby clothes to fall out."

Katie grimaced at the present. "Why is it blue?"

"Because Lisa had a baby boy, and boys like blue."

"Not girls," Katie stated emphatically. I'd have to work on that. Someday she might want to wear a pair of jeans, but for now she was an all-pink girl and shunned any other hue.

Lisa welcomed us inside her cappuccino-scented home and let us each hold baby Ryker.

Katie didn't have him for more than two seconds before pushing him away. "I'm done with the baby, Mommy," she said, scampering off to play.

"Lisa, he's precious!" I exclaimed as I brought him into my arms. "I can't believe how tiny he is."

"He's the smallest baby I've had," she said. "But way better natured! He's so sweet."

Little Ryker was so little I could hardly believe Katie had ever been that small. As I held him and stroked his fragile, downy-soft cheeks, I filled up with emotion that was hard to repress. All the intense feelings I'd experienced when Katie was born flooded my heart.

"He's like a bit of heaven," I said almost reverently. Touching Ryker's tiny, wrinkled fingers, I suddenly ached for another baby of my own and wondered if it would ever happen.

"Speaking of heaven," Lisa said, "I'd love it if you can come to his blessing next month. We go to Faith Lutheran."

"Lisa, I'd be honored."

"You know where it is?"

"Yeah, right behind Holiday's and the fire station?"

"That's it."

"Just tell me the day and time, and we'll be there."

"Awesome." Lisa's delighted smile wavered when she saw the way I held Ryker so tenderly. She moved to sit beside me on the sofa. "Remembering?" she asked quietly.

I smiled sadly. "A little. I don't know if I'll ever have another baby."

"Of course you will," she groaned sympathetically, putting her arms around me. "You'll get married again and have fourteen more."

I laughed. "Not that many, please." The very thought made me laugh again. "Hey, are you putting Lily in preschool this fall?"

"Yeah, I almost forgot! Let me show you the paper!" She ran to the kitchen and brought back a bright-yellow sheet of paper. "Look, I found a place with a couple of openings, so I signed Katie and Lily up in case you were interested. If not, it's fine, I just thought it would be fun for them to go together."

"You did that for me? Oh my gosh, it's perfect! Thank you."

"No problem. You're my friend, and my friends mean a lot to me."

I looked up at her and had such an overwhelming feeling of trust and gratitude fill my heart. "Me too."

I had a sense that Lisa was one of those gifts from heaven, my personal angel to lift me on a hard day. I only hoped that someday I'd be able to do as much for her as she had done for me.

*****

Saturday was a day of California sunshine, blue skies, and clouds shaped like dollops of whipped cream. On the ground, dry golden grasses swayed like rolling waves. Smokey the Bear's forestry sign alerted drivers that fire danger was high. But as Matt drove north on the Grass Valley Highway, I felt peaceful—like everything in my life was going to turn out okay.

We drove past ranches and farms where future fruit stands would sell their harvest, continuing uphill through undulating, yellow grassy hills topped with clusters of oaks that looked like patches of overgrown broccoli. With an increase in elevation came more forested areas and mountain vistas.

When we reached Grass Valley, Matt pulled off the road near a creek.

"We can eat here," he said, pointing to the thick, wooded area.

He'd brought us sub sandwiches, chips, and a drink, which we ate quietly near the water. Everything was perfect about the food, the day, the setting. But I didn't feel like I should be there.

"You know what?" Matt said, after taking a swig of Sprite.

"Hmm?" I mumbled, still working on my sandwich.

"I really like being with you, Ashlyn."

I swallowed hard. "I like being with you too, Matt."

"You're so easy to get along with. You don't stress me out or make me feel nervous. I can be myself around you, and I really like that."

I tried not to look shocked when he leaned over and kissed my cheek. He was so laid back that I wasn't expecting it. But it was a simple, short kiss. More of the touch of friendship than passion. I decided that the calm, comfortable feeling I had being with Matt was important and that I should listen to those feelings.

*****

The following weekend, Matt took me to the movies. He held my hand for the first time and bought me a huge bucket of popcorn with extra butter. His kiss that night made me realize that he cared for me much more than I'd realized. He was more reserved with his affections, so what he did offer was truly meaningful.

I thought about the way he interacted kindly with Katie when he came to visit recently. I thought about his stability and good job. When I was with him, I had the feeling of being taken care of, feeling sheltered and safe. I didn't know if that was an answer, but there was one place I believed I could find out. I'd be going to the temple in a week!

One day Megan brought me some earth-shattering news as well. "Ash, I want to go to the temple with you," she told me.

"Walking the grounds with Katie?"

"No, I want to go through the temple for the first time with my favorite sister. Would you be okay with that?"

"Of course, Megan, that's wonderful! But does this mean . . . ?"

She couldn't hold in her laughter. "I'm doing it! I'm going on a mission!"

"You're kidding. When did this happen? Do Mom and Dad know?"

"Yeah, they're doing mental backflips over it. I've been praying about it a lot lately, and"—she shrugged—"it feels right."

"What about dating?" I asked gently.

"Drake never made a move, and you know how things turned out with Ryan. So I'm going."

So my crazy, unpredictable sister and I both prepared ourselves the best we could for the big day. I had prayed a lot and believed that all the questions I had about my life would be answered once I started going to the temple. Including what to do about Matt.

The clear, sunny day we drove to the Sacramento temple, I was surrounded by family. Brother and Sister Loveless were there, as well as Aunt Linda and Uncle Ray. Shaun and Karen's kids watched Katie while we went through the endowment session.

I couldn't believe how glorious it was! There were no words to accurately describe what I felt. It was like being in heaven. My gratitude for life and all its blessings escalated incalculably. I wished John could have experienced a fraction of what I felt—then nothing would have kept him from taking us to the temple. I was at peace about Katie too. I felt that, in time, I would be sealed to her.

Back at my parents' house, when things had settled down and Katie had fallen asleep on my old bed, Megan took off to go shopping with a friend. I realized it was just me and my parents.

"Hey, Mom, where's Dad?" I asked, drying the last casserole dish on the counter.

My mom answered from inside the pantry. "Watching TV, I think. Do you need him?"

"I wanted to talk to you—to both of you—if that would be okay."

"Sure, honey. Let me go get him."

She walked off, and I sucked in a deep, steadying breath. After going to the temple, I knew I could do this. I was a daughter of my Heavenly Father, who loved me! Had I forgotten that over the years? And now I was endowed with power from on high, and I knew I could do great things. Hard things. Anything I needed to do! Because God was on my side and would help me. I felt new and revived and wonderful, ready to face everything the rest of my life had to bring.

I followed my mom and found her in the family room dusting knickknacks while Dad gathered up all his remotes. "Hi, guys." I couldn't help smiling at their image of domestic tranquility.

"How's my girl?" Dad asked, coming over to give me a hug. "Mom says you'd like to talk to us?"

"I do if you have a minute."

"For you, I have *two* minutes."

"Oh, Gerald." Mom sighed. "Just sit down."

We sat together on the big sofa—the same way we had the time Ryan had come over. I thought about how I couldn't look at him that night but wondered what he was doing. I felt almost the same way now. Could I ever approach him again after everything that had happened? Would he even want to see me?

"What's on your mind honey?" Dad asked, reaching for my hand.

I glanced at them both then plunged in. "Remember, Mom, how I told you about John? How busy he was?" She nodded, and I kept going. "He took business trips and worked all the time. He wasn't home very much." I turned to my Dad to make sure he was on board with the story. He nodded as well. "So at his funeral, I noticed this woman crying and, at first, didn't really pay any attention to it because I was already devastated. But later I realized it was someone John worked with in the office. When I went through his wallet one night"—my chest hurt, but I pressed on—"I found a note this woman had written. John was having an affair before he died."

Dad now had his arms around my shoulders, and Mom had hers around my middle.

"Are you sure? Could there be some mistake?" Mom asked.

"No, I made sure. I asked the woman."

"Why didn't you tell anyone?" Dad asked. "We could have helped you!"

"I'd already done everything wrong—dating John, marrying outside the temple—it would have been one more thing to add to my pile of failures. A huge thing. I didn't want you to know the extent of my bad choices. I'm sorry."

Dad became a bit enflamed. "John's bad choices, not yours, sweetheart! I don't know what was going on between you, but if he chose to stay at work rather than come home to his family, it's not your fault. If he put himself in a position that would result in this affair, it was his doing, not yours. So you don't need to be carrying around any more guilt for what he did. Do you understand me?"

"I do."

"Your father is right, Ashlyn. Let go of the guilt. And remember today how everyone talked about returning to the temple often? It's true. It will help."

"Absolutely," Dad agreed. "Ashlyn, I want to promise you something. The more you go to the temple, the more you will heal. Go there seeking that blessing, and the Lord will heal any wounds in your heart. He is always there."

Chapter 27

"I HOPE I GET CALLED somewhere like Tahiti. Or Russia," Megan said, stuffing one of Mom's famous peanut butter cookies into her mouth.

My dad heartily laughed in his La-Z-Boy chair, where Katie sat on his lap waiting for him to finish reading a story. "The similarity between Tahiti and Russia being . . . ?"

"They're foreign," Megan quipped, tossing him her don't-make-fun-of-me look.

"Canada's foreign," he bantered.

"Dad." She scolded. "I'm talking *foreign* foreign. Madagascar, Korea, Finland—" She threw me an immediate "Sorry!" at the mention of Finland. Megan had been acting weird lately—different in a way I couldn't quite pinpoint. She was so gung-ho about her mission now, which was great. But she was also ultra-concerned about my feelings for Ryan—which was also great, it was just weird. How did she get over guys so fast?

"Honey," Mom called to my dad from the kitchen, "you know Megan will go wherever she's called to serve."

Setting my mother's favorite glass bowl in the antique hutch, I daringly asked, "What happens if the Lord calls you to serve in Winnemucca, Nevada?"

"Winnemucca?" Megan barked. "I am *not* going to Winnemucca!"

"No, I know," Dad guffawed. "How about Tijuana!"

Now all of us were laughing, and I needed a good laugh. I walked over to the large family room window and looked down at the lake, visible through the lacy pine trees. The afternoon sun was settling in the sky, casting a glow on the rust-colored shoreline. As the conversation continued behind me, I took a long, deep breath, and my thoughts drifted away.

Three weeks. I hadn't seen him for three weeks, and I thought I'd die. But I couldn't think about it. It hurt too much. I still went out with Matt once in a while, but he moved so slowly that it drove me crazy! I'd been to the temple so many times, trying to figure out what I should do, but when I prayed in the celestial room, the same thing always happened. As my eyes would wander over the exquisite gold scrollwork overhead, gleaming from sunlight filtering through massive arched windows, the same answer would come. Wait.

The word implied patience, which I didn't have in abundance. I didn't know specifically what I was supposed to wait for, but I finally understood what my heart was trying to tell me all along. Why did it take me so long to figure out? And now it was probably too late. If I loved Ryan as much as I believed I did, I could have given him more trust. Maybe he wouldn't do the same things John had done.

But I didn't want to move away from Meadow Vista! Especially not out of state. It was important to me to be near my family, and I didn't want to give that up. When you gave someone your heart, did you have to make sacrifices that big?

I saw a dark bird swoop down over the lake then disappear from my view. Why were answers so elusive? I continued my perusal of the wooded slope as though I'd find what I sought out there.

"Still at it?" Megan asked quietly beside me. I hadn't realized she'd come over.

"At what?" I asked, still gazing out the window.

"Pining."

I sighed.

"Ash, if you hurt this much, isn't it obvious what you should do?" She knew enough about what had happened between Ryan and me to have an opinion. But she felt bad that her "knife-stabbing pain" remark had come true.

I turned to the window again. "I'm going to go down to the lake," I said. "I need to think for a while." I just didn't know if there was anything that would fix my predicament.

Megan looked at me helplessly then nodded. "I'll keep an eye on Katie."

I escaped into the wooded backyard and walked down the steep, terraced path of steps to the lake. I sat down on one of the beat-up old Adirondack chairs near the water's edge where we had a sandy play area. Other than a lonely bird call, the gentle rustling of oak leaves, and the calm sloshing of water, it was quiet. I loved this secluded spot. I'd found solace here in my topsy-turvy teenaged years and hoped it would do the same for me now.

I leaned my head back against the chair and watched the clouds drift ever so slowly to the right. I remembered wishing that John could sit back and watch the clouds instead of rushing all the time. Maybe he could do that now. Although I couldn't picture it. I could see him just as busy up there with other pursuits. I sighed. Forgiveness was a long process, but I was working on it and felt so much lighter.

I thought about the life I'd created for Katie and me in Meadow Vista and felt good about all we'd accomplished so far. But my thoughts strayed to Ryan, and a sharp pain sliced through my chest.

I'd been trying to push out thoughts of Ryan, not allowing them to take up residence in my mind, where they could hurt me. Now, as I looked at the gossamer clouds overhead, I allowed myself to bring him back—everything that was part of who he was.

My mother once said that Ryan had made me feel and that after being dead inside, it was good for me to feel again. Was that his only purpose in coming into my life? To prepare me to move on so I could meet and marry someone else?

I used to think I'd never marry again. With Ryan, I actually wanted it but was too afraid to let him in. I squeezed my eyes shut, picturing a life with him, imagining Katie rushing into his arms when he came home from work. I pictured us having more children and growing old together. Those mental pictures were so easily filled now. Why was I so afraid to make them a reality before?

Help me, Heavenly Father.

I half prayed, half deliberated, searching for an answer. When I opened my eyes, I saw a butterfly dance overhead then land in front of me on the ground. As I studied its speckled wings, I heard a crunch of brush behind me. I turned toward the sound, thinking that Katie must have discovered my hiding place. Someone was coming down through the thicket. I peered more closely and decided that maybe it wasn't Katie, but who was—

A sudden thudding erupted inside my chest, the kind of wild thudding that only happened with one person. What was he doing here? I shot out of my chair with a frantic impulse to hide, but I knew he'd seen me. His long legs worked their way down the hill. About ten feet away, Ryan stopped, searching my face.

"Hello, Ashlyn," he finally murmured.

"Hi." I blinked and stared at him.

He walked toward me, as if in slow motion, yet my heart accelerated to a riotous tempo. A multitude of emotions crossed his face—uncertainty, pain, longing, and something else I couldn't define. While I tried to understand his intense expression, his eyes never left mine. He stopped when there was only a breath of air between us.

"Hi," he said.

"Hi." I blinked at him, at a loss for words.

"Am I too late?"

I could barely speak with my heart pounding that way. What was he talking about? And what was he doing down here? Did my family send him down?

My entire body was affected by his nearness. He looked amazing. He smelled amazing. The touch of his hands felt amazing. The longing in my chest went full throttle.

"I heard there's someone else," he said. The distress in his voice was audible, as though he'd been suffering as much as I had—or more.

When I registered the fact that he was talking about Matt, my wandering thoughts came to an abrupt halt, and I pulled my hands away. "Ryan—"

"Is it serious?" His expression was pained.

I swung away, to collect my thoughts.

"Ashlyn, wait."

I glanced at the ground near his shoe.

"I know I've been stupid, but I have something to say. There's something I *need* to say . . . if you'll give me the chance."

Almost fearful of what he would say, I hesitantly turned back.

"I've been such an idiot," he said, bringing one hand to my arm. "I should never have—" He swallowed and shook his head. "I shouldn't have done a lot of things. Starting with taking you to that stupid party! I thought it would be good because you totally blow all the other girls out of the water; you're so beautiful. I probably should've said it that night, but I wasn't sure how. But you need to know that you are completely and utterly desirable as a woman—in every possible way—and always have been. As a teenager I used to fantasize about you as only a sixteen-year-old can, and I didn't stop dreaming about you for years after we moved away! From the day I saw you again, those feelings only multiplied—exponentially."

Already self-consciously biting my lip, I couldn't help looking away when Ryan stopped for breath.

"You're not used to hearing it, are you?" he ventured, gently turning my cheek back with the palm of his hand. "He should have told you every day, Ash. I'm sorry that he didn't, and I'm sorry that he hurt you."

"It's okay, Ryan. And about the night of that party, it was my fault for harassing you about commitment in the first place. I was kind of psycho and ruined everything all on my own. I'm sorry I didn't trust you, that I thought you could be like John. Will you forgive me?"

He crushed me into his embrace. "Of course." He held me close, and I felt the rise and fall of his chest with each breath. "I've missed you so badly," he said. "How have you been?"

"I'm good." I smiled hesitantly. "I finally went through the temple."

"You did?" he exclaimed. "That's awesome."

"Yeah, and it's really helping me with a lot of things."

He gave me another bear hug. "I'm so happy for you, kulta!" Just as quickly and cautiously, he pulled back. "So you've been going a lot?"

I nodded happily.

His eyes clouded over as he took a step back. "And you've been going with . . . this other guy?"

"No, with Megan." I laughed.

He scrunched up his forehead. "But she told me things were getting serious with him."

"With Matt? Megan talked to you?"

"Yeah, I thought—from what she said anyway—you were getting close and that I'd better—"

"Better what? What has she been saying?"

He gave me a look full of regret. "I made such a big mistake that I don't know if you can ever forgive me. It was way too soon to be talking to you about the job in Virginia and marriage and everything else. I took the best offer I'd been given and hoped everything would work out in the end."

"So you didn't trust me, and I didn't trust you."

"But, Ash, I went out to Virginia to see the company and meet people I'd work with. Every wonderful thing out there I wanted to share with you. Every bad thing I wanted to laugh about with you. Because you are the most important part of my life, not a job. So I made a decision. I turned the job down."

"What!" I couldn't believe what I was hearing.

"I didn't sign anything," he continued. "I decided that I needed to come back, to ask you a very important question." My heart thundered in my chest as he took both my hands in his. "Ash, I always keep my promises, but there's one promise I don't want to keep anymore." As he took a step closer, I felt his warmth and wanted to feel it surround me. He lifted a hand to caress my cheek. His thumb brushed down along my jaw and over to my lower lip, where it lingered. "Will you please let me—"

I pulled his head down and kissed him. How I loved this man! How I wanted him to be mine! Ryan responded with ninja-quick reflexes and kissed me back with enough passion and eagerness to lift me off the ground—but thrown off balance, it knocked us both down to our knees, where we struck the arm of the Adirondack chair and toppled onto the ground. We broke apart laughing and rolled onto our backs.

"Wooh!" Ryan exclaimed, looking up at the sky. "Now that was a kiss! Are you okay?"

"Mmmm . . . never better," I answered breathlessly.

He turned toward me, tangling one leg over mine. His lips brushed lightly over mine, once, twice, and again a third time, adding a little more pressure with each kiss. "Your kisses knock me out."

I laughed again and sighed blissfully. "Ryan?"

"Hmm?" he murmured as he scattered kisses along the side of my face.

"What does *kulta* really mean?"

He laughed a little next to my ear. "In Finnish it means *gold*, but it also means *honey*, *baby*, *sweetheart*, or *love*."

"You told me it didn't really mean anything!"

"Oh, it meant something all right. A little more than I could say for a while. It's always been my perfect name for you, Ashlyn. You *are* my gold, and I love you."

"I love you too, Ryan."

He narrowed the sliver of space between us, and I surrendered to the pressure of his parted lips, his breath mingling with mine. It amazed me that I could feel so complete lying on an unglamorous, lumpy spot by the lake with my hair in the sand and brush. After several enchanted minutes, we both suddenly stopped, out of breath, looking into each other's eyes.

"We better get up," we said at the same time. Once Ryan helped me to my feet, we had to brush off all the natural debris from our fall.

"Let me get this lovely twig." He grinned, reaching into my hair. "And the dry leaves over here . . ."

"Am I that bad?" I asked, brushing sand off my bum.

"No. You're perfect." He took both my hands in his own, becoming serious again. "Ashlyn, I mean it. To me, you are perfect. You're everything I could ever hope for, and I love you and Katie more than I can say. I never imagined I could love a little girl like that, but I do. The thought of losing you both has been the worst thing I've ever gone through. I would do anything to have you both be part of my life forever."

"Oh, Ryan." I felt love flow through me, my heart completely given. I wrapped my arms around his neck, letting my fingers glide through his hair. "You will always have my heart."

Cupping my face with both hands, he dropped his lips to melt against mine, and I savored the kiss that was once forbidden. It was long and lingering, making my knees go weak beneath me. The feel of his mouth on mine made me feel loved and desirable. "Ash," Ryan whispered against my lips, "I need to ask you something."

Not wanting to pull away, I looked into his eyes. "What is it?"

"The most important question I'll ever ask," he said, his hands threading through my hair. "I royally botched this last time, so if you'll let me have another go . . ." He drew a quick, rough breath. "Ashlyn, I've waited a long time for you, and you really are the only one for me. I want to spend the rest of my life making you feel important and beautiful and loved. I want to have more children with you and to grow old with you. You're my life, and I love you with all my heart." Moisture filled his eyes as he dropped to one knee in the sand. He reached into his pocket and slipped out a beautiful diamond ring. "Ashlyn Rose Carter, will you marry me?"

I laughed and sobbed all at the same time. "Yes, I will!"

Ryan swooped me into his arms and crushed me against him like he'd never let me go. He cradled my head in one of his hands, and I reveled in feeling completely cherished. This was where I belonged, the only place I wanted to be.

"I love you," I said, swiping at a tear.

"I love you too. Oh, I forgot to put your ring on. Here, do you want to try it on?"

"Yes, it's gorgeous!" As he slid the ring onto my finger, I could hardly believe he'd chosen such a spectacular setting.

"The jeweler helped me design it with a vintage feel."

"I love it!" I said, back in his arms. "I can't believe this. Katie's going to flip out when we tell her you're going to be her daddy. She absolutely adores you."

"Actually, I have a confession to make. She kind of . . . already knows."

"What? How?"

He grinned sheepishly, rubbing his nose against mine. "Up in the house, before I came down here, I asked her permission to marry you and to become her daddy."

"And what did she say?" I laughingly asked, tangling my arms around his neck again.

"Not much, actually. She sort of strangled me with those cute little arms, kind of like you're doing right now. I had to promise her a piggyback ride before I could pry her off me." We both laughed, and Ryan pulled me even closer. "She was so happy," he whispered tenderly against the side of my face.

At that moment, everything made sense. I knew I was in the right place—the only place I truly wanted to be. I hadn't mastered trust, but I knew that I could trust Ryan with my heart and my life because I knew he was the right man for me. There wasn't even a hint of doubt in my mind, and it filled me with joy and light to be so sure.

"Ash?" Ryan nuzzled my neck with warm kisses.

"Hmm?"

"I'd marry you right now if I could."

It was a long time before either of us could speak again.

Life certainly had a way of taking you places you never planned to go. I'd slid into a deep ravine of sorrow after John died. I'd climbed steep hills of experience as I learned to move on. And now, in this moment, I was ready to take a new, unexpected path because I knew I'd be taking that path with my greatest treasures. Here in the Sierras, I'd found my true gold.

About the Author

JEANETTE MILLER WAS BORN IN Northern California but spent most of her childhood in Guatemala, Puerto Rico, and Costa Rica, where her father worked. She cherishes her experiences of living in Latin America. In her teenage years, she dreamed of becoming a teacher and a published author. Jeanette attended Brigham Young University, where she earned a degree in elementary education. After graduating, she taught third grade for four years in the Spanish Immersion program. There, she enjoyed writing and directing plays for her students.

As a young mother, Jeanette started writing in moments snatched between changing diapers and making peanut butter sandwiches, whenever her nose wasn't in a book. She loves all things Jane Austen and Charlotte Bronte's *Jane Eyre*. She loves starting new projects rather than finishing them, hiking, snowshoeing, and really good chocolate. She dreams of traveling all over the world someday. Jeanette and her husband, Michael, have six children. She would love hearing from readers at konablos@ yahoo.com.